THE
C·L·U·B

Jane Heller

THE
C·L·U·B

KENSINGTON BOOKS

KENSINGTON BOOKS are published by

Kensington Publishing Corp.
850 Third Avenue
New York, NY 10022

Copyright © 1995 by Jane Heller

LIBRARY OF CONGRESS CARD CATALOG NUMBER: 95-076005

ISBN 0-8217-4988-9

First Printing: July, 1995

Printed in the United States of America

ACKNOWLEDGMENTS

♦

A heartfelt thanks to those whose advice and expertise proved invaluable while I was writing this book: Michael Barrett, Jane Dystel, David Goldener, Ruth Harris, Ann LaFarge, Bob Patent, and Edwin Shmerler.

Special gratitude to my husband, Godie, and to my family and friends, who cheered me on and made me feel that I wasn't in over my head.

For my father, Mort Reznick,
a golf lover and a great guy.

PART
O·N·E

CHAPTER ONE

♦

"You're fired."

Is there a more dreaded sentence in the English language? Sure, "You've got six weeks to live" is right up there on the All-Time Dreaded Sentences List. So is "I'm leaving you for somebody else." But "You're fired" really, really hurts if: (a) you're a loyal and long-time employee of the company; (b) you're good at your job; and (c) you make a point of never letting your boss know how profoundly incompetent you think she is.

To be fair, my incompetent boss, Leeza Grummond, the vice president and associate publisher of Charlton House, didn't exactly say "You're fired." She opted for the cozier "We're going to have to let you go."

Let me go, my ass. Twenty-six-year-old Leeza was canning thirty-nine-year-old me. I was in shock. Total shock. I was in such shock that my mouth dropped open and stayed that way for several seconds, and I began to drool all over my robin's egg blue, just-back-from-the-dry-cleaner, Anne Klein II silk blouse.

I must be dreaming, I thought, aware of the cliché but in too much pain to come up with a fresher explanation. Yes, that was it. I was dreaming that Leeza Grummond, my nightmare-of-a-boss, was firing me.

"Last year's merger with Pennington Press has necessitated a reevaluating and refocusing of our publishing program," Leeza explained as I continued to stare at her in disbelief. "We've decided to return to Charlton House's roots, to revitalize the company's literary legacy."

What would you know about the company's literary legacy, I wanted to say to Leeza, who graduated at the top of her class at Harvard Business School but hadn't read a novel since high school. The little shit talked incessantly of focus groups and direct respondents and profit and loss statements but was speechless on the subject of literature. Sure, she had expertise in the selling of toothpaste. But she knew as much about the book business as my mother, whose idea of "business" was what you did in the bathroom, not the boardroom.

"Charlton House published Henry James and F. Scott Fitzgerald," she was saying, as if I didn't know. "But somewhere along the way we lost our reputation as a quality publisher."

Yeah, bitch. When *you* showed up, fresh from Procter & Gamble in your androgynous suit and androgynous hair, and made us the joke of the industry.

"We've decided that 1995 will mark our renewed commitment to our heritage," she droned on. "The Pennington Press division of our company will publish the more commercial, mass market titles, while the Charlton House imprint will be devoted to books with literary appeal, books that will endure." She paused, letting her words hang in the air like bad perfume. "Which brings me to you, Judy." She cleared her throat. "I regret to say that cookbooks won't be part of this new publishing mix. You've been a fine editor, but we just won't be needing a cookbook editor any longer."

"But I've been here eight years," I managed to say. "And I've made money for this company. A lot of money."

In the past couple of years alone, I'd edited half a dozen bestselling cookbooks. No, I wasn't Julia Child's editor or Martha Stewart's editor or even The Frugal Gourmet's editor. I was a scrappy sort of editor who found cookbooks where others wouldn't think to look. For example, when George Bush let it be known that he hated broccoli, I moved quickly to publish *The I Hate Broccoli Cookbook,* which hit *The New York Times* bestseller list and stayed there for two months. And when *USA Today* ran a front-page story on the health benefits of garlic, who do you think was the genius who signed up *So Your Breath Smells—You'll Live Longer!* And then, of course, there was my real blockbuster, *Valerio's Kitchen.* It was I who saw the "singing restaurateur" on "Regis and Kathie Lee" and contacted him about doing a cookbook for Charlton House. The book sold a hundred thousand copies in hardcover and Valerio became a household name. He was so grateful to me for discovering him that he insisted he was in love with me. "You're not in love with me," I told him. "You just think you're in love with me, the way patients think they're in love with their doctors." Undaunted, Valerio held fast to his love and continued to propose marriage to me, even though I was married to someone else.

"Yes, Judy, you have made money for Charlton House," Leeza acknowledged. "You've been a very valuable member of our team."

Our team. The woman ran the company like a dictator of a third world country.

"You've been so valuable to us," she said, "that we're giving you three months' severance."

"Three months' severance?" Was she kidding? I was worth much more than that.

"Yes, three months," she said as she straightened her bow tie and flicked a speck of lint off her skirt. "In exchange, we'd like you to stay for a couple of weeks. To make the transition easier."

"Easier for whom?" I said, trying not to sound shrill. "For you? For the person who'll be taking over my office? For the accounting department?"

"For all of us, frankly," she said. "We don't want there to be any bumps."

Bumps? My career had been reduced to bumps? *I* was being reduced to bumps? What was there left to say? To do? Crying in front of Leeza was out of the question. I was a professional, after all. So was stabbing her with the sterling silver letter opener on her desk. And I certainly wasn't going to beg her to reconsider. Obviously, her mind was made up to fire me. Still, there was a tiny part of me that kept waiting for her to say, "April Fool's," even though it was March, and hand me a bonus check instead of a pink slip.

I looked at her expectantly, but she only blinked a couple of times, then checked her watch. I was keeping her from something. Something extremely important, no doubt. Perhaps there were other employees to fire, other hearts to break, other lives to ruin.

I stood up and made a move to leave her office.

"I won't be staying for a couple of weeks," I said, my voice quivering but clear. "Or even for a couple of days. I'll be out of here within the hour."

Now it was Leeza's turn to look shocked. "I'm afraid you can't just leave," she said when she recovered. "What I mean is, there's still the matter of your interfacing with Human Resources. For your exit interview."

Interfacing. Human Resources. Exit interview. What had Charlton House come to? What had corporate America come to?

"Goodbye, Leeza," I said, as I gave her one last look. "I hope you realize what a terrible mistake you've made."

I turned and stormed out of her office, my eyes flooding, my heart pounding, my stomach churning. Down the hall I marched, ignoring the stares, the questions, the whispering. I was desperate to reach the safety of my little office, where I had happily spent most of my adult working life. When I got there, I locked the door and began to pace, back and forth, back and forth, back and forth. Since my office was the size of a hamster's cage, my pacing took the form of very short laps and, before long, I was dizzy.

I sat at my desk and began to sob.

What will I do without my job? I blubbered. It's my identity. My power base. My source of income.

Well, it wasn't my only source of income, I reminded myself. There was Hunt's income from his job as the head of the commodities department at Fitzgerald & Franklin, the stuffy, old-line investment banking firm that kept promising to make him a partner and never did. But I couldn't live off Hunt. In the seven years of our marriage, I'd never lived off Hunt. We'd always been a two-career couple, pooling our resources to buy cars and houses and trips to the Caribbean, a modern couple who split all our expenses, even groceries. We needed my income to keep things balanced. If I suddenly had no pay check, what would become of our lifestyle? What, for example, would become of our membership in The Oaks, the country club Hunt had insisted we join so he could network on the golf course, male-bond on the tennis court, and schmooze in the swimming pool? He'd said joining the club was his last shot at making partner at F&F. Personally, I thought country clubs were a total anachronism. They were exclusionary and cliquish and harkened back to the days when white Anglo-Saxon Protestant men ruled the world, and they had nothing I wanted or needed out of life. Even the athletic facilities held no lure for me. I didn't care about sports (my idea of exercise was REM sleep). I didn't play golf, was never very good at tennis, and because I feared what the chlorine would do to my frosted blond hair, I avoided swimming pools.

Still, Hunt had been persuasive. "If you don't belong to a club, you're out of the loop, Judy," he'd said. "Getting into a prestigious club like The Oaks, where most of the members are CEOs of Fortune 500 companies, can mean a big boost to a guy's business."

"Sure," I'd smirked. "If the guy is an undertaker. The people at The Oaks are so old that when you first meet them, the initials that come to mind are CPR, not CEO."

Hunt had accused me of exaggerating, and he was right, of course. There *were* some young people at The Oaks. They just acted old.

My musings were interrupted by a knock on my office door.

"Judy?" came a voice. "It's Arlene. Let me in, okay?"

Arlene was my best friend at Charlton House. She had been the company's romance editor as long as I had been its cookbook editor. We were the only two editors whose books made any money for the place. And now I'd been fired. I guessed Arlene had heard the news and come to console me.

I unlocked the door and motioned for Arlene to enter. Her eyes were red and swollen and she looked paler than I'd ever seen her. Obviously, she had heard about my firing and was not taking it very well.

"Please don't be upset," I said, patting her on the back. "We'll still see each other. You'll come up to Connecticut for the weekend, and I'll come into the city for lunch. It'll be just like the old days. You'll tell Loathsome Leeza stories and I'll tell Loathsome Leeza stories and we'll have a good laugh."

"You don't understand," she said gravely.

"Of course, I do," I said. "We were soul mates. Buddies in a storm. Editors in a sea of number crunchers. I know it's very difficult for you to deal with my getting fired."

"It's not your getting fired that's upsetting me," she sniveled.

"Then what is it?" I asked.

"It's *my* getting fired," she said and began to cry.

"You too?" I couldn't believe it.

"Leeza called me in a few minutes ago. I thought she was going to congratulate me about *The Duchess and the Delivery Boy* making the *Times'* bestseller list. But no. She didn't care that the book is selling better than any other romance novel out there right now. What she wanted to tell me was that the company was downsizing and I was getting downsized."

I sat at my desk and tried to take it all in. "How could anybody be that stupid?" I asked. "Downsizing or not, you and I bring in best-seller after bestseller and instead of giving us a raise, Leeza fires us."

Arlene shook her head. "She said the company is going in a different direction."

"Yeah, down the toilet," I said. "Doesn't this idiot know that sex and food are the only things that sell in a troubled economy?"

With her shaggy brown hair and poignant, thin face, Arlene looked like a lost puppy, and no wonder. She didn't just edit romance novels; they were her life. Thirty-eight and single, she buried herself in the books instead of going out and trying to meet a man. Night after night, in her Laura Ashley–decorated, one-bedroom apartment on the Upper West Side, she imagined herself lassoed by a cowboy or kidnapped by a pirate or seduced by a half-breed Apache, just like her favorite heroines. Every so often, I'd tactfully point out that life wasn't nearly as dramatic as the stories she loved and that, perhaps, she was losing her sense of reality. "Reality is overrated," she'd say.

The woman had a point.

"Feminism sucks," I said suddenly.

"Why?" said Arlene.

"Because of the Leeza Grummonds of the world," I said. "Feminism has unleashed these women, who have MBA degrees but no common sense, to run our big companies. Well, if they're the best thing feminism can come up with, we should all go back to the kitchen. We can do less damage there."

Arlene tried to smile. "Speaking of the kitchen," she said, "I know you'll get another job, Judy. You're a great cookbook editor. You have a real understanding of food."

"Thanks, Arlene. I appreciate that."

I suppose I did have a real understanding of food, what with my family history. On my mother's side were the eaters—big, fat women who ate and ate and ate and always wondered why they were so fat. On my father's side were the food purveyors. My grandfather, Milton Millstein, arrived in this country from Germany, shortened his name to Mills and opened a butcher shop on Long Island. When he retired, my father took over the running of Mills's Prime Meats. He made such a success of the operation that he opened two more stores. Then two more. Then, some advertising genius suggested my father should appear in his own TV ads, like Frank Perdue and Tom Carvel. My father loved the idea and, thanks to the power of television, went from being an anonymous butcher to being "Mr. Butcher." He made a lot of money being Mr. Butcher, but the whole experience did something to his mind: he started speaking in cuts of meat. He called his brother Louis's daughters a pair of rump cuts. He called his brother Louis's wife a beat-up old brisket. He called me, his only daughter, a tenderloin. It wasn't until I went off to college that I realized that when men call a good-looking woman a "ten," it isn't short for "tenderloin."

"You'll find another job too," I told Arlene. "You're the best romance editor in New York."

"Maybe so, but the job market isn't what it used to be," she said. "There were so many mergers and takeovers in the eighties that there are only six publishing houses left in the business. I just got fired from one of them, so that leaves five."

"What a nightmare," I said. "I'm going down to the mailroom to see if they have any cartons. Then I'm packing my stuff up and going home."

"I'll see you, Judy," Arlene said wistfully.

I gave her a hug. "Of course you will. We'll probably find jobs at the same company. It'll be just like it was at Charlton House—only better."

She managed a weak smile and left.

I returned from the mailroom fifteen minutes later and found that I had a couple of visitors.

"May I help you?" I said to the two security guards who stood on either side of my desk.

"No," said one of them. "We're here to help *you.*"

"Help me what?" I said.

"Pack up and leave," said the other. "We're here to make sure everything goes nice and smooth."

I was outraged. "Why wouldn't everything go nice and smooth? Do you expect me to set fire to the place?"

No response.

I decided to ignore them and began packing up my personal belongings—my Rolodex, my Filofax, the philodendron plant Hunt had given me, the crystal paperweight the author of *The Psychic Cook* had given me. I was about to reach for the Charlton House coffee mug on my desk when one of the guards stopped me.

"What do you think you're doing?" I asked, peeling the man's hand from my shoulder.

"The mug's company property," he said. "It stays here."

Oh, so that's it, I thought. This isn't a dream. It's an episode of "America's Funniest Home Videos." Someone is videotaping this and sending it to the network.

"How about these?" I said to the guards as I opened my desk drawer and pulled out a handful of Charlton House pencils. "These okay?"

"Nope," one of them said and grabbed them.

God, they're not kidding, I realized. Leeza is some piece of work. She fires her most successful editors—women who actually make money for the company—and she's worried about a bunch of number two pencils!

"I guess I won't even try to take those with me," I said, pointing to the file cabinet in the corner. I had hoped to pack up a few important files—files that might help me get another job.

The guard smiled. "Not a chance."

I smiled back. It was either smile or slit my wrists.

"Well, that about does it," I said, surveying my office for the last time. I swallowed the giant lump in my throat as I took a long, hard look around the room in which I'd spent so many wonderful hours. Suddenly, I spotted the needlepoint sign on my wall and scurried over to take it down.

"Sorry, Miss Mills," one of the guards said as he tried to stop me. "That's a no-no."

I spun around to face him. "Get out of my way," I said, steel-eyed. "The sign on the wall is *mine.*"

I pulled the sign off the wall and placed it gently in a carton.

They could take my job but they couldn't take my sign, which Hunt had given me on our first wedding anniversary. He'd asked his secretary, a whiz at needlepoint, to make it for me. It read: LOVE MEANS NEVER HAVING TO SAY YOU'RE HUNGRY—NOT WHEN YOU'RE MARRIED TO A COOKBOOK EDITOR!

Corny, maybe. But it was Hunt's stab at humor, and since he wasn't exactly the most humorous guy on the planet, it meant a lot to me.

I gathered my belongings, wished the security guards a nice life, and went home.

CHAPTER TWO

♦

"Belford. Next stop," boomed the conductor.

I checked my watch. How weird is this? I thought. It's 11:38 on a Friday morning, and while everybody I know is at work, I'm taking the Metro North train home. Talk about depressing.

I'd never taken the train home in the middle of the day, except once, two years before, when I'd gotten a terrible head cold. I was running a fever and could barely talk, but even then, I hadn't wanted to leave the office. I loved my job at Charlton House *that* much.

Stop torturing yourself, I thought. You got fired. Deal with it. Take the weekend off and start hustling for another job on Monday.

I peered out the window and watched the Connecticut landscape go by. Greenwich. Stamford. Noroton Heights. Darien. Every town looked as forlorn as I felt, what with its bare trees, brown grass, and gray sky. Nobody should have to lose their job in March, I thought, not when the Northeast is about as welcoming as an unemployment office.

"Belford. Next stop," the conductor boomed again.

He didn't have to boom; I was the only one on the train.

I regarded the conductor for the first time during the sixty-five-minute ride. He was pretty cute, I realized. Medium height, stocky, red handlebar mustache, wire-rimmed glasses. Not my type, but then "my type" had, of late, come to mean "any type." I'm ashamed to admit this, but in the past year I'd found myself lusting after all sorts of men in a way I hadn't since college. I never acted on the lusting (adultery sounded wildly romantic but in the end required far too much calculation), but it worried me all the same. First I had sexual fantasies about Mark, Charlton House's director of sales. Then I had sexual fantasies about Richard, the author of *How to Find Resonance in Risottos*. Then I had sexual fantasies about Chuck, the man who came to adjust the air-conditioning duct in my office. What was going on? I asked myself. Why was I acting like a Dirty Old Woman? Was it the fact that I was about to turn forty and going through a "passage"? Was it my hormones? Or was it that my marriage was stale?

Stale as week-old zucchini bread, that's what it was. I had to face facts: Hunt and I had been growing apart. After seven years of marriage, we had reached that inevitable fork in the road where we were either going to rediscover those lovable little traits that had attracted us to each other in the first place or get a divorce.

The thought of divorce made me cringe. I had no interest in throwing myself back into the singles' scene. For one thing, I'd be yet another middle-aged divorcée in a market glutted with middle-aged divorcées. For another, men were so . . . so . . . confused these days. They were either confused about their sexuality or confused about their attitudes toward success or confused about whether it was okay to cry. They were even confused about how much aftershave lotion they should wear, which was why there was an inordinate amount of Drakkar Noir floating around. God, it was a jungle out there.

But the thought of reviving the passion of my marriage . . . well, it wasn't impossible. I still loved Hunt and I felt sure he still loved me. The question was, How do people rekindle that first spark, that wonderful giddy feeling when everything the other person does is miraculous?

You enter into a bizarre sort of bargain when you fall in love: if your beloved watches football games on television, you watch football games on television; if your beloved eats Indian food, you eat Indian food; if your beloved spends New Year's Eve with his old Army buddies, you spend New Year's Eve with his old Army buddies. And then the novelty of the relationship wears off, and you never do any of these things again.

Of course, in Hunt's case, it wasn't football, Indian food, or even New Year's Eves with Army buddies that tried my patience; it was Kimberley, Hunt's ten-year-old daughter from his first marriage to a sometime actress named Bree. When he was a mere twenty-two, Hunt had met Bree through a friend he no longer speaks to. Bree was blond and long-necked, just like her idol Meryl Streep, but the comparison ended there. Thanks to a very limited range and a tinny, thoroughly irritating voice, she couldn't get a part in a movie no matter how many producers and directors she slept with. Currently, Bree spent her time reading *Variety,* collecting alimony payments from Hunt and badmouthing me to her daughter.

Her daughter. I sighed when I thought of Kimberley, the child I wanted so desperately to love. When I got engaged to Hunt, I was a fledgling cookbook editor at Charlton House, all naive and dewy-eyed about life. I thought it was incredibly worldly of me to involve myself with a man who had an ex-wife and a young daughter.

"I'll be a stepmother!" I told my mother excitedly when I called to announce my wedding plans. I had visions of being Superwoman, running home from the office, whipping up nutritionally correct dinners for my little family, helping my stepdaughter with her homework and tucking her tenderly into bed.

"You'll be a doormat," my mother said, never one to mince words. "You'll beat your brains in trying to win her affection and she'll shit on you. Both of them will."

"Both of them? You mean Kimberley and her mother?" I asked.

"No, no," she clucked. "The mother won't shit on you. She'll just poison the little girl against you."

"How comforting," I said.

"I meant Hunt. The minute you open your mouth to discipline his daughter, he'll take *her* side and you'll be the odd one out."

"Oh, Mom," I said. "That doesn't sound like Hunt. He'd never take Kimberley's side against me."

My mother knew what she was talking about, I realized later. When I married Hunt and inherited his daughter, I found that every time I told the kid to clean up her room, turn the radio down, or take her feet off the kitchen table, Hunt would get that pathetic, guilt-trip look and tell me to back off.

"She's only a child," he'd say. "She doesn't know any better."

"How's she going to know any better if nobody tells her?" I'd say.

The situation only got worse as Kimberley got older. When a little kid misbehaves, you giggle and say goo-goo and chalk it up to the fact that little kids don't know right from wrong. But when a *big* kid misbehaves, you say, "That kid's a pain in the ass." There's nothing cute or cuddly about a big kid who misbehaves, especially when the big kid's misbehaving comes between you and your husband.

I missed the way Hunt and I used to be, before I saw how Kimberley manipulated Hunt, before I watched him cave in to his ex-wife every time she needed money or said she did, before we allowed our marriage to go stale. I longed for the days when just the thought of him would get my heart racing. But my heart hadn't been doing any racing lately—at least not for him. My heart only raced when I thought of Mel Gibson and Kevin Costner and railroad conductors with red handlebar mustaches.

As for Hunt, I knew what got *his* heart racing—his country club. Sure, we were having problems before he joined The Oaks. But since then, he'd become a person I hardly recognized. Yes, he wanted to make partner at F&F, and yes, there were influential and important business types at The Oaks. But did my nice, normal husband have to metamorphose into a back-slapping, approval-seeking, pink-and-green-plaid-panted golf nut? I had heard The Oaks had an exquisite, eighteen-hole course. *Golf Digest* called it the most challenging, "visually eventful" course in Connecticut. But after joining the club, Hunt became positively bewitched by golf. He was so bewitched by the game that he often taped tournaments on our VCR and watched them before he went to sleep. He was so bewitched by the game that he often wore neckties with little white golf balls on them. He was so bewitched by the game that he often chose golf over sex, the result being that the only head and shaft that saw regular action belonged to his putter, not his pecker. In other words, our sex life, once so rich and rewarding, had slowed to a crawl. "A guy only has so much energy," Hunt explained.

"Belford station," boomed the conductor.

Shit. I didn't want to get off the train in the worst way. I wanted to stay in my seat in the nice big choo choo and think and daydream and never have to face the fact that my job was gone and my marriage was stale.

"Bel-fooord," the conductor said again.

"I'm going, I'm going," I muttered as I gathered my belongings and stepped off the train onto the empty platform.

I suddenly wished I'd called Hunt at his office to tell him what had happened. I should have asked him to meet me at Grand Central and take me home. But there was always the chance he'd say, "Sorry, Judy. Got a big pork bellies meeting this afternoon." Better not to be rejected, I decided. I'd been rejected enough for one day.

♦

When the taxi pulled up in front of my house, the driver looked at me in his rearview mirror and said, "Nice house."

I thanked him, paid him, and walked up the flagstone steps to my nice house—my nice house that, without my pay check, would be a stretch for us to afford.

The house was a bona fide antique colonial circa 1810, known around town as The Ichobod Townsend House for some crazy old bastard who shot a band of marauding Indians right on the front lawn and became a local hero. Consequently, the house was one of Belford's prized pieces of real estate, according to the realtor who sold it to us without mentioning that the place was full of squirrels— squirrels who were so comfy up in the attic that they didn't want to leave no matter what we did. Since we were as environmentally cor- rect as a modern couple could be, we wouldn't let our exterminator poison the little rodents. Instead, we decided to share the house with them: they got the attic and we got the rest of the place.

I put my key in the door and let myself in. "I'm home," I said to no one in particular.

We had bought the house six years ago, in the second year of our marriage. It was Hunt who'd suggested we move out of the city. "We need more space," he'd said. "Besides, it'll be fun riding in on the train together." Commuting together into Manhattan from our an- tique house in Connecticut with its wooden ducks, patchwork quilts, and American flags sounded just ducky to me, only it turned out to be something we rarely did: Hunt liked to take the seven o'clock express train with all the other guys from F&F; I preferred the 8:02. So much for togetherness.

The woman who owned the house before us had done a good deal of renovation, albeit some of it nonsensical. I mean, would you install an elevator in a cozy, 1810 colonial? Apparently, she'd taken a fall on the rickety old stairs and put the elevator in so she could travel more easily between the house's three floors. On our first night in our new home, Hunt and I made love in the elevator. It was exciting, but not so exciting that we ever did it again. Mostly, we used the elevator as a kind of mechanical hamper—a handy gadget for transporting our dirty clothes from the bedroom on the second floor to the laundry room in the basement.

I dropped my things on the kitchen counter and heaved a deep sigh. What should I do now? I asked myself. It was only noon. There was a whole day staring me in the face.

I was dying to call somebody, to tell somebody I'd been fired, to "share my pain," as they say on "Oprah." But who? All my friends in publishing would be at lunch, eating "spa food," sipping mineral water, and chewing on the latest, juiciest gossip.

I considered calling my mother, but she and my father wouldn't be home. Ever since they'd retired to Boca Raton, where they bought a four-bedroom "Mediterranean-style" house in a country club community called Point O' Palms, they had led an incredibly active lifestyle. Their country club wasn't a country club in the same way that The Oaks was a country club—i.e., there was no trick to getting into their country club; all you had to do was open your checkbook—but it had tennis courts, two golf courses, and a marina, and my parents felt at home there the way I never would at The Oaks.

I considered calling Hunt's mother, but she and I didn't get along any better than Kimberley and I did. She was cold and distant and painfully monosyllabic. A real chore to be around. She'd just sit there, smug in the knowledge that chatty types like me would rush in and fill the dead air. And her husband wasn't a gabber either. Spending an evening with them was about as much fun as watching an icicle melt.

I considered calling someone I knew from Belford, but I didn't know anyone from Belford except our plumber, our exterminator, and the teller at our bank's drive-in window, none of whom were the stuff of bosom buddies. A rural yet sophisticated town in affluent Chesterfield County, Belford wasn't the friendliest town in the world unless you had kids—kids who lived with you full time.

I considered calling Kimberley, but she was at Nightingale-Bamford School, on Manhattan's Upper East Side, where the girls wore starched uniforms and spent summers at their families' chateaux in the south of France and were fonder of their au pairs than they were of their parents. Three years ago, Bree had insisted on sending Kimberley there, despite the ridiculous tuition, and Hunt, ever passive when it came to his ex-wife and daughter, had paid the bill. I remember how we fought over it. I called him a wimp and he called me a nag; I told him to wise up and he told me to butt out; then I stormed into the kitchen and he went off to play golf. As I said, I missed the way Hunt and I used to be.

♦

Hunt came home at seven-thirty. I could tell he was in a good mood because he kissed me on the lips when he saw me. That's one of the first things to go in a marriage, you know: kissing on the lips—slow, meaningful kissing on the lips. Oh, you still hug and cuddle and even have sexual intercourse every now and then, but you stop kissing each other on the lips once you've been married a few years—unless, of course, one of you is drunk.

"How was your day, Jude?" he asked as he hung his coat in the foyer closet and ran his fingers through his wavy blond hair. His *natural* blond hair. Hunt was a pure-bred WASP—a blond-haired, blue-eyed, small-nosed Episcopalian. Hunter Dean Price III was his full name. He was long-legged and long-waisted and had only recently started to grow a paunch. He had the look and the manner of a man who'd grown up with money, even though he hadn't. What he'd grown up with was a father who had failed at every business he'd ever gotten involved in; a father who felt like such a failure that he was determined his son would succeed where he had not. Indeed, I often wondered whether Hunter Dean Price *II* wanted that partnership for Hunt at F&F even more than Hunt himself; whether Hunt's relentless campaigning and networking and sucking up had more to do with old Dad than with his own personal satisfaction.

"You really want to know how my day was?" I asked him.

"You bet," he said. "How about a drink first?"

I nodded.

I followed Hunt to the wet bar in the library, a warm, dark green room off the kitchen. He poured me a glass of Pouilly Fuissé and made himself a Tanqueray gin and tonic, a libation known affectionately around the house as a T 'n' T. I sat on the loveseat; Hunt sat at the leather-top desk.

"Something happen today?" he asked.

I took a deep breath. "You could say that," I said and started to cry. I had promised myself I wouldn't, but I was overcome with feelings of sadness and loss. Having to tell Hunt what Leeza had done to me only made it seem more real, more horrible.

Hunt got up from his chair and sat beside me on the loveseat. "Judy? What is it?" he asked.

"I was fired," I said and started sobbing on his shoulder.

"Fired?" said Hunt as he pulled me off him. I couldn't tell if he was upset by my news or afraid I'd soil his suit.

"Leeza Grummond said Charlton House is taking the high road,"

I said. "From now on they're going to publish 'literature.' " I rolled my eyes. "No more cookbooks. No more romance novels either."

"Arlene Handlebaum was fired too?" Hunt asked.

I nodded.

Hunt was speechless and expressionless. He just sat there, pulling on his left earlobe and working his jaw muscles, the way he always did when he was upset.

"They're giving me a whopping three months' severance," I went on. "Big sports, huh?"

He continued not to speak.

"Hunt?" I said. "What are you thinking?"

He cleared his throat. "I'm thinking that I can't believe what I'm hearing," he said, "and I'm thinking what a raw deal you got." He paused. "I understand that they've got to trim the fat. All the big companies are cutting back. But letting you and Arlene go is pure stupidity. You two are terrific editors."

"I couldn't agree more," I said sadly. "Oh, Hunt. What am I going to do? I loved working at Charlton House. I feel lost already."

Hunt put his arms around me and held me. "Everything's going to be okay," he said as he rocked me. "I have faith in you. I know you'll find another job very quickly."

"Really? How?" I said. "The whole industry is downsizing. It's the nineties, remember? There aren't exactly a million jobs out there now."

"You're good at what you do," he insisted. "That has to mean something."

"It didn't mean anything to Leeza Grummond," I pointed out. "She told me I was good at what I did and then fired me."

Hunt shook his head. "I still can't get over it," he said.

"Join the club," I said. "What are we going to do about money?" I said. "No job, no paycheck."

"We're not exactly destitute. I make enough to support us," said Hunt.

I nodded. Hunt was right, of course. His salary had always dwarfed mine, even with my yearly raises. But my salary had made me feel worthwhile, as if I were a true partner in the marriage. I didn't want to mooch off him.

"Look," he said. "Give it a day or two to sink in. Then on Monday you can start networking and figuring out your next move. You'll get another job, Jude. I know you will. You're bright and clever and very talented, and talent always wins out."

I looked up at Hunt and felt a surge of love for him. Sure, he could be a boob sometimes. And sure, his obsessions with his pork bellies and his country club and his golf got on my nerves. But the man was loyal and true and a good husband. How could I even think of divorcing him?

I spent the next twenty minutes venting my spleen about Charlton House and their new publishing program and Leeza—most of all Leeza. It felt so satisfying to be able to tell Hunt how I felt about the wunderkind of the Western world, sort of like having a really bad case of poison ivy and finally being able to scratch.

When I'd said enough about Leeza for one evening, I suggested we rustle up something to eat for dinner.

Hunt said he had to make a phone call but would join me soon.

I kissed him (on the lips) and went into the kitchen. A few minutes later, he reappeared.

"I found some leftover veal marengo in the refrigerator," I said. "Want to nuke it?"

"Sounds fine," Hunt said, and I knew he meant it. Any kind of food was fine with Hunt, as long as it didn't have anchovies in it. Here I was, a Jewish foodie who spoke of polenta and pancetta and penne puttanesca, married to a goyish guy whose idea of a gourmet meal was gorgonzola on his cheeseburger instead of Velveeta. What's more, he didn't care if he ate. He could skip meals and not even know that he skipped them, while I hadn't missed a meal since I was nine.

I heated up the veal and set the little table in our eat-in kitchen.

"Who'd you call?" I asked Hunt as we ate.

"Call?" he said.

"Yeah. Before. You said you had to call someone."

"Oh, that. Just a client."

I nodded and went on eating. "New client?" I asked.

"Yeah," said Hunt. "How'd you know?"

"Because you seemed like you were in a good mood when you first came home. That can only mean one of two things: you got a new client or you had a big day on the links. Since it's March and you aren't playing golf yet, I'm betting it's a new client."

He smiled. "I'm that predictable, huh?"

" 'Fraid so," I said and drained my wineglass. "Want some more wine?" I asked as I got up to retrieve the bottle from the refrigerator.

"Sure," said Hunt.

I came back to the table and refilled both our glasses.

"So who's the new client?" I asked, a forkful of veal en route to my mouth.

Hunt sipped his wine but didn't answer.

"Who's the new client?" I asked again. Like his parents, Hunt wasn't the world's greatest conversationalist, but he usually held up his end better than this.

He put down his glass and stared at his plate.

"Leeza Grummond," he said finally, looking guilty but not guilty enough.

It took me a second to process the information. Then I exploded. "You're telling me Leeza Grummond is your new client?" I laid down my fork and put my hands in my lap so I wouldn't strangle him.

"It's your fault," he had the nerve to say.

"How do you figure?" I said.

"Remember how you got that big Christmas bonus last year?" he said.

"How could I forget," I said. "It paid for this table we're sitting at."

"*Part* of it paid for the table. The other part went into the commodities market, into an account at F&F that I set up for you."

"Yeah? So?"

"Remember how much money you made from that account? And how you went around telling everybody at Charlton House that they should give me their money to invest?"

I nodded. I'd wanted everybody at work to know what a smart commodities trader my husband was. So I shot my mouth off. So what.

"Well, Leeza heard you. She called and said she wanted to invest in crude oil and natural gas and pork bellies, just like you did."

"That twit. That fucking twit. How dare she fire me and then hire my husband? Does that take the cake or what?"

Hunt took a sip of wine. "She gave me a lot of money to invest, Jude," he said. "And every time I get a new client I score points with the partners, you know?"

I looked at Hunt and all I could see was *traitor!* Well, *asshole* also came to mind. "So you'd screw your wife just to impress the partners?" I said.

"Of course not," he said. "I took Leeza Grummond on as a client because I want to move up in the firm—for *both* our sakes. You like our lifestyle as much as I do. Don't you want to be able to maintain it? Especially now that you've lost your job? Think about it."

All I could think about was that my husband would be making money for Leeza. It was too gruesome a thought to bear. I had to leave the room. I was afraid that if I didn't, I'd say something really nasty and insulting to Hunt, something I wouldn't be able to take back.

"I hate today," I said as I stood in the doorway. "If I go to sleep now, today will be over."

"Do you hate me too?" he asked.

I considered the question. "Yes," I said.

Hunt's face fell.

"But I'll get over it," I added and went to bed.

CHAPTER THREE

♦

I spent Monday morning on the phone with my friends in publishing, all of whom expressed shock and indignation over my firing but none of whom knew of any job openings.

Don't worry, I told myself. Something will turn up.

I was right: something, or should I say some *one*, did turn up—my loyal author and relentless suitor, Valerio. When he heard I'd gotten the ax, he was so enraged he called Leeza to tell her he was taking his next cookbook to a rival publisher. But he never got to deliver his message because good old Leeza wouldn't even take his call! So what did he do? He turned up at my house, bearing gifts and lots of sympathy.

"You're sweet," I told him as we sat in my living room one Wednesday afternoon, drinking Bellinis and reminiscing about our salad days at Charlton House.

"Eeet has nutting to do weet being sweeta," said Valerio, his accent thick with his native Italy. I had to hand it to the guy: he could turn that accent on and off at the drop of a hat. When he was in serious contract negotiations, for example, he could make the accent disappear. "Don't you hondle me, buster," he'd say, without a trace of the Old Country. "No escalator clauses, no deal!"

"I'm not sweet at all," he continued. "I am een love with you, Judy."

I had given up trying to talk Valerio out of his ardor. My current strategy was to ignore it. "Have you heard anything new about Charlton House?"

I bit my lip as I spoke the name of my former employer. I felt like some jilted lover who wishes she never met the guy who dumped her but asks everyone who knows him how he's doing.

"No," Valerio said. "But you don't needa that place. You will get a job with a publishing house that appreciates your brains and beauty."

He reached over and grabbed my hand, then kissed it.

Such a Casanova, that Valerio. I looked at his hands, which were now on my thigh. The tips of his fingers were their usual bright pink, and the thought of them on my body made me laugh. I mean, would *you* take a guy seriously in the love object department if his fingertips were stained with pistachio nuts? Never mind that pistachios were the "secret ingredient" in his now-famous signature dishes. He was a terrific cook and an even more terrific talk show guest, but he wasn't for me, not even in my present, highly vulnerable state.

He stayed until Hunt came home. The two men chatted for a few minutes, while I went to the bathroom. When I came back, I walked Valerio to the front door.

"Your husband is okay," he whispered, minus the accent. Apparently, he was now in his deal-making mode. "I used to think he didn't know a thing about food and wondered how you could be married to him. But you should have heard him go on about corn and wheat and soybean oil. He said corn's the place to put my money now. He said he'd handle my account, no problem."

Leave it to Hunt, the commodities broker. The man never stopped hustling.

"Maybe you two should have lunch," I said as I ushered Valerio out the door.

"Only if you come with us, my sweeta," he said and kissed my hand.

"Can't," I said. "Got to get a job."

I tried to get a job, I really tried, but nobody was hiring. I'm not saying there weren't openings. I'd hear that this cookbook editor was leaving to have a baby and that cookbook editor was leaving to go into rehab. The trouble was, their companies weren't replacing them; they were *downsizing*. God, what an awful word.

Then one day I took the train into the city to have lunch with Arlene. She looked even paler and more haunted than usual so I asked her if she was taking care of herself.

"Oh, sure," she said. "But I miss my job."

"I know how you feel," I said. "I'm going crazy sitting at home."

"Same here," she said. "If it weren't for my six favorite romance novels, I don't know what I'd do."

"Your six favorite romance novels? You mean you keep rereading the same books?"

"Sure. Why not?"

I wanted to say, "Because you should find a *real* boyfriend instead of mooning over fictional men," but I just shrugged and kept my mouth shut. The trouble with Arlene was that no mortal man could possibly live up to her favorite romance heroes. I'd tried to fix her up with a couple of Hunt's friends from F&F, but she wasn't interested in meeting either of them. "Just because they're not dukes or counts or knights doesn't make them bad people," I'd pointed out.

After we ordered lunch, Arlene told me she'd heard a rumor that Beach Reads, a paperback house that published the occasional cookbook, was looking for an editor. It seems the previous cookbook editor had gone to India to live in an ashram.

"That's great!" I said enthusiastically. "I'll call them the minute I get home. Thanks for the tip."

"I just hope it pans out," said Arlene. "Beach Reads isn't a very classy outfit, so don't expect much."

"I won't," I said.

Beach Reads published a lot of sleazy, pornographic novels. The employees the company attracted weren't exactly the cream of the crop, but hey—a job was a job.

The morning of my interview at Beach Reads, I regarded my reflection in the mirror and thought, Okay, you're not twenty but you look pretty good for a girl who'll be forty in three months. I was still a size eight, although my clothes were a tad too tight, what with my hanging around the house and eating way too many Pepperidge Farm cookies. My eyelids were drooping a bit, and my thighs had sprouted some nasty varicose veins, not to mention cottage cheese, but all in all, I was still a tenderloin. At least, I hoped so. There was my long, frosted-blond hair and my almond-shaped hazel eyes and my full, pouty lips, which had embarrassed me as a kid but were now all the rage. And then there were my very perky breasts, which were the envy of my friends and the pride of my husband, who had once suggested I have them insured the way dancers insure their legs. "Are you serious?" I'd said. "No, I was just kidding," he'd said. That was the trouble with Hunt. As I told you earlier, he wasn't the most humorous guy on the planet, so when he *was* making a joke, you couldn't exactly tell.

I was early for my interview, but there was no excuse for my having to wait forty-five minutes to see the Director of Human Resources.

"Come on in," she said finally, introducing herself as Ms. Rothstein. She wore blue jeans with holes in the knees, black high-top Reeboks, and a T-shirt that read: AEROSMITH—1992 TOUR." Her long black hair was pulled behind her ears, presumably to show off her lobes, each of which had been pierced three or four times. She couldn't have been more than twenty-five, and she certainly wasn't my idea of a personnel director, but I tried to maintain a positive attitude.

It was difficult, though, especially since Ms. Rothstein didn't even bother to look at my résumé.

"Where are you from, Ms. Mills?" she asked.

"Shirley, Ms. Rothstein," I replied.

"You want me to call you by your first name? That's cool, Shirley. Call me Linda," she said. "Now, where are you from?"

"Shirley," I said.

"Right. So what town are you from?" she said.

"Shirley," I said again. The conversation reminded me of Abbott and Costello's Who's on First routine. "Shirley is a small town on Long Island," I explained. "Not far from the Hamptons."

"The Hamptons. Oh, cool," said Linda. "What was your major in college?"

Did we really have to go back that far? I wondered. I had a dozen bestselling cookbooks to my credit. What the hell did my college major have to do with anything?

"Greek and Latin," I answered anyway, trying to stay focused.

"Cool," said Linda. "We have a bunch of cookbook authors who are Greek and Latin. There's Arianna Stavros, who did *Fun with Feta Cheese,* and Pablo Bournino, the pasta guy who—"

"I meant *ancient* Greek and Latin. As in the classics," I interrupted. "You know, *The Iliad, The Odyssey,* stuff like that?"

Linda gave me a blank look.

We chatted for several more minutes. Then Linda took a phone call from her boyfriend, an aspiring rock guitarist named Pain (that was only his stage name, she explained; his real name was Howard).

"Now," I said when they hung up fifteen minutes later. "About the job. Is there someone else I should see? The publisher? Or maybe the editor-in-chief?"

I didn't want to spend another minute at Beach Reads, let alone work there, but I had promised myself I would take any publishing job that came along and I was sticking to it.

"Not yet," said Linda, who reached into her desk drawer, pulled out a half-eaten bag of trail mix, and offered me some.

"No thanks," I said.

"I'll call you if anybody here wants to see you," she said, giving me no indication whether I had made the first cut.

She stood, shook my hand, and showed me out.

That night Hunt asked me how my interview went.

"I have no idea," I said. "We barely discussed cookbooks. I never got to tell her about the bestsellers I had at Charlton House."

"She'll find out about all that from reading your résumé," he said. "Maybe for the interview she just wanted to get a sense of you as a person."

"Maybe. We'll see."

We saw. Linda Rothstein never called. After two weeks, I broke down and called her.

"It's Judy Mills," I said. "I was just wondering, have you made a decision about your cookbook editor?"

"Oh hi, Judy," said Linda. "Yeah, the publisher made a decision. He hired someone else."

I was disappointed and very relieved.

"But I never even got to talk to him," I said. I'd heard Beach Reads' publisher, Sam Spellman, was a real cheepskate, the type who never pays people what they're worth.

"That's because Sam decided to promote from within," Linda explained.

"Oh, you mean there was an editor there who'd already worked on cookbooks?" I said.

"No," she said. "Sam gave his wife the job."

"His wife? Is she an editor there?"

"No, she's never worked in publishing. But he likes her cooking so he hired her."

Talk about promoting from within. I didn't have a chance.

I thanked Linda, hung up the phone, and tried not to be discouraged. It was only one interview. There would be others.

There were others. There was the interview at Save the Manatee Press, publishers of books about the environment. They were looking for an editor to oversee their line of vegetarian and health food cookbooks. Hey, so I was a beef lover whose idea of heaven was a luscious, velvety filet mignon, charcoal grilled medium rare. So what? The people at Save the Manatee would never have to know, as in: "Don't Ask. Don't Tell."

The good news was that the issue of my own eating preferences was never raised during the interview. The bad news was that the interview lasted only a minute and a half. I made the colossal and irrevocable mistake of showing up in my sheared beaver coat, the coat I'd bought with my Charlton House Christmas bonus two years before. Yeah, I know, it wasn't a swift move to wear fur to an interview with a publisher whose name was Save the Manatee. But it was an absolutely freezing day in March, and the sheared beaver was the warmest coat I owned.

After two months' worth of dead-end interviews with cookbook publishers, I decided it was time to venture outside the book industry. I interviewed at *Gourmet* magazine. I interviewed at *Bon Appétit.* I even interviewed at Kellogg's, where they were looking for someone to edit the little recipes they put on their boxes of All Bran. None of the interviews amounted to anything more than a "You're not right for *this* job but we'll call you if anything else opens up." It was depressing, let me tell you.

But the most depressing interview of all—the utter nadir, to be honest—was the one I had at MTV. Yes, the music video cable channel. It seems that one of the geniuses over there decided they should have a regular feature teaching America's young people how to cook. They were calling the show "MTV Cooks" and were looking for a recipe consultant. Since I was known for my somewhat gimmicky cookbooks, the producer got my name and called me. I was thrilled.

I went to the interview full of hope, bursting with ideas for instilling in the Guns 'n' Roses generation a deep and abiding appreciation for confit de canard, broccoli rape, and anything with fennel. Unfortunately, the producer of "MTV Cooks" had more low-rent dishes in mind for his young audience—dishes like nachos, English muffin pizzas, and chicken wings fried in beer batter. When I suggested that

MTV would be promoting junk food if it went the nachos, pizza, and fried chicken wings route, he laughed and said, "You haven't been watching your MTV, baby. Junk food is what we're all about. You think Pearl Jam's latest video isn't junk food? I hate to dis you, baby, but we need someone younger for this job, you dig?"

I dug, all right. Right into a world-class black hole. I had no job, no prospects of a job, and no one to commiserate with. Arlene had gotten a job a month ago and was so busy proving herself to her new employer she didn't have time to listen to my kvetching. Even Valerio was suddenly too busy for me; he was on the phone to Hunt six times a day, checking on his latest transactions in the commodities market.

Speaking of Hunt, I left my interview at MTV and went straight to a pay phone to call him at his office, which was only a five-minute walk from Grand Central Station. I was dying for him to take me to lunch at some dark, wildly sophisticated restaurant where I could sit among people who were writing off their meal on their expense account. I wanted to feel like I was a member of the work force again, like I was still part of the action. I felt so isolated since losing my job, so relegated to the suburbs, so excluded, as if I had suddenly been booted out of a club. So when I dialed Hunt's number and listened to his secretary tell me he had taken the rest of the day off to play golf at *his* club, I felt even more alone.

I couldn't blame Hunt, of course. It was mid-May, and while The Oaks didn't officially open until Memorial Day weekend, the golfers had been out on the course since April.

I took the train back to Connecticut. When I got home, I made out my shopping list, hopped in my car, and went grocery shopping. That's how I got through every day that I didn't have a job: I went grocery shopping and then came home and cooked Hunt and me a spectacular dinner. I didn't know what else to do with myself or how else to prove my worthiness. Night after night Hunt would walk in the door and be welcomed by a five-star gourmet meal, a meal most men would be grateful for. Not Hunt. Gourmet meals went right over his head. Not only that, they made him angry. At least, mine did.

"You're wasting our money on this stuff," he said of that evening's meal, cornish game hens stuffed with basmati rice and shitaki mushrooms. "You know I can't tell a shitaki mushroom from the fungus that grows in our backyard. And what's more, I don't want to."

"Not very open-minded of you," I scowled.

"Maybe not, Judy, but we can't afford this kind of dinner every night. Not on only one paycheck."

"I'm well aware that I'm not contributing a paycheck," I said defensively. "That's why I'm cooking these dinners. They're my way of contributing."

"Judy," Hunt said in his most tolerant voice, "I don't want you to cook. I want you to work. I've never known you not to work."

So that was it. When Hunt fell in love with me, I was a big-shot career woman. Now I was a big-shot career woman without a big-shot career and he was feeling cheated. Well, too bad. I wasn't going to be made to feel worse about myself than I already did.

"It's not as if I'm not trying to get a job," I said. "I wasn't the one who was at The Oaks today, playing golf."

Hunt smiled. He couldn't help himself. The word "golf" nearly always made him smile. It was a knee-jerk reaction, a Pavlov's dogs thing.

"Where were you?" he asked.

"I was interviewing for a job at MTV," I said.

"MTV? That's great, Jude," he said, full of sudden admiration for me.

"Yeah, well, I didn't get the job," I snapped. "But I was out there trying, while you were out there trying to hit a stupid little ball into a stupid little cup."

"Come on."

"Come on, yourself. The minute The Oaks opens for the season, you turn into some dopey, golf-crazed, country club person."

"Thank you."

"You're welcome."

Hunt walked over to me and draped his arm around my shoulder. "Let's not do this, okay?" he said.

I nodded halfheartedly. "You've got to admit you're really into that club," I said.

"It's a terrific place. Why shouldn't I be into it?" he said, pulling his arm off me.

"Because the people there are numbingly dull, not to mention snobby, small-minded, and completely out of touch with reality."

"How would you know?" Hunt said. "You never go to the club."

"I don't have to. I already know that there's nobody there I would ever want as a friend."

"Really? Who would you want as a friend, Judy? Those publishing types you call friends? Those people who dropped you the minute you lost your job at Charlton House? Aside from Arlene and Valerio, your 'friends' haven't been acting very friendly lately."

Hunt had a point. "That doesn't mean the people at The Oaks aren't a bunch of drips," I said, remembering my brief contact with them during the weeks they were deciding if we were qualified to join the club.

We had been proposed for membership by Perry Vail, the head of F&F's estate planning department and a complete horse's ass. As his family had belonged to The Oaks for three generations, he knew everything about everybody there. He was a terrible gossip—a "wash woman," my mother called such men. It was he who had first invited Hunt to play golf at The Oaks. Hunt had come home that afternoon raving about the course; it was love at first hole, let me tell you. The next thing I knew, Dexter "Ducky" Laughton, F&F's vice president of operations and a member of the club's Finance Committee, was agreeing to be our co-sponsor. As The Oaks was one of America's last bastions of WASP wealth and privilege, there was a long waiting list to get in. But Ducky maneuvered Hunt and me to the top of the list, and after two ghastly dinners with the Laughtons and the Vails, we were visited by three members of the Membership Committee. God, what torture. Someone named Duncan Tewksbury, a stooped, sun-spotted man in his late seventies who had greasy gray hair, wore a rumpled, seersucker sport jacket, and looked as if he hadn't brushed his teeth since the invention of the cotton gin, introduced himself as the chairman of the Board of Governors. Also along to check us out was Pete Barr, a fortyish, steroid-engorged man whose neck was the size of my hips and whose hips were the size of my neck. And then there was Addison Bidwell, who was in his thirties but had not a trace of youthfulness about him. He was thin-lipped and narrow-eyed and had an Alfalfa-esque cowlick, not to mention the tightest sphincter in Belford.

Hunt had said that they were only going to stay for an hour or so; that the "at-home visit" was just a silly formality; that we were as good as in.

"What makes you say that?" I'd asked. "The Oaks is a WASP club. The minute they find out I'm Jewish, you'll be blackballed."

"How will they find out?" Hunt had said.

"Kimberley will tell them," I said.

"Kimberley won't be here when they come," Hunt pointed out.

"Yeah, but once you start bringing her to the club, she'll tell them. She loves to cause trouble for me."

"That's ridiculous, Jude," said Hunt, ever protective of his daughter. "She's just going through a stage."

"Yeah, well, the 'stage' has lasted as long as I've known her," I said. "Haven't you noticed how she's always running to you with bulletins about my shortcomings? She wants everybody to hate me as much as she does."

"Kimberley doesn't hate you, Judy. Deep down, she cares for you very much."

"It must be *way* deep down."

"If she showed how much she cared, she'd feel disloyal to her mother."

"Look, all I know is that the first time you take her to that club she'll walk right up to Duncan Tewksbury, the chairman of the Board of Governors, and say, 'My stepmother's Jewish. Na-na-na-na-na.' "

Hunt arched an eyebrow at me. "Kimberley would never do something like that," he said. "She'll keep her mouth shut and so will I and everybody at The Oaks will assume you're Episcopalian."

I thought it was funny at the time—the idea of my trying to "pass" as a Gentile. I mean, what did I care? Hunt wanted to join the club so badly that hiding my heritage was the least I could do for him. But then the three Membership Committee members showed up at our house for their "at-home visit," and after determining that I had not gone to Farmington with someone named Bootsie Mills, nor had I served on the Belford Historical Society with someone named Flossy Mills, nor was I related even in the most distant way to jolly old Hayley Mills, they forced me to answer questions like: "Do you play croquet? Do you sail? Do you ride?"

Do I ride, give me a break. I could no more picture myself sitting atop a horse than I could picture myself spending two minutes with the members of The Oaks.

The men asked me nothing about my career. They were so behind the times when it came to women that when I mentioned the feminist book *Backlash,* they probably thought I was talking about a kink in Hunt's golf swing.

After the at-home visit, a letter went out to the club's 300 members stating that Mr. and Mrs. Hunter Dean Price III had applied for membership and inviting the members to come forward with any blemishes in our background. None of them did, so we were asked to come to the club for a meeting with all fifteen members of the Membership Committee. Two weeks after that, we were notified by mail that we'd been accepted into The Oaks.

"We are delighted to inform you," the letter read, "that the Membership Committee has recommended you for membership in The

Oaks. Welcome! Enclosed is our 1995 Directory, which explains our Membership Classifications, lists forthcoming Social Functions and sets forth our House Rules. Also enclosed is an invoice for the first installment of your initiation fee. Annual dues must be paid in full. Please remit both at your earliest convenience. On behalf of the Board of Governors of The Oaks, I wish you a healthy and happy membership. If I can be of any further service to you, I hope you will let me know. I look forward to seeing both of you at the club. Sincerely, Lloyd Wright, Secretary. The Oaks."

"We made it!" Hunt had exclaimed when he read the letter. "This is gonna do big things for us, Jude. Big things!"

As it turned out, the only big thing it did for us was to give us something else to fight about. Hunt spent all his free time at The Oaks. I spent all my free time avoiding the place. Not a good way to promote intimacy and closeness.

"People ask me if my wife is sick," he'd reported one Friday night, after he had taken the day off from work to play eighteen holes with Perry, Ducky, and a client. "They're trying to figure out why you're never there."

"Tell them I have a job," I'd said sweetly. "Remind them that twentieth-century women often have jobs."

"Not on weekends," Hunt had countered. "Surely you could show up on a Saturday or Sunday and try to make friends with the wives."

"Oh, Hunt," I'd sighed. "What could I possibly have in common with those women? Even the ones who work are throwbacks to the fifties. Their idea of women's liberation is going a whole day without wearing control-top pantyhose."

Hunt had laughed in spite of himself. But he wasn't laughing now, now that I had no career to throw up to him. Now he was angry.

"All you do is make fun of the club," he was saying as I shoveled what was left of our cornish hens dinner down the garbage disposal. "I joined The Oaks because I wanted to make business contacts, so I could go further in my career, so I could build a better life—for us."

"I know, I know," I said. "But have you made these terrific business contacts?"

"You're damn right I have."

"Name one."

He thought for a second. "Clark Haverford. He's a cardiologist. He's given me a lot of money to invest."

"Okay. Name two."

He thought for another second. "Nelson Phipps. He's the CEO of Texoil, Judy. The CEO, for Christ's sake!"

I was impressed. "This Nelson Phipps is a client of yours now?"

"Not exactly. But I'm getting close. I've seen him on the golf course a couple of times. In the Men's Grill too. He remembers my name now. Before you know it, I'll be reeling him in."

I looked at Hunt. When had his quest to become a partner at F&F become so calculated, so desperate? Did he sense that time was running out for him there? That if he didn't make partner in the next year or so, he'd be mired in Middle Management Hell for the rest of his working life?

And what about me? I was getting pretty desperate myself. If I didn't get a job soon, I didn't know what I'd do.

"If you ask me, Judy, I think you should quit dumping on The Oaks and the people who belong there and give the place a try," said Hunt. "The season starts the weekend after next. Your birthday weekend."

My birthday. God, in two weeks I'd be forty. How was that for a kick in the teeth?

"Spend the weekend of my fortieth birthday at The Oaks?" I scowled. "Talk about a double negative."

For some reason that remark seemed to infuriate Hunt.

"Has it occurred to you that maybe you should get your ass over to that club and make some business contacts of your own? You're the one without a job, babe. Maybe you should get over there and find one."

He stormed out of the kitchen without even waiting to see what super-duper concoction I'd whipped up for dessert.

I opened the refrigerator, reached in for the Tiramisu, and placed the bowl on the kitchen counter. I had an urge to stick my head in it, to drown myself in lady fingers and chocolate shavings and marscarpone cheese. What a way to go, huh? I wondered if Jack Kevorkian had thought of it.

Instead of killing myself, though, I decided I would take Hunt's advice and spend some time at The Oaks over Memorial Day weekend. Maybe he was right. Maybe I was too hard on the place. Maybe I'd make some great contacts there and land the job of my life. Yeah, sure.

CHAPTER FOUR

♦

I turned forty the Friday of Memorial Day weekend. I was now a mid-dle-aged person, a person for whom the next stop was senior citizen-ship—if I was lucky.

I had always assumed that by the time I was forty, I'd have Found Myself. But there I was, still struggling with my place in the cosmos, still wondering who I was and why I didn't have a job and why I was married to a man who had begun treating me like an old golf shoe.

Oh, I don't mean to suggest that Hunt ignored me. He took me to the Belford Inn for my birthday dinner. The Belford Inn was one of those quaint New England hostelries where everywhere you looked there was pewter this and copper that and fish bowls full of potpourri. And the waitresses! God, they were so maternal they practically sat you on their laps and fed you.

"Here. For you," Hunt said as he handed me a small gift box. We had just sat down at our table and ordered a bottle of champagne.

I held the box next to my ear and shook it. "Hmm." I smiled. "It's smaller than a bread box but bigger than a container of dental floss."

Hunt laughed. "Open it," he said. "I think you'll like them."

"Them?" I said, arching an eyebrow.

I tore off the wrapping and beamed when I saw Tiffany's famous blue box. I lifted off the top: inside was a little black jewelry case. "Oh, Hunt," I said. "This is so nice of you."

I felt a pang of guilt. Here I had been so down on Hunt, so critical of his unsympathetic attitude toward me. Now look. The man had gone out and bought me a pair of earrings from Tiffany. At least, I assumed they were earrings.

I opened the jewelry case. Yup, they were earrings all right. Eighteen karat gold hoop earrings. Classic, simple, elegant. Totally my taste. They were so totally my taste that I already owned them: Hunt had given me the very same earrings for my thirty-fifth birthday.

"What's wrong?" he asked when he saw my face fall. "Don't you like them?"

"Oh, I like them," I said dully. "In fact, I almost wore them tonight."

"What do you mean you almost—" He stopped. "Oh, Judy. I can't believe I did this."

I didn't answer. I couldn't. It was an honest mistake on Hunt's part. I mean, it wasn't as if I wore the earrings every day. It was understandable that he'd forgotten that I had them or even that *he* had been the one who'd given them to me. I'd given *him* the same Ralph Lauren shirt twice, hadn't I? But still. A woman likes to feel her husband cares enough to remember the jewelry he's given her, especially if he's the sort of husband who doesn't buy her jewelry very often.

"Please forgive me," he said, taking my hand. "It's just that I—"

"Don't worry about it," I said, trying to act mature, like the forty-year-old I had just become. "I know how busy you've been, what with golf season starting and all."

"That's no excuse," he scolded himself. "First thing Monday morning I'm going back to Tiffany and returning these." He slipped the jewelry case into his jacket pocket. "I'm going to pick out something else, something you don't already have."

"Maybe I'd better come with you," I said, half in jest.

"I can manage," he said. "Oh look. Here's our champagne."

The waitress had arrived with our Perrier-Jouet. She showed Hunt the label, waited for him to nod his approval, and when he did, she popped the cork—right into my left breast.

I was in agony, as if a bullet had ripped through me. But it wasn't the pain of the wayward cork that sent me into the ladies' room sobbing. It was the torrent of champagne that soaked my Calvin Klein linen suit, the suit I'd just bought myself for my fortieth birthday. When things go bad, they really go bad.

◆

I chose the next day for my long-awaited debut at the club. I had promised Hunt I would start showing up there, cultivating business contacts the way he did. So, true to my word, I went.

Hunt had informed me that he had a 7:00 A.M. golf game with Perry Vail, Ducky Laughton, and Addison Bidwell, and that if I wanted to ride over to the club with him, I'd have to be ready by six-thirty.

"Never mind," I said. "I'll take my own car."

"You sure?"

"I'm sure. I said I'd put in an *appearance* at The Oaks. I didn't say I'd *live* there."

Hunt kissed me. "Why don't you call Larkin or Nedra and see if you can get a tennis game?"

Larkin Vail was Perry's wife. She had platinum blond hair, a deep tan, and a terrific figure, despite having given birth to five children. She was a full-time wife and mother if you didn't count the seven hours a day she spent on the tennis courts at The Oaks, where she reigned as the women's singles champion and made it known that she intended to hang on to her crown until the day she died. She was also the doubles champ with Nedra Laughton, Ducky's wife. Nedra had stick-straight, chin-length, coal-black hair and spoke with a vaguely foreign accent I couldn't place. One minute I guessed Prague, the next Pago Pago, the next Peoria. She intended to appear worldly and sophisticated, I supposed, what with her kissing people on both cheeks and her constant chatter about her sex life. But her most curious trait was her jealousy: if Ducky even looked at another woman, she went berserk. The whole thing seemed rather high schoolish to me, but Ducky, apparently, found it a turn-on.

"I can't call Larkin or Nedra," I said.

"Why not?" said Hunt.

"For one thing, I haven't seen either of them since those awful Let's-get-to-know-Hunt-Price-and-his-wife dinners last year. For another, Larkin and Nedra are excellent players. They're not going to play with me. I haven't hit a tennis ball in years."

"Sure, they will, Jude. The Oaks is a very friendly club. Look at how easy it's been for me to get golf games."

"Sure, it's been easy. In golf you're competing against yourself; the other members of your foursome don't care if you're a lousy player.

But in tennis you're supposed to hit the ball back to the people across the net. If you don't, they tend to get a bit churlish."

"Look, Jude. I've got to go. Give Larkin and Nedra a call, huh?"

He kissed the top of my head and took off.

I stared at myself in the bathroom mirror. "Okay, so you're not Steffi Graf," I addressed my reflection. "Get over to that club and start networking."

I made a stop on my way to the club. Realizing I had nothing to wear on the tennis court, I walked into the Wimbledon Shop on Main Street in Belford, asked to see the latest in tennis clothes, and walked out wearing a hot pink Ellesse outfit, complete with matching top, skirt, socks, wristbands, and lace panties. Valerio would have loved it—I looked like a walking pistachio nut.

The entrance to The Oaks was marked by stone pillars, one of which was embedded with a small bronze plaque that read: PRI-VATE—MEMBERS ONLY. No name. No identification. Just a tasteful fuck-off to the riffraff.

My BMW and I made our way up the long, winding driveway, past the stone walls and beneath an archway of sixty-foot, century-old oak trees, to the sprawling, Tudor-style clubhouse, which loomed over the club's nearly three hundred acres like a grand nineteenth-century English estate. As I'd discovered from my one and only evening at The Oaks, back when Hunt and I were still being considered for membership, the building housed a large and very formal living room, the walls of which were covered with murals depicting ladies and gentlemen of the turn of the century engaging in a variety of not-very-strenuous sports; a sitting room, paneled in mahogany and lined with bookcases; a main dining room, which overlooked the golf course's eighteenth hole; a Men's Grill, a dark, clubby dining room from which women and children were aggressively barred; a dining terrace, shielded from the elements by a green and white striped awning; men's and ladies' card rooms, which erupted with activity on Thursday nights when many of the members played bridge; and a ballroom, which was used for weddings, debutante balls, and of course, the Memorial Day Dance.

I pulled up in front of the clubhouse and waited for someone to help me out of my car and park it. No one did.

"Excuse me," I said to the elderly woman who finally emerged from the building. She wore a baggy cotton dress, sneakers without socks, and bobby pins in her matted gray hair. I guessed she was one of the club's maids. "Is this where I leave the car for valet parking?" I asked her.

The woman flared her nostrils, as if I'd stepped in dog doo and she'd just caught a whiff. "Valet pahking? At The Oaks? How obsuhd," she said in an unmistakable WASP lockjaw. She walked away, shaking her head and muttering to herself. I later learned she was Mrs. Whitman Tuttle, one of the club's most revered members.

Revered maybe, but the woman wasn't going to make anyone's Best Dressed List; that much I knew.

And what was this no valet parking bullshit? My parents' country club in Boca Raton had valet parking. The attendants there not only parked your car, but shampooed and waxed it.

I parked my own car and found my way to the white clapboard tennis house, which overlooked the club's sixteen Har-Tru courts. A half-dozen women were huddled around a water fountain. They wore white shirts and white skirts and white socks, and they looked like a huge bar of Ivory soap. One of them spotted me and nudged the others, and before I knew it they were all staring at me, their gaze as withering as I had ever endured.

I felt my cheeks grow hot. Was my slip showing? I wondered. No, I wasn't wearing a slip. So what was the problem?

I decided not to let them intimidate me and stared right back. Upon closer examination, I noticed that Larkin Vail and Nedra Laughton were among the group. I took a deep breath and walked over to say hello.

"Oh, look everybody," said Larkin as I approached them. "It's Hunt Price's wife."

She remembered me. Or at least, she remembered Hunt.

"Hi, Larkin," I said. "Nice to see you again."

"Yes," she said simply.

"And you're Nedra, right?" I said, turning to Ducky Laughton's wife.

"It is true," she said in that continental way of hers. She kissed me in that continental way too, first on the left cheek, then on the right. "Everybody, meet June," she said.

"Judy," I corrected her.

"Oh, sorry," she said. *"Judy."*

Call me paranoid, but it sounded like she was saying Jew-dy.

Nedra introduced the others as Weezie Evans, Bailey Vanderhoff, Lacey Hilliard, and Penelope Etheridge.

"Who's going to tell her?" Bailey Vanderhoff asked, eyeing me.

"Tell me what?" I said.

"It's the pink," said Larkin.

"The Oaks has an all-white rule," said Nedra.

"You mean, like South Africa?" I said.

The women looked at each other and shook their heads, as if they couldn't believe they were in the presence of such a hopelessly dense person.

"Everyone has to wear white on the tennis courts," Larkin explained. "It says so in the club directory."

"Oh," I said, looking down over my hot pink Ellesse outfit, which the saleswoman at the Wimbledon Shop had said looked very "smart" on me. Smart. I was so smart I'd never bothered to read that damn club directory. But it had never occurred to me that The Oaks wouldn't allow its members to wear pink on the tennis courts. My parents' club didn't have a dress code on the tennis courts or anywhere else. You could show up there in a magenta roller blading outfit and none of the women would mind—unless, of course, one of them was wearing the very same outfit, in which case you'd be blackballed for life.

"If you plan on playing today, Judy, you might try the pro shop," said Larkin. "They sell white tennis clothes."

Yeah, and judging from the white tennis clothes you're all wearing, the pro shop's merchandise must be about as stylish as a nurse's uniform.

"Thanks, Larkin," I said. "I certainly don't want to break any rules. Not on my first day anyway." I smiled jauntily, trying to make light of the situation. Hey, the situation *was* light. I mean, we were talking about tennis clothes, not world peace.

"How's that adorable husband of yours?" Nedra asked.

"Who's her husband again?" asked Weezie Evans.

"Hunt Price," Larkin said.

"Hunt Price?" said Lacey Hilliard. "He's *sooo* sweet."

"And those dreamy eyes," added Penelope Etheridge.

Adorable? Sweet? Dreamy eyes? *My* Hunt?

What are you so surprised about? I asked myself as they began to debate the merits of Har-Tru tennis courts versus the faster-drying all-weather, then flitted from one insignificant subject to another. Have you forgotten how charming you used to find your husband? How you used to think his earnest, uncomplicated personality was such a refreshing change from all the intense, self-involved assholes out there? How his golden blond hair and twinkling blue eyes and tall, long-waisted body used to make you weak in the knees? Have you really forgotten all that?

"So, Judy," said Nedra, turning the conversation back to me. These women had the attention span of a gnat. "Are you here to play tennis?"

No, I'm here to make new business contacts, I laughed to myself. "Yes, I'm here to play," I said.

Larkin looked stricken, then recoiled from me as if I'd eaten a dozen garlic cloves for breakfast. Perhaps she saw me as a threat, someone who might whip her butt on the court and challenge her sovereignty as The Oaks's best woman player.

"I'm here to play," I said again, "but not with you ladies. I haven't hit the ball in years, and even then I was only a 'C' player."

She breathed a sigh of relief. "Maybe you should take a lesson," she suggested. "The head pro's great. His name's Johnny. He used to be ranked."

"Or you could take an hour with Rob, the assistant pro," Nedra smiled lasciviously. "He's *very* good."

Rob turned out to be twenty-one, well built, and very hands-on. Ten minutes into the lesson, I could see why Nedra enjoyed being under his tutelage. When he wanted to demonstrate, say, the backhand grip, he held you from behind, wrapped his hands around yours on the grip of your racquet, and nuzzled his face between your head and neck as he whispered instructions in your ear. Then he showed you how to execute the perfect swing, and if you followed his instructions correctly, he rubbed your back. Hmm, I thought. If the assistant pro's reward for good play is a back rub, how does the head pro show his approval?

After my lesson I took a quick swim, changed clothes, and drove home. I had promised Hunt we could go to the big Memorial Day Dance that night and I needed a nap before heading back into the trenches.

I had no idea what to wear to The Oaks's Memorial Day Dance, especially after the fiasco with my pink tennis outfit. I knew that the affair was black tie, but I also knew that when it came to sensing what people at The Oaks considered "appropriate dress," I was at a loss.

I threw on the most conservative, understated thing I could find in my closet: a midcalf, black linen dress with short sleeves and a white lace collar. It was more suitable for a funeral than a country club dance, but at least it wouldn't offend anybody.

Imagine my surprise when I arrived at the dance and found that all the women—even the old bats—were dressed to kill. I had never seen so many heaving bosoms. Everywhere I looked there was cleavage and bare backs and slits up the sides of gowns.

"I don't think I'll ever get this right," I sighed as Hunt and I stood in the foyer of the clubhouse.

"What's to get right?" said Hunt. "This is going to be a great party. Enjoy yourself."

A great party. Fat chance. As the theme of the dance was "The Motown Sound," the club had hired a live band composed entirely of white people, performing songs by the Temptations and Four Tops, who were black people. It was The Oaks's idea of multiculturalism.

"Shall we go in?" Hunt said, offering me his arm.

"If we must," I smiled weakly, linking my arm through his.

As we walked through the clubhouse en route to the ballroom, I surveyed the rooms and wondered what the club did with our money. I mean, the walls needed a paint job, the floors were completely carpetless, and the place smelled as musty as my attic. They obviously didn't apply our steep initiation fees and annual dues to the sprucing up of the clubhouse. I guessed it all went to the golf course, knowing nothing about golf courses except that they obviously required more maintenance than the average backyard.

Hunt had reserved a table-for-six with Larkin and Perry Vail and Nedra and Ducky Laughton. Swell.

Nedra waved as we approached the table.

"Hey, everybody. How are ya?" said Hunt as he waved back.

What I didn't realize was that when Hunt said, "Hey, everybody," he didn't just mean the Vails and the Laughtons. He meant everybody in the goddamn room. I'm telling you, the man stopped at every single table to say hello to somebody or other. There had to be nearly three hundred people there, and Hunt seemed to know every one of them! What's more, they seemed to know him. And like him! They joked about his golf game. They inquired about his sore shoulder. They commented on his whimsical cummerbund, a black silk sash with—what else?—little white golf balls on it. My husband really *had* made a lot of contacts at The Oaks. I was impressed. But there was something so nauseating about the obviousness of it all, something so pathetic about the way he slapped backs and laughed too hard at jokes and sucked up to complete strangers.

Or was I just envious? Was I envious of the fact that people were paying attention to my husband and not to me? Was I feeling competitive with him, now that he had friends and I did not? That he had contacts and I did not? That he had a *job* and I did not?

We sat down at the table. Boy girl boy girl boy girl. I was sandwiched between Perry and Ducky.

Perry had shaggy, prematurely gray hair, a hoarse, raspy voice, and as I mentioned earlier, a penchant for knowing everybody's business and sharing it. Ducky was my favorite in the group, although "favorite" might be overstating the level of my affection for him. It was just that he seemed more "real" than the others. He had thinning, wispy brown hair, chubby chipmunk cheeks, and a warm, avuncular manner. It was Ducky who asked me about my career as a cookbook editor; Ducky who confided he was The Oaks's only liberal Democrat; Ducky who joked about the food at the club.

"Awful, isn't it?" he laughed, after taking a bite of his dinner. The menu for the Memorial Day Dance consisted of clamless New England clam chowder, rubbery chicken cordon bleu, and apple pie à la WASP—i.e., with a slice of Velveeta on top. "Even after three drinks it's awful."

"Why doesn't the club fire the chef and get somebody in here who can cook?" I asked.

"Because good chefs are expensive," Ducky explained. "The members would much rather spend their money on a new sprinkler system for the golf course. Besides, Brendan was brought in by the chairman of the Board of Governors, Duncan Tewksbury."

"Brendan's the chef?"

"Right. Duncan likes to tell everyone how he 'stole' Brendan away from The Belford Athletic Club. Now we're stuck with him *and* his rubbery chicken cordon bleu."

For the next hour or so, the men spoke of commodities and the women spoke of shopping. I was so bored I thought I'd cry. Then Addison Bidwell, looking more funereal than ever, his cowlick sticking up like a pitiful erection, walked over to our table to drop a bombshell.

"Claire Cox has joined The Oaks," he told us. "Say goodbye to everything that was good and honorable and right about our club."

I was speechless. Everyone was. Claire Cox was America's best-known feminist, a Gloria Steinem for the nineties. Beautiful and brilliant, she was a lawyer-activist who crusaded tirelessly for women's rights. Everywhere you looked, there she was: on "The Today Show," on "Donahue," on "MacNeil/Lehrer," on "Nightline." The woman was a dynamo. But unlike some of her famous sisters in the Movement, she wasn't a man-hater. On the contrary, her liaisons with some of America's most powerful men made headlines. Tall and lean and graceful, she had long, flowing auburn hair, creamy white skin, and huge green eyes. She looked like the classic forties movie star, with her shoulder pads and pleated slacks and Katharine Hepburn ease. Like Hepburn, Cox was also said to be quite the athlete. She played golf and tennis and was a fabulous swimmer.

But why on earth would someone as sharp and forward-thinking as Claire Cox want to join a club where women were treated like second-class citizens? After showing up at the tennis courts earlier in the day in my hot pink, against-the-rules Ellesse outfit, I'd come home and read that dopey club directory and was shocked: according to the bylaws of The Oaks, men and women were *not* created equal. We weren't allowed to eat in the Men's Grill. We weren't allowed to use the golf course on Wednesday, Friday, Saturday, and Sunday mornings. We weren't allowed to play tennis on Courts 1 through 4 on Friday, Saturday, and Sunday mornings. We weren't allowed to wear slacks in the dining room—even if the slacks were palazzo pants from Giorgio Armani. And worst of all, we weren't allowed to serve on the Board of Governors and certain other committees or vote on matters affecting the membership. Hell, women weren't even allowed to be full members. It was our *husbands* who were full members, while *we* were referred to as "associate members." What's more, single women couldn't join the club under any circumstances. Apparently, the men didn't want women hanging around the golf course, and their wives didn't want *single* women hanging around their husbands. It was that simple. But if single women couldn't join the club, how had Claire Cox gotten in?

"She can't possibly have joined," I said. "Single women can't."

"She got in on a technicality," said Addison, looking terribly defeated. "She's Duncan Tewksbury's grandniece."

"He's the chairman of the Board of Governors," Hunt whispered.

"Yes, I know," I said.

"He's also on the Membership Committee," Hunt added.

"Right," I said, "but I still don't see what that has to—"

"Duncan's a past president of the club," Perry jumped in. "Most important, his older brother Justin was the club's founder *and* Claire Cox's grandfather. That means she's a legacy."

"Exactly," Addison sighed forlornly. "There's a clause in the bylaws stating that a legacy, or descendant, of the founder *has* to be granted full membership, single woman or not."

"How's Duncan taking the news?" Perry asked.

"He's mortified," said Addison.

"Why should he be mortified?" I asked. "I would think he'd be proud that he has such an important relative. If you ask me, Claire Cox will be an asset to this club."

"Oh, please," Addison sighed again. "She's going to turn this place into a women's lib colony."

Ducky laughed. "Don't listen to him, Judy," he said. "He and the others are afraid Claire will drag everybody into the twentieth century. They're afraid she's going to destroy their grand old traditions."

"Would that really be so bad?" I asked.

"To them it would," said Ducky. "The older members are absolutely terrified of change. They want to be able to count on the fact that Jimmy, the general manager, will remember the names of their children and grandchildren; that Rick, the starter, will know what time they like to tee off; that Margaret, the hostess in the Men's Grill, will bring them their favorite drink before they even ask for it. They don't want anything to change, especially not the rules involving women. These guys are in the Dark Ages, Judy. The club is sacred to them, and they'll be damned if they're going to let someone like Claire Cox tell them what to do."

"There goes our resident liberal," Perry pointed at Ducky. "That bleeding heart of his never stops bleeding."

"It has nothing to do with his liberal politics," Nedra snapped, her eyes blazing. "He had a fling with Claire Cox when they were college students at Berkeley. Tell everybody how much you two meant to each other, Ducky. Tell them."

We all looked from Nedra to Ducky then back to Nedra, who was red-hot with jealousy. The woman was like something out of an Italian opera.

"Let's not go into that, huh, Nedra?" Ducky said. "It happened a long time ago."

"Yes, but how will you feel now that she's back in your life?" asked Nedra. "Will you talk to her? Eat with her? Play golf with her? Will you?"

"Speaking of golf," said Perry in a valiant attempt to move the conversation in another direction, "let's just hope Ms. Cox doesn't try to stick women on the course on Saturday and Sunday mornings. It's crowded enough on weekends."

"Why shouldn't women play on weekends?" I said.

"I agree with Judy," said Hunt.

"I'll tell you why," said Addison. "They talk too much, they play the course too slowly, and they clog things up. Let them play during the week."

"That's not fair," Hunt argued. "There may be some women at the club who work during the week."

"Not only that, it's against the law to discriminate against women," I said, getting angry now. "I, for one, am excited about Claire Cox coming here. I hope she shakes the place up."

"Here, here," said Ducky. "I'm looking forward to seeing her again."

"I'll just bet," said Nedra as she elbowed her husband in the ribs.

"What do you think, Larkin?" Hunt asked her.

Larkin pouted, then said, "She's supposed to be a sensational tennis player. If she enters the women's singles tournament this year, I won't have a prayer of winning."

Eventually, Addison went back to his table, we finished up our coffee and dessert, and the conversation reverted back to less controversial matters, like gun control, abortion, and Bosnia.

When we got home from the club, Hunt said he was so tired he wanted to take the elevator up to our bedroom. But he couldn't have been that tired, because after climbing into bed, he turned on his reading lamp and immersed himself in *Harvey Penick's Little Red Book* for the hundredth time.

Slightly intoxicated and more than slightly horny, I snuggled next to him and started nibbling on his earlobe. "Kiss me," I whispered after several minutes.

Hunt put the book down and kissed me. Once.

"Sorry, Jude," he said. "Early tee time tomorrow morning."

CHAPTER FIVE

♦

I gave The Oaks another try on Sunday, hoping to network or, at the very least, find someone I could relate to.

First I took a lesson with Rob, the touchy-feely tennis pro. Then I changed into my bathing suit and headed for the pool. I found an empty chaise longue near the deep end, stretched out, and closed my eyes. When I opened them a few minutes later, I discovered that everybody in the place was staring at me. What have I done this time? I wondered. Does The Oaks have a dress code for the pool too? No, I told myself. It has to be something else.

It *was* something else: people were staring at me because—are you ready?—I was *new!* They were staring and squinting and trying to figure out who I was and what I was doing there because they were old members and I was a new member and because they had nothing better to do! Talking about people is sport at country clubs, just like golf or tennis. But I didn't like being talked about. I felt so claustrophobic I could barely breathe.

I was about to get up and leave when three women sat down in the chaises next to mine and started chatting—with each other and with me.

"How many children do you have?" one of them asked me.

Not "Do you have children?" but "How many children do you

have?," as if it were inconceivable that I wouldn't have a fifties, Leave-It-to-Beaver life just like hers.

"I have a stepdaughter," I said, bracing myself for more shunning, then added, "And I have a career." Well, I used to.

"What sort of career?" one woman asked.

"I edit cookbooks," I said.

"What fun!" she said. "What super, super fun!"

"Deep down, women don't really want to work outside the home," another woman chimed in. "As Marilyn Quayle said, 'Women do not wish to be liberated from their essential natures.' "

I stared at these women and felt like the proverbial fish out of water. One of them assumed that I had kids. The other assumed that having a career was one big garden party. And the third assumed that I would come to my senses someday, get in touch with my essential nature, and give up my silly old career.

I don't remember ever feeling so alone, so isolated. There I was, trying unsuccessfully to relate to women who had never worked a day in their lives. At the same time, I was having trouble relating to my friends in publishing, who were so busy networking and deal making that they'd forgotten all about me. The fact is, I didn't belong in either group. The realization made me so sad that I bid the ladies a much-too-abrupt farewell and beat the hell out of the place.

My spirits rose a bit on Sunday afternoon, when Hunt came home with an interesting piece of news.

"Guess who played in Perry's foursome today," he said.

"Who?" I said.

"Guess," he said.

"The Reverend Jesse Jackson," I deadpanned.

"Nope. Wrong color," said Hunt.

"Okay. The Pope," I said. "I hear he's a scratch golfer."

"Wrong again," said Hunt.

"I give up," I said.

"George Stanton," Hunt said.

"Who?" I said.

"George Stanton. The number-two guy at Shilton & Company."

I drew a blank.

"Shilton & Company," Hunt said again. "The parent company of Davidson House."

Davidson House was, along with Charlton House and Pennington Press, one of America's best-known book publishers.

"Is this George Stanton a member of The Oaks?" I asked with growing interest.

"You betcha. What's more, his wife plays tennis. Maybe you could set up a game with her, score a new business contact, do some networking."

"I just might. What's her name?"

"Perry told me and I wrote it down." Hunt pulled a piece of paper from his pants pocket. "Porter," he said. "Porter Stanton."

Monday was Memorial Day, and the tennis courts at The Oaks were hopping. I had a lesson with Rob, but before we began, I asked him if he knew Porter Stanton.

"Sure," he said. "She's right over there."

He pointed to a short, plump, fiftyish woman over by the vending machine. She didn't look like much of an athlete, but then I didn't exactly have the body of an Olympian.

"Have you ever given Mrs. Stanton a lesson?" I asked Rob.

"Yeah," he said. "She's about your speed. No backhand. Weak forehand. Weak serve."

"Perfect." I smiled, ignoring Rob's unflattering assessment of my tennis game. "Would you mind introducing me to her?"

"Now?"

I nodded.

"What about your lesson? You paid for an hour."

"I know," I said. "But introduce me anyway. Okay?"

Rob shrugged and walked me over to Porter Stanton.

"Mrs. Stanton, meet Mrs. Price, one of our new members," he said smoothly, then added before leaving us alone, "she's looking for a game and I thought you two might be evenly matched."

Porter Stanton smiled and extended her hand. "Please call me Porter," she said.

"And I'm Judy," I said as we shook hands. So far so good.

"I'm really not much of a tennis player," she said apologetically. "Clumsy as all get-out. My husband tells me I have the grace of a hippopotamus."

Nice guy, our George. "Well," I said, laughing, "I'm not exactly a pro myself. I'm not in Larkin Vail's league, that's for sure."

"Yes, but Larkin works so hard at her game," Porter said. "I just can't bring myself to care about tennis the way she does. She practically *lives* on those courts.''

How refreshing! A woman for whom the club wasn't the end-all be-all. "Yes," I said. "And she's very competitive. The season's just starting and she's already worrying about winning the women's singles tournament in September.''

She laughed. "How about some soda, Judy. My treat.''

"Thanks," I said. "I'll take a Sprite.''

Porter dropped money into the machine and handed me a can of Sprite. Then she got herself a Coke.

"So you just joined The Oaks?" she asked.

"Actually, we joined a couple of years ago," I explained. "My husband has been playing a lot of golf, but this is my first real weekend at the club.''

"Why is that?''

"Because until recently, I had a full-time job. *In book publishing.*"

No, I didn't scream it out, but I made sure old Porter couldn't possibly fail to catch my drift.

"Book publishing? What a coincidence," she said. "My husband's company owns Davidson House.''

"Really? That *is* a coincidence.''

"You said you had a full-time job—until recently?''

"Yes. I was a cookbook editor at Charlton House," I told Porter. "But they're downsizing. I got laid off a few months ago.''

"I'm sorry," said Porter.

"Thanks. I've been interviewing at other houses, but nothing's clicked yet.''

"Have you tried Davidson House?" she asked.

"No," I said. "I don't really know anyone there." Hint hint.

"Well, I can certainly help you with that, Judy. I'll speak to my husband. I'm *sure* he'll see you.''

"Oh, Porter," I said, grabbing her hand and pumping it. "I'd be very grateful if you'd tell him about me. Davidson House has such a wonderful reputation. I'd be honored to have the opportunity to work there." Grovel, grovel. Shovel, shovel.

"Not to worry," she said. "I'll get right on it.''

The woman was a sweetheart. I wanted to kiss her. Instead, I suggested we play tennis.

"How about it?" I said. "It sounds like we're both a couple of hackers, so why don't we get out there and hack away?''

Unfortunately, that's exactly what I did: hack away—at Porter Stanton's nose.

We'd been warming up for ten minutes or so when I suggested we play a set. Porter agreed. We split the first four games and were on serve in the fifth when she decided to rush the net. I should have taken her at her word when she said how clumsy she was, but how was I to know she meant it? People were always saying self-deprecating things about themselves, especially when it came to sports. So how was I to know she was *seriously* clumsy?

There she was, rushing the net at the very moment I picked to hit the ball as hard as I had ever hit it in my life. But instead of positioning her racquet in front of her face to protect herself or, God forbid, to return my shot, she just stood there gawking at me, her arms at her sides, her legs bolted to the ground. I mean, the woman seemed incapable of getting out of the way of the ball!

I'll spare you the gory details of what happened next. Suffice it to say, an ambulance carried Porter off to Belford Hospital, where the doctors set her broken nose, kept her overnight for observation, and sent her home. She was told she couldn't play tennis for the rest of the summer. I tried to visit her in the weeks after the accident, but she wasn't too keen on seeing me. I took that to mean she would not be speaking to her husband, the publishing mogul, on my behalf. I was right. Hunt saw George Stanton on the golf course and the man said he wouldn't hire me for a job at Davidson House if I were the only cookbook editor on the planet.

The second Friday in June, Hunt was asked to join the Finance Committee. Apparently, one of the old geezers on the committee, Chester Babcock, croaked in the saddle—i.e., he was having sex with a waitress from the Men's Grill when his heart gave out—and Ducky recommended Hunt to fill Chester's spot. Boy, was he excited. He was so excited he actually ran into the kitchen to tell me the news.

"Do you know what this means?" he said as he hugged me.

"It means you get to spend even more time at that delightful club," I said dryly.

"Jude, it means new guys to network with. And more clients. And before you know it, a partnership at F&F."

"Maybe. Maybe not. Now that you're on the Finance Committee, can you get them to kill that ridiculous three-million-dollar assessment for the new kitchen?"

The club had recently sent around a letter informing members that they were each being assessed ten thousand dollars for the renovation of the kitchen. It all seemed a little weird to me, since no one at The Oaks wanted to spend a dime on anything but the golf course. What's more, after we coughed up three million for a new kitchen, we'd still be stuck with Brendan, the chef who couldn't cook his way out of a pastry bag.

"I hear Duncan Tewksbury thinks three million is a good price," said Hunt. "Ducky's grumbling, but everybody else on the Finance Committee approves. The contractor the club is going with uses only the highest-quality materials."

"Yeah, but who needs a diamond-studded stove?"

"Jude."

"Sorry." I kissed Hunt. "I'm proud of you," I said. "So proud that *I'll* pick Kimberley up at the station tomorrow morning." Normally, Hunt picked his daughter up when she came for a visit, but since Saturday morning was prime golf time, I offered to do the honors.

"It's been a few weeks since we've seen her," he said. "It'll be great having her with us again."

"Yeah, great," I said, faking a smile.

Kimberley came in on the 10:02. She was wearing white shorts, red Keds, and a pale blue Izod shirt. Very preppy. She had her father's looks (golden hair, thin hips, long legs) and her mother's attitude (rotten). When she saw that *I* was to be her chauffeur and not Hunt, she scowled. I pretended not to notice.

"Hi, sweetie," I said cheerfully as I loaded her belongings into the car. She permitted me to kiss her. "Train ride okay?"

"No, we crashed head-on into a stalled school bus. There were no survivors."

Ahh, so it was going to be one of *those* weekends. One of those fabulous, fun-filled weekends where my stepdaughter treated me as if I had Malomars for brains.

Actually, I *acted* as if I had Malomars for brains when she was around. There was something about her disapproving glares and snotty remarks that made me feel so constrained, so uptight that I was often reduced to the role of idiot stepmother, carping and sniping instead of loving.

"I thought we'd go over to the club today," I said as she stared out the car window. "How does that sound?"

"Weird."

"Why weird?"

"Because you never go to the club."

"That was last year, Kimberley. This summer I'm using the club."

"My mother says it costs a lot of money to belong there."

"That's really none of your mother's concern, Kim."

"She says Daddy should be saving his money so he can send me to college."

"You'll be able to go to college. Don't you worry."

"How do you know?"

"Because your father works very hard so he can send you to college."

"What if he gets fired?"

"He won't. He's good at his job."

"*You* got fired. Weren't *you* good at your job?"

"Not good enough, apparently." I was exhausted, and I'd spent only five minutes with the kid.

"That's what my mother says."

"What?"

"That you weren't good at your job."

"Would you tell your mother something when you see her?" I said as I gunned the accelerator. "Tell her that actresses who can't get acting jobs shouldn't cast aspersions."

"What are ass-persions?"

"You're a smart girl. Figure it out."

Kimberley figured it out all right. The three of us had dinner at the club that night, and the food was as ghastly as ever. My appetizer, an avocado stuffed with shrimp salad, was so mayonnaise-y you needed a team of divers to locate the shrimp. And my entrée—ha! It was Brendan's so-called specialty: Blackened Crab Cakes. I defy anyone to tell me there was a single morsel of crabmeat in those hockey pucks. What's more, Brendan's idea of "blackened" was overcooking food to the point where it looked and tasted like charcoal. We were just about to order dessert when Kimberley reported to her father that, earlier in the day, during our ride home from the station, I had called her mother a curse word. Hunt said nothing. Neither did I. But after we got home and put Kimberley to bed, he lectured me on the responsibilities of parenthood. Then I denied that I had used foul language in front of his daughter. Then he lectured me on the responsibilities of stepparenthood. Again I denied that I had used foul language in front of his daughter. Then he lectured me on the responsibilities of marriage, at which point I used the foulest lan-guage—and gestures—I could think of and announced that I was going to sleep.

On Sunday, Kimberley said she wanted to stay home and watch TV.

"But it's a beautiful day," Hunt said. "Don't you want to go swim-ming at the club?"

She shook her head. "I don't like it there," she said. So Kimberley and I finally had something in common.

"Why don't you like it there?" Hunt asked.

"They make you wear a bathing cap if you go in the pool."

"Who makes you?" he asked.

She shrugged. "Some old guy."

"Do you remember his name?" asked Hunt.

"Yeah, it was something like Pukesberry," said Kimberly.

I stifled a laugh. "Must be Duncan Tewksbury," I said.

"All right, honey," Hunt told his daughter. "You don't have to go to the club if you don't want to." He turned to me. "I've got a golf game, Jude. Would you mind staying here with her?"

"Sure," I said. "Arlene's coming for lunch. Kimberley can help me cook."

"I changed my mind. I want to go to the club with *you*, Dad," she said quickly. Anything not to be alone with me.

"What about the bathing cap problem?" Hunt asked.

She smiled. "What bathing cap problem?"

Arlene was in great spirits—for her. She liked her new job very much, she said, and was making terrific money. As a result, she felt she could finally afford psychotherapy.

"It's time I learned how to have a rich, full life," she said. "I want a husband and children."

I was dying to tell her that having a husband and children weren't all they were cracked up to be, but I kept quiet. After all, I'd been the one who'd spent years trying to talk her into finding a man. What right did I have to talk her out of it?

She told me all about the people she worked with, the books she was editing, the restaurants she was eating lunch at. Then she asked *me* what was new.

"Not a thing," I admitted. "Not a damn thing. No interviews. No meetings. Nothing."

"I'm sorry," she said. "I wish I could do something."

I patted her shoulder. "You *are* doing something," I said. "You're having lunch with me. All my other friends have dropped me like a ten-ton manuscript."

"I'm sorry," she said again. "So what are you doing with yourself? How do you keep busy?"

"I've been hanging out at our country club," I said. "Swimming. Taking tennis lessons. Trying to meet people."

"Anyone there worth meeting?" she asked.

"Only if you're doing a study of people who never made it out of the 1950s. Either that, or you need material for a TV sit-com."

She laughed.

"Actually, I just found out that Claire Cox has become a member," I said.

"Wow. I'm impressed," said Arlene. "Have you met her yet?"

"No, but I'd like to."

"You two would have a lot of common."

"Why? Does she have a disagreeable stepdaughter too?"

"No, silly. She's a food maven. Like you."

"Really?"

"Yes. She's a great cook, practically a professional. Haven't you read about those weekend get-togethers she has at her Connecticut house?"

I thought for a moment. "Now that you mention it, yes. Once a month she invites important women like Janet Reno and Barbra Streisand to her house for these fabulous, six-course meals."

"Right. And *she* does all the cooking. You should get friendly with her, Judy. Maybe she'll add you to her guest list."

"Maybe I should," I said.

Then suddenly, an idea came to me. An idea that would change my whole life.

"If Claire Cox is such a great cook, she should write a cookbook," I said.

Arlene smiled. "There's the Judy Mills I know," she said. "The Judy Mills who saw cookbooks where nobody else would think to look."

"I mean it, Arlene. If Claire Cox really cooks all those terrific meals for Diane Sawyer and Nora Ephron and women like that, she must know her way around the kitchen. And if she knows her way around the kitchen, she should share her techniques and recipes with the public at large. Think of the promotional possibilities! Claire Cox whipping up soufflés on 'Good Morning America'! It's dynamite, pure dynamite."

"Yeah, but Claire Cox doesn't strike me as someone who would go on a talk show to hype a product."

"She wouldn't hype a product, but she'd sure as hell hype a cause."

"You've lost me."

"What if she donated the profits from the cookbook to one of her pet causes? She'd hype it then, wouldn't she?"

"I think you're on to something, Judy. But how do *you* fit into the picture?"

"A big-shot feminist lawyer like Claire Cox would never have time to write a cookbook herself. She'd need a collaborator. Someone to help her write and edit the book, then package it for a publisher. I could do that for her, couldn't I?"

"Damn right you could," said Arlene, her eyes twinkling.

"I can see it now," I said. "We'll call the book *Cooking with Claire.* Or *Food for Feminists.* Or *Smart Women, Scrumptious Courses.* It'll be big, Arlene. Bigger than *The Art of French Cooking.* Bigger than *The Silver Palate.* Bigger than *Martha Stewart's Entertaining.*"

Arlene nodded enthusiastically.

"All I've got to do is meet her, get friendly with her, and talk her into doing the book—with me. Then we'll sell it to a publisher and watch the money roll in. Everyone will see my name attached to the project and my phone will start ringing off the hook. I'll be turning down offers. Even Loathsome Leeza will call, *begging* me to come back to Charlton House. I'll tell her to go fuck herself and take a job somewhere else. This book will represent my triumphant return to the industry, Arlene. I'll be back! Oh, God, I'll be back!"

Okay, so I got a little carried away. I couldn't help myself. I saw Claire Cox as my return ticket to the land of the working. I would get her to write a cookbook if it killed me. I would get her to write a cookbook if it killed her.

CHAPTER SIX

♦

On Monday morning I went down to the kitchen to make breakfast for Kimberley, who was taking the train back to the city with Hunt. I always felt a keen sense of regret when she was about to leave after yet another failed weekend, regret that I was unable, once again, to bridge the gap between us.

Was it simply that I was unlovable as far as she was concerned? Or rather, that she was unlovable as far as I was concerned, and knew it? Why couldn't things go better between us? Why did she have to treat me with such disdain, such resentment? And why couldn't I win her over? "Try acting like a normal person," she told me once when I'd asked her why we couldn't seem to get along. "But I do," I'd protested. "No, you just think you do," she'd said. "What you act like is a stepmother." She had me there. I *was* a stepmother. *Her* stepmother. And not a bad one, all things considered. I kept her bedroom spotless. I bought her little goodies whenever I went shopping. And I cooked for her—in spite of her horrendous manners. And what did I get for it? Grief. Nothing but grief.

"Oh, yuk," she said when she sat down at the kitchen table and saw the plateful of food I'd prepared for her that Monday morning.

"Is there a problem?" I asked, knowing the answer.

"Yeah. The problem is: What is *that*?" She pointed at her plate.

"You know what it is, Kimberley. It's scrambled eggs and English muffins. I sprinkled a little paprika on them, that's all. Just for color. Now, how about eating them while they're hot."

"But I hate scrambled eggs. I'm into poached eggs," she said.

"Since when? I've never seen you eat a poached egg."

"I do a lot of things you've never seen me do."

I know I was supposed to ask "What things?," but I wasn't in the mood to play. It was too early in the morning.

"Taste the eggs," I said. "I made them mushy. Just the way you like them."

"The way I *used* to like them. When I was a *kid.*"

I looked at Hunt's daughter, who was all of ten years old. She had the face of an angel. And the personality of a Gila monster.

"Kimberley," I said patiently. "Your dad will be down in a few minutes and he wants to make the 8:15 express train. Now that I know you like *poached eggs,* I'll be sure to make them for you the next time you visit us. But just this once, for old times' sake, how about polishing off these scrambled eggs, huh?"

"My mother says eggs are bad for you," she said as she picked up the fork and began to play with her food.

"They *are* high in cholesterol," I conceded. "But every now and then, it's all right to indulge."

"My mother says cholesterol causes heart attacks and strokes. She says millions of people die from too much cholesterol in their diet."

"You won't die from eating scrambled eggs," I said. "At least, not today. So come on, Kim. Your breakfast is getting cold. Eat up."

"My mother says—"

"Kimberley! Enough! Please eat your breakfast!"

I left the little darling in the kitchen and walked outside to get the newspaper. Hunt never took the train into the city without his *New York Times,* and I never let him take it without reading it first.

I unfolded it as I walked back into the kitchen and set it down on the counter. And then I gasped. Right there in the bottom right section of the front page was the headline CLAIRE COX FIGHTS SEX DISCRIMINATION AT CONNECTICUT COUNTRY CLUB.

I grabbed the paper off the counter, sat down next to Kimberley, and devoured the article, which read, in part:

> . . . Feminist lawyer Claire Cox says she has received many letters from women who want to join a country club but lack an essential requirement for membership: a husband.

"These women are capable of running their own businesses but not of joining a country club? That's absurd," stated Ms. Cox in an interview late Friday. "It's not only absurd. It's illegal."

Technically, there is no federal law against sex discrimination by private clubs, but several cities have passed laws banning discrimination, and still others have threatened to take away a club's tax benefits or revoke its liquor license if there is evidence of discrimination.

"Exclusion from clubs limits women's economic opportunities," Ms. Cox argued. "Men conduct business on the golf course. Golf is a sport that promotes business relationships. So why shouldn't women have access to it? How can women be cabinet members and corporate leaders and presidents of colleges and universities and not be allowed membership in country clubs? How can we allow men to continue to close the door in our faces? We can't. Not anymore."

In addition to turning down applications from qualified single women, many clubs, according to Ms. Cox, discriminate against their existing women members by barring them from men's grills, not permitting them to tee off on weekends and restricting their memberships to "associate" status. Ms. Cox intends to focus the public's attention on these practices by challenging the bylaws of The Oaks of Belford, Connecticut, the country club founded by her late grandfather, Justin Kennelworth Tewksbury. Ms. Cox explained that her primary reason for joining The Oaks last month was to put pressure on the club's Board of Governors to change its antiquated and discriminatory bylaws.

"The other reason I joined was to play lots of golf and tennis," she said. "The facilities at The Oaks are absolutely first-rate."

Duncan Tewksbury, a spokesman for The Oaks and Ms. Cox's great-uncle, said the club would have no comment . . .

"Hunt, look at this!" I said as he entered the kitchen. "There's an article in the *Times* about The Oaks."

"Impossible," said Hunt. He kissed the top of Kimberley's head, then reached into the refrigerator for some orange juice and poured himself a glass. "The members of the club would rather die than see their names in the newspaper, Judy. You know that."

I *did* know that. People at The Oaks were such privacy nuts that they didn't allow cameras on the premises, not even my measly little Kodak Instamatic.

"Read it," I said and handed Hunt the article.

"I'll read it on the train," he said, swallowing the last of his juice and checking his watch. "Come on, Kim. We gotta go."

"But Kimberley hasn't touched her breakfast," I said.

Hunt looked at his daughter. "Not hungry, pumpkin?"

Pumpkin shook her head and pouted. "Judy says I have to eat these eggs, even though eggs give people heart attacks."

"Oh, Kimberley," I sighed.

"Leave the eggs," Hunt told her, refusing to support me, as usual. "I'll buy you a muffin at the station."

"Oh, thank you, Daddy," she cried, smiling, then hopped off her chair into his arms.

I nearly got sick. One of these days, I thought angrily as I watched them leave the house together. One of these days I'm going to tell Hunt that if he doesn't stop undermining my authority over Kimberley, if he doesn't stop coddling his precious little pumpkin, if he doesn't stop acting like a guilty, divorced father, I'll walk. I'll walk and I won't look back. I'll walk and I'll start a new life. I'll walk and I'll find somebody else. Somebody who thinks I'm attractive and sexy and a great cook. Somebody who appreciates me. Somebody who would rather get laid than play golf. In the meantime, I'll put Kimberley's breakfast in the microwave, nuke it, and eat it myself.

The article in the *Times* threw the old guard at The Oaks into a state of panic. Lose their tax benefits? Their liquor license? Get dragged into a messy lawsuit? See The Oaks's name sullied in the press? The very idea! On the other hand, how could they let themselves be bossed around by some ball-breaking feminist? Even if she *was* Duncan Tewksbury's grandniece.

There were feverish meetings late into the night, according to Hunt, who was now on the Finance Committee and involved in nearly every aspect of club business. Duncan, Addison Bidwell, and Curtis Lamb were violently opposed to amending the bylaws. But several others felt that, in order to avoid a protracted and expensive legal battle, it was in the club's best interests to change the rules. In the end, the membership of The Oaks decided to cave in to Claire Cox's demands and admit single women for the first time in its fifty-year history, as well as remove all barriers to female equality at the club. The whole thing was vaguely reminiscent of the tearing down of the Berlin Wall.

"I can't wait to meet Claire Cox," I said to Hunt. "She must be an amazing woman."

I told Hunt about Claire's culinary skills and about my idea for a cookbook that I would help her write.

"Sounds great," he said. "But you've never even spoken to the woman."

"No problem," I said. "I'll follow her around that club until she begs me to talk to her."

"Jude?"

"Yeah?"

"Just don't ask her to play tennis."

"Why? Because she's a great player and I stink?"

"No. Because you've already broken one nose this summer. Don't try for two."

My first sighting of Claire Cox came the following Saturday afternoon. I had decided to venture into the new, supposedly female-friendly Men's Grill, which, at Claire's insistence, had been renamed simply The Grill. Yes, things were changing quickly at The Oaks, despite the grumblings of the old guard, who could only watch in horror as their precious club marched into the nineties.

On one side of the dark, publike dining room sat several men in plaid pants, one of them Duncan. On the other side sat a group of women in business suits, one of them Claire. The men were drinking scotch and glowering at the women. The women were eating salads and talking about the stock market.

I laughed when I remembered that, only two weeks before, I had been thrown out of the very same room. My mere presence had provoked the sort of angry, lynch-mob response usually reserved for child molesters and people who stand in supermarket express lines with more than ten items in their shopping cart. But now here I was. No scenes. No fuss. Just a little hostility, but that was to be expected.

I sat at a table about halfway between the men and the women and ordered lunch. Several minutes later, as I was wrestling with my rock-hard cantaloupe, Claire got up and walked over to her great-uncle's table. She was lovely in her mint green silk suit and lacy white blouse. Her hair looked like something out of a magazine ad, all thick and lush and shiny. And the way she carried herself. Shoulders back. Head high. Eyes bright and smart and knowing. She exuded a kind of self-confidence I'd always wished I'd had.

"Hello, Uncle Duncan," I heard her say.

Duncan rose from his chair, as did his cronies. "Claire." His lip curled when he uttered her name. How he must despise her, I thought. She's made him look like an impotent old fool.

"Please don't get up," she told the men, who remained standing anyway. "Playing golf today?" she asked Duncan.

"No, the course is full—of women," he said, his nostrils flaring, his eyes narrowing with resentment.

"That's a shame," she said. "Well, give my best to Aunt Delia, will you?" She patted him on the shoulder and walked back to her table.

Duncan and his pals sat down. He lifted his glass and took a long sip of his scotch. His hand trembled as he set the glass down on the table. And when the man seated next to him nodded in Claire's direction and mumbled, "Fuckin' dyke," Duncan chuckled in agreement.

Of all the nerve, I thought. Claire was a member of his family, after all.

Claire resumed her conversation with her friends. I leaned toward them and strained to hear what they were saying.

"I want to thank you all for coming," I heard her say, "and for letting me 'recruit' you. You're just the sort of members we need at The Oaks, and I hope you will decide to apply for membership. Especially now that you've seen the club for yourselves, had lunch, walked the grounds, etc." She paused. "Now I know what you're thinking— that the food's god-awful here—but I'm working on that. I'm looking into a replacement for the chef."

"Good move," said one of the women. She was heavyset, with short dark hair, bushy eyebrows, and a faint mustache. I vaguely remembered seeing her on "Court TV" prosecuting somebody or other for first-degree murder.

"You've got to change the menu too," said another woman, an African-American with Whoopi Goldberg dreadlocks. "It's nothing but honky stuff."

"My lunch wasn't bad," said a beautiful redhead whom I recognized as a local TV weatherwoman. "But I'm more interested in hearing about tennis at The Oaks. There are sixteen courts, right?"

"Yes. And they're very well maintained," said Claire. "The only problem with tennis is the assistant pro. A guy named Rob. He's next on my hit list."

"Why?" asked Ms. Dopler Radar. "Bad teacher?"

"No, bad guy," said Claire. "He puts his hands all over the women who take lessons from him. We're talking sexual harassment here."

So Claire was trying to get Brendan, the chef, and Rob, the assistant tennis pro, canned! Boy, she wasn't wasting any time turning the club around. I had to meet this woman. I just had to. But how? I couldn't go waltzing over to her table and introduce myself. Not in front of her friends. I'd have to wait until she was alone to tell her about my cookbook idea.

I hung around until Claire and her guests got up to leave. Then I signed my check and hurried outside after her.

Perfect, I thought as I watched her shake each of their hands and point them toward the parking lot. They were leaving and she was staying. Maybe she'd have a few minutes to chat with me after all.

She took off in the direction of the tennis courts, walking so fast I was forced to trail several paces behind her, which is what I get for being the only person on the planet who has yet to discover the charms of the Stairmaster.

I was in hot pursuit of Claire when she turned off toward the locker rooms. I followed her around the corner and would have barreled right into her—into them!—if I hadn't heard voices that stopped me cold.

"Claire!"

It was a man's voice. I ducked behind the side of the building to listen.

"Yes?" she said.

"Don't you recognize me?" said the man. "Have I changed that much, Clissy?"

Clissy?

"Oh, it's Ducky Laughton, isn't it," she said, somewhat unsteadily, it seemed to me. "Nobody's called me Clissy in years."

So it was the Duckster, Claire's classmate at Berkeley. Nedra said they'd been college sweethearts. But then wouldn't Claire have recognized him? And wouldn't she have reacted with more enthusiasm?

"I've been hoping to run into you," he said. "More than you can imagine. You were my Grand Passion, you know."

What was Nedra, chopped liver?

"Really, Ducky," Claire said. "I don't think it's a good idea to—"

"To what? To stir up old memories?" he said. "I disagree. I've been waiting twenty-five years to tell you how I feel about you, about what happened between us."

Uh-oh.

"Well, it was a very long time ago, wasn't it," she said. "And you've gotten over it, judging by that wedding ring on your finger."

"Yes, Nedra and I are happy," he said. "But I still think about you. About what might—no, *should*—have been."

Oh, God. So Nedra had reason to be jealous. The man was a cad.

"Why would you think about me now, so many years after the fact?" said Claire. "Surely, your life is full?"

"You're an unforgettable woman, Clissy," Ducky said. "You taught me everything I know about believing in a cause, about fighting for change, about standing up for peace and love and equality for all."

Jesus. Did he really think that, if he made himself sound like Gandhi, he'd win her love? At this stage of the game?

"I'd like us to have dinner together," he went on. "We have so much to catch up on, so much to reminisce about."

"I don't think so, Ducky," said Claire, sounding incredibly uncomfortable. Reunions with old lovers could be so excruciating, especially old lovers who were revisionists.

But Ducky wasn't giving up. "It'll be just like the good old days," he insisted. "Some wine. Some candles. Some music. You remember those evenings, don't you, Clissy? Before the trouble? Before I went away?"

"Listen, Ducky," said Claire. She had had enough, I could tell. "I don't want to relive those times, and I wouldn't think you would either. We're both members of this club now. That means we'll be running into each other from time to time. I'd like to keep things cordial, okay?"

"Cordial? After what we had together?" he said.

God, he was pathetic.

"Yes, cordial," she said. "Now, I'm supposed to play tennis and I haven't even changed my clothes."

"Who are you playing with?"

"A woman named Larkin Vail," she said. "Frosted blond hair. Big forehand. Big first serve. The pro thought we should play each other."

"Only if you're prepared to fight to the death," Ducky laughed. "Larkin approaches every tennis game as if it were her last. The only thing worse than losing to her is beating her. She doesn't like to be beaten."

"Good. Neither do I."

"So when will I see you?" asked Ducky, sounding like a love-struck teenager.

"I don't know," she said. "Let's just leave it at that, okay?"

"For now," he said.

"Bye, Ducky. Take care," said Claire, and off she went into the ladies' locker room.

I was about to follow her inside when I narrowly missed a head-on collision with Ducky.

"Oh, hi," I said, an awkward, embarrassed smile on my face.

"Judy, hi," he said. I could sense that he was dying to know if *I* knew that he had just made an ass of himself in front of Claire.

"How've you been?" I said.

"Fine," he said. "You?"

"Fine," I said.

Stimulating, huh? I was itching to get away from Ducky and resume my pursuit of Claire.

"Oops," I said after checking my watch. "Gotta go."

"Me too," he said.

And one of the world's great nonconversations came to a merciful end.

I hurried after Claire, who was now decked out in her tennis outfit and heading over to the courts. When she got there, she walked straight onto the teaching court, where Rob was giving Bailey Van-derhoff a lesson—and a back rub—and she insisted that he remove his hands from Bailey's body immediately.

"That's just my teaching style," Rob protested after Claire accused him of sexually harassing Bailey.

"Then your teaching style is against the law," Claire said. "Putting your hands all over a woman's body is not part of your job."

"But they like it," Rob said.

"Then they should make an appointment with you after hours," said Claire. "You were hired by this club to teach tennis, not give massages."

"Says who?"

"Says I. I'd start looking for another job if I were you."

"Another job? What for?" Rob said smugly. "The *real* women at this club like the way I teach tennis. *They're* not gonna let me go."

"We'll see," Claire said as she walked past a dozen gaping stares, including mine.

Everyone was buzzing about the incident until Claire took on her next victim: Larkin Vail, The Oaks's reigning women's singles champion and the favorite to win the tournament in September. All eyes were on the two women as they settled onto Court 1 and began smacking shot after shot at each other. And that was just the warm-up! Once the actual match got under way, they battled each other for two and a half hours. Larkin won the first set. Claire won the second—and the third, in a tiebreaker. Larkin was so undone by her defeat that she smashed her racquet against the fence until she bent it—and the fence. Then she stalked off the court muttering something about retribution.

I hurried after Claire as she made her way toward the clubhouse. God, she walked fast. I could hardly keep up with her. She turned off into the ladies' locker room, so I followed her in there, even though the ladies' locker room was my least favorite spot at The Oaks. I just couldn't get used to stripping in front of a bunch of strange women. The ladies' locker room at my parents' club in Boca Raton had private, plushly carpeted changing rooms, with full-length mirrors and portable hair dryers and all the comforts of home. But The Oaks, that bastion of shabby gentility, offered no such amenities. Its ladies' locker room was one big space that was decorated in "early high school gym." In other words, you stood at your little locker and changed into your bathing suit and tried to act nonchalant about the fact that a dozen eyes were checking out your cellulite. It was the sort of togetherness I could have done without.

On that particular afternoon, however, I welcomed the intimacy and closeness of the setting, because guess who was standing stark naked right next to my locker as I walked into the room: Claire Cox. Alone at last! And what a body. I tried not to look, really I did, but how could I not? She was athletic and tight and nothing sagged, not even her ass. I wondered if she was into fitness videos and, if so, which one. I wondered if she had a personal trainer. I wondered why I was wasting time pondering her exercise regimen when I'd finally gotten her alone.

"Excuse me," I said, trying not to look anywhere but at her face. "I've been hoping to talk to you. My name is Judy Mills."

"Hi," she said, seeming not the least bit modest. "Claire Cox. Nice to meet you."

"I know this is going to sound tacky," I began, "but I have a business venture I'd like you to consider."

Claire raised an eyebrow and looked at me. "My agent handles things like that," she said.

"Yes, but this is something I'd like to discuss with you personally."

She slipped into her black, one-piece bathing suit and said, "I'll tell you, Judy, with all my lectures, television appearances, and fundraising activities, I'm kind of overcommitted. Maybe some other time."

"I've read that you're a great cook," I blurted out as she was about to leave the locker room.

She turned to face me, then threw her head back and laughed. "Don't tell me you want an invitation to my weekend retreats. Is that it?"

"No," I said, a little insulted that she thought I was some groupie hoping to mooch a meal. "I've read that you're a great cook and I wondered if you'd ever thought of writing a cookbook."

She laughed again. "No. I can honestly say I've never given the idea any thought."

"May I tell you something about my background?" I said, then, without waiting for a reply, I gave Claire Cox a thumbnail sketch of my history in book publishing.

"Sounds like you're a shrewd editor, Judy," she said. "But I'm not sure I understand why you're—"

"I think you should do a cookbook," I interrupted. "A cookbook that presents all the recipes you prepare for your famous women friends at those weekend retreats. You could include anecdotes about the people you've cooked for, about the causes you've fought for, whatever you want. Most importantly, you could donate the profits from the book to breast cancer research, abortion clinics, you name it."

The last sentence hooked her, I could tell. She was a sucker for projects that raised money for her causes.

"It's not the worst idea I've heard lately," she admitted.

"I'd like you to think about it," I said, trying not to act too excited or pushy. "Think about how you might group the recipes, whether the book should be illustrated, what kind of title you'd like, that sort of thing. We can talk more specifically about the project once you've had time to consider the idea."

"Yes, yes," she said, nodding her head. "I will think about it. There's just one thing, Judy. How do you fit in?"

"I'll be your collaborator—your co-author, editor, whatever you need me to be," I said. "I'd help you write the book, shape it, test the recipes, bring it up to speed so it's ready for publication."

"Well, it's an intriguing idea," she said. "Do you have a card?"

I fished around in my purse and handed Claire one of my business cards. It still said Charlton House, so I crossed out my old office number and filled in my home phone.

"Great," she said as she stuffed it in her purse and locked it in her locker. "I'll call you."

♦

Claire did call—that very night. She asked if we could have lunch at the club the next day. There was hope for me and my career yet!

We met in The Grill. Claire ordered the pasta special, which bore an uncanny resemblance to Chef Boyardee Ravioli, and I chose the BLT, which had plenty of L and T but no B.

"Have you noticed that the food here isn't what it should be?" I asked.

Claire rolled her eyes. "That's all going to change," she said. "But first, I'm getting rid of Mr. Testosterone."

"Who?"

"Rob, the tennis pro with the groping hands. Then, I'm going to see that Brendan is replaced by a *real* chef. There's no point in spending the members' money to renovate the kitchen while he's in charge. He's hopeless."

For the next hour, Claire and I chatted like old friends—about her work, about my work, about the lack of romance in her life, about the lack of romance in my life. She was charming and open and I found her a refreshing change from the other female members of The Oaks.

Eventually, we got down to the reason for the lunch: the cookbook.

"I called my agent last night," said Claire.

"Your agent works on Saturday night?"

"She's a close friend as well as my agent," she explained. "I told her about your idea and she thinks it's terrific. She says it will be good for my image to show my less serious side for a change. She's going to call you Monday to discuss money. When all that's settled, we'll get to work. What do you say?"

"What do I say? I say I'm ecstatic," I said. "This cookbook of ours is going to reopen doors for me. I'm really looking forward to working on it."

"Same here," she said. "Now my agent can get very busy, so if you don't hear from her by, say, Wednesday, call me." She handed me her business card, with both her Manhattan and Connecticut numbers on it.

"I'm giving a lecture in Stamford on Wednesday morning, then I'll stay up in Connecticut through the July Fourth weekend."

"Will you be coming to the club's July Fourth party next Monday night?" I asked. "The theme is the Wild West. A logical way for New Englanders to celebrate America's birthday, don't you think?"

She laughed. "Actually, I *am* planning to go. I'm bringing a few women friends who've applied for membership."

"I hope they eat burgers, franks, and baked beans," I said. "The club is describing the menu as 'Wagon Train Food.' Hunt and I are bringing his daughter and his parents. Wagon Train Food is their idea of haute cuisine."

I must have made a face because Claire asked me if I got along with Hunt's parents and daughter.

"About as well as the Israelis get along with the Palestinians," I said. "In other words, they're not my biggest fans."

"It's no fun to have people gunning for you," said Claire. "I know. I've gotten hundreds of death threats."

"Really? I've only gotten one."

"From whom?"

"My stepdaughter."

"What did you do to deserve that?"

"I existed."

CHAPTER SEVEN

♦

Claire's agent called the next day and offered me a terrific deal: instead of paying me a flat fee as a consultant on the book, they wanted me to be the co-author and split all profits fifty-fifty. If the book sold well, I'd make big bucks! Even if it didn't, I was sure to net a tidy sum on the advance. After all, Claire Cox was a celebrity, and publishers saw celebrity books as a hot commodity—even cookbooks.

I ran to the phone to call Hunt at his office, but as I started to dial, I changed my mind and hung up. What if he was unimpressed by my cookbook deal, the way he'd been unimpressed by everything else I'd told him lately? Take my news about Ducky and Claire. "Ducky's dying to get into Claire's pants," I'd said. "No way," Hunt had said. "I'm telling you, I heard him," I'd said. "You must have been imagining things. Ducky's not like that," he'd said. "Not like what?" I'd said, then added, "some men actually have sex once in a while. Some men actually think it's fun to get laid." "Are you suggesting I sleep with other women to prove to you that I'm a *real* man?" he'd said. "No," I'd said. "I'm suggesting that you sleep with me." Hunt did not take me up on my suggestion, and life went on.

So it was with some reservation that I finally dialed his number at the office to tell him I was back in the book business at last.

"That's great, Jude," he said. "I'm really proud of you, of the way you went after this thing."

This thing. Nice.

"Thanks," I said, trying to stay upbeat. "Want to celebrate tonight? Just the two of us?"

"I wish I could, but Bree wants me to have dinner with Kimberley tonight. She's feeling kind of blue."

"Who? Bree or Kimberley?"

"Kimberley. Susie died."

"Susie? Was she a classmate of Kimberley's?"

"No, Susie was Kimberley's gerbil."

"My condolences. Should I send flowers or a donation to Susie's favorite charity?"

"Jude."

"Sorry. I'm being selfish. I wanted you to take *me* to dinner tonight."

"I know, but Kimberley needs me."

So do I, I wanted to scream into the phone. And I have for months. I need you so much I fantasize about divorcing you.

"I'm going to be working late tomorrow night and Wednesday night," said Hunt. "And then there's a meeting of the Finance Committee on Thursday night. Why don't we celebrate on Friday night?"

"I can't," I said. "I'm having dinner with Arlene on Friday night. She's feeling kind of blue. Her rabbit died."

"Jude. There's no need to play tit for tat."

"Who's playing tit for tat? Arlene's rabbit *did* die. She's pregnant."

"You're kidding."

"You're right, I am. I was playing tit for tat."

"Jude."

"I'll see you at home later," I said and hung up.

Since Kimberley wasn't due to arrive in Connecticut until Sunday and Arlene was spending July Fourth weekend in the Hamptons, Hunt and I invited Valerio up for the early part of the weekend. I cooked dinner for us on Friday night, and we took Valerio to The Oaks for dinner on Saturday night.

"So thees eez the cluba," he said as we were shown to a table in the main dining room.

"Super place, isn't it?" said Hunt as he surveyed the room. People at several tables waved.

"Eet's nice," said Valerio, who grabbed my hand and kissed it while Hunt wasn't looking. "But a leetle plain, no?"

I laughed, thinking of Valerio's restaurant on the Upper East Side of Manhattan. It was the antithesis of "plain," with its heavy drapes and tassled lamp shades and thick shag carpet that was such a loud red you could dump a gallon of marinara sauce on it and never see it.

While we all sipped cocktails and Hunt discussed the finer points of commodities trading, I was busy peeling Valerio's hand off my thigh, which he kept trying to squeeze under the table.

Then our dinner arrived. I had warned Valerio that the food at The Oaks wasn't up to his standards, but when he tasted his steak, he reacted with horror.

"Thees eez sheeta," he said.

"Then send it back," I suggested. "You ordered it medium rare. It looks well done."

"It isn't that," he said, abruptly losing his accent. "It's the meat. It's not prime beef."

"Of course it's prime," said Hunt. "Judy's right, though. If it isn't cooked the way you ordered it, send it back."

Valerio shook his head. "It's not prime," he said. "It's a shitty grade of beef. I can tell by the taste and by the ratio of fat marbling to red meat. Believe me, I know food."

Hunt looked peeved. "I'm on the Finance Committee here," he explained to Valerio, "and I'm telling you, The Oaks pays for prime meat. Not choice. *Prime.* I see the bills after they've been approved by the chef and signed by the treasurer."

Approved by the chef. If Brendan was as lousy a food purveyor as he was a food preparer, God knows what garbage we were eating.

"Let me tell *you,* Hunt," said Valerio. "You're paying for quality you're not getting."

"Valerio," I said, "why don't we send your entrée back and get you something else?"

He agreed. We called the waiter over and explained that our guest was unhappy with his dinner. Valerio took another look at the menu and chose the rack of lamb. When it arrived twenty minutes later, we went through the same scenario.

"The lamb is shit too," said Valerio, thoroughly disgusted. "You may be paying for prime, but you're not getting it. You're not even getting choice."

Valerio said he was no longer hungry. So did Hunt. I, on the other hand, ate virtually every morsel of my dry, overcooked Dover sole. As I said earlier, I never passed up a meal, even one of Brendan's.

I was in remarkably good spirits as I dressed for the club's Wild West July Fourth party on Monday night. Yes, despite the fact that I'd be spending the evening at a place I despised with my recalcitrant, manipulative stepdaughter, my remote, humorless in-laws, and my inattentive, golf-obsessed husband, I was feeling happy and optimistic for the first time in months. It had occurred to me that perhaps I didn't need a job at Charlton House or any other publishing company; that if the cookbook I was writing with Claire sold even half as well as *Valerio's Kitchen,* I'd never have to work for the Leeza Grummonds of the world again. The idea was incredibly liberating.

"Almost ready?" Hunt asked as he entered the bedroom.

I took one look at him and burst out laughing. He was supposed to be dressed as a cowboy, but he was the preppiest cowboy this side of Brooks Brothers. I mean, when was the last time you saw a cowboy wearing *white* pants—pleated and with cuffs?

"My jeans seem to have shrunk" was his explanation.

"Maybe your waist expanded" was mine.

He shrugged. "Like the hat?"

Along with the white pants, he was wearing a blue denim work shirt (Ralph Lauren), white boating shoes (Topsiders), and an authentic cowboy hat (Billy Martin).

"The hat's just great," I said. "You're the spitting image of Lee Majors on 'The Big Valley.' "

He grinned, and for a moment, he did look every bit the handsome TV star. I felt a sudden attraction toward him and was flooded with memories of how it used to be with us. For despite the distance between us, despite the months of benign neglect, despite the fights and the silences and the tentative truces, I still found the man appealing. He had glorious golden hair and earnest, kind eyes and the whitest, straightest teeth I'd ever seen. And then there were his lean but muscular legs that I used to love to be entangled by. Even his hands turned me on. They were the hands of an artist, not a pork bellies trader—elegant, strong, nimble. I sighed as I thought back on the steamy, endless nights of our courtship, when those hands played magic tricks with my body. I missed *that* Hunt, that man whose love I felt with such force it used to take my breath away, that man who—

"Where's the rest of your costume?" he asked, interrupting my reverie, which was just as well.

"Here." I lifted my Davy Crockett 'coonskin hat out of the box and put it on my head. The rest of my outfit consisted of a midcalf blue jeans skirt, a red-and-white-checked shirt, and cowboy boots. Not very original, but what do you expect? I couldn't go dressed as an Indian, not in these politically correct times and not when I had been the household's most vociferous critic of the Tomahawk Chop.

"What do you say, Davy?" Hunt smiled. "Shall we go?"

"Is Kimberley ready?" I asked. My stepdaughter had decided not to dress in costume. She'd said the idea of a July Fourth Wild West party at the club was weird. I couldn't argue with her there.

"Mother and Dad are meeting us at the club," said Hunt.

"Good," I said and meant it. The less time I had to spend with my in-laws, the better.

It was a beautiful, crystal-clear July evening, with the temperature hovering around seventy degrees and the humidity low and comfortable. There was no threat of rain, the mosquitoes were tolerable, and the club's manicured grounds looked positively pristine. Thanks to the great weather, the party was set up outside, on the terrace by the pool. When we arrived, the band—six men in denim overalls who called themselves The Cowpokes—were entertaining the members with their rousing rendition of the theme from "Bonanza."

Our table, I was pleased to discover, was only a few feet away from Claire's, and you'll never guess what she came dressed as: an Indian! Of course, she described her costume as "the authentic garb of a Native American medicine woman," which only goes to show that political correctness is as political correctness does.

She stopped by to say hello as we were having cocktails.

"Here's to America's independence," she said, then shook hands with each of us.

Hunt told Claire how thrilled he was about our cookbook, which was something he'd neglected to tell me. I told Claire that I hoped we could finish the outline for the book within the next few weeks. Kimberley asked Claire if she had ever met Oprah Winfrey and, if so, whether she looked fatter or thinner in person. And Hunt's parents never opened their mouths, even to say hello. Eventually, Claire went back to her table, where she held court with four single women who had applied for membership in The Oaks and were waiting to hear if they'd been accepted. They were all very young and attractive, and they drew daggers from some of the established members—male and female.

I spotted the Duncan Tewksburys and their guests, Larkin and Perry Vail with their five children, and Ducky and Nedra Laughton with the Vanderhoffs and the Etheridges. I also noticed that Brendan, the chef, was busy toting large silver platters onto the buffet table, and I wondered if he suspected that Claire was doing her best to have him fired. Ditto: Rob, the tennis pro, whom we passed in the parking lot as we arrived at the club.

"So, Mom and Dad," I said to my in-laws, "how've you both been?"

Hunt's father, Hunter Dean Price II, had taken the club's invitation to dress in Western clothing seriously. He had come as a ranch hand, complete with leather chaps and a lasso. The outfit was perfect, except for those white socks, which he wore everywhere, even to bed.

Hunt's mother, who was called "Kitty" by her husband and "Betty" by everyone else, had chosen not to come in costume, but wore a sleeveless cotton dress with a floral print, white sandals, and a pearl necklace. She was dressed not for a Wild West party but for church. As I've said, my mother-in-law was not a barrel of laughs.

"How've you both been?" I asked again, having not gotten a response the first time.

"Well," said Hunt II.

I assumed my father-in-law's "well" was a prelude to the rest of his answer, as in: "Well, we've been just fine." But it turned out that "well" *was* his answer, as in: "Fine."

"How about you, Mom?" I asked Hunt's mother. "Are your cataracts still giving you trouble?"

"Yes," she said.

And that was the end of that. Oh, I could have pressed on. I could have said daughter-in-lawish things like: "I'm sorry to hear that, Mother dear." Or: "Can I drive you to the eye doctor next week?" Or: "Would you like me to switch seats with you so the moonlight isn't in your eyes?" But why bother? I decided. Let Hunt be the sport. She's *his* mother. *My* mother didn't make people work so hard. If you asked Lucille Mills about her cataracts, she'd *tell* you, probably much more than you'd ever want to know. But then my parents were as different from Hunt's parents as bagels and Wonder Bread. When the two couples met at our wedding, they came to the swift and unspoken conclusion that they had nothing in common; that they would never play bridge together, never take transatlantic cruises together, never get together to giggle over our baby pictures. The only time they communicated with each other was at Christmas, when my father, the former "Mr. Butcher," always sent Hunt's parents a package of freeze-dried Omaha steaks, and Hunt's parents, people of few words, always sent my father a one-line thank-you note.

"When's dinner?" Kimberley asked as she sucked the last of her Shirley Temple through the straw and made obnoxious, slurping noises in the process. When I asked her to stop, she began to play with the book of matches on the table, then lit one and blew it out.

"Kim, please don't do that," I said, since no one else did.

She looked over at her father, who was busy waving at Addison Bidwell and his wife. Then she looked back at me and asked again about dinner.

"I think it's a buffet," I said. "Why don't we all get in line?"

I'd always thought buffet dinners were incredibly uncivilized. You had to slough your way through food that had already been picked over by dozens of other people and was inevitably ice cold, except when it was supposed to be. Still, buffets served their purpose: they provided an escape from one's dinner companions—a respite from having to sit at the table and make conversation with people whose idea of small talk was speaking in monosyllables.

We ate cheeseburgers and baked beans and cole slaw (the mayonnaise-y kind Hunt loved), and for dessert, we had make-your-own ice cream sundaes. Kimberley knocked hers over as she was taking her first bite, and I agreed to walk over to the buffet table to get her another one. As I passed Claire's table, I noticed that she wasn't there. Then one of the women waved me over.

"Excuse me," she said. "I saw Claire talking to you earlier."

"Yes, I'm Judy Mills. Claire and I are writing a cookbook together," I said proudly. I still couldn't get over the fact that *my* name was going to be linked with Claire's for all eternity.

"Hi, Judy. I'm Sharon Klein, Claire's accountant." We shook hands. "We're all a little worried about Claire," she went on. "She told us she had to meet someone and would be back in plenty of time for dinner."

"Someone here? At the club?" I asked.

"Yes. She said it would only take a few minutes." She checked her watch. "But that was over an hour ago."

My face flushed as I thought of Claire and Ducky. Had he talked her into a quickie on the golf course? No, neither of them was *that*

tacky. Besides, it had sounded to me like Claire didn't want anything
to do with Ducky.

"We don't know anyone here, since we're not members yet," said
Sharon. "But we saw Claire talking to you, so we thought maybe you
could give us some idea of where she might have gone."

I shook my head. "I don't have a clue offhand," I said. "But let me
get my stepdaughter her ice cream sundae and I'll take a look
around."

"Thanks, Judy."

"Sure."

Boy, that was strange, I thought as I waited on the dessert line for
twenty minutes and then heaped hot fudge sauce and chopped
M&Ms and whipped cream and slivered almonds on a scoop of va-
nilla ice cream. When I brought the sundae back to Kimberley, she
took one look at it and said, "You forgot the cherry!"

No, I didn't throw the sundae at her, much as I wanted to. But I
didn't run and get the cherry either. I told Hunt to do it, then I ex-
cused myself and went to look for Claire.

First I checked the powder room. Then the ladies' locker room.
Then every room in the clubhouse. Then I walked over to the parking
lot to see if Claire's car, a white Range Rover with a "Pro Choice"
bumper sticker on it, was still there. It was. Where on earth could she
be? I wondered.

I decided to return to the party in case Claire had come back. But
when I approached her table, I saw that her place was still empty.

"Jude? What are you doing?" Hunt asked.

"I'm trying to find Claire," I said. "She's missing."

"What do you mean 'missing'?" he said, in that exasperated tone
meant to suggest that I was imagining things again.

"Just what I said, Hunt. Her friends say she's been gone for over an
hour."

"So? Maybe she's been on the phone all that time," Hunt said.
"She's a lady with a lot going on."

"I checked the phones," I said.

"How about the bathroom?" said Hunt. "Maybe the Wagon Train
menu didn't agree with her."

"She never got around to sampling the Wagon Train menu," I
said. "She left before dinner was served."

"She could be anywhere," said Hunt. "The Oaks is a big place."

"I know. That's what worries me," I said. "I think we should call the police. Maybe she fell and hurt herself. Or maybe she's been kidnapped.''

"Kidnapped? Oh, cool," said Kimberley.

"Jude, sit down and have some coffee," said Hunt.

"I don't want coffee," I said. "I want to find Claire."

"I'm telling you, she'll turn up," said Hunt. "Let's not spoil our evening, huh?"

Maybe he was right, I thought. Maybe Claire had simply gotten into a long conversation with someone and had lost track of time. Or maybe she *was* in the bathroom. I didn't peek under every stall, for God's sake. Maybe she was fine. Maybe she *would* turn up.

I sat back down at the table and tried to make light banter with my in-laws, which is like trying to squeeze orange juice out of a baseball. Another half-hour went by and still Claire had not returned to her table.

"Hunt," I said. "We've got to do something."

"Like what?" he said.

"I don't know. Maybe tell Duncan. He is her relative, after all."

We both glanced over at the Tewksburys' table. Delia Tewksbury was there, but her husband was not.

Hunt nodded, took my hand, told the others we'd be back in a minute, and led me over to the Tewksburys' table.

Delia Tewksbury, a tall, big-boned woman, had hair that could best be described as "skunklike." It was worn in a tight French twist—always—and was very dark, except for the streak of silver that ran from her widow's peak down to her left ear. She had pale, heavily powdered skin, with little dots of rouge on her cheeks, and she often smelled of rose petals—not the real ones but the kind that came in cans of Glade Air Freshener.

"Hello, Mrs. Tewksbury," I said, then introduced myself to her for the umpteenth time. So did Hunt.

She smiled and said hello but showed no signs of having met either of us before.

"We hate to disturb your dinner," said Hunt, "but we're a bit worried about your grandniece, who seems to have disappeared from the party."

"Claire? Disappeared?" She seemed genuinely alarmed. Perhaps she had a greater fondness for Claire than her husband did.

Hunt shared our concerns with her and she suggested we tell Duncan about them when he returned from the men's room. "He will know how to handle the situation," she said. I suspected that she had never handled a situation in her life, not if she could help it.

When Duncan returned, Hunt told him about Claire. Unlike his wife, he seemed unperturbed.

"If you know Claire, you know how unpredictable she is," he chuckled.

"Really?" I said. "I wouldn't call her unpredictable at all. She seems pretty consistent in what she does."

Duncan chuckled again. He was one of those perpetual chucklers, I had discovered the night of our interview with the Membership Committee. He chuckled when he was amused and he chuckled when he wasn't. His chuckling was his cover, his way of making us think he was urbane and witty and a good sport, when what he really was, I guessed, was a sad old man who clung to a lifestyle that had long become as obsolete as he was becoming.

"I think we should put together a search party," I suggested. "Or call the police and let them do it."

"The police? At The Oaks? Nonsense," he said. "We don't want a fuss."

"Your grandniece has vanished," I said firmly. "Fuss or not, we've got to do something."

Duncan looked at Hunt with an expression that said, "Can't you handle your wife, sonny boy, the way I handle mine? What kind of a man are you?"

"I agree with her, sir," Hunt said. "We've got to do something. Claire is missing and we really should try to find her."

I smiled at Hunt. Maybe there was hope for him yet.

We all agreed that there was no point in alarming the rest of the members, as the party was winding down and they'd all be going home anyway. So we enlisted the help of Perry, Addison, and several of the dining room staff, who were dispatched into the kitchen for flashlights.

Kimberley went home with her grandparents, while nearly a dozen of us combed the grounds in search of Claire. It was close to midnight when we heard someone shouting.

"I think the voice is coming from the fourth," said Hunt as we stood near the approach to the golf course.

"The fourth what?" I asked.

"Hole," he said. "It's a par-3. A *long* par-3. Boy, it's treacherous. It runs over water and offers a rock-wall plunge protecting forward pin positions, but the green is so big that back cup locations take the—''

"Hunt, please," I said. "This isn't the time for a hole-by-hole assessment of the course. Let's just find out where the voice is coming from, okay?"

He nodded, took my arm, and guided us across his beloved course. Despite the full moon and our flashlight, the night was dark, and we had trouble finding our way over the fairways and greens.

"Over here! Over here!" someone shouted.

"That's Perry," said Hunt.

We ran toward the voice, which, we discovered, was coming from a sand trap. The rest of our search party had already gathered there in a little semicircle.

"You found her?" Hunt asked them.

They stepped back and pointed to the body lying facedown in the sand. I gripped Hunt's arm and shielded my eyes.

"Is it . . . Claire?" I asked him.

"Dear God, it sure looks like it," he said. "It sure does."

"Oh, no," I wailed. "It can't be."

"I'm afraid it is our poor, poor Claire," said Duncan Tewksbury, who sounded as if he cared.

"Has anybody tried to turn her over?" Hunt asked the others?

"No," said Perry. "I, for one, didn't want to touch anything. The police always say not to."

"What if she needs help?" I said, still hiding my face in the crook of Hunt's arm. "What if she's still alive?"

"I took her pulse," said a member of the kitchen staff. "There wasn't any. She's dead all right. And judging by that gash on the back of her head, she's—"

"Gash?" I said, looking up finally. I forced myself to confront Claire's body. It was she, all right. I'd recognize that Native American medicine woman costume anywhere. And there *was* a gash—and it was mean and bloody. But who would want to hit her on the back of the head and why?

"I'll call the police," said Hunt.

"No!" said Duncan. "I should be the one to call them. I was her great-uncle after all."

Duncan put his hand to his forehead in a gesture meant to suggest his pain and suffering.

"Why don't you go inside the clubhouse with him," I whispered to Hunt. "In case he becomes overcome with grief."

"Right," said Hunt. "Want to come with me?"

I shook my head. "I'm staying with Claire," I said, tears welling up in my eyes. "Oh, Hunt. It's so awful."

I began to cry. Hunt took me in his arms and rocked me, smoothing my hair off my face and kissing my forehead. "We'll find out who did this," he vowed. "Don't you worry."

"But I still can't believe she's dead," I said. "Just a few hours ago, I was talking to her, laughing with her, planning our cookbook . . ."

It suddenly hit me: Claire was dead and so was our cookbook. Whoever killed her also killed any hopes I had of resuming my career.

"Hey, look at this," said Perry as he pointed to the golf club lying several feet away from the sand trap.

Hunt and the others went over to get a closer look but didn't pick it up.

"It's Henry's pitching wedge," he said.

"It's what?" I called out, then went over to see for myself.

"It belongs to Henry Bradford, the golf pro," Hunt explained. "It's his pitching wedge."

"How do you know?" I asked.

"Because of the angle on the head of the club," he said. "That's what a pitching wedge looks like."

"No, I meant how do you know it belongs to the golf pro?" I said.

"Look at the shaft," Hunt pointed. "It's got Greg Norman's autograph on it: 'The Great White Shark.' Henry was very proud of that club."

"Was Henry angry at Claire?" I said.

"Henry is out of town," said Duncan. "He didn't do this if that's what you're thinking, Mrs. Price. We don't employ criminals at The Oaks. Whoever hurt my grandniece must have been an outsider."

"Perhaps," I said. "I just thought that since it was Henry's pitching wedge that seems to have been the murder weapon, we should—"

"Henry's clubs are for the members' use," said Duncan. "They're in his office, for teaching purposes. Everyone at The Oaks has access to them."

"There's no point in our speculating," said Hunt. "The police will figure out who did this to Claire. Duncan? Are you ready to go inside?"

Duncan nodded.

"Be back in a few minutes, Jude," said Hunt.

"Before you go, may I have this?" I reached up to lift the cowboy hat off his head.

"Sure," he said. "But what do you want with it?"

I walked over to Claire's lifeless body, her face encrusted with sand, her hair matted with blood, and placed the cowboy hat gently over the back of her head, shielding it from the night air and our curious eyes.

"You're not supposed to disturb anything," said Perry. "Not when there's been a homicide."

"Oh, come on," I said. "That's not one of The Oaks's dopey bylaws, is it?"

I crouched down in the sand, very close to Claire's body, and said my goodbye.

"Farewell, my friend," I whispered to her. "We didn't know each other long or well, but I promise you I'll make sure they find out who did this to you. Meanwhile, I hope that wherever you are now, wherever your soul has journeyed, there is no war, no famine, and no Men's Grill."

PART
T·W·O

CHAPTER EIGHT

♦

The country was grief-stricken over Claire Cox's death. Reports about it were all over the media—from the morning news programs, during which political pundits from both parties debated her place in history, to the evening news shows, on which Hillary Clinton, Gloria Steinem, and other female luminaries said how much they admired and respected her. Newspapers and magazines offered moving retrospectives of her life and times. Photos pictured her with the likes of Anita Hill, whom she had supported during the Clarence Thomas hearings; Nebraska senator Bob Kerrey, whom she dated after he broke up with Debra Winger; and Warren Beatty, with whom she had a relationship in the late 1970s. The tabloid media covered her life and death as if she were another Amy Fisher. All three networks were scrambling to produce TV movies based on her story.

Who would want to kill her? I asked myself over and over. Who would want to end the life of a woman who had accomplished so much—and had so much more to accomplish? Who would want to kill her at *my* country club? In *my* little town?

I shuddered when I thought about the fact that the killer was still on the loose and that the intrepid Belford Police Department hadn't handled a homicide in nearly a half-century. Would they be up to the challenge of solving the case? Would they conduct a thorough investigation? Would they leave no stone unturned?

I had my answer on Tuesday morning—the day after the club's Wild West July Fourth party, which, of course, turned out to be wilder than anyone could have predicted. Hunt had taken the train into the city with Kimberley, and I was at home making the beds. The phone rang at about nine-thirty.

"Mrs. Price?" said a male voice.

"I'm not interested," I said. God, those telephone salesmen were a pain. They were interrupting you in the middle of dinner or bugging you first thing in the morning, and they were never selling anything you were remotely interested in buying.

I was about to hang up when the caller introduced himself as Thomas Cunningham—*Detective* Thomas Cunningham of the Belford Police Department.

"Oh," I said. "I thought you were trying to sell me a Discover card."

"No," he said gruffly. "I'm trying to solve Claire Cox's murder."

"Oh," I said again. "Please excuse me. You see, the only people who call me Mrs. Price are telephone salesmen, my husband's parents, and members of my country club."

"What does everyone else call you?" he asked.

"Judy. Judy Mills."

"Mills is your maiden name?"

"Yes. I was never big on hyphenated last names. I've always felt that you either take your husband's name or you don't—and I didn't."

Silence, then: "So your full name is Judy Mills?"

"No. My full name is Judith Rifka Mills."

"I didn't catch the one after Judith."

"Rifka. It's Hebrew for Rebecca. You know, like Becky?"

More silence. I had a hunch that Detective Cunningham was really sorry he'd started this. "Look, Ms. Mills," he said. "I'd like to talk to you about Ms. Cox."

"You mean, because I was one of the people who found her body?" I asked.

"Yes," he said, "and because one of the women who was having dinner with her last night told us that you and Ms. Cox were writing a book together."

"Yes," I said sadly. "A cookbook."

"Could you come down to headquarters this morning? Say around ten-thirty?"

I thought for a minute. I didn't have anything scheduled for ten-thirty. As a matter of fact, I didn't have anything scheduled for the foreseeable future, except a gynecologist appointment two weeks from Wednesday and a periodontal checkup three weeks after that. I was jobless and appointmentless and directionless, and going down to police headquarters and talking to a cop sounded like a welcome change from sitting at home and waiting for the phone to ring. "Ten-thirty will be fine," I said. "Just fine."

I arrived at the police station and was directed to the cubicle-size office of Detective Thomas Cunningham and his partner, Detective Jake Creamer, who was not present at the time of my visit.

"Sit there," said Detective Cunningham as he pointed to the chair next to his desk.

I sat and stared at the detective as he went through a pile of pink "While You Were Out" message slips and tossed most of them in the garbage.

Gee, I thought. He's not bad-looking. Not bad at all. Thirty-five-ish and ruggedly handsome, he had a lean, sinewy build, a cleft in his chin, gleaming brown eyes, and hair that was so dark it was almost comic-book blue-black. And then there was his nose, which, judging from the right turn it took at the bridge, had been on the receiving end of one too many fists. I'm embarrassed to admit I checked out his left hand: no wedding band. I guessed he had a girlfriend, a manicurist he'd met in the bar of the local Pizza & Brew, and that they often spent the night at his house, having rough sex and watching professional wrestling matches on Pay Per View.

"Thanks for coming, Ms. Mills," he said, finally looking up at me.

"You're welcome," I said, transfixed by the way the cleft in his chin moved as he talked.

"I'll need your address and date of birth," he said as he pulled out a notebook and pen.

"I live at 42 Beaverbrook Road. Belford."

"Date of birth?"

"Is that absolutely necessary?"

Okay, so I was being a little sensitive about my age. It's not easy to admit you're forty when you're sitting with a very attractive younger man.

"Yes, it's absolutely necessary," he said, revealing a hint of a smile.

"May thirtieth, 1955."

"Now, tell me about your relationship with Ms. Cox."

I gave Detective Cunningham the whole sad story—how I was fired from my job at Charlton House, how I hadn't been able to find another job, how my husband had suggested I start networking at our country club, how I had previously avoided the club like the plague but took his advice anyway, how I met Claire there, how we decided to write a cookbook together, how I spoke to her at the party the previous evening and how I was one of the group who found her body.

"How long have you and your husband been members of The Oaks?"

"About two years."

"You said you avoided the club. You don't like it there?"

"In a word: no."

"Why not?"

"There's no valet parking."

Detective Cunningham looked up from his notepad.

"Well," I said, "that's not the main reason."

"What's the main reason?"

"The people are a bunch of phonies. The food's not so hot either."

"Is there anything you *like* about The Oaks?"

"Yes. The facilities are very well maintained. If I brushed my teeth as often as they brush those tennis courts, I wouldn't have any enamel left."

"Did Ms. Cox have many friends at The Oaks?"

"No." Well, there was Ducky. But I didn't see the need to mention their history together. It was such a long time ago.

"She wasn't very popular with the established members?"

"God, no. She wanted to change things at the club. She thought women should be allowed to eat in the Men's Grill and things like that."

"The what grill?"

"The Men's Grill. It used to be the club's men-only restaurant."

"Oh, yeah. My father's club has one of those."

Detective Cunningham didn't strike me as a man whose father was into country clubs. "What club does he belong to?" I asked. Rotary? Elks? Knights of Columbus?

"Actually, he's on the Board of Governors at The Westover Country Club."

"Really?" The members at Westover were rich Catholics who tried to get into The Oaks but couldn't.

"Did Ms. Cox have any enemies at The Oaks? Anyone who might want to harm her?"

I thought for a minute. "Well, a lot of people were against her joining the club," I said. "She was the first single woman to get in. Even her great-uncle didn't want her there."

"Would that be Duncan Tewksbury?" he asked.

I nodded.

"So no enemies that you can think of?"

"Enemies? It's hard to say," I said. "At country clubs you can't really tell your enemies from your friends. The guy who plays golf with you one day could be the guy who hits you over the head with a pitching wedge the next."

Detective Cunningham stopped writing and looked up. "What do you know about that pitching wedge, Ms. Mills?"

"You mean the one we found near Claire's body?"

"Yeah."

"Nothing, except that it belonged to Henry, the golf pro. It was one of his teaching clubs."

"Did you ever see any of the members playing with that club?"

"No, but then I make it a point never to see the members playing with *any* club. I hate watching golf. It's a really boring sport, if you ask me. Right up there with fly fishing."

Thomas Cunningham stared at me. Clearly, I was not his run-of-the-mill interviewee.

"I think we're just about finished here," he said.

"Oh?" I was disappointed. I had enjoyed having Detective Cunningham ask me questions, listen to my answers, ask for my opinions.

Detective Cunningham gave the notes he'd taken during our interview to a secretary, asked her to type them up, and when she did, he handed me the pages and told me to read them over.

"If everything's correct, sign here," he said.

I signed.

"Thanks for coming in." He shook my hand and allowed himself a smile.

My eyes went straight to the cleft in his chin, and the oddest thing happened. I began to imagine myself inserting my tongue in that cleft, in and out, in and out, in and out. Yes, I was horny, and yes, my marriage was stale, and yes, I'd always thought men with cleft chins exuded a certain animal magnetism, but to have fantasies right there in the police station—during a murder interrogation, no less—was humiliating and not a little disrespectful to the murder victim.

You need to get a job, I told myself as I left police headquarters. You need to get a job and you need to get laid.

I went home and sulked. How on earth was I going to get a job when there weren't any? That very morning *The New York Times* had reported that Charlton House was laying off another twenty employees and that Gaines McGrath, another trade book publisher, was dismissing fifty of its Manhattan-based workers. I didn't have a prayer of getting hired.

I started to cry—big, dopey tears that ran down my cheeks into my shirt collar. Talk about feeling sorry for myself. I was the picture of self-pity. Why did Claire have to get murdered, I sobbed. Why couldn't she have lived, so we could have written our cookbook? Why couldn't we have written the cookbook and watched it hit the bestseller list? Why? Why? Why?

In an attempt to calm myself, I flipped on the television set and channel-surfed until I came to a station that was broadcasting a rerun of "Mannix." Before I knew it, I was glued to the episode, which found macho, dark-haired Detective Mannix, aka Mike Connors, solving the murder of a kindly pediatrician who had witnessed a hit-and-run accident. I thought of Detective Cunningham and decided he was much handsomer and sexier than Mannix. I wondered if he had found me the least bit attractive during our interview that morning. I wondered if his girlfriend was attractive. I wondered if she minded that he was a cop or if she was the type who was turned on by men with dangerous jobs. I wondered if I'd ever see him again.

I hardly ever went to the club. Just thinking of Claire's body lying in that sand trap made me wary of ever setting foot in the place again. Besides, I found it hard to deal with the members, who, with the exception of the handful of women who had respected Claire's accomplishments, were more insufferable than ever. Talk about denial! A murder had been committed on the grounds of their goddamn country club and yet they acted as if nothing very significant had happened. Instead of being helpful and cooperative with the police, who had the daunting task of interviewing every single person who attended the July Fourth party, they bitched and moaned about having to schlep down to headquarters and answer a bunch of questions. Some of them complained that a fifteen-minute interview with the police would screw up their golf game or bridge game or both. Others were concerned that their names—and that of the club—would be forever linked with a murder. Still others said they felt harassed by the very police force they'd supported with their extraordinarily generous tax dollars. Even Hunt seemed irritated when Detective Creamer called and said it was his turn to be interviewed. "Why are these local characters wasting our time when the FBI should be handling a case of this importance?" he grumbled.

Then one day Arlene called and asked if she could be my guest at the club.

"My therapist says country clubs are a good place for meeting men," she explained.

"So you haven't met anyone you really like?" I asked.

"I've met men I like, but none that look like Fabio," she sighed.

"I've got a bulletin for you, Arlene," I said. "You won't find anyone who looks like Fabio at The Oaks. You won't even find anyone who looks like Fabio's great-grandfather."

Undaunted, Arlene spent the following Saturday with me at the club, and I couldn't get over the change in her. This woman, who used to dress like a vestal virgin, had transformed herself into Ms. Hot Stuff—tight skirt, tight blouse, loose look. As we ate lunch in the terrace dining room, I noticed that every man I introduced her to eyed her lasciviously—even Ducky Laughton, who was married to Nedra, the sexpot, and grieving over the death of his old love Claire.

"It's a pleasure," he said, shaking her hand and looking straight at her cleavage. The man could barely keep his tongue in his mouth.

"Thank you," said Arlene, batting her eyelashes. "Judy has told me so much about you. I feel as if I know you somehow."

I nearly gagged. I hadn't told Arlene a thing about Ducky except that he was the one member of The Oaks who didn't make my skin crawl.

Ducky bowed. "I hope we'll meet again, Arlene," he said. "Now that the club is accepting single women at long last, perhaps you'll think about becoming a member. It's what Claire would have wanted, don't you think, Judy?"

I nodded.

"Well, I'll leave you two to your lunch," said Ducky.

"Goodbye," said Arlene as she uncrossed her legs, then crossed them again.

When Ducky was gone, I leaned over and whispered to her. "Don't take this the wrong way," I said. "But I think you're being a little obvious."

"Obvious? How?" she said.

"You know. The clothes. The hair. The makeup. Guys are turned off by women who come on strong."

"Says who?" she said. "I've had six dates in the last two weeks. None of them complained."

I shrugged and changed the subject. What did I know about men? My husband barely knew I was alive.

Arlene and I talked about my inability to find a job, about my inability to get anyone to meet with me, about my inability to get anyone to return my phone calls. Then we talked about how tough it was to earn a living in the post-Recession nineties.

"How's the money situation?" Arlene asked at one point. "Is it tough on a marriage to live off one person's income?"

"Everything's tough on a marriage," I said ruefully. "But to answer your question, money doesn't seem to be a problem. We're still members of this obscenely expensive club, as you can see. And we're certainly not starving. Actually, our financial life hasn't changed much at all since I got fired, which is almost the most depressing thing about my getting fired. I always believed that my contribution to our income meant something, that without it Hunt and I wouldn't be able to enjoy the Good Life. But it turns out that we do just fine without my money, that life goes on, that our membership in The Oaks goes on, even though I'm not bringing in one red cent."

"Weird, isn't it?" said Arlene. "You're being supported by your husband, which is something millions of women would die for, yet you feel totally disposable, discarded, worthless . . . without any sense of identity . . . like some pathetic hanger-on . . . dependent . . . needy . . . unable to—"

"I get the picture, Arlene," I said, despising her for knowing exactly how I felt. "But enough about me. How's your job?"

"Fabulous," she said. "I adore it. The people I work with are great, and I just got a promotion *and* a raise."

I mumbled a "congratulations," but my heart wasn't in it. Friendship schmiendship. It's hard to be happy for someone who's having the success you think you deserve.

♦

I was moping around the house one morning, trying not to think about the torrid sex Detective Cunningham and I would have if we were both free, when the detective himself called me.

"Yes, Detective. Of course I remember you," I said, my heart doing little pirouettes as I wound the telephone cord around my finger.

"I'd like to see you," he said.

Did I sense a certain urgency, a certain huskiness in his voice, or was it just wish fulfillment on my part?

"When?" I said, trying not to pant.

"How about in twenty minutes?" he said.

"That would be fine," I said. "You have the address."

"Yeah. See ya."

He hung up. I hung up. Then I caught a glimpse of my reflection in the hall mirror. Brother, I was still wearing my ratty bathrobe *and* the plastic bite plate that was supposed to prevent me from grinding my teeth at night.

I hurried upstairs to freshen up and change, and tried to stay calm. But I was nervous. The last time I'd been home alone with a man other than my husband was when Valerio came to visit, and that didn't count.

I jumped when the doorbell rang.

I let Detective Cunningham in and suggested we sit in the living room. I offered him coffee. He said he'd rather just talk.

"Now, Ms. Mills," he began. "I hope you won't be shocked by what I came to ask you to do."

Now, I was really nervous. I'd been fantasizing about the man for days. Had he been thinking about me too? Was that why he had come? "Ask me," I said.

He cleared his throat. "I'd like to make you a proposition."

I was stunned. He was propositioning me. Be careful what you wish for, my mother always said.

Okay, so he was sexy. And sure, I was aching for a little action. But as I said earlier, I wasn't the adulterous type, not really. I wasn't clever enough for adultery. Adultery takes cunning. You've got to plan ahead. You've got to find a trysting place. You've got to remember to shave your legs. I didn't have the time or energy for all that. I had to throw everything I had into finding a job.

"As I said, Ms. Mills, we'd like to make you a proposition."

Ms. Mills? Under the circumstances, shouldn't he be calling me

Judy? And what was all this "we" stuff? Was Detective Cunningham actually proposing a ménage à trois?

"The answer is no," I said firmly.

"But you haven't even heard what we want you to do."

"All right," I said, "say what you came to say." How awful could it be to have to sit and listen to a handsome hunk confess his passion for you?

"We'd like to offer you a job."

"A job?"

"Yeah. With the Belford Police Department."

I was confused. "The police department wants to do a cookbook?"

I had once edited a cookbook that was put together by the New York City Fire Department. It had recipes for things like Firehouse Chili and Smoky Barbecued Chicken, and raised money for some charity or other. But a local police department's cookbook? It didn't sound like a huge seller.

"Are you thinking of a book that's sort of a cross between Joseph Wambaugh and Julia Child?" I asked.

"No, no. You don't understand," he said.

"What then? Joseph Wambaugh and Jacques Pepin?"

He shook his head.

"Daryl Gates and Jacques Pepin?"

"Look, Ms. Mills."

"Judy."

"Judy. While we're exploring all aspects of this case and following up on each and every lead, we think it's possible that a member of your country club was responsible for Claire Cox's death."

"Oh?"

"We want you to help us find out if the killer *was* one of the members, and if so, *which* member." He paused. "We want you to be our informant."

I was dumbfounded. "You want *me* to help you solve Claire's murder?"

"That's right. Ms. Cox was a big celebrity, and the federal boys would love to get their hands on the case. But it's *our* jurisdiction, *our* case to solve. Well, actually it's *my* case to solve. Mine and my partner's. And our boss wants us to solve it yesterday. You understand?"

"Not really."

"Okay, let me try again. The Belford Police Department isn't a huge force. We're a small-town force, 'small' being the operative word here. We can't put every single guy on this one case. So my partner and I are kind of handling it the best we can. We've got hundreds of interviews to do, hundreds of leads to follow up on, hundreds of leads that have nothing to do with The Oaks. At the same time, we—or should I say I?—am interested in getting information about some of the members of The Oaks, to determine if one of them had a motive for killing Ms. Cox. But I don't want to go in there and upset everybody. You know how bent out of shape they get, right?''

"Do I ever. I hear some of them gave you a hard time when you asked them to come down to headquarters.''

He rolled his eyes. "That wasn't the half of it. You should have seen what happened when we asked for a list of all the members.''

"What? Nobody would give you one?''

"Oh, they gave us one, but only after we got a subpoena for it. Then we started calling the members on the list and found out that a quarter of them were dead. No, I wouldn't say the people at your club have been especially forthcoming.''

"I'm not surprised.''

"So, what we need right now—and I know this is a little out of the ordinary—is for someone to help us get information about The Oaks's members and their relationship with the deceased. Someone who's an insider, someone who could hang out there without arousing suspicion. We think *you'd* make a perfect informant.''

"Me? Why?''

"Because you're a member of the club but you hate the place.''

"I don't hate . . . well, I see what you're getting at.''

"Good.''

"What exactly would you want me to do?''

"The same thing you've been doing. Go to the club. Play golf—''

"I don't play golf.''

"Sorry. I forgot.'' He smiled. The hole in his chin danced. "Then play tennis, swim, whatever. The important thing is to just *be* there, keep your eyes and ears open, tell us if you see or hear anything suspicious.''

"I see and hear suspicious things all the time at The Oaks.''

"Like what?''

"The members cheat—at everything. The golfers doctor their score cards, and the tennis players call every close ball in their favor. There's no such thing as sportsmanship at The Oaks.''

He laughed. "It's not their lack of sportsmanship I'm concerned about. It's their possible connection to Claire Cox's murder.''

"So you're saying you want me to spy on my friends at The Oaks?''

"You said you didn't have any friends at The Oaks."

"Good point." My mind was racing. "But my husband does. He's Mr. Popularity at the club. He'd be furious if he found out I was doing anything to jeopardize his membership. He uses the club to network. He's trying to make partner at Fitzgerald & Franklin, the investment banking firm. He's—"

"Then don't tell him," said Detective Cunningham.

"Don't tell him?" What an idea. I told Hunt everything, or at least I used to. How could I possibly be a police informant and not tell him?

"Look, Ms. Mills."

"Judy, remember?"

"Sorry. Judy. And I'm Tom."

"Tom."

"It's up to you whether or not you tell your husband. I just want to know if you'll do it."

"Be an informant, you mean."

"Yeah."

"How would it work exactly?"

"First, you'd come down to headquarters so we could run your prints, that kind of stuff."

"Run my prints?"

"Yeah, the lieutenant is pretty strict about prints. He says if I'm going to go out on a limb and hire you, I've got to get you finger-printed, make sure you are who you say you are. Then I'd give you a beeper so we could always be in touch with each other."

Always be in touch with each other. That had a nice ring to it.

"So I'd be working directly with you?" I asked.

"Only with me," he said. "You have a problem with that?"

"No, no problem," I said.

"As far as money goes, you'll be paid about $200 a week for as long as we need you."

Paid? That did it. Income and Tom Cunningham too.

I took a deep breath. "Tom," I said. "Meet your new informant."

"So you're taking the job?"

"Yes."

"Good."

"I hope so."

CHAPTER NINE

♦

What does one wear when one goes to the police station to begin a job as an informant?

That was the question I pondered as I rummaged through my closet that Friday morning. I had no idea how to dress for the occasion. I was an out-of-work cookbook editor. What the hell did *I* know about being an informant? On the other hand, I'd had all those years in publishing, an industry full of gossips and rumor mongers and people who allowed themselves to be quoted in newspaper articles only if their names weren't used. Maybe I knew more about being an informant than I thought.

I tried on a few outfits and settled on one that I thought looked very country club-ish: white skirt, navy blue and red "nautical" shirt (it had little gold anchors on it), red sandals, and a white headband. All the women at The Oaks wore headbands, usually black velvet or some milky pastel. And when they didn't wear headbands, they wore visors, which made the act of air-kissing nearly impossible. I mean, have you ever seen two visor-wearing women trying to air-kiss each other? They have to bob and weave like a couple of prizefighters trying to land a punch.

"Where are you off to?" Hunt asked as he watched me dress. He was working at home that morning, then playing golf at the club in the afternoon.

"I'm . . . uh . . . going to talk to some people about a job," I said. Not a lie.

"Who?"

"Who?"

"We sound like a couple of owls."

I laughed. "Sorry. I'm a little distracted this morning."

"Probably the heat," said Hunt. "It's supposed to hit ninety today."

Ninety. Ugh. I hoped the Belford Police Station was air-conditioned.

"So who are you interviewing with?" Hunt asked again. "You're dressed kind of casually for a job interview."

"Oh, well it's a real low-key company. Family owned."

"What's the name?"

"Uh . . . Food Data Systems." Sounded good to me.

"Never heard of it."

"They're new. Small. Not publicly traded."

"What do they do?"

"Well, they . . . uh . . . compile recipes from cookbooks and put them on computer disks." I hoped the questions would end here. I knew as much about computers as I knew about police work.

"What do they do with the computer disks?"

"They sell them to . . . um . . . people who are interested in food. It's a mail-order kind of thing."

"Big market?"

"Absolutely. People are always misplacing their favorite recipes. Remember when I couldn't find my mother's recipe for stuffed cabbage?"

Hunt nodded, even though there was no such recipe. The only thing my mother stuffed was herself.

"Well, by putting recipes on disks, people will have permanent access to them," I went on. I didn't have a clue what I was talking about, but Hunt didn't seem to notice. Perhaps I was born for undercover work.

"What would you do for this Food Data Systems?" Hunt asked.

"Help gather the recipes from various cookbooks, acquire the electronic rights, things like that."

I couldn't believe Hunt was asking me so many questions. He wasn't usually so inquisitive. But then husbands always surprise you.

When you want them to give you their undivided attention, they run off to play golf. When you want them to run off to play golf, they give you their undivided attention.

"How did you hear about the job?" he asked.

"From Arlene," I said, trying to mask my impatience. "But listen, Hunt. I've really got to get going. My interview is for nine o'clock."

"It's eight forty-five now," said Hunt after checking his watch. "I hope for your sake this place is nearby."

"Yeah, it's right off I-95."

I gave Hunt a quick peck on the cheek and took off.

Sure, I felt guilty about lying to my husband. Very guilty. I'd spent the previous night tossing and turning and agonizing over whether I should tell Hunt about my deal with Detective Cunningham. Ultimately, I'd decided that it was better all around if I didn't tell him, and the decision had given me a bad stomachache. Still, there was something oddly thrilling about deceiving him. Stomachache or not, I hadn't felt so alive in months.

"Good morning," I said to Tom Cunningham as I walked into his office at eight-fifty.

He nodded and introduced me to his partner, Detective Jake Creamer, a blond, heavyset man with a Marine-style crew cut and a ruddy complexion. Detective Creamer nodded at me too. Neither cop was especially friendly, but it wasn't even nine o'clock yet. Maybe they weren't morning people.

"We won't keep you more than a few minutes," said Tom, who hadn't gotten any less attractive in the twenty-four hours since I'd last seen him. He was wearing blue jeans, a faded blue denim work shirt, and a pair of high-top Reeboks, and he *was* much sexier than Mannix. "But first we've got to get you fingerprinted and photographed."

"Photographed?" I'd been so concerned about leaving the house without Hunt finding out where I was going that I hadn't paid much attention to my hair and makeup.

"Yeah, photographed," said Tom. "Like a *Sports Illustrated* swimsuit model." He smiled at his joke. We were making progress.

Tom took me down the hall for my photo shoot. It turned out that the guy who photographed me was the same guy who took all the mug shots of criminals. His work made passport photos look like Scavullo portraits.

Getting fingerprinted wasn't a picnic either. I broke a nail, forgot to wash the ink off my finger, and got black smudges all over my white skirt, not to mention my face.

"Here," Tom laughed as he handed me a damp paper towel. "Clean yourself up."

I tried to wipe the ink off the tip of my nose, but without a mirror it was difficult.

"Let me," said Tom, taking back the paper towel.

He stood facing me, his body just inches from mine, and dabbed at my nose with the steady hand of a painter. I could feel his nearness, sense his manliness, smell his breath. Onion roll, I deduced. The man had definitely eaten an onion roll for breakfast.

As we walked back to his office, I asked Tom if he had specific instructions for me as I prepared for my life as an informant.

"Just go to The Oaks and keep your eyes and ears open," he said. "We'll probably meet once a week, unless you call me with something sooner. I'm counting on you, Judy."

I gulped. I suddenly realized that this was not a lark I was entering into. This was serious business. Belford's Finest were counting on *me!*

"I won't let you down," I said solemnly. "If Claire's murderer is anywhere near The Oaks, I'll find him."

Tom nodded, then handed me a beeper, which he alternately referred to as a pager. I'd seen beepers before, of course. Several people at The Oaks had them—the macho corporate types who loved getting "beeped" on the tennis courts or the golf course to remind us how important and indispensable they were. I always suspected that it was really their wives who beeped them, to remind them to bring home a pint of milk.

"Your beeper comes with the vibrator option," Tom said with a straight face.

"The vibrator option?" Perhaps police work would expand my horizons in more ways than one.

"The purpose of the vibrator option is to eliminate noise," Tom explained with a wry smile. "There'll be times when you won't want to get beeped. So you just flip on the vibrator switch, and instead of getting beeped, you get vibrated."

"Oh," I said and tried not to imagine Tom Cunningham getting vibrated. This wasn't the time or the place.

"Any other questions?" he asked.

"Yes," I said as I put the beeper in my purse. "You haven't mentioned whether you have any suspects in Claire's case. Is there anyone in particular you'd like me to keep my eye on?"

"I'll be honest with you, Judy," he said. "There were no finger-prints on that pitching wedge, which was bent and nearly broken. Whoever used it to kill Ms. Cox hit her over and over before calling it a night."

I shuddered.

"In addition to there being no fingerprints on the murder weapon," he continued, "there were no discernible footprints around the crime scene, because your little search party went into that sand trap and obscured whatever evidence there may have been. As for suspects, no terrorist group has claimed responsibility for the murder. No motive has been established. We're nowhere on this in-vestigation. Nowhere. You'd be doing us all a giant favor if you came up with a motive for one of these people at your country club. Some-body had a reason for killing Ms. Cox, or thought they did."

I heaved a deep sigh.

"What's the matter?" he asked. "Cold feet?"

"No," I said. "I was just wondering: what if it turns out that *several* people at the club thought they had a reason for killing Claire?"

"Then you'll be a very busy lady."

He smiled and showed me the door.

For the next week I was The Oaks's most omnipresent and enthusias-tic member. I played tennis. I used the pool. I ate lunch on the ter-race with the girls and dinner in the main dining room with my husband. I even—get this—took golf lessons. Hunt was overjoyed. He said if I showed a facility for the sport, he'd buy me my own set of golf clubs. Hubba hubba.

During a lunch with Bailey Vanderhoff and Penelope Etheridge, I learned a very interesting tidbit. We, or should I say they, were gossip-ing about Larkin Vail, who was often gossiped about at the club be-cause of her prominence as the top woman tennis player. Generally, the way it works at clubs is that when you're a mediocre player, every-body likes you but nobody wants to play with you. When you're the club's best player, everybody wants to play with you but nobody likes you. That rule was especially true in Larkin's case. Six or seven years before, she was a so-so player with a wide circle of friends. Now that she was a whiz on the courts, she was down to a single friend: Nedra Laughton, her doubles partner. I tried to act riveted as Bailey and Penelope ripped her to shreds.

"Don't you despise the way she bounces the ball five times before she serves?" said Bailey. "I mean, is that pretentious or what?"

"I don't know about pretentious, but it's definitely malicious," said Penelope.

"Malicious?" I said. "Isn't that overstating it?"

"No way," Penelope insisted. "When she pulls that five-bounce routine, she's deliberately trying to unnerve her opponent. Well, I, for one, refuse to stand for it."

"What do you do?" I asked.

"I cough or adjust my visor or bend down to tie my shoelace," she said. "It throws off her rhythm and makes her double fault."

"Gee, that's inspired," I said and tried to look as if I meant it.

"What I don't get is how nobody's ever tried to run her out of the club," said Bailey.

"For bouncing the ball five times before she serves?" I asked, incredulous.

"No," said Bailey. "For her off-the-court behavior."

"What's wrong with her off-the-court-behavior?" I asked. On the court Larkin was a monster, the classic example of a poor sport, but off the court she always seemed pretty normal. Relative to everybody else at The Oaks, that is.

"You haven't heard?" said Penelope.

"Heard what?" I said.

"About the match last year against the Westover Country Club," she said. "We play them twice a summer."

I nodded and thought of Detective Cunningham's father. "Go on," I urged Penelope.

"Well, Westover's number-one player on the women's A team is June Douglas," Penelope went on. "Larkin had to play her and had a hissy fit."

"Why?" I asked.

"For the same reason Larkin always has hissy fits: she hates to lose," Bailey offered.

"It was the day of our tournament against Westover," Penelope continued. "We were all sitting there drinking Gatorade and trying to make conversation with the Westover players before the matches started. Before we knew it, June Douglas was drunk as a skunk. The poor woman could barely walk, let alone play tennis."

"Drunk? From drinking Gatorade? How could that happen?" I asked.

"Ask Larkin," Bailey snickered.

"I'm asking you guys," I said.

"It was Larkin who went inside the tennis house and came back with June's Gatorade," said Bailey. "June drank it and got drunk. Doesn't that say it all?"

"You're not suggesting that Larkin spiked the woman's drink," I said.

Penelope and Bailey nodded.

"But surely this June Douglas would have smelled the alcohol before she drank it," I said.

"Not if Larkin spiked the Gatorade with vodka," Penelope countered. "It doesn't have a smell—especially if it's Absolut, the kind Perry Vail happens to drink."

"I find it very hard to believe that Larkin would do something like that, competitive though she may be," I said.

"You may find it hard to believe, Judy, but June Douglas is sure that she was sabotaged," said Bailey. "She told her husband, who told my husband, who told me."

"Then how come nobody else noticed what was going on?" I asked.

"Who knows?" Bailey said. "Larkin could have brought a flask to the club and slipped the vodka into June's cup without the rest of us noticing. All I can say is that June had to default the match, which gave Larkin the automatic win."

"Larkin's a terrific player," I said. "She doesn't have to drug her opponents to beat them."

"She couldn't beat Claire Cox a couple of weeks ago, remember?" said Bailey.

Yes, I did remember. Not only that, she'd gone ballistic when she'd lost to Claire. Still, Larkin couldn't possibly care enough about winning a dopey tennis match to drug June Douglas . . . or bludgeon Claire Cox to death, could she? The idea was absurd, but then many things about The Oaks were absurd.

I decided to have lunch with Larkin and get my own impression of her psyche.

"How've you been?" I asked her. She looked tanned and fit and ready for a couple of sets of tennis.

"I'm super," she said, taking a bite of her New Potato Salad. I had ordered the New Potato Salad too, only to discover that there was nothing "new" about it; the potatoes were so old they had liver spots.

During most of the meal, Larkin gossiped about Bailey and Penelope and all the people at the club who gossiped relentlessly about her. In fact, Larkin was a world-class gossip, especially when it came to everybody's tennis injuries. If you had even the slightest case of tennis elbow, she knew all the details—including which elbow. She ate very quickly, and when she had finished her lunch, she announced that she had to leave.

"What's the rush?" I said.

"I have a game with Nedra at two-thirty," she said.

"But it's only one-fifteen," I said.

"I know, but I want to be over at the courts by one-thirty. Nedra and I like to warm up before we play."

"For an hour? That's a lot of warming up."

"Yes, but you've heard the old saying: 'You can never be too rich, too thin, or too warmed up.' "

No, I hadn't heard that old saying. "Before you go," I said, "how's your tennis game going? You seem to be playing well this summer."

"Pretty well," she said. "I'm having a little trouble with my drop shot, but otherwise I'm on course."

Spiked anybody's Gatorade lately? I wanted to ask her. "Have you lost any matches so far?" I asked her instead.

She thought for a minute. "No," she said finally.

"What about that match against Claire Cox?" I asked. Apparently, it had slipped Larkin's mind.

"Oh that," she said. "I had my period that day. I wasn't playing my best."

"Claire was a good player, though, wasn't she?"

"She had good strokes but she didn't know where to place the ball."

"So you didn't see her as competition for the women's singles tournament later this summer?"

"I see everyone as competition."

"It's too bad about what happened to Claire, isn't it?" I asked. It was time to stop pussyfooting around.

"Horrible."

"And to think it happened at our club. During the Wild West July Fourth party."

"Dreadful."

"You and Perry were sitting near the Laughtons, right?"

"Yes."

"Did you enjoy the party?"

"Very much. Perry and I thought the band was exceptional, especially when they played 'The Achy Breaky Heart.' "

"Did you happen to see Claire or talk to her during the evening?"

"No."

"Really? You couldn't miss her. She was the only Indian medicine woman at the party."

"Well, I didn't see her."

"Do you have any thoughts on who might have killed her?"

"Probably someone from one of those Right to Life groups."

"I don't think so," I said. "I think the killer is someone who had a personal grudge against Claire."

"Oh, you mean like a love affair gone sour?"

"Maybe."

"Aha! Then I bet Ducky Laughton did it."

"Ducky? How can you accuse him of being a murderer?"

"Because he used to have a thing for Claire Cox, according to Nedra."

"Yes, but he's your best friend's husband. The four of you are inseparable." Did the woman have no loyalty?

"Fine. So it wasn't Ducky. Maybe it was Nedra."

"Nedra?" I was aghast that Larkin could stab her best friend in the back. If she could stab Nedra in the back, maybe she could hit Claire over the head.

"Come on, Judy," she said. "You've seen how jealous Nedra is. Maybe she lost it when she realized her husband would be sharing a golf course with his old lover."

I stared at Larkin. I knew I was supposed to be concentrating on the fact that she was a possible suspect in Claire's murder, but I was fixated on what a rat she was, on how effortlessly she accused her only ally at the club. "Do you have any qualms about talking to me about Nedra this way?" I asked.

She shrugged. "Life's a lot like tennis," she said. "You have to play the ball wherever it lands."

I shuddered as I watched her get up to leave for her hour-long, prematch warm-up session with her best friend Nedra. Maybe she was the murderer and maybe she wasn't. But one thing was certain: with friends like her, who needed enemies?

I called Tom Cunningham when I got home from the club, but the department secretary said he was out on a case. Apparently, someone had robbed the Belford Hardware Store and taken, among other things, a Weber grill and a large bag of charcoal. The cops had already dubbed the thief the Barbecue Bandit.

"Why didn't you beep me?" Tom asked when he reached me about six o'clock. "If I'm not at the station, you're supposed to beep me."

"It wasn't an emergency," I said. "I'm not even sure it warranted a phone call."

"Meet me in fifteen minutes and we'll see," he said.

"Where?" I said. Hunt would be home soon. We were supposed to be having dinner with Nedra and Ducky at the club.

"The parking lot of Stop 'n' Shop," he said.

"How will I find you?" I asked. "That parking lot is always full, and I don't know what kind of car you drive."

"Not a problem," he said. "I'll find *you.*"

At six-twelve, Tom drove up in his white unmarked Chevy Caprice and parked alongside my BMW. He motioned for me to get into his car, so I did.

"What's up?" he asked.

He was wearing blue jeans and a Hartford Whalers T-shirt. His face bore the hint of a five o'clock shadow, and his coal-black hair had curled up the back of his collar from the summer heat and humidity. He smelled sweaty, manly, sexy. I tried not to notice.

"During our first conversation you mentioned that your father was on the Board of Governors at the Westover Country Club," I said.

"Right."

"So he must know the other members at Westover pretty well."

"Sure."

"Well, there's a woman there named June Douglas. A good tennis player. Do you think he might know her?"

"Probably. What's your point?"

"There's a rumor going around The Oaks that one of the members, Larkin Vail, may have spiked June Douglas's sports drink before an interclub tennis tournament last summer."

"Why would she have done that?"

"To eliminate the competition. This Larkin Vail is a real piece of work. Totally obsessed with winning every tennis match she plays."

"Yeah, but would she actually drug her opponent? Just to win a tennis match? It sounds pretty far-out to me, even for a country club."

"Fine. I'm just telling you what I heard. It occurred to me that if

Larkin did tamper with June Douglas's Gatorade, she might also have tampered with Claire Cox's life. Claire would have beaten Larkin in the club championship tournament this year—if she'd lived.''

"So you want me to consider Larkin Vail a suspect in the case?''

"She was at the July Fourth party at the club, and she had a motive," I said. "A lame one, I admit. But people have killed for less.''

Tom's expression turned serious. "You don't have to tell me," he said.

"Oh, you mean because you're a cop?''

"Yeah, and because my wife was killed for no reason. No reason at all.''

"Killed? Your wife? You were married?'' I had taken Detective Cunningham for the singles' bar type.

"Yeah, Sarah and I were married when we were twenty. We were in the city one night. It was our first anniversary, and I'd gotten us tickets to see a show. We were on our way back to the garage around ten-thirty when a guy mugged us at gunpoint. I gave him my wallet, no questions asked, and told Sarah to give him her purse. But she hesitated—just for a half a second—and he shot her. She died in my arms.''

"Tom. How awful." I was stunned. I had never known anyone who had lost a loved one through violent crime, and I couldn't imagine enduring such trauma. "Is that what made you become a policeman?''

"I guess you could say that," he said. "I had planned to go to law school. But after Sarah died, I lost interest in the idea of practicing law. Police work seemed like it would give me more instant gratification. I wanted a hand in keeping scumbags like the guy who shot Sarah off the streets, so others didn't have to suffer the way I did.''

I nodded.

"That's one of the reasons why this Claire Cox case is so frustrating," he went on. "I hate to see women being brutalized. Every time I do, it's like Sarah dying all over again. I want the guy who killed Claire Cox, Judy.''

"So do I," I said. "So do I.''

I looked at Tom and saw the hurt in his eyes. It was still there, despite the mischievous grin and tough talk. I felt sorry for him and attracted to him at the same time—a dangerous combination for a married woman.

"Now, getting back to Ms. Vail," he said.

"Yes, well I thought you might ask your father if he heard anything about the June Douglas incident. Maybe the story about her is just country club gossip, nothing more. On the other hand, if it's true . . ."

"There are two things wrong with your little plan."

"What?"

"First of all, even if your friend did put something in Ms. Douglas's drink, there's no way to prove it. Not a year after the fact. There's no evidence, no substance to analyze, no nothing."

"What's the second thing?"

"I don't speak to my father."

"You two don't get along?"

"Nope. Not since I became a cop. He hates the idea."

"Why? What does he do for a living?"

"He's in the media. He's William Cunningham—Wild Bill Cunningham of Pubtel."

"Bill Cunningham is your father?" I was stunned again. Pubtel was Charlton House's parent company—a media conglomerate that also owned a record company, a magazine division, and a couple of cable television channels. I'd never met Bill Cunningham but I'd seen him once, at a book convention. Nobody had ever said anything about him having a son who was a police detective in Belford.

"You seem surprised," said Tom.

"Surprised? I'm floored," I said.

"Why? Because I'm a cop with a rich father?"

"Frankly, yes," I admitted. "And because your father runs the company I used to work for—the company that fired me."

"Really? Small world," he said.

"Sure is," I agreed. Then the bitter irony hit me. I had finally networked my way to the head of Pubtel, a man who was Leeza Grummond's boss's boss's boss. But I couldn't get to him because he and his son were having a family tiff. Talk about a bad break!

"Dad wanted me to be a lawyer," he explained. "Like he was. But after Sarah died, as I said, I had no appetite for it. I wanted to be a cop and that was that."

"And your father didn't understand that?"

"My father doesn't understand a lot of things," he said. "But hey, he's my problem, not yours."

"Oh, it's my problem too."

"What do you mean?"

"Nothing."

"Look, Judy. About this Westover thing. I'll check it out the best I can. Meanwhile, you keep snooping around at The Oaks."

"Okay. I'm having dinner tonight with two other suspicious characters."

"Yeah?"

"Yeah. I'll let you know if I come up with anything."

I sensed that our meeting was over, but neither of us suggested that I leave.

"Judy?" said Tom after a few seconds of awkward silence.

"Yes?"

"I didn't mean to dump my problems on you."

"Don't be silly."

"It's just that you're easy to talk to, ya know?"

"My husband doesn't think so."

Tom looked at me with raised eyebrows. "Want to tell me about it? It's your turn."

I shook my head. "Thanks anyway," I said. "Maybe some other time."

A perfect exit line. I started to get out of the car, but Tom Cunningham put his hand on my arm.

"Judy?" he said.

"Yes?"

"You're okay."

"Did you expect me not to be?"

"Yeah."

"Because?"

"Because I thought you were one of those snooty Manhattan types that move up to Belford because it's so cute and quaint and New England-y, then shit all over the locals."

"That's not a very nice picture."

"They're not very nice people."

"You shouldn't generalize. None of us should."

"Yeah, but cops see people at their worst, day in and day out. After a while, it's hard not to write everybody off."

"Well, don't write me off," I said. "Not while I'm sticking my neck out, snooping around The Oaks for *your* murderer."

"That reminds me," he said. "You're being careful at that club, right?"

"Careful? You mean, am I waiting a half-hour after lunch before going swimming?"

He laughed. "I mean that I don't want our murderer figuring out what you're up to."

"Why would he figure out what I'm up to?"

"I don't know. Maybe you're going around asking a lot of questions, meddling in people's business."

Now it was my turn to laugh. "You don't know country clubs, buster. You can't belong to a club unless you meddle in people's business. It's in the bylaws."

CHAPTER TEN

♦

The Laughtons were twenty minutes late for dinner, and when they arrived, they seemed very angry with each other. And let me tell you something: if you want a bad case of heartburn, eat dinner with a married couple that's having problems. Every word is loaded; every gesture is fraught with hostility. The tension is so thick it covers everyone at the table like Alfredo sauce. Here's an example:

"Have you two seen any good movies lately?" I asked the Laughtons.

"Ducky see a movie?" Nedra scoffed. "He never understands the dialogue. The only movies he can understand are foreign films. They have subtitles."

"At least I don't talk during the movies," said Ducky. "Nedra can't keep her big mouth shut. Ever."

"That's because I'm starved for intelligent conversation," Nedra sniped. "God knows, I don't get it at home."

"You wouldn't know intelligent conversation if it hit you in the face," Ducky countered.

"You'd like to, wouldn't you?" said Nedra.

"Like to what?" said Ducky.

"Hit me in the face," said Nedra.

And on it went. Even the subject of Claire's murder provoked bickering between them.

"You knew Claire years ago, right, Ducky?" I asked, knowing the answer but trying to raise the issue gracefully.

"Yes," he said dejectedly. "At Berkeley." He seemed to be taking Claire's death hard. Perhaps that was why Nedra was so angry with him.

"They were lovers," Nedra snapped. "Ducky was quite the cocksman in those days."

Ducky sighed. "What Nedra is *trying* to say is that Claire and I dated in college."

"Was it serious?" I asked. I was dying to see how Ducky would describe his relationship with Claire, seeing as he'd told her she was his "grand passion."

"Not really," he said. "We were campus activists together. We were both vehemently opposed to the Vietnam War. Our relationship was based on politics, not romance."

Yeah, and I'm a potted plant. The man was lying, but why? To keep his jealous wife from foaming at the mouth? Or was there a more sinister reason?

"I still can't believe she was murdered," said Hunt. "Here at The Oaks, of all places."

"I know," I said. "Did you see or talk to her the night she was killed, Ducky?"

"Yes," he said. "We ran into each other on the buffet line and reminisced about the good old days."

More lies! Claire never made it to the buffet line, according to her friend Sharon. What's more, Claire didn't have the slightest interest in reminiscing about the good old days, and she'd told Ducky as much. She hadn't wanted anything to do with him.

"This must be painful, Ducky, seeing as you and Claire were old friends and all," I said. "But do you have any guesses as to who may have killed her?"

He thought for a minute. "I hate to say this, but it could have been one of the Neanderthals at The Oaks," he said. "They were terrified of Claire, terrified that she'd change the club rules."

"Yes, but she already *had* changed the rules," I said. "If they were going to kill her, why didn't they do it *before* she became a member?"

"Judy's right," said Hunt. "If you ask me, I think an outsider did it. Someone who sneaked into the club and dragged her off to that sand trap. You can't go anywhere in this country anymore without fearing for your life. Even on a golf course."

"The police don't agree," I said. "They think the killer is probably a member here."

"How do you know that, Jude?" said Hunt. "The newspapers say the police don't have any idea who did it."

Okay, Judy. Get yourself out of this one. "Well . . . I uh . . . heard that from the woman who cuts my hair," I said. "Her husband's on the Belford Police Force."

Saved by the bull.

There was more talk of the murder, then the conversation turned to golf. Blah blah blah. I was so bored I agreed to keep Nedra company when she went to the ladies' room. While we were freshening up, I asked her what was wrong between her and Ducky.

"Nothing that a good fuck won't cure," she answered and changed the subject.

The next day Nedra got her curative fuck all right—but it wasn't with Ducky.

I was playing a set against Bailey Vanderhoff on Court 16, the farthest court from the tennis house, when I hit the ball over the fence, into the woods. Obviously, the tennis lessons I'd taken hadn't done much for my game.

"I'll get the ball," I yelled to Bailey. I wasn't wild about venturing into the woods, not with all that poison ivy back there, but since I was the one who'd hit the ball, and since Bailey was the one who'd brought the new can of Wilsons, I felt it was my duty to retrieve it.

I was well into the woods, about a foot from where our ball had landed, when I heard moaning. I stopped and listened. The sound was coming from the bushes to my right.

"Oh, baby. Oh, baby. Don't stop. Don't stop."

It was a woman's voice, and even a straight-arrow like me could tell she wasn't talking to the mosquitoes.

"Oh, yes. Oh, yes. Oh, yes," she moaned.

I was frozen to my little spot on the ground, riveted. I chastised myself for being so voyeuristic, but I couldn't help myself.

"Oh, God. Oh, God. Oh, God."

It was a man's voice this time. Men always invoked the name of the Lord during sex.

"Ahhhhhhh," they cried out in unison.

Boy. This couple must have had some practice, I thought. To pull that off while rolling around in grass and dirt and pine needles takes real concentration.

When I heard Romeo and Juliet getting up, I grabbed the tennis ball and raced back to Court 16.

"What's the matter?" Bailey asked when she saw me. "You look flushed."

"Just a little winded," I said. And disappointed that I hadn't learned the identity of the lovers. Some sleuth I was.

My disappointment faded about ten minutes later. Bailey and I had finished our match and had walked over to the tennis house for a soda.

"Oh, there's Nedra," Bailey said. "Over by the water fountain talking to Rob."

I turned to look, saw Nedra and Rob, and waved. They waved back. Then they walked away from us, down the stairs toward Rob's teaching court.

"What did *they* sit in?" Bailey laughed.

The backs of Nedra and Rob's tennis whites were grass stained. Seriously grass stained.

So Nedra was having an affair with the assistant pro. The very assistant pro that Claire had tried to fire. How long had the affair been going on? I wondered. Was it Nedra's way of paying Ducky back for his interest in Claire? Or was Nedra and Ducky's supposedly torrid sex life a sham, as well as Nedra's jealousy? Were they one of those couples that couldn't stand each other but stayed together for the sake of the country club?

A few nights later, I met Hunt in the city so we could have dinner with Arlene and her date, a man whose name was Randy and whose hair was longer and blonder than mine. He and Arlene had been introduced at a romance book convention. Apparently, Randy was a model who posed for romance book covers. Apparently, Randy was in his forties but looked much younger. Apparently, Randy was a former Peace Corps volunteer who'd come to the conclusion that making big money was ultimately more satisfying than saving the world.

"How did you come to work for the Peace Corps?" I asked Randy.

"I was a sixties person," he said. "Protest marches, sit-ins, demonstrations, you get the picture. Everybody at Berkeley was into the peace-not-war thing."

"Berkeley? Did you happen to know Claire Cox?" I asked, assuming she and Randy were about the same age.

"Who didn't?" he said. "She was a star on campus. Very activist. Very charismatic. Very beautiful."

"Did you know a guy named Ducky Laughton?" I asked. "He was at Berkeley around the same time."

"Yeah, sure," said Randy. "He and Claire Cox had a thing going for a while."

"So I understand," I said. I was about to pump Randy for more when he volunteered it.

"We were all surprised when he transferred out," he said. "To U.Va., of all places. Not exactly a hot bed of political activism."

Hunt and I looked at each other. "Ducky graduated from the University of Virginia?" Hunt asked. He'd known Ducky longer than I had, and he seemed surprised by the information.

"Yup," said Randy. "He got into trouble at Berkeley at the end of his junior year. When we came back in the fall, he was history. No one knew exactly what happened—it was all kind of hush hush—but the rumor was that his father, a U.Va. man, made some kind of a deal with the dean and Ducky was shipped off to Charlottesville for his senior year."

"Interesting," I mused. "That must have put a damper on his romance with Claire."

"I think they had broken up before that," said Randy. "She started going with a Russian exchange student."

I nodded, and tried to look fascinated as Randy, Arlene, and Hunt entered into a heated discussion of Boris Yeltsin's economic policy, but my mind was stuck on Claire and Ducky and what might have occurred between them twenty-five years ago. According to Randy, who may or may not have been a reliable source, Claire had gone out with Ducky, then dumped him, then he was kicked out of Berkeley and hustled off to his father's alma mater. Did the trouble he'd gotten into have anything to do with Claire? Was he angry that she dumped him? Had he hung on to his anger all these years? Did seeing Claire again at the club make him even angrier? Was he the one who killed her?

"Not likely," was Detective Cunningham's response when I told him my theory.

I had beeped him in the morning, and we'd arranged to meet in the parking lot of Stop 'n' Shop. We were sitting in his car. It was raining heavily and the windows were fogged. The air was sticky or sultry, depending how you feel about summer humidity.

"Why couldn't Ducky have done it?" I said. "He was a spurned lover. Isn't that a motive for murder?"

"Not when the spurning happened over twenty years ago," he said. "From what you tell me, Mr. Laughton hadn't been in touch with the deceased in all that time. He'd gotten married, gone to work for a respected investment firm, become a member of a prestigious country club. If he had wanted to kill Claire Cox, why wouldn't he have done it back at Berkeley when she broke his heart?"

I shrugged. "Maybe he had a delayed reaction," I said.

"Good try," said Tom. He smiled and patted my shoulder. Electrical currents surged through my body. I mean, there we were, just the two of us, sitting in his car with the windows rolled up, breathing each other's air, looking into each other's eyes, listening to each other's theories about a murder case. It was the stuff of High Drama, but it made me laugh, seeing as I wasn't the High Drama type.

"What's so funny?" Tom asked.

"This," I said. "The fact that I'm doing this."

"What's 'this'? Working on a murder investigation or being here with me?"

"Both."

His dark eyes penetrated me. I felt a trickle of sweat form on my upper lip.

"Do I make you uncomfortable?" he asked.

"Of course not. It's just that I'm not used to working this closely with a man I hardly know. The authors I used to work with always submitted a detailed biography with their proposals before we actually got down to business."

He smiled. "I don't have a detailed biography, but if I tell you more about myself, would that make the job easier?"

"No. I was kidding. Please forget I said anything."

"Let's see," he said, ignoring me. "I'm allergic to penicillin. My favorite movie is *Casablanca*. I'm a big Boston Celtics fan. And I love meat loaf. What else would you like to know?"

"Who cooks you meat loaf? Is there a woman in your life now?"

"No one special. Ever since Sarah died, I've been kind of here and there. My work makes it hard to get attached. I'm always rescuing damsels in distress and falling a little bit in love with them."

I swallowed hard as I pictured Tom rescuing me. Falling a little bit in love with me.

Snap out of it, I commanded myself. Get back to the job you were hired to do.

"As I was saying about Ducky Laughton," I continued, "I don't trust the man at all."

"Why not?"

"I told you. He lied about college. He lied about his relationship with Claire. And he lied about talking to her in the buffet line the night she died."

"So the guy's a liar. That doesn't make him a murderer."

"What about that trouble he got into at Berkeley? Once a troublemaker, always a troublemaker."

"Nah. He was a kid then. Now he's vice president at Fitzgerald & Franklin. A member of The Oaks's Finance Committee. A real pillar of the community."

"Okay. What about this? One minute his wife acts like they have this hot sex life, the next minute she acts like they never have sex at all."

"Be more specific."

"The other day I heard her having sex in the bushes with the tennis pro at the club."

Tom laughed. "You're taking this informant thing seriously, aren't you, Judy?"

"I heard them by accident," I said. "And I was shocked, let me tell you. Nedra had always seemed so happy with Ducky."

"So she likes to get laid. Who doesn't?"

My husband, I almost said.

"Doesn't any of this sound suspicious?" I asked, growing a bit exasperated by Tom's refusal to take my theories seriously.

"Look, Judy, as far as Mr. Laughton is concerned, I doubt whether he killed Ms. Cox over a twenty-year-old failed love affair. Her murder wasn't a crime of passion. It was planned, premeditated. Our killer knew Ms. Cox was going to be at that party and probably arranged to meet her on the golf course at a specific time. She didn't strike me as someone who would walk out on her dinner guests and take a little stroll in a sand trap all by herself."

I nodded. "Then maybe Ducky had another reason for killing Claire."

"Either that or he's not the killer."

I sighed. "Back to the drawing board," I said.

"Hey, cheer up," said Tom as he touched my shoulder again. "There are three hundred members at The Oaks. You've already checked out Larkin Vail and Ducky and Nedra Laughton. Only two hundred and ninety-seven more to go."

Later on in the summer, my parents flew up from Florida so my father, a Mets fan, could go to some games at Shea Stadium. My mother didn't care about baseball but she cared very much about food, so she went to the games for the hot dogs, which she enjoyed so much she brought several of them home with her and reheated them in my microwave. Unlike me, my mother was not much of a gourmand. She was more like Hunt in her lack of discrimination regarding food. The greasier and more laden with preservatives, the better. She'd actually go to Chinese restaurants and tell them to put in *extra* MSG.

She and I were in the kitchen one morning, debating the age-old question, "Which tastes better: Hellman's Mayonnaise or Kraft Miracle Whip?," when she said suddenly, "So who's the fella?"

"Excuse me?" I said.

"You can't fool your mother, Judy," she said. "There's hanky panky going on around here. Don't try to deny it."

I laughed nervously. "I don't know what you mean," I said. "Hunt and I are as happy as we've ever been."

"You don't want to tell me? Don't," she said.

"There's nothing to tell," I said. "Really."

"You and Hunt are having problems," she said. "I can see it on your faces. Either he's fooling around or you are."

"Hunt? Fooling around? Nah, that would take time away from his golf," I said.

"Then you're the one who's got someone."

"Why do you say that, Mom?"

"Because you've got that look."

"What look?"

"That guilty-secret look. When a woman's got a guilty secret, it's either one of two things: either she's spent money she shouldn't have or she's having an affair. You're out of a job, so you're not throwing your money around. That can only mean one thing: you're having an affair."

"I like your logic, Ma," I laughed. "But I'm not having an affair." Not yet anyway.

"See that you don't," she said. "Hunt's a nice boy. Not a ball of fire, but a nice boy. Nice appearance. Nice manners. Nice job. You could do worse."

"I'll tell him you said so."

"I mean it, Judy. The grass always looks greener, but the grass you've got here is green enough."

Yeah, green with a few brown spots. Maybe Hunt and I didn't need a session with a marriage counselor; we needed a house call from the Lawn Doctor.

The Mets lost five games in a row and my father threatened to become a Yankee fan. He thought his defection might wound his team so profoundly that they'd come to their senses and regain their old form. The strategy didn't work. The Mets kept losing and my father kept kvetching. I suggested we take his mind off baseball and try to lift his mood by bringing him and my mother to The Oaks for dinner.

"No valet parking?" my mother asked when we pulled into the parking lot.

"No, Lucille," said Hunt. "That would be an unnecessary expense for the club."

"Hunt's on the Finance Committee here," I explained. "He knows how every penny is spent."

"From the look of the place, I'd say that pennies is all they spend," said my mother, a firm believer in the old adage, "if you've got it, flaunt it."

We walked to the clubhouse, where my mother pointed to the creaky, carpetless floors, the frayed fabric on the sofas, and the plaster cracks in the ceiling and said, "Who's their decorator, the Salvation Army?"

"Now, Mom," I said. "Behave."

"The Oaks is one of the most prestigious country clubs in America," Hunt added defensively. "George Bush was once a member."

"I'm not surprised," said my mother. "You saw what he and his wife did to the White House. Shabby this. Shabby that. Thank God the Clintons came in and redecorated the place."

Heads turned as we entered the dining room and were shown to our table. At first I thought heads turned because Hunt was so popular at the club. Then I realized heads turned because my mother's outfit was garish by club standards: gold jewelry, purple dress, purple hair. Yes, purple hair. It used to be a very tasteful silver, but the hairdresser in Boca Raton had suggested a lavender rinse, something special for my mother's trip north. "They like variety up in New York," the woman had assured my mother, who forgot that Connecticut was worlds away from Manhattan when it came to things like variety.

We ordered our entrées (Broiled Swordfish for Hunt and me, Steak Diane for my mother and father). When they arrived, nobody was happy with his meal, not even Hunt.

"It's overcooked," he complained of his swordfish.

"It must be really overcooked," I said. "You never complain about food."

I took a bite of my fish and winced. "This baby wasn't broiled, it was cremated."

Then it was my parents' turn.

"Where's the rest of it?" my mother asked as she looked down at her pathetically small piece of steak and almost cried. As I indicated earlier, it was quantity, not quality, that mattered to her, when it came to food. As long as the portions were plentiful, she was happy.

My father, already in poor humor as a result of the Mets' losing streak, chewed a piece of his steak and then spit it into his napkin.

"Dad!" I said, horrified by his bad manners.

"I know, I know," he said, shaking his head. "But this meat isn't fit for dogs."

Here we go again, I thought, remembering Valerio's reaction to the meat at the club. Hunt and I had chalked that outburst up to the fact that Valerio was a star and a prima donna and a know-it-all about food. But now my father was reacting the same way.

"Who's in charge here?" he said.

"The chef's name is Brendan Hardy," said Hunt. "He buys all the meat for the club."

"Yeah, well he's buying cutter," said my father, the butcher.

"What's cutter?" asked Hunt.

"Dog meat," said my father. "The lowest grade you can get."

"But that's impossible, Arthur," said Hunt. "I see the bills, and I can tell you The Oaks buys prime meats."

"You may be paying for prime, but you're not getting it," said my father, echoing Valerio's remarks.

"Didn't Ducky tell us that Duncan Tewksbury brought Brendan into the club a few years ago?" I asked Hunt.

"Yes," said Hunt. "He used to be the chef at the Belford Athletic Club."

"Their loss, our gain," I said.

"My steak was delicious—what there was of it," said my mother, who had cleaned her plate while the rest of us were talking. "I think I'll have seconds."

When Hunt and I were in bed that night, I asked him if he had ever met Brendan Hardy.

"Once or twice," he said. "He takes a break from the kitchen sometimes and watches us tee off. Perry says he's a pretty good golfer."

"Interesting. Does he do all the buying for the dining rooms?"

"You mean the food and beverage buying?"

I nodded.

"Sure. Then he gives the bills to Jimmy, the general manager, who approves them and sends them on."

"To whom?"

"To Evan Sutcliffe, the club treasurer and our committee chairman. Evan signs the checks and pays the suppliers. Why all the questions, Jude?"

"Just curious."

"About The Oaks? Since when?"

"Since . . . well, since you became a member of the Finance Committee, sweetheart."

I never called Hunt sweetheart, but he didn't seem to notice.

"Gee, if you're really interested in what we do in the Finance Committee, I'd be glad to tell you all about the way we oversee the budget and—"

"No, that's okay," I said, eager to ward off what I knew would be a hopelessly boring recitation of the club's bookkeeping practices. "It must be very involved."

"It is, but we leave the tough stuff to the accounting firm. They come in once a year to clean things up," said Hunt, who punctuated his remarks with a loud yawn.

I nodded again. "Getting back to Brendan," I said, "does he seem like a nice fellow? What I mean is, does he have a friendly way with the members? Is he receptive to criticism? Does he mind if people make suggestions about the menu? Some chefs can be awfully touchy about their creations. I was just wondering if Brendan struck you as the sort who balks at interference."

I went on and on about the chefs I'd known and worked with, hoping Hunt would jump in and offer some insightful commentary on The Oaks's chef. But when I looked over at him, I realized that there was no point in continuing the discussion. Discussions take a minimum of two people, and I was the only person doing any discussing. Hunt was sound asleep, and his snoring would have drowned me out anyway.

I rolled over on my side and thought about Brendan Hardy. Had he known that Claire was intent on getting the club to replace him with another chef? Had he feared that if he lost his job at The Oaks, he'd never get another one, given his spotty reputation? Had he gotten a look at the reservation list for the Wild West July Fourth party, seen Claire's name on the list, and lured her onto the golf course? Could it be that it was an employee of The Oaks, not a member, who killed her? Could it be that a country club chef bludgeoned a famous feminist to death?

I tried to make myself think, tried to put myself in Brendan's shoes, tried to imagine how panicked I'd be if some bitch set out to fire me.

Then I lit on the irony of the whole thing. I *was* in Brendan's shoes. I *had* been fired by a bitch. But as much as I despised Leeza Grummond, I'd never once been tempted to hit her over the head with a pitching wedge. Not even after she hired my husband as her commodities broker.

"Jude?"

It was Hunt, but he was still asleep. I could tell he was asleep because his mouth was slack and his eyeballs were rolled back in his head. During the seven years we'd been married, he often called out my name in his sleep, and I'd learned not to make more of it than it was: a reflex. Sure, I wished his "Jude?" was a prelude to seduction, a sign that he was about to sit up in bed, pull me toward him, and make mad, passionate love to me, over and over until the sun came up. But I knew Hunt's sleep patterns. That's what marriage is all about: knowing your partner's sleep patterns. Knowing that he snores. Knowing that he drools. Knowing that he likes two pillows instead of one, one blanket instead of two, and sheets that are cotton, not polyester. As mundane as it must sound, there is something to be said for all this knowing, something reassuring, comforting.

"Jude?" he mumbled again.

"Yes, Hunt. I'm here," I said as I watched his chest rise and fall with each breath. "I'm right here."

CHAPTER ELEVEN

◆

Brendan lived at the club, in a small white cottage behind the kitchen. According to one of the waitresses, he was single, did not have pets, and liked to play golf on Mondays, when employees were permitted to use the facilities. When I caught up with him, he was sitting at a table in the main dining room, smoking a cigarette and reading *People* magazine. It was ten-thirty on a Tuesday morning, and I supposed he was taking a break from his prelunch preparations.

"Excuse me," I said. "I'm Judy Mills. My husband is Hunt Price. From the Finance Committee?"

"Sure, sure," said Brendan distractedly. He was chubby—maybe two hundred pounds—and had shaggy brown hair and a ruddy complexion.

"Would you mind if I sit down?" I asked.

He seemed surprised by the question. Perhaps The Oaks had a rule about members fraternizing with The Help. But he pulled out a chair and motioned for me to sit next to him.

I guessed he was about fifty, and despite his somewhat doughy body, he wasn't unattractive. Just bleary-eyed, as if he'd been chopping onions all night.

"I'd like to talk to you," I said.

"About what?" he said.

"Well, my husband and I enjoy the meals at the club tremendously," I said with a straight face. "In fact, I was saying to Hunt just the other day, 'I've got to introduce myself to the chef and get his recipe for that delicious rice pudding.' "

Brendan laughed. I suspected that no one had ever complimented him on his food before, except Duncan Tewksbury, who was probably born without tastebuds.

"You like that rice pudding, huh?" He grinned, then drew on his cigarette.

"Oh yes. Very much," I lied. I had tried Brendan's rice pudding once—and that was enough. It was a gooey, sickeningly sweet pudding, with very little rice. And the rice that *was* in it wasn't even cooked. In fact, if you weren't careful, you could break a tooth on it. I'd joked to Hunt that I thought Brendan's rice pudding, like many of his dishes, should come with a warning label from the Surgeon General.

"I appreciate the compliment," said Brendan, "but I never give out my recipes."

"Oh, that's a shame," I said, trying to look grief-stricken. "Let me ask you something else then. I've been in the cookbook business for several years, and my latest project is a theme cookbook."

"A what?"

"A theme cookbook. You know, a book that tells how to throw themed parties. A Romantic Valentine's Day Dinner for Two. A Family Christmas Brunch. A High School Graduation Barbecue. That sort of thing."

Brendon nodded but looked incredibly bored. I couldn't blame him, but I pressed on.

"I was so impressed with that menu you came up with for the Wild West July Fourth party that I wondered if you'd let me include it in the book."

"You mean the Wagon Train Menu?" he said.

"Exactly."

"But that was just chili and hot dogs. No big deal."

"Yes, but it was the *way* you pulled the party together, the effortless execution of the menu, that impressed me. It's no mean feat to serve chili and hot dogs to three hundred people and make it look easy."

"Well, the whole thing did take some planning," he conceded.

"Exactly. And that's just what my readers would want to know about: how you planned the party—from A to Z. Which dishes you prepared ahead of time. Which dishes were made just before the party began. How you juggled your duties as chef with the job of over-seeing the staff. Where you were every minute of the party."

"Where I was every minute of the party?"

"Yes. In Martha Stewart's books, she always gives her readers a complete account of her movements during a party. Organization and planning are very important aspects of entertaining, as you must know."

Brendan said nothing, but appeared to be mulling over my questions, especially the one regarding his whereabouts the night of the party.

"For example," I went on, "give me an idea of what you did after the chili and hot dogs were set up on the buffet table."

"What I did?" he said.

"Yes, what you did," I said.

He scratched his head. "Well, I guess I went into the kitchen and checked on the desserts."

"Great. Now you're getting the idea. Then what?"

"I . . . uh . . . well, to tell you the truth, I think I ate a couple of hot dogs."

I smiled. "So you took time out to sample your own cooking. Yes indeed, Martha Stewart says one must always taste one's creations."

Brendan nodded. He was a bit slow, I realized. Not what you would call a quick study.

"Now then," I continued, "after you ate a hot dog, did you go back outside to supervise the meal or did you stay in the kitchen?"

"I don't remember exactly."

"Do you remember being at the buffet table when the desserts were served?"

"Yeah, I was there."

"The whole time?"

"No, not the whole time. I had a headache. I went back to my cottage to get some aspirin."

Aha. The old I-had-a-headache alibi. I was betting that the real reason Brendan disappeared from the party was to follow Claire to the sand trap and kill her.

"Don't tell me you had a headache too," I played on, hoping Brendan was on the verge of incriminating himself. "I thought I'd never recover from the band's drum solo. My head was pounding for days."

"What drum solo? I didn't hear any drum solo."

"Gee, that's funny. It was deafening."

Interesting. So Brendan hadn't heard the drum solo. Was that because he was down on the golf course, giving Claire Cox the headache of her life?

"We had all started on our chili and hot dogs when the Cowpokes' drummer started doing a little Led Zeppelin," I said. "It didn't do much for my head or my digestion."

"Yeah, well, I must have missed it," said Brendan, beginning to understand that he had just admitted something he hadn't intended to admit. The fact was, he couldn't have missed the drum solo unless he was a good distance away from the band—like in a sand trap.

"What did you do after you got your aspirin?" I asked.

"Hey look, Mrs. . . . . What did you say your name was?"

"Mills. Ms. Judy Mills."

"I don't think I want to be in your book after all." Brendan's expression had turned sour.

"Oh, I'm sorry to hear that," I said. "I was hoping we could give the readers a real feel for your Wild West July Fourth party."

"Nope. I don't like talking about my work. I'm a chef, not a celebrity. You like my food? I'm flattered. But that's it, okay?"

"Well, I suppose if you're—"

"Now if you'll excuse me, I've gotta go back to the kitchen."

He started to get up from the table.

"Brendan?"

"Yeah?"

"I'm glad we had this talk. You've been much more helpful than you can imagine."

He gave me a puzzled look, scratched his head again, and went back to work.

After my chat with Brendan, I debated whether I should run to the phone in the ladies' locker room and beep Tom. I was eager to tell him about Brendan's admission that he had wandered far enough away from the party to miss the band's ear-splitting drum solo, but I was supposed to meet Nedra at the pool and didn't want to arouse her suspicion by not showing up. Unfortunately, it was Nedra who didn't show up. I guessed she was in the bushes somewhere with Rob, practicing her strokes.

I found a chair near the deep end of the pool, deposited my towel, beach robe, and purse there, and walked down to the shallow end. I always went into the water at the shallow end, where you could tiptoe in with all the other wimps, little by little, inch by inch. Sure, I felt like a jerk as I watched the more daring souls do back-flips off the diving board. But how else could I avoid getting my hair wet?

I was about halfway into the water when I heard an incredibly annoying beeping noise coming from a chair near the deep end. I assumed it was somebody's beeper, or one of those black Casio watch alarms that people are always programming to go off every hour on the hour. But nobody ran over to claim responsibility for the noise, and the little beep kept going for what seemed like an eternity. Suddenly I realized that the little beep was *my* little beep, that it was coming from *my* beeper, which was in *my* purse lying on *my* chair! All eyes were on me as I hurried out of the pool, opened my purse, shut the beeper off, and read Detective Cunningham's display message asking me to call him as soon as possible.

Some informant I was. Now everyone at the club would wonder why I, an out-of-work cookbook editor, would need a beeper. Maybe they'd be so curious they'd ask Hunt, who'd ask me, and then what would I do? If only I'd switched the beeper to the vibrator option the way Tom had suggested. Then I wouldn't have everybody staring at me—including Duncan Tewksbury, who had shown up at the pool and plunked himself down on the chair next to mine.

"What was all that about?" he asked, as if I'd polluted his air.

"Must have been a wrong number," I shrugged and hurried inside to call Tom.

"Isn't there somewhere else we could meet?" I asked Detective Cunningham. We were sitting in his Chevy Caprice in our usual haunt, the parking lot of the Stop 'n' Shop.

"You don't like Stop 'n' Shop?" he said. "How about Waldbaum's or maybe the A&P?"

"I had something more exciting in mind. Something more police-y."

"Police-y?" He laughed. "You crack me up."

"Thank you," I said, assuming he meant it as a compliment. "In the movies, the cop and the informant meet in mysterious, out-of-the-way places."

"Yeah, only this is the suburbs, not the movies," he said. "But hey. You want police-y? I'll give you police-y."

Tom turned on the ignition and drove us out of the parking lot so fast I nearly herniated a disk in my neck.

"Where are we going?" I asked.

"You'll see," he said.

He sped along Route 1, heading north, darting in and out of traffic, weaving in and out of lanes. I wasn't surprised when he got stopped for speeding several minutes into our ride.

"Umm, we've got company," he said as he looked into his rearview mirror and saw a patrol car's lights flashing behind us.

He pulled over onto the shoulder and waited.

"You *were* speeding," I said. "The speed limit's thirty-five here. I'm pretty sure you were doing sixty."

He didn't seem the least bit concerned.

A state trooper came up to his side of the car and asked to see his license and registration. Instead, Tom showed the officer his badge.

The cop took a quick look at it and smiled. "Have a good day, Detective," he told Tom, then winked at me and walked back to his car.

"Hey," I said. "He didn't give you a ticket. He didn't even give you a lecture."

"Professional courtesy," Tom said and started the car. "It's one of those police-y things you were talking about before."

"Are police informants eligible for this professional courtesy?" I asked. "I sure could use it. I got stopped a couple of weeks ago for going forty miles an hour in a fifty-mile-an-hour zone. I couldn't believe it. 'How can you give me a ticket when I'm not even going the speed limit?' I asked the cop. And do you know what he did?"

"Yes," Tom said. "He checked out your legs."

"How did you know?" I said, amazed.

"Professional courtesy." He grinned. "Cops know each other's routines. When a cop stops you for driving *under* the speed limit, he just wants to check out your legs."

"How did he know I was wearing a skirt from three cars back?" I asked.

"Instinct," said Tom. "Cops are born with it."

Tom turned off Route 1, and a few minutes later, we were on a winding country lane that led to an even more winding country lane. We went up a hill and down a hill and ended up on a tiny dead-end street that backed up to the Sasquahonek River. The view was dramatic and, if you weren't crazy about heights like I wasn't, a little scary.

"What are we doing here?" I asked after Tom had turned off the ignition.

"You wanted something exciting and police-y," he said.

"Exciting, I understand. This is a fabulously atmospheric spot. But police-y?"

"You should see it at night," said Tom. "Big make-out place. The police are always chasing couples out of here."

"Oh, you," I said and swatted Tom's thigh.

Tom's thigh. Talk about fabulously atmospheric spots. Muscular. Tight. So near and yet so far. I looked up at his face and felt my own flush.

This is dangerous, I said to myself. You're having problems with your husband. You're feeling undesirable, unloved. And you're sitting in a car with a very attractive single man who's probably yearning to rekindle the passion he shared with his dearly departed wife. It's a scenario that can only lead to one thing. And you're not the adulterous type, Judy, remember?

"So why did you beep me?" I asked Tom in an effort to get down to business.

"I wanted to check out your legs," he said.

I took another swipe at his thigh. "Seriously. Why did you want to see me?"

"I looked into that business at Westover," he said. "About June Douglas, the woman who said Larkin Vail tried to get her drunk."

I nodded.

"It turns out that Ms. Douglas has a reputation for boozing it up," he said. " 'A real lush,' people say. So maybe Larkin Vail spiked her Gatorade, and then again, maybe not."

"Just to be safe, I think I'll get my own drink before I play against Larkin in the Tennis Tussle on Friday night. Maybe she's moved from vodka to strychnine."

"Tennis Tussle?"

"Yeah, it's one of the club's most popular events. Every Friday night there's a mixed doubles tournament, followed by Bloody Marys and barbecued chicken."

"You country club kids sure know how to have fun," Tom smirked.

"Don't we?"

"Yeah, while you're out there tussling with each other on the tennis courts on Friday nights, I'm out on the streets, tangling with criminals."

"Aww, poor thing. Listen, from the look of things, you may be a lot safer on the streets than I am at the club. I still think Larkin might be our murderer. But I have another suspect for you to chew on."

"Yeah? Who?"

"Brendan Hardy. He's the chef at The Oaks and a really lousy cook."

"If he's so lousy, how does he keep his job?"

"Good question. He was hired by Duncan Tewksbury, Claire's great-uncle and the chairman of the Board of Governors. Whenever someone complains about the food, Duncan defends him. It's weird."

"What makes you think Brendan might have killed Claire Cox?"

"Because Claire was determined to upgrade the club's food, which she found embarrassingly poor. There she was, trying to convince all these hot-shit women to join The Oaks, and she couldn't even offer them a decent meal."

"Did Brendan know she wanted him out?"

I shrugged. "My guess is that she spoke to her great-uncle about it, and that Duncan might have passed the information along to Brendan."

"Why would he do that?"

"Because Duncan and Brendan are a gruesome twosome at the club. I always see them huddled together, probably conjuring up new ways to give the members indigestion."

"Refresh my memory. Duncan Tewksbury didn't get along with Ms. Cox, right?"

"Right. When Claire got into the club, it spelled the end of Duncan's reign of chauvinism. He lost out to her on the issue of admitting single women. He lost out to her on the issue of the Men's Grill. He lost out to her on just about every issue that mattered to him—except the issue of the chef. Claire wanted Brendan out. Duncan wanted Brendan to stay. Now Claire is dead, and Brendan's still in the kitchen turning out meals you wouldn't feed your worst enemy. What's more, I had a little chat with Brendan and it seems he can't account for his whereabouts the night Claire was murdered."

"That's not what he told my partner. He said he was in the kitchen cooking dinner for three hundred people."

"Yes, but then he left the party. He said he had a headache and went to his cottage to get some aspirin."

"So?"

"So his cottage is directly behind the kitchen, which is right next to where the band was playing. Brendan says he never heard the drum solo. And trust me, you couldn't *not* hear that drum solo, unless, of course, you were way down on the golf course, hitting a woman over the head with a golf club." I paused. "Oh, and another thing: Brendan loves to play golf. And guess whose golf clubs he plays with? The golf pro's—including the golf pro's pitching wedge.''

Tom turned to face me, then nodded his approval.

''I'm not bad at this informant stuff, am I?'' I asked, feeling as if I had finally impressed Detective Cunningham with my sleuthing.

''Not bad at all,'' he said, then reached out to pat my knee.

The minute he touched me, my leg shot straight out, like when the doctor tests your reflexes with that dopey little hammer. I was so embarrassed I wanted to crawl under the seat of the car.

''Easy,'' he said. ''I'm not gonna bite you.''

''Sorry. It's been so long since a man touched me I forgot how it felt.''

As soon as the words were out of my mouth, I regretted having said them. The last thing I wanted to do was burden someone else with my problems, someone I barely knew, someone who had hired me to perform an important job. How unprofessional can you get!

Still, when Tom started asking me to elaborate on my remark, when he seemed so interested, so caring, so sympathetic, I couldn't resist opening up about my private life. Maybe it was the fact that he had lost his wife, that he understood pain and suffering, that we were alone together in his car in the middle of nowhere that had loosened my tongue. All I knew was that I found myself going on and on about Hunt, about our seven years together—especially the last couple of years when things had begun to disintegrate between us, about Kimberley, Charlton House, F&F, and the rest of it.

''What a waste,'' said Tom, shaking his head, his eyes boring in on me. ''You're a fantastic woman, Judy. A man would have to be crazy to neglect you.''

I blushed at the compliment.

''Really,'' he went on. ''You're a special lady. Don't you know that?''

He touched my hand. I melted. Flattery always made me melt. So did being touched by a handsome man with whom I was alone in a car.

Tom looked at me with soulful eyes and shook his head again. ''Such a waste,'' he said, then took my hand in his. I thought he was going to kiss me as he drew me closer. But he reached up and brushed away a lock of hair that had fallen against my cheek. I didn't flinch this time. Perhaps I was getting more comfortable with his touch, more comfortable with the idea that a man who was not my husband was touching me.

God, what was happening to me, to my marriage? First I lied to Hunt by not telling him I was working for the police. Then I blabbed to another man about our marital problems. Now I was allowing this other man to touch me in a way that was sure to lead to trouble. I considered getting out of the car right then and there, but I didn't exactly have another ride home, did I? What's more, I didn't really want to go home.

"Remember when I told you I was a sucker for damsels in distress?" he said.

"Yes."

"I meant it. You sound like you need someone, Judy. You sound like you need a *man*."

Oh, God, I thought. Now I'm in trouble.

Tom inched his face closer to mine. I could feel his breath on my skin. No onion rolls this time.

It would have been so easy to let it happen, so easy to just go ahead and let him kiss me. He was handsome and virile and sexy—straight out of one of Arlene's romance novels. And I was very attracted to him, no question. But I couldn't get my jerky, plaid-panted husband out of my mind. Not for one second. He might as well have been sitting in the back seat of Tom's Chevy, watching us. It was no use.

"I think we should head back," I said, breaking the spell of the moment. "Hunt will probably be home by now."

"So? From what you told me, it doesn't sound like he'll care whether you're there or not."

"Maybe not, but I still think I should get going."

Tom shrugged, started the engine, and drove us back to Stop 'n' Shop.

When we pulled up next to my BMW, he told me he would run a check on Brendan, to see if The Oaks's chef had ever been in trouble with the law.

"While I'm doing that, you check out Duncan Tewksbury," he instructed me.

"Duncan? You really think Duncan could have killed his brother's granddaughter?" I asked.

"Why not? You said he resented her, that she had shown him up in front of his friends at The Oaks."

"And he *was* at the July Fourth party," I added, "and had access to the golf pro's office."

"Right. So while I'm checking on Brendan, you check on his pal Duncan."

I opened the car door and stepped out.

"Thanks for . . . listening," I said into the open window.

"You're welcome," said Tom. "Take care, okay?"

"You too."

"And don't forget. If you need anything or want to talk some more, I'm only a beeper away."

"I won't forget," I said and got into my car.

CHAPTER TWELVE

♦

"Kimberley," I said when I walked in the door. "What a surprise."

I tried to conceal my disappointment that Hunt had neglected to tell me he was bringing his daughter home with him, but I doubt I was successful.

It was so typical of him lately. In the old days he would have checked with me, asked me if it was all right to have Kimberley spend a few days with us. But then Hunt rarely communicated with me about anything anymore, I thought sadly. It was as if I had no say, no importance, no leverage in the household, now that I no longer had a job or a paycheck.

I shook my head as I watched Hunt and Kimberley huddle together on the floor of the library. It appeared that they were engaged in a rousing game of Monopoly. I couldn't remember ever feeling so left out, and I fought the urge to beep Tom and beg him to come and rescue me.

"Jude," said Hunt as he shook the dice. "Where've you been?"

"Stop 'n' Shop," I said.

"Stop 'n' Shop?" said Kimberley without looking up. "Did you buy me some pretzels? The kind that come in little sticks?"

Give me. Buy me. Do for me. Was that what stepmothering was

about? What ever happened to: Hi, nice to see you. Or: Would you like to join us in a game of Monopoly?

"No, I didn't buy pretzels," I said, trying to control my anger. "I had no idea you'd be here when I got home."

"My fault, Pumpkin," Hunt said to his daughter. "I forgot to tell Judy you were coming. I'll buy you the pretzels on our way to the club in the morning."

"You're taking Kimberley to the club?" I said to Hunt. He and I had talked about spending some time alone together over the weekend. Apparently, he had forgotten.

"Yup," he said. "I thought it was time she learned how to swing a golf club. We're going to hit the driving range first thing in the morning and see if she's got the right stuff."

"Isn't she a little young for golf?" I said.

"I'm ten," Kimberley said. "That means I'm a teenager."

"Right," I said. "Well, I'd like to go over to the club tomorrow morning too. How about we all drive over together?"

"Fine with me," said Hunt, as he moved his piece around the board. A few minutes passed as he and Kimberley made their real estate deals. I could have been a piece of furniture for all they cared.

"Call me when you're ready for dinner," I said as I started to leave the room. "I'll come down and rustle us up something to eat."

"Not necessary," Hunt said as he glanced at me then returned his gaze to the game. God forbid he should break his concentration. "Kimberley and I had a bite before we left the city."

I stared at the two of them, my eyes burning with anger and resentment. It hadn't even occurred to them to include me in their plans.

"Is something wrong?" Hunt asked me.

"Yes," I said, "and it has been for a very long time."

As I stormed out of the room, I heard Kimberley tell her father to go directly to jail without passing Go. If she hadn't been around, I would have told him where else he could go.

The next morning, Hunt tapped on the bathroom door as I was brushing my teeth.

"Jude? Can I come in?" he said.

"What is it?"

He opened the door and stepped inside, then whispered, "Kimberley woke up on the wrong side of the bed this morning."

"How can you tell?"

"Jude, please. She's upset because she left her makeup in the city."

"Her makeup? The girl's ten years old."

"I know, but her mother lets her wear lipstick now and then."

"Yeah, well, her stepmother doesn't. Kimberley is way too young to wear lipstick."

"I agree with you, but she says she wants to wear it to the club."

"Hunt," I said as patiently as possible. "Repeat after me: 'I'm Kimberley's father and I'm allowed to say no to her.' Can you do that?"

He sighed. "You're right. I've got to be stricter with her. It's just that I don't see her very often, and I don't want to ruin her visits by playing the heavy."

"You'd rather *I* played the heavy?"

"Of course not."

"Okay, then you'd rather ruin Kimberley's life?"

"What do you mean by that remark?"

"I mean that if you keep wimping out every time you should be disciplining her, she's going to grow up to be one of those people who shoots at strangers from roofs of tall buildings. What's more, she's going to have a pretty low opinion of men."

"The way you have of me?"

I turned away from him. I wanted to scream, *Yes! Exactly the way I have of you, because you've changed from the man I adore to the man I abhor!* I especially wanted to scream if after I realized that it rhymed.

"Look, Jude, I don't want to fight," he said, reaching out to touch my shoulder and then thinking better of it. "If you don't want to lend Kimberley your lipstick, that's up to you. I'll see you downstairs."

He walked out of the bathroom and left me staring at my reflection. Was I a wicked stepmother? I asked myself. Was I a nagging, shrewish wife? Was I the bitch Hunt and Kimberley made me feel I was? I couldn't tell anymore. I really couldn't tell.

During the ride over to the club, Kimberley kept asking me if she could borrow my lipstick and I kept saying no. She had an amazing capacity for getting on a person's nerves, honest to God.

When we arrived at The Oaks, she and Hunt headed in the direction of the driving range, while I went straight to the pool. We agreed that they would join me there when they'd finished their father-daughter golf lesson.

There were plenty of empty chairs around the pool, as it was still well before the noontime rush, so I had my pick—and I picked one right next to Delia Tewksbury. She was sitting under an umbrella, reading a novel by Belva Plain. She wore a black, two-piece bathing suit, the bottom half of which had a little pleated skirt. I guessed it was at least thirty years old.

"Hello, Mrs. Tewksbury," I said. "Mind if I join you?"

She put her book down and stared at me as if she'd never seen me before. We went through this every time, so I introduced myself once again.

"Oh, yes, Judith," she said. "Lovely to see you, dear."

"Thank you," I said. "You know, Mrs. Tewksbury, I don't believe I've had the chance to personally express my sympathies over the loss of your grand-niece Claire. Please accept my condolences."

"That's very thoughtful of you," she said. "My husband and I are so lucky to have the support of our fellow club members."

"Yes, that must be very comforting, especially since the police don't seem to know who was responsible for your loss." I paused, not knowing how much Delia Tewksbury knew about her husband's run-ins with Claire. She seemed so out of touch. "Does Mr. Tewksbury have any idea who the murderer might be?"

"He thinks it was some outsider." She sighed. "As do I. We've never taken security measures at The Oaks, not in all the years the club has been in existence. But I suppose it's time to follow the lead of the Jewish clubs and barricade ourselves in. Some of their clubs actually have gatehouses with twenty-four-hour guards." She sighed again. "Perhaps if we'd adopted similar security measures at The Oaks, Claire would still be with us." Delia's eyes welled up and she dabbed at them with a lacy handkerchief she pulled from her purse.

"I didn't mean to upset you," I said.

"No, no," she said. "It's all right. It's just that Claire was like a daughter to us."

"Really? I thought she and your husband didn't get along all that well."

"Oh, nonsense," she scoffed. "That was country club business, nothing more. We adored Claire, especially since we had no children of our own. I'm barren, you know."

"No, I didn't know." And furthermore, I didn't want to. I'd always assumed one's barrenness was something one kept to oneself.

"Ah yes," she said, and sighed yet again. "The sadness still overwhelms me. When a woman is unable to bear a child, she dies little deaths every day of her life."

"My, that *is* sad." Well, what else was I supposed to say? "What about Mr. Tewksbury? Did he want children as badly as you did?"

Delia Tewksbury's eyes misted again and her lower lip quivered. "No," she said firmly. "No, he didn't."

She began to cry—big, noisy tears. Clearly, she was an emotional wreck. The handful of people around the pool turned to see what was going on, and what was going on was that I, Ms. Police Informant, had just made the wife of the Chairman of the Board of Governors cry.

"Please, Mrs. Tewksbury," I said, patting her arm. "I didn't mean to cause you any undue pain." The woman was in her seventies, for God's sake. Wasn't it a little late to be weeping over her barrenness?

I offered to get her a glass of water and went into the terrace dining room to fetch it. When I returned, she was gone—Belva Plain novel and all.

I drank the water myself and sunbathed until Hunt and Kimberley showed up an hour later. By that time, the pool was crowded—so crowded that Kimberley and I had to share a chair.

"How was the golf lesson?" I asked.

"Kimberley shows real promise," said Hunt. "She has a natural swing."

"That's great," I said. "Kimberley, did you enjoy your lesson?"

"Yeah," she said. "But I would have enjoyed it a lot more if I'd been allowed to borrow your lipstick."

I shook my head. The kid never stopped.

"I'm boiling. Who wants to go in the water?" I asked.

"I think I'll wait awhile," said Hunt.

"Me too," said Kimberley.

"Then I guess I'm on my own," I said. "The chair's all yours, Kim."

I got up, walked toward the shallow end of the pool, and submerged myself (up to my neck) in the cool, blue water. Then I did a few laps of the dog paddle, my one and only stroke. I was paddling toward Hunt and Kimberley, hoping one of them would remember I was alive and wave to me, when I saw Kimberley pick up my purse, unzip the top, and reach inside.

The little shit! She was going for my lipstick, even though I'd told her sixteen times she couldn't borrow it! And what was Hunt doing? He was taking a nap!

Aw, what the hell, I thought. Let her wear the damn lipstick. Why spoil a perfectly delicious swim by rushing out of the pool to scold her?

I watched as Kimberley fished around in my purse for my makeup kit . . . as she pulled the black case out and examined it . . . as she held it up to her ear and shook it. Shook it? What on earth was she doing?

I swam a little closer. She seemed to be holding the black case and peering at it as if it were a—

"Hey!" I yelled when it dawned on me that she had my beeper, not my makeup case, in her hot little hands. "Leave that alone!"

God, if Hunt found out I was snitching for the police—snitching on his buddies at The Oaks—he'd be so furious he'd . . . I didn't know what he'd do.

I dog-paddled fast and furiously to the edge of the pool, leapt out, and hurried over to my chair.

"Give me that, huh, Kim?" I said breathlessly.

"You're dripping all over me," said Kimberley, who clutched the beeper to her chest when I made a move to grab it from her.

"Give me that," I said again, holding out my hand. "Now."

Kimberley shook her head. Somehow, she knew she had me. She'd been waiting seven years to make me squirm, and her wish was finally coming true.

"Kimberley, I'm asking you nicely," I tried again. "Please give me the beeper."

She refused, so I attempted to wrestle it out of her grip.

"Dad! Judy's hurting me," she squealed. Apparently, I had pinched her arm during our little tug-of-war.

Hunt roused himself from his nap. "What's going on here?" he asked.

"Nothing," I said. "Go back to sleep."

"She won't let me see this thing," Kimberley whined.

"What thing?" said Hunt.

"It's just a little gizmo that Arlene gave me," I said as I continued to try to wrest the beeper out of Kimberley's small but very strong hands. "Everyone in publishing's got a beeper now. It's the latest craze."

"But you're not in publishing anymore," Hunt couldn't resist reminding me.

"I know, but Arlene didn't want me to feel left out," I said.

"That was nice of her. Let me take a look at it," said Hunt, who managed to pry Kimberley's fingers off the beeper.

Okay, I said to myself as I tried to stay calm. At least Hunt's got it now. There shouldn't be any problem getting him to give it to me.

"It's a little thing, isn't it?" said Hunt as he rested it in the palm of his hand. "Really compact. And look at this window. Is this where the message comes in, Jude?"

"Yes," I said. "Now, why don't I put it back in my purse, so it doesn't get wet or broken?"

"Good idea," Hunt said.

He was about to hand the beeper over to me. No muss. No fuss. No begging. No pleading. But then, in the millisecond *before* he was about to hand the beeper over to me, it beeped. Well, actually it vibrated.

"Whoa, I'm getting a message *and* a massage," Hunt quipped, laughing as the beeper sent tiny vibrations into his palm.

"Perfect timing," I giggled, trying desperately to appear light-hearted and casual. "Now why don't you give me the beeper so I can put it away?"

"Aw, come on, Jude," said Hunt. "I want to see the kind of girl-talk you and Arlene send along the phone waves."

You know the rest. It was ugly. First, I couldn't get Hunt to hand over the beeper. Second, Tom chose that particular moment to send me a suggestive message. (He asked me to meet him at the make-out spot by the river—the same make-out spot he'd taken me to the day before. He said he wanted to discuss Brendan. He also mentioned something about my having great legs.) Third, I had no explanation for any of it—not the beeper, not the message, nothing. At least none that Hunt would buy. Oh, I tried to fast-talk my way out of the situation. I told Hunt that Tom was one of Arlene's new boyfriends, someone she'd met at work. I said, "Oh, that Tom. He was probably sitting in Arlene's office, reading from one of her romance novels when he decided it would be fun to beep me."

"Bullshit," Hunt said as several sunbathers looked on. "Who is this guy, really?"

"I told you," I said. "He's Arlene's new boyfriend."

"What was that business about meeting you by the river, where he'd taken you yesterday?" Hunt said angrily.

"Who knows?" I shrugged. "As I said, he was probably reading a passage from one of Arlene's bodice-rippers."

"There's one way to find out," said Hunt, getting up from his chair. "I'll just go inside and call the number *Tom* left."

"But wait! You have no right," I cried. We were creating quite a scene around the pool.

"I have every right," Hunt snapped. "You're my wife and you just got beeped by a strange man."

I had never figured Hunt for the jealous type. Of course, I'd never given him any reason to be jealous. I'd never flirted with other men in front of his nose, or dressed suggestively, or flaunted my curvaceous and, I suppose, fetching figure. No, I'd always been Little Miss Faithful, saving all my loving for my husband—the very same husband who was suddenly displaying a keener interest in me than he had in months.

He stalked off, taking his suspicions and my beeper with him. I was left with a curiously speechless Kimberley.

"You okay?" I asked her as I pulled a towel around me and sat down in Hunt's chair. It occurred to me that Kimberley had never seen her father and me fight. Any harsh words between us were always spoken behind our bedroom door.

She looked up at me. "You and Dad aren't getting a divorce, are you?" she said.

"Why? Because of a silly little misunderstanding?" I said.

"No, because it's been weird between you for a while."

So Kimberley hadn't bought our act.

"I'm sorry," I said. "Your father and I have been under a lot of stress lately, what with my losing my job and not being able to find another one."

That seemed to satisfy Kimberley for the moment. We sat together in silence. Then she suddenly began to cry.

"What is it, hon?" I asked, drawing my chair closer to hers.

"Nothing," she said, tears running down her freckled cheeks.

"Kim?"

"I don't want to talk about it."

"But you're upset."

"I said I don't want to talk about it, Judy. Please leave me alone."

I lay back in my chair and waited for Hunt to return. I didn't know what else to do. In just under an hour, I had made two people cry—first Delia, now Kimberley. Not a good sign.

About fifteen minutes later, Hunt did return and he didn't look any happier than his daughter. He announced that he wanted to go home, which astonished me. He never left the club in the middle of the day, not when there were hours of networking left.

When we arrived at the house, Hunt called his parents and asked if he could bring Kimberley over for an impromptu visit. Apparently, they said yes, because he and Kimberley were out the door in a matter of minutes.

"Don't go anywhere. I want to talk to you," he said before slamming the door in my face.

When I was sure they were gone, I ran to the phone to beep Tom. I was dying to know what he'd told Hunt. I was also dying to know why he had beeped me at the club and what kind of dirt he'd dug up on Brendan. But as I dialed Tom's beeper number, it occurred to me that he might not call me back right away; that by the time he did call me back, Hunt would be home. I didn't want to make things worse, so I hung up the phone and waited.

Twenty minutes later, Hunt returned.

"Is Kimberley all right?" I asked.

"I don't want to talk about Kimberley," said Hunt. "I want to talk about you and . . . and *Tom.*"

"Look, Hunt, if you reached Detective Cunningham, he probably explained to you that the reason he was—"

"He didn't explain anything," said Hunt. "Your boyfriend held fast to your secret."

"He's not my boyfriend and there is no secret," I said. "At least, not the kind of secret you're alluding to."

"Really? Then why don't you tell me what kind of secret you and Tom have together." He stood in the kitchen with his arms folded across his chest. His cheekbones bulged as he worked his jaw.

"All right," I said. "I'll tell you everything." I took a deep breath. "Just after Claire's death, Tom Cunningham, one of the Belford police detectives assigned to the investigation, asked me to come down to the station to answer a few questions about Claire and the night she died."

"I remember."

"During that interview, I must have given him the impression that I wasn't a fan of the people at The Oaks."

"No news there. You trash the club any chance you get."

"Do you want to hear my explanation or don't you?"

"Go on."

"Tom called a couple of weeks later and asked if he could come and talk to me. I said yes."

"He came here? To our house?"

"Why shouldn't he? He's a cop investigating the death of the woman I was planning to write a cookbook with."

"I suppose."

"He came here and said he thought the person who killed Claire might be someone from the club but that he couldn't arrest anybody until he had a motive for the murder. He asked me if I'd be interested in helping him."

"In helping him? How?"

"By working as a police informant." There, I said it.

"You're telling me this detective asked you to work for the police?"

"Yes. And I accepted his offer. I thought it would be a great way to help bring Claire's murderer to justice, make a little money, and give me something to do while I waited for a publishing job to open up."

"But a police informant? What does that involve?"

"It involves spying on the members of The Oaks. It involves trying to help Tom—Detective Cunningham—figure out which one of the members had a motive for smashing Claire on the back of the head with that pitching wedge."

Hunt looked sick.

"Let me get this straight," he said, his face as chalky as Rolaids. "You've been snooping around the club, feeding this cop with damaging and incriminating information about people I consider to be my friends, people I play golf with, people I'm trying to get as clients?"

I nodded.

"And then you've gone running off to secret meetings with the guy?"

"The meetings are part of the job," I said. "I can't exactly have tea with him at the club."

"I can't believe all this. I really can't." He pulled on his left ear lobe. "Where do you meet him?"

"Usually at the Stop 'n' Shop."

"Yeah, right. In the frozen food section, I'll bet."

"No. We meet in the parking lot."

"What about your little spot along the river? The 'make-out' place *Tom* took you to yesterday?"

"That was a special thing," I said. "Tom wanted to show it to me. So I went."

"Yeah? What else did he want to show you, huh, Judy?"

"Hunt, it's not what you think. Really."

"How about his crack about your legs?"

"I have nice legs. Tom noticed, unlike other people I know."

Hunt flinched as if I'd hit him. "Do you deny that you're sleeping with the guy?"

"Yes."

"Then why didn't you tell me about your little 'arrangement'? Why did you lie to me, Judy?"

"I'm sorry," I said. "It was wrong of me not to tell you I was working with the police. But I knew how much you valued your membership at The Oaks. How could I tell you I was hired to get dirt on the members there?"

He shook his head. "I'm your husband. I can't believe you'd do something like this behind my back. I can't believe you'd jeopardize all the contacts I've made at the club. I can't believe you'd jeopardize your life, for Christ's sake."

"My life?"

"Yeah. Police work is dangerous business. You could get hurt."

"Would you care?"

"Of course I'd care."

"That's the nicest thing you've said to me in months."

"That's what all this is about, isn't it, Judy," Hunt said, his voice rising. "You think I'm a boring clod who doesn't know how to show his wife he cares. Well, here's a bulletin for you: I *am* a boring clod. I am not some hot-shit bachelor cop with a thrill-a-minute job, I'm a commodities broker with a wife and a kid and a mortgage. Not very glamorous, I admit, but that's the way it is. What's more, you never used to mind. In fact, you never used to mind that I didn't take you to make-out spots along the river. You didn't need Hallmark greeting card shit like that to know I loved you. You never used to accuse me of not caring." He stopped to wipe some spittle from the corner of his mouth. "And speaking of not caring, do you think your constant jabs and barbs and relentless sarcasm go right over my head? Do you think I don't know how dull you find me? How frustrated you are with me? How ineffectual a parent you think I am? Do you think it doesn't hurt when you put down every fucking thing that gives me pleasure—my work, my golf, my club, even my daughter?"

He sat down on one of the kitchen chairs and put his head in his hands. I prayed he wouldn't cry. If he cried, that would mean I'd made three people cry in one day.

"Hunt," I said, "hasn't it occurred to you that the reason I didn't tell you about my job with the police was that you and I have drifted apart—dangerously apart? We live in the same house, but we're strangers. We don't connect. We don't communicate. We don't have sex."

"And I suppose Detective Cunningham is better at all that than I am?"

"God! You can be so dense! Listen to me! I am not having an affair with Tom. I am working with the man. Why can't you get it through your fucking head that the person I want to connect, communicate, and have sex with is *you*?" I slammed my hand down on the kitchen counter for emphasis and regretted the gesture instantly. Not only did it hurt my hand, it knocked the salt shaker off the counter and spilled salt all over the floor.

Neither of us made a move to clean it up. Then both of us did. We nearly collided. Under other circumstances, I would have laughed.

"Let me," I said. "I'm the one who spilled it."

"Fine," said Hunt. "Be my guest."

I wiped up the salt.

"Maybe we need some time apart," said Hunt.

I gulped. I'd been thinking the same thing, of course, but when he said it, a large lump formed in my throat.

"If that's what you want," I said.

"I'm sorry, but I can't seem to get over the fact that you didn't tell me about your deal with the police; that you've been hanging around the club, not to please me, as I'd allowed myself to believe, but to gather incriminating evidence against my friends and business associates; that you put your life in danger and didn't think to discuss it with me."

I couldn't respond.

"How did we get here?" he asked, rhetorically, it seemed. "We were so happy, weren't we?"

I still couldn't speak. The lump was choking me. So was the irony that, in the past few minutes, Hunt and I had said more to each other than we had in months; that in the very process of accusing me of adultery and of acknowledging our problems, he had finally shown some real emotion.

"Why don't we think about what we want," he said.

"You mean, what we want out of the marriage or what we want out of life?" I managed.

"Both," he said. "I know *I* have a lot of thinking to do."

He started to leave the kitchen, then turned to face me. "I think I'll do some work upstairs," he said and left the room.

We didn't talk much for the rest of the day. Hunt said he didn't want dinner, so I ate alone in the kitchen. At about ten, he announced that he was going to sleep—in the guest room.

"I think it's best," was his explanation.

Alone in our king-size bed for the first time in years, I slept fitfully. I was so tired when I finally got up in the morning that I took the elevator down to the kitchen. Hunt was long gone, but he'd left a note: "Kimberley's staying with my folks. Went into the office. Won't be back until late. Don't wait up. Hunt." No "Love, Hunt." No XXXes and OOOs. Nothing. Not even a little face with a smile on it.

I took a shower, ate breakfast, and called Tom.

"You okay?" he asked.

"Not really," I said.

"I'm so sorry I beeped you when I did, Judy."

"Listen, it wasn't your fault. It was mine. I should have told Hunt what I was doing."

"Can you meet me in about fifteen minutes?"

"Sure. Where?"

"The usual. From the sound of your voice, I don't think this is the day for anything too wild and crazy."

When I pulled into the Stop 'n' Shop parking lot, Tom was there waiting for me. I parked my car and got into his.

"You look tired," he said.

"I am."

"You think you and your husband will work things out?"

"I don't know. But I think I discovered something yesterday."

"What?"

"I *want* to work things out. Hunt's terribly upset with me now, because I didn't tell him about my police work, but I have a feeling the whole incident woke him up. Maybe he won't take me for granted now."

"He's nuts to take you for granted," said Tom.

"Listen, before I start blabbing about my marriage again, tell me why you beeped me at the club yesterday. Your message said something about Brendan."

"Yeah, I checked out Mr. Hardy, like I said I would, and guess what?"

"What?"

"He's had a couple of scrapes with the law."

"Like what?"

"A little armed robbery here, a little extortion there."

"My God. How could The Oaks have hired a chef with a background like that? The club is so picky about the people it allows on the premises. You should have seen the way Duncan Tewksbury and his pals grilled me when I was applying for membership. They asked me everything but my bra size."

"Well, they weren't as tough on Brendan."

"I wonder why."

"I'll tell you why. I have a buddy who can find his way into all kinds of records and files. One of the things he came up with was Brendan's birth certificate.''

"How juicy could that be? Did Brendan lie about his age or something?"

"No, but the birth certificate did turn up a very interesting tidbit concerning Brendan's parentage.''

"His parentage? Is the senior Mr. Hardy a notorious serial killer?''

"No. There is no senior Mr. Hardy. According to the birth certificate, Brendan Hardy's father goes by a different name.''

"Which is?''

"Tewksbury. Duncan Tewksbury.''

CHAPTER THIRTEEN

♦

As I drove home from my meeting with Tom, I kept thinking about his little bombshell: Duncan Tewksbury was Brendan's father! No wonder he always stuck up for Brendan! But why did they keep their relationship a secret? Who was Lorraine Pennock, the woman listed on the birth certificate as Brendan's mother? And how did poor Delia Tewksbury, a woman so depressed about her barrenness that she was still crying about it, feel about the whole thing? Did she even know that Brendan was her husband's son? And what about Claire? She was a member of the family. Did she know that Brendan was her relative and try to get him fired anyway?

God, I felt like I'd stepped into a Tennessee Williams play. My mother always said that WASPs had tangled family histories and that you never could tell which were the sisters and which were the cousins. Of course in my mother's family, you could always tell which were the sisters and which were the cousins, because the sisters were the ones that were never speaking to each other.

At about noon, Hunt called.

"I won't be home for dinner," he said, sounding very cool and distant. "I'm having dinner with a client."

"Yes, you mentioned in your note that you'd be home late," I said. "Who's the client?"

"Leeza Grummond."

I felt my stomach turn. So that's how he was paying me back.

"Give Leeza my worst," I said.

"Very funny."

"Hunt? How long is this big chill going to last? You buried yourself in work yesterday. You slept in the guest room last night. You left before I was up this morning. And tonight you're staying in the city to have dinner with my sworn enemy. Don't you think we should talk? Try to work things out?"

"Try to work things out? You're the one who lied, who went behind my back and—"

"Hunt, there's no point in going over it again," I interrupted. "I've already explained why I didn't tell you about my arrangement with Tom. I didn't want to ruin your friendship with people at the club, and I didn't think you cared what I did. You've been treating me like a piece of cheese lately, and I felt that you—"

"Oh, now we're back to what *I* did to *you?*"

It was Hunt's turn to interrupt me. Interrupting the person you're fighting with is dirty pool, but all married couples do it—unless, of course, they've graduated from one of those How-to-Save-Your-Marriage seminars where husbands and wives are taught to sit and listen to their spouse say horrible and disgusting things about them without ever interrupting. These couples swear by the technique and come out of the seminars smooching and cuddling and claiming they've seen The Light. But I'd like to track some of them down, say, five years after the seminar, and see how they're doing. I'll bet you nine out of ten of them are up to their old tricks, fighting and cursing and interrupting, just like the good old days.

"Look, Hunt. We need to sit down together, face to face, and talk calmly, rationally, like adults. I happen to think that the incident with the beeper at the pool yesterday might have been just the catalyst we needed to nudge us out of our rut."

"Our rut? Is that what you call what we've been in? When a wife lies to her husband, I don't call that a rut, I call that a betrayal."

"Oh, Jesus. Hunt, I really think you're overreacting here. I mean, I didn't commit a crime. Quite the contrary. I agreed to help the police *solve* a crime."

"Without telling me."

And around and around we went.

"Let's table this until you get home," I suggested.

"Fine. I've got a meeting now anyway."

"Then I'll see you tonight?"

"Right. Bye."

"Hunt, wait—I want you to know that I still love—"

Click. He had hung up before I could get the words out.

I made myself a sandwich and drove over to the club, hoping to learn more about the Duncan-Brendan connection. As luck would have it, I ran into Delia Tewksbury in the ladies' locker room.

"Hello, Mrs. Tewksbury," I said and got her usual blank stare. "I'm Judy Mills. Hunt Price's wife."

"Yes, of course," she said.

"You know, I've been thinking about you, ever since our little chat yesterday."

"Chat?"

"Yes, by the pool." Was Delia Tewksbury an Alzheimer's sufferer or just dotty? Or was she the sort of woman—and there were several at The Oaks—who displayed her superiority by *acting* forgetful, as if to say to the world: "I'm so important I couldn't possibly be expected to remember someone as insignificant as you."

"We were discussing your grandniece, Claire," I reminded her, "and your maternal feelings toward her."

"Oh, yes. I remember now."

"And then you expressed your sorrow about not having had a child of your own, while your husband didn't share your desire for children."

"Yes, I recall saying all that," said Delia as she smoothed the sides of her already impeccably rendered French twist.

"Well, the reason I bring it up is that my husband and I are going through the very same ordeal. I desperately want children, but Hunt does not."

"Pity."

"Yes. You see, he already has a child, by another woman." Just like *your* husband, Delia. Now let's see if you know the truth about Brendan and if you'll admit it to a perfect stranger, like you admitted your barrenness. "It's not an easy situation to deal with," I went on. "Knowing your husband has a child that isn't yours."

"No, I suppose it isn't," said Delia. "Still, a child is a child. How I wish I'd had one. But as I told you, I was unable to conceive and my husband was against adoption. He maintains that, with adoption, you never know what you're getting. Questionable gene pools and that sort of thing."

Aha! So Delia didn't know that Brendan was her husband's son. If she had, wouldn't she have said something? I'd given her the perfect opening. But how was it possible that she didn't know? Could Duncan have kept a secret like that from his wife all these years? Could he have kept her from knowing that he had fathered a son and hired that very son to work at his country club? A son with a shady past? Or was it that Delia Tewksbury was cagier than she seemed? Maybe she knew everything and wasn't telling. But why?

"Now, if you'll excuse me, dear. I must use the telephone," said Delia. "Bridge game to cancel, you know."

"Right. Well, it was nice seeing you," I said and left old Delia to her phone call.

I was suddenly dying for an iced tea so I headed for the terrace dining room, where I spotted Duncan Tewksbury at a table for two, probably waiting for his wife to join him. I couldn't resist stopping by his table to see how he'd react to questions about his son.

"Hello there, Mr. Tewksbury," I said.

"Hlloo," he slurred. He appeared to have had several gin and tonics.

"I have a friend whose son is interested in apprenticing in the kitchen here, under Brendan," I said, not really sure where I was going. "But before he fills out a formal application for employment, I wanted to be able to tell him something about Brendan's background. You know, where he trained, where he worked before coming to The Oaks, that sort of thing."

"Why don't you ask Brendan himself?" Duncan suggested, then hiccuped.

"He seems so busy all the time," I said. "I hate to bother him."

"Well, I don't remember where the heck he trained," said Duncan.

Does Leavenworth ring a bell? "But you were the one who brought him here, right?" I asked.

"That's right," said Duncan. "He was working at the Belford Athletic Club. We had an opening, and Brendan filled it."

"What happened to the chef he replaced?" I asked.

"He was killed," said Duncan. "In a car accident. Dreadful business."

"I'll bet," I said, wondering if Brendan had anything to do with his predecessor's demise and whether Claire's death was merely another on a long list of his murder victims.

"Oh, here comes Mother," said Duncan as he eyed his wife bustling toward us.

Mother? Don't you just love men who call their wives "Mother"? I mean, how weird is that?

"I'd better run," I said, not wanting Delia to think I was insinuating myself in her life yet again. "Ta ta."

I walked over to the tennis courts and signed Hunt and me up for the Friday Night Tennis Tussle, just in case we reconciled and he felt like a little Friday Night Networking. Then I decided to go home. I wasn't really in the mood for more snooping. Snooping, I'd discovered, was far more demanding than gossiping, a skill I'd mastered during my years in book publishing. Unlike gossiping, where you merely had to repeat stories about people you barely knew, snooping required the ability to uncover stories about people you barely knew—*before* they became gossip. And I was just too tired for that. I hadn't slept the night before and my eyelids were heavy. Besides, it was hard to concentrate on Claire's murderer when my marriage was in shambles.

The parking lot at The Oaks was huge, so there was never a problem finding a spot. But there were a handful of spots that the members literally fought over—the coveted parking spaces that were in the shade, under a row of towering Oak trees. I say "coveted," not because the members were desperate to keep their cars out of the sun, but because they were desperate to keep their *dogs* out of the sun. That's right, their dogs. The Oaks had a rule that forbade members to bring their dogs to the club, but several fanatical dog owners—including Nedra Laughton, who owned a Yorkshire terrier named Bartholomew in spite of the fact that Ducky was allergic to dogs—couldn't conceive of leaving their precious pets home alone while they went off to play eighteen holes. So they'd show up at the club at the shriek of dawn, secure one of the shady parking spaces, and leave poor Fido in the car with the window open—all day. It was inhumane, if you ask me.

As I walked to my car, past the row of shady parking spaces that Thursday afternoon in July, I noticed that one of the dogs was barking nonstop: "Yip! Yip! Yip! Yip!" Thinking the poor pooch might be sick or hurt, I approached the car he was yipping from to see if I could help. The car, it turned out, was Nedra's big black Mercedes.

"Hi, Bartholomew," I said, peering into the car. The windows of the Mercedes were tinted that God-awful limousine dark-gray, so I practically had to plaster my face up against them to see inside. And when I did, I got the gist of what was making Bartholomew bark: it seems that while he was yipping away in the front seat, Nedra was performing fellatio on Rob in the back seat. In fact, at the very moment my hot breath was making circles of steam on the tinted glass, Nedra's hot breath was making Rob yip even louder than Bartholomew.

"Uh-oh, we've got company," she groaned to Rob when she saw me leaning against the window. Apparently, the tinted glass didn't make it hard to see out, just in.

She quickly disentangled herself from her lover and ordered him to pull his tennis shorts on. Then she hopped out of the car. Rob lingered in the back seat.

"Well, if it isn't The Oaks's little snoop," said Nedra as she stood there eyeing me, her hands on her hips. Her face was flushed with afterglow. She smelled of sex, reeked of it. I was filled with envy.

"I wasn't snooping," I said. "I heard a dog barking, and I came over to see what the problem was."

"Good try," she said. "I know you were snooping. You've been snooping around the club for weeks. Everybody's talking about what a busybody Hunt Price's wife turned out to be."

"Everybody?" I was aghast. People were saying I was a busybody? I hated busybodies. On the other hand, having them think I was a busybody was better than having them think I was a police informant, hired to find out which of them was a cold-blooded killer.

"I suppose you're just dying to run off and tell people about Rob and me," said Nedra. "For all I know, you'll tell Ducky, too."

"Why are you putting *me* on the defensive?" I asked. "I'm not the one who was screwing the tennis pro in the middle of the parking lot."

She smiled, then licked her lips. "No, honey. You weren't. Jealous?"

I scowled. Okay, so Nedra felt no remorse for her actions. No embarrassment either. Was she in love with Rob? Was that why she was so desperate to be with him that she couldn't wait until they got to some seedy motel, so desperate that she had to have sex with him in the bushes behind the tennis courts, in the parking lot of the country club? And where would they strike next? I wondered. On the golf course? On the putting green? In a sand trap?

A sand trap? Suddenly, a thought came to me with an electric jolt: suppose that Nedra and Rob were the ones who beat Claire with the pitching wedge and left her for dead in that sand trap.

I had first put Nedra on my list of possible suspects, because I'd thought she was jealous of Claire and threatened by the fact that Ducky's old girlfriend had come back into his life. I had first put Rob on my list of possible suspects, because I knew how angry he was at Claire for accusing him of sexual harassment and trying to get him fired from his job. But the revelation that Nedra and Rob were lovers put a new spin on things. Maybe Rob had told Nedra that Claire was out to get him. Maybe Nedra didn't want to lose her boy-toy at the club. Maybe the two of them decided to put a stop to Claire's plans by bashing her over the head with a golf club. Nedra did have a volatile temperament, after all. And what did I really know about Rob? Just that he was an eager beaver who hoped to parlay his job as a tennis pro into his own sporting goods store someday—maybe sooner rather than later. They were both at the club the night of the July Fourth party. I'd seen Nedra sitting with Ducky and two other couples. And I'd seen Rob in the parking lot as we were arriving at the club. Maybe they'd rendezvoused while everyone else was having cocktails and had lured Claire onto the golf course. Then while one of them talked to her, the other one bopped her over the head.

"So can I assume you're going to tell Ducky about this, Judy?" Nedra said as my mind raced.

"I have no intention of telling your husband," I said. "However, there is something you can tell me."

"Let me guess: you want to know if Rob has a friend."

"A friend?"

"Yes, for you. I saw the way you drooled at us through the window, honey. I have a hunch that you and Hunt haven't exactly been burning things up in the bedroom."

I felt my face burn up. "What on earth makes you say that?" I asked.

"Just a guess," she said. "If Hunt is anything like Ducky, he thinks making partner at F&F is the end-all be-all. I wouldn't be surprised if Hunt is as apathetic about sex as Ducky is."

I was angry now. My sex life was none of Nedra's business. "Has it occurred to you that Ducky's apathy may have coincided with Claire Cox's arrival at the club?" I asked. "You always struck me as the jealous type, Nedra. Perhaps you had a reason to be jealous where Ducky and Claire were concerned."

"Meaning?"

"Meaning that Ducky seemed pretty shaken by Claire's death. Maybe you and Rob weren't the only ones having parking lot sex at the club. Maybe Ducky and Claire had an affair before she was murdered."

"Ducky? Don't make me laugh," she said. "Ducky doesn't have parking lot sex or any other kind. His rocket hasn't been launched in years."

"But . . . I don't understand. It always seemed as though you and Ducky had the hottest—"

"Look, Judy. Things are never what they seem. Ducky Laughton's not a sexual animal. He just isn't. He gets his rocks off in other ways."

What other ways? I was dying to ask but didn't, because Rob picked that very moment to emerge from Nedra's Mercedes—and he had a big guilty smile on his face, the kind that said, "I'm embarrassed that I was caught having sex with the wife of one of the members, but I can't wait to do it again."

"Hi, Mrs. Price," he said, appearing a little wobbly in the legs. I guessed Nedra had sucked the life out of him.

"Hello, Rob," I said.

"Judy promises that she's not going to tell anybody about us," Nedra said to him. "Right, Judy?"

"Right, Nedra, *if* you tell me whether you and Rob were already seeing each other in the beginning of July." Before the night Claire was killed, for instance.

They looked at each other.

"What makes you ask that?" she said.

"Just curious. I wondered how long you two had been together."

Rob draped his arm around Nedra's shoulder. "About a year," he said proudly. "My job at the club makes it pretty easy for us to see each other. Everybody assumes Nedra's wild about tennis, when what she's really wild about is me." He grinned on the word "me." The guy was obviously very taken with himself and with the fact that he had found a woman who was rich, socially prominent and sexually promiscuous, not to mention a respectable tennis player.

Nedra grinned back at Rob. " 'Wild' doesn't begin to cover it, baby."

"I think I see things clearly now," I said.

"And *I* see things clearly, too," said Nedra. "I see that people around here were right about you, Judy. You *are* a busybody. You ask a lot of questions and you stick your nose where it doesn't belong."

I smiled and looked at the two of them. "I wouldn't talk about sticking things where they don't belong," I said, then walked toward my car and headed for home.

Instead of going straight home, I took a detour to the Stop 'n' Shop. No, not for a meeting with Tom, but to buy myself something to eat for dinner, since Hunt was staying in the city to dine with Loathsome Leeza. I figured I'd tell Tom all about my theory about Nedra and Rob tomorrow, when I felt more rested.

The supermarket was packed, and I had to wait in the checkout line for what seemed like an eternity. Of course, there were compensations: I got to leaf through *The National Enquirer* and *The Star* and *The Globe,* and find out more than I ever wanted to know about Burt and Loni, Oprah and Stedman, and a 100-year-old woman who gave birth to a dinosaur.

I pulled into our driveway at about six o'clock and parked in front of the large red barn that doubled as our garage. I gathered my packages and carried them to the back door that led directly into the kitchen. Balancing both bags in one arm, I fumbled around in my purse for my key, which I found and inserted into the lock.

"That's weird," I mumbled. "It's already open."

Had I forgotten to lock the door as I sometimes did, especially when I was in a hurry?

I proceeded inside with some trepidation, hoping that the house hadn't been burglarized. Fortunately, everything seemed perfectly in order, and I came to the conclusion that *I* must have left the door open. I *was* exhausted when I'd left the house, I reminded myself, and not a little anxious about the state of my marriage.

I put the groceries away and pushed the "call" button for the elevator. Yeah, I know. I should have *walked* upstairs to the master bedroom. It would have been so much more aerobically correct. But I had very little energy, and all I could think about was letting the elevator carry me up to my bedroom so I could take a nice little nap before dinner.

The elevator arrived at the first floor and I walked in, flipped on the light, closed the gate and the elevator door, and pressed the button for the third floor. I leaned against the wall and closed my eyes as I ascended slowly through the house—and I do mean slowly. The woman who'd installed the elevator hadn't cared about speed; consequently, riding between the three floors often felt like creeping along I-95 in rush-hour traffic.

So there I was, riding in my painfully slow elevator, nearly falling asleep standing up, when I suddenly felt a jolt! The elevator had stopped, somewhere between the second and third floors! What's more, the light on the ceiling had gone out. I was stuck in the elevator in the dark, with no light and no air.

"Help!" I screamed. "Somebody help me!"

I started to hyperventilate and my heart sped. Then I remembered the phone that Hunt had insisted on putting on the wall of the elevator. "In case somebody gets stuck," he'd said. "Who's going to get stuck?" I'd said, thinking he was being overly cautious. "You never know, there could be a power outage," he'd said. "With a phone in the elevator, you can always call for help."

Bless you, my darling husband, I said silently.

I was about to reach for the phone when it rang! I was so surprised I actually jumped. Maybe it's Hunt, I thought, telling me he's changed his plans and will be home for dinner after all.

I lifted the receiver eagerly, grateful for the opportunity to ask whoever it was to rescue me.

"Hello?" I said.

"Good evening, Mrs. Price."

It was a strange voice. A high-pitched, singsong voice. A voice that could have belonged to either a man or a woman.

"Yes?" I said tentatively.

"It's very hot and dark in that elevator, isn't it, Mrs. Price? A little claustrophobic, too, wouldn't you agree?"

A chill ran through me. A cold terror I had never experienced in all my life. A realization that my little rest stop in the elevator was no mechanical mishap or fluke of nature; it had been planned—by the person on the phone. The same person who had evidently broken into my house and waited for me to come home and was now calling me on our other line. God, there was a real-live wacko somewhere in my house at that very moment!

"Who . . . who is this?" I said. I could barely get the words out. Fear was strangling me.

"A friend," said the voice, which I now realized was disguised. "Someone who just wants to send you a little message, Mrs. Price."

Mrs. Price. As I told you earlier, no one ever called me "Mrs. Price" except Hunt's parents, telephone salesmen, and members of The Oaks.

Members of The Oaks! The elevator disabler had to be someone
from the club! But who? Had Nedra and Rob driven over to my house
after our little scene in the parking lot? Or had Brendan come to shut
me up? Or was it the Tewksburys? And what about Ducky? And Larkin?

"Mrs. Price? Are you there?" said the eerie, sickeningly sweet
voice.

"Yes," I said, trying not to let hysteria overwhelm me. "I'm here."

"Good. Now, I'll just say what I came to say and leave."

I waited, my anxiety building.

"Stop asking so many questions at the club, Mrs. Price. If you
don't, you'll be sorry."

Jesus. I was sorry already. Sorry that my snooping had gotten back
to Claire's killer and that he or she felt the need to pay me a visit.

"I'll stop," I said. "No more questions."

"That's a good girl."

"Now, whoever you are, won't you please let me out of here?" The
walls of the elevator were beginning to close in on me and I'd only
been in there for a matter of minutes.

"You know, Mrs. Price, I *was* going to flip the circuit breaker back
on," the creepy voice continued, "but I don't believe I will."

"Why?" I wailed. "I said I'd stop snooping around the club. You
can't leave me in here."

"I'm afraid that's exactly what I'm going to do—just to make sure
we understand each other. Have a pleasant evening, Mrs. Price."

"No! Don't go! I can't breathe—"

Click. The voice had hung up.

I pressed my ear against the wall of the elevator and listened carefully. A few minutes later, I heard a door slam. The voice had left the
house, and I was still stuck between floors!

Wait, I calmed myself. The phone.

Now that Claire's killer was gone, the phone was free. I could beep
Tom and he'd come and rescue me. Then I'd tell him what happened and he'd go and arrest the person. End of story. Case closed.
And best of all, the whole thing would be settled in time for me not to
miss the dinner I'd bought myself at the Stop 'n' Shop.

I reached for the phone, lifted the headset off the wall, and dialed
Tom's beeper number. Then I held the phone next to my ear and
waited. Nothing happened. No ring. No recorded message. Nothing.

I hung up and dialed again. Still nothing.

Then I held the headset to my ear. Shit. There was no dial tone.

The phone was dead! The line had been cut! Now I had absolutely no way out of the elevator!

In a total state of panic, I began to pound on the walls of the elevator.

"Help! Help!" I shouted, knowing full well no one would hear me. Two-hundred-year-old houses are built like fortresses—at least ours was. Besides, our closest neighbor was four acres away.

I wracked my brains for a way out of the elevator. I checked the ceiling to see if there was a trap door. I checked the panel to see if there was an emergency power switch. I checked the floor to see if the squirrels had eaten a hole in it—a hole big enough for me to crawl through.

Just as I was standing back up, I developed a terrible cramp in my calf muscle and fell to the floor.

"I've fallen and I can't get up," I yelled, imitating the lady in the TV commercial for those medical alert bracelets. If I'd been wearing one, I could have set off the alarm and a kindly EMS person would have rescued me. It was something to consider for the future—*if* I had a future.

"Help! Help!" I screamed in vain.

Overcome by fear and fatigue, I curled up on the floor in a little ball, my knees tucked under my chest. I tried to calm myself, but my mind ran wild. What if Hunt decided to stay in the city overnight, as he occasionally did when he was working late? What if I couldn't get out of the tiny, claustrophobic elevator, with no light, no air, and no place to lie down? What if Claire's killer came back to the house to bash me over the head with a pitching wedge?

I checked my Rolex, the face of which lit up in the dark. Six-thirty, it said. Even if Hunt's dinner with Leeza only lasted until nine, he wouldn't be home for hours.

I almost cried as I considered my predicament, then I decided against it. I didn't want to sap my strength. I had seen a movie once where these guys from Kentucky were trapped in a coal mine and told not to cry or even breathe hard if they wanted to make it out alive. But trust me, it's hard not to cry when you realize that, even though you're a forty-year-old with no history of bladder control problems, you nearly wet your pants!

Focus on something pleasant, I commanded myself as I sat on the floor of the elevator, trying to ignore the heat and the dark and the lack of ventilation, not to mention the fact that a cold-blooded killer had just broken into my house and threatened me. Think about the dinner you'll have when you get out of here.

I closed my eyes and conjured up images of the meal I had planned for myself: of that sirloin steak, so juicy and tender and flavorful; of those luscious roasted potatoes, all crunchy on the outside and moist on the inside; of the sautéed zucchini, redolent with olive oil and garlic and chopped, vine-ripened tomatoes; of the crisp, dry Merlot I would wash it all down with.

What if I die right here in this elevator and never get to sink my teeth into a meal like that again? I thought suddenly.

And then I cried.

CHAPTER FOURTEEN

♦

I slipped in and out of a kind of haze, never sure if I was asleep or awake. I was conscious of feeling very hot, though, and very closed in, as if a grand piano were standing on my chest.

Once I realized that fantasizing about food only made me depressed, not to mention hungry, I began to concentrate on Hunt—specifically, how we met and fell in love, a period I like to call: "Hunt and Judy: The Good Times."

It all began eight years ago at Karen Benzinger's wedding at Tavern on the Green. I wasn't looking forward to the wedding, because Karen and I were no longer friends. Sure, we'd been pretty chummy in college, but then I'd gone on to a career in book publishing and she'd gone on to an obsession with finding a husband. She wasn't interested in hearing about my cookbooks any more than I was interested in hearing about her blind dates, so we'd drifted apart. Then an invitation came in the mail one day: "Mr. and Mrs. Oscar Benzinger Request the Honour of Your Presence at the Marriage of Their Daughter, Karen Roberta, to Seth Alan Lieberman, at Tavern on the Green . . . blah blah blah." So, she finally hooked one, I remember thinking as I read the wedding invitation and tried to come up with a really good excuse not to go. I mean, who wants to go to one of those circuses where the parents invite everyone they've ever said hello to and the bride and groom invite everyone they've ever said hello to and none of the guests really gives a shit about anything except whether the hors d'oeuvres are any good? But as the date rolled around, I found myself trudging over to Bloomingdale's bridal registry and asking to see what the happy couple had selected and buying them the very thing I hoped no one would buy me when I got married: a crystal bowl. I ask you: in the larger scheme of things, what good is a crystal bowl and how many of them can you really use?

The wedding was on a Saturday night, and since I wasn't a member of the family or one of Karen and Seth's married friends, I was stuck at what is commonly referred to at these affairs as "the singles table." There I was, seated between a slick, game-show-host type, who said he owned time shares in a condo in the Poconos and tried throughout the evening to sell me one, and a thin, intense man whose idea of table talk was: "I think that's *my* water glass you're drinking from; yours is to your right." But the evening wasn't a total loss because sitting right across the table from me, sandwiched between a pair of identical twins named (no kidding) Jan and Fran, was Hunt, looking as miserable and out of place as I felt. About midway through the soup course, approximately five minutes into the band's dreadful rendition of the already dreadful "Close to You," he got up from his seat, walked over to me, and asked me to dance.

I had been eyeing him, of course, willing him to rescue me from Mr. Time Share, who at that very moment was describing the heart-shaped Jacuzzi that came with the condo.

Hunt was so handsome in his tuxedo—his golden hair gleaming, his blue eyes sparkling, his teeth whiter than white. Suddenly, there he was, offering me an escape. "Dance?" he'd said simply. "Please," I'd replied, a little too eagerly, I imagine.

Then off we went, onto the dance floor, where we were nearly crushed to death by men who couldn't manage a simple fox trot and women who were wearing too much makeup and not enough clothes. Hunt was a wonderful dancer, I learned, as he navigated us through the crowd. We talked as we danced—the basic stuff like: "How do you know Karen and Seth?" And: "What do you do?" And: "How long do you think it will be before they cut the wedding cake and this thing will be over?"

It turned out that Hunt had played racquetball with Seth, who was a dentist, twice. "Twice? And he invited you to his wedding?" I said. "Yes," he said. "And now that I've met you, I think he did me a favor."

Oh, boy, I thought. The blond god likes me.

We remained on the dance floor through "Feelings," through "You Are the Sunshine of My Life," even through the more up-tempo "Mustang Sally," which the lead vocalist had retitled "Mustang Karen" after being told that a Mustang was what the groom had given the bride for a wedding present. Eventually, the band took a break so the main course could be served. We went back to our table, and Hunt asked Mr. Time Share if he would switch seats. I was ecstatic. For the rest of the night, we sat next to each other, ate, danced, talked about ourselves, talked about world problems, talked about when we could reasonably leave the party without offending our hosts. By the time the bride and groom finally cut the cake, we were in love. I mean it. Yes, it was fast, and yes, we hardly knew each other, but it happened—for both of us. I had just broken up with an aspiring movie critic named Greg, who, because he couldn't get a job criticizing movies, criticized me instead. Boy, did my self-esteem take a bruising in that relationship! Hunt had just broken up with the lovely and talented Bree, who threatened to make his life miserable if he ever remarried, which he had no intention of doing. But then he met me—and I caught Karen's bouquet. So much for intentions.

He took me home from the wedding and moved into my apartment two weeks later. We were happy. Ecstatically happy. Deliriously happy. Hunt was the nicest, sweetest, most considerate man I'd ever met. A real gentleman, except in bed, where he threw caution—and manners—to the wind and made love to me the way I'd always dreamed about. No, he wasn't Mr. Personality and he tended to wimp out when it came to his ex-wife and he couldn't tell a joke to save his life, but he was honest and true and very different from all the weirdos I'd been meeting, and he made me feel loved in a way I can hardly describe.

When did things begin to change between us? I wondered as I sat on the floor of the elevator and tried not to pass out. The air was fetid and stagnant. I couldn't remember ever feeling so uncomfortable. When had my marriage begun to—

Oh my God! What was that?

I listened. I could have sworn I heard a noise. A car outside? A door opening? What?

I checked my watch. It was nine-fifteen. Too early for Hunt to be home.

I summoned all my strength and stood up. Then I pressed my ear to the wall of the elevator and listened.

Another noise. It *was* a door opening! Someone was in the house! The question was who? Had Claire's killer come back to torture me some more? Should I call out? Or stay quiet? I was paralyzed.

I sank back down on the floor, terrified that the psycho from The Oaks had returned to finish the job.

Please, God, I prayed, sweat pouring down my face. Please let me be saved. I know I haven't been a perfect wife, and I haven't been patient enough with Kimberley, and I haven't lifted a finger to help the starving people of Rwanda. But please don't let me die in this elevator. Please help me—

Footsteps! I heard them! They were coming from the floor below!

I began to shake uncontrollably, the terror so overwhelming I couldn't make it disappear, even for a second. Visions of a gun, a knife, a pitching wedge, flooded my mind. Then blood—lots of blood. Mine.

More footsteps!

I huddled in the corner of the elevator, my heart beating so loud it—

"Jude? Are you home?"

Oh, thank God! It was Hunt!

"Yes! Yes! I'm here!" I screamed and pounded on the walls. I had never been so happy to hear Hunt's voice. Never. Not even when he'd stood in front of that half-drunk Justice of the Peace and said "I do."

"Jude? Where are you?" he called out.

"In the elevator!" I yelled to him. "I'm trapped! Turn the circuit breaker back on and get me out of here!"

I heard Hunt run down to the basement. A few minutes later, the light in the elevator went on and I felt a jolt as I began to ascend to the third floor, as per the original plan.

Hunt must have raced up the stairs because he got to the master bedroom before I did. When he opened the elevator door and saw me curled up on the floor, he gasped.

"Jude! How long have you been in here?" he said, then came to me, helping me up. I collapsed in his arms.

"My God," he mumbled. "You're half-dead!"

"Maybe two-thirds." I tried to smile. "You're a sight for sore eyes, you know that?"

He gathered me up in his arms and carried me out of the elevator, over to the bed, then let me down carefully.

"I'll get you some water," he said and ran down to the kitchen.

Within minutes he was back with a tall glass of ice water, which I gulped down so fast I started to burp.

"Excuse me," I said.

"Don't worry about it," he said. "Just tell me what happened."

"First, I've got to call Detective Cunningham," I said.

"What's he got to do with this?" said Hunt.

"Someone broke into the house and was still here when I came home this afternoon," I said. "Whoever it was hid while I got into the elevator to go upstairs and then he—or she—turned the circuit breaker off. The elevator stopped between floors with me in it."

"Jesus, I don't believe this," said Hunt as he pulled on his left earlobe.

"It gets worse," I said. "Our little mischief maker called me in the elevator from our second line."

"Called you? Why?" he said. "What kind of a kook—"

"The kind that plays golf at The Oaks," I said.

"Aw, Jude. Don't start that stuff. Not at a time like this."

"Listen to me, Hunt," I said. "It was Claire's killer who broke into our house and trapped me in the elevator. He called me on the phone and told me he was sending me a message."

"A message?"

"Yeah. That if I didn't stop asking questions and snooping around at the club, I'd be sorry."

Hunt's jaw dropped.

"I'm going to call Tom," I said as I started to get up off the bed.

"No," he said, stopping me. "I'll call him. You drink your water and rest."

"All right, but you'll have to go downstairs to call him. The phone line up here has been cut."

"Oh, so that's why I couldn't get through."

"You tried to call?"

"Yeah. Several times. I wanted to tell you I canceled my dinner plans with Leeza. When I couldn't get through, I called the operator and she said there was trouble on the line. I figured I'd better come home and see what was going on. I would have been home sooner, but the train broke down in Norwalk. We sat on the tracks for forty-five minutes."

"It doesn't matter," I said. "At least you're home now." I patted Hunt's hand. "Why did you cancel your dinner, by the way?"

Hunt lowered his head. "I've been a mess all day," he admitted. "I couldn't get my mind to focus on business. I couldn't think about anything but you and me, about how we were going to fix the marriage. I love you, Judy. I'm so sorry if I haven't shown it."

He put his head on my stomach and cried. We both did. After months of acting like two shits passing in the night, we had finally connected, finally reached out, finally gotten in touch with each other. It was a poignant and powerful moment—a scene straight out of a TV infomercial during which contentious couples have a tearful reconciliation and then endorse a series of self-help videotapes.

"If anything ever happened to you, I'd die," he sobbed as I stroked the back of his head.

"Nothing's going to happen to me," I reassured him.

"You're damn right," he said. "This is the end of that job of yours. No more police work."

I took my hand off his head. "No more police work? Are you kidding? We're so close to catching Claire's killer now. The guy is panicking. He's going to reveal himself any day."

"Great, but he's not going to reveal himself to my wife. I love her too much to see her hurt."

"I love you too," I said. "Come lie down next to me for a minute."

He climbed onto the bed next to me and we held each other. Neither of us spoke for a while. Then he broke the silence.

"I'm sorry I didn't believe you about the club," he said. "Obviously, someone from The Oaks did kill Claire, no matter how badly I didn't want it to be true."

I nodded.

"And another thing," he said. "I'm sorry I've been so wrapped up in making partner at F&F that I've been blind to how badly our marriage has eroded."

I nodded again.

"And one more thing," he said. "I'm sorry I've been so passive in terms of Bree and Kimberley. I hate myself for the way I've been letting them manipulate me. But all that's going to change. I promise."

I nodded again, then said, "May I ask what provoked all these 'I'm sorry's'?"

"Yes," he said. "Finding out about you and Detective Cunningham. About your *working* for Detective Cunningham. It made me see how far apart we'd drifted. You wouldn't have kept all that a secret from me if we'd been close, the way we used to be."

"No, I wouldn't have. I'm glad you see that now."

He kissed me. "I see it," he said. "But that doesn't mean I approve of your being a police informant. I don't approve of anything that might put you in danger, Jude.''

"I love you," I said again. "I always have. Even when you were being a boob." I kissed him. "But working with Tom has given me something important to do, made me feel like I'm contributing to the public good in some small way. Think about it. Think how *you* would feel if you could help the cops catch the person who murdered somebody. Wouldn't it make you feel worthwhile?''

"Of course it would. It's just that I want to protect you.''

"Oh, Hunt. That's really sweet.''

"Just like I protected you eight years ago. From Mr. Time Share, remember?''

We looked at each other and started to laugh, recalling Karen Benzinger's wedding. "Do I remember?" I smiled. "I was thinking of Mr. Time Share only an hour ago. It's what got me through my evening in the elevator.''

We clung to each other and began to kiss, first tenderly, then feverishly, with more urgency. I had forgotten how warm and soft Hunt's lips were, how succulent, how—

"Whoa, Jude," he said, pulling away. "Before we get carried away, we'd better call your friend the detective. The sooner we report what happened, the sooner he can catch the guy.''

So much for feverish. "You're right," I said with obvious disappointment.

"But the minute he's out of here," Hunt added, "I'm going to make mad, passionate love to you, Judy. I just hope you have the strength after what you've been through tonight.''

"Oh, I have the strength, don't you worry," I said, brightening. "You know the old saying: 'Where there's a will there's a lay.' ''

Tom came rushing over after I told him about my adventure in the elevator. Along for the ride were his partner, Detective Creamer, and several other officers, who combed the house for fingerprints, hair fibers, whatever.

Hunt, Tom, and I sat in the living room, while I gave both of them a play-by-play of my eventful day. Then Tom and I went over the list of suspects from the club and discussed which of them may have broken into the house. Hunt remained silent until Ducky Laughton's name came up.

"Now wait a minute," he said. "Ducky's a business associate of mine. And a golf buddy. He's a darn nice guy."

Hunt said things like "darn nice guy." But hey, nobody's perfect.

"According to Judy, Mr. Laughton had a relationship with the deceased," Tom pointed out.

"That doesn't mean he killed her, for God's sake," said Hunt.

"Calm down, honey," I said. "We don't really know what happened between Ducky and Claire all those years ago. But it didn't end well, that we know. And he didn't stay at Berkeley, we know that too. He was kicked out because of some 'trouble' and never saw Claire again, until they ran into each other at the club."

"So?" said Hunt.

"So, your wife is simply saying that there may be more to Mr. Laughton than meets the eye," said Tom.

"Look, Detective," said Hunt. "I don't need an interpreter to understand my wife. Besides, I know Ducky Laughton. He's a vice president at Fitzgerald & Franklin. He's a member of the club's Finance Committee. He's—"

"Mr. Price," Tom interrupted. "You said you were in your office all day today. Was Mr. Laughton there too?"

Hunt thought for a minute. "Actually, no, not all day. I saw him in the morning, at about ten-thirty, but he left the office after that. He said he had some personal business to take care of."

Tom and I looked at each other.

"What could be more personal than trapping your friend's wife in her elevator?" I said.

Hunt shook his head. "I don't know what to believe anymore," he said.

"Look, everybody, let's not jump to conclusions," said Tom. "It will be easy enough to find out where Mr. Laughton was this afternoon. The same goes for all the other people you suspect, Judy."

"All the other people? How many are there?" said Hunt.

"Half a dozen," I said.

Hunt turned to Tom. "It sounds like my wife has been doing the police's job," he said. "May I ask what *you've* been doing to solve this case?"

"Sure. I've been interviewing everybody who had anything to do with Claire Cox," said Tom. "Do you have any idea how many people that woman associated with? Well, I'll tell you: hundreds! And I'll tell you something else: this is a big case and my boss would really like to solve it—soon. I'm being pressured like you can't believe. But now, after what happened here today, I think we can narrow the suspects list down to the people at your club. Somebody there threatened Judy, somebody who didn't want her snooping around in his business."

"That doesn't mean the guy killed Claire Cox," Hunt said. "Maybe there's something else he didn't want Judy to find out about."

"Like what?" I said. "That he went in the pool without showering first?"

Hunt shrugged.

"Listen, we're all tired," said Tom, who turned to me. "Judy, the next time you go to the club, try to find out where—"

"The next time she goes to the club?" Hunt said. "You don't expect her to continue this informant thing after what's happened, do you?"

"Yes," Tom said, "but a little more subtly. She's about to help us solve the case. She's got the murderer scared enough that he risked getting caught. Next time he's going to make a mistake. And then we'll nab him."

"What if the mistake he makes is killing Judy? Then what?" said Hunt.

"I'm going to put a guy outside your house," said Tom. "For protection. Nobody's going to break in, believe me. I don't want Judy hurt any more than you do, Mr. Price."

"I appreciate that, Detective, but what about when she leaves the house?" said Hunt. "What about when she goes snooping around at the club again? Who's going to protect her then, huh?"

Simultaneously and without missing a beat, Tom and I looked at Hunt and said, "You are."

Surprisingly, Hunt went for it. No, not at first, but gradually, after Tom and I convinced him that helping me with my informant duties wouldn't be a betrayal of his friends at The Oaks but rather a chance for him to protect me and help the police with their murder investigation, he agreed. He *was* on the club's Finance Committee, after all, and had a much wider circle of contacts there than I did. With his help, the murderer might be brought to justice that much sooner, Tom pointed out.

"Just think! We'll be working together to solve a crime," I said to Hunt as we lay in bed an hour or so after Tom and the other cops had left. "We'll be like Robert Wagner and Stephanie Powers on 'Hart to Hart.'"

"What's the matter with Nick and Nora Charles?"

"Nothing. We'll be like them too."

I hugged Hunt. He was being a good sport. I knew how much he loved the club, how hard it would be for him to finger one of the members as Claire's murderer.

"Boochie?" I said as I snuggled next to him under the covers. "Boochie" was the little love name we called each other when we were feeling amorous. Sometimes we shortened it to "Booch" and sometimes we lengthened it to "Boochikins," but you get the point.

"Yes, Booch?" Hunt said as he kissed the tip of my nose.

"I love you," I said.

"I love you too," he said.

"I love you as much as ever," I said.

"I love you more than ever," he said.

"I love you in ways that—"

Hunt silenced me by pressing his lips on mine. For the next fifteen minutes or so, we did nothing but give each other wet, sloppy, over-heated, groin-stirring soul kisses, one overlapping into the next. There was barely time to breathe! It was wonderful, as if we couldn't get enough of each other, couldn't tear our mouths away from each other. I knew I'd missed having intimate contact with Hunt, but I hadn't realized how much until those kisses.

"I want to touch you," Hunt murmured. "All over."

He began to undress me, and I began to undress him. Never very adept at this part of the sex act—the undressing one's partner part—Hunt fumbled with the buttons on my blouse and I fumbled with the buckle on his belt. Then I fumbled with the buttons on his shirt and he fumbled with the hooks on my bra. Eventually, we got where we wanted to be, which was naked.

"Oh, you are so beautiful, Boochie," said Hunt as he appraised my body. "I'm a lucky, lucky man."

Boy, did flattery turn me on. I reached out and touched Hunt's throbbing, outstretched manhood.

"No," I purred. "I'm the lucky one."

We made love for what seemed like an eternity, although the entire thing probably lasted no more than twenty minutes.

"We really should do this more often," said Hunt as we lay in each other's arms, basking in the afterglow.

"How much more often?" I asked.

"Oh, I don't know. Maybe two, three, four times a day. Something like that," said Hunt.

"What about your golf?" I asked. "How will you fit me in?"

He rolled over and kissed me. Then he put my hand on his sex organ, which, I was surprised to find, had bounced back in a big way. "No, Booch," he whispered in my ear. "The question is, How will *you* fit *me* in?"

"I don't know, but I'm willing to give it a try," I said. "Come here."

We were up to our old tricks, Hunt and I, making love, then making jokes, then making love all over again, just like we used to. When I finally fell asleep, after another, especially satisfying go-around, Claire and The Oaks and my aborted elevator ride were the farthest things from my mind. What was on my mind, as I passed into dreamland, was that I had my husband back, and that together, we could solve anything—even a murder.

CHAPTER FIFTEEN

♦

Tom stopped by at nine o'clock the next morning. He wanted us to know that he'd put a man outside to watch the house. He also wanted to give us some advice.

"Don't tell anyone about the break-in," he said. "Especially anyone at The Oaks. Just go there and make small talk and see what happens. I'm betting that whoever gave you that warning in the elevator is getting very nervous. And if he's nervous, he's going to make a mistake and reveal himself."

"Or herself," I added.

"Herself? Do you really think one of the women at the club could have killed Claire?" asked Hunt.

I shrugged. "Larkin's a nut case when it comes to tennis. I wouldn't put it past her to knock off her only real rival. And then there's Nedra. First I thought maybe she wanted Claire out of the way so Ducky wouldn't start up with her again. Now I think Nedra doesn't give a damn about Ducky. Maybe Nedra and Rob were worried that Claire would get him fired and ruin their cozy little arrangement. Maybe they were the ones who killed her—and broke into our house. Let's not forget that it was Nedra who chewed me out for being such a busybody at the club."

"What about Ducky?" said Hunt. "You two mentioned him as a

possible suspect, but he couldn't have killed anybody. I've known him for years and he's a super guy. Easygoing, no temper. He doesn't even get mad on the golf course—and that's saying something.''

"I agree with you, Mr. Price," said Tom. "I don't think he's a killer either. All we've got on him is that he and Claire were lovers years ago and that she broke it off. Not a big deal. I'm more interested in Brendan, the chef, and the fact that he's the secret son of a big shot at The Oaks—a big shot who happened to be a relative of the deceased. Something's fishy there.''

"We'll do our best to find out what it is, Detective," said Hunt, showing off his new cooperative spirit. It's amazing what getting laid after a long drought can do for a person's mood. Hunt was positively buoyant—for him.

"Please call me Tom, Mr. Price," said Tom.

"Sure, Tom. And I'm Hunt," said Hunt.

"And I'm going into the kitchen to make coffee," I said, and left the two of them to chat. When I came back into the living room, they were smiling and patting each other on the back and acting like long-lost buddies.

"He's not a bad guy," Hunt acknowledged when we were alone. "Did you know he was Bill Cunningham's son? Bill Cunningham, the guy from Pubtel?''

I nodded. "I think they're estranged though," I said.

"Estranged or not, Tom comes from money. He told me he's thinking of getting into the Market. We decided that when this case is all over, I'm going to set up an account for him at F&F."

I looked at Hunt and shook my head. The man had tunnel vision when it came to people: anyone who breathed was a potential client.

"I still think he's got the hots for you, Jude," he went on. "I can tell by the way he looks at you.''

"Don't be silly," I said. "He's just lonely. His wife was killed, and I don't think he's been serious about anyone since.''

"Killed? What a tough break," said Hunt as he put his arms around me. "If he loved her half as much as I love you, he must be very lonely. I'd be lost without you, Booch.''

"Not to worry," I said. "I'm not going anywhere.''

After a man from Southern New England Telephone came to restore our severed phone line, Hunt spent a couple of hours talking to his office and giving whoever was on the other end very specific instructions regarding cattle and corn and soybeans. On our second line, I called Valerio, to whom I hadn't spoken in a week or so.

"How eez my beautiful Judy?" he asked. "Eez she ready to divorce that husband of hers?"

"I'm fine, how are you?" I said, ignoring the Casanova routine as I always did.

"How am I?" he said. "Righta now, not so good."

"What's wrong?" I asked.

"I caught my sous-chef with his hand in the cookie jar," he said.

"He was stealing money from the restaurant?"

"That's right. Not only that, he was making me look bad to my customers. I'm telling you, Judy, running a restaurant eez no picnic."

"I'm sure it isn't. How did you find out what he was up to?"

"I tasted his bolognese sauce."

"I don't understand."

"Eet was sheet."

"So?"

"So I make my bolognese sauce with ground veal. Eet gives a richer tasta. But this guy used grounda beef. Chopped chuck, would you believe!"

"Valerio, just because he deviated from your recipe doesn't make him a thief."

"You don't get it," he said, impatient and accentless. "I buy the best, most expensive milk-fed veal you can get, and this guy packs it up, takes it home, and serves the chuck to *my* customers!"

"That's terrible," I said. "I hope you fired him."

"Of course, I fired him. But now I have to find somebody to replace him."

"That shouldn't be hard, should it? I mean, there are so many people out there looking for jobs in this age of consolidating and downsizing and laying off. I should know."

"Yes, but it's hard to find an *honest* person in the restaurant business. Everybody lies and cheats and steals. There are scams going on all the time. I'm thinking of selling the restaurant and devoting all my time to writing cookbooks, going on talk shows, and letting your husband make me rich in the commodities market."

"Selling the restaurant? But you put your life's blood into that place."

"Yeah, and now I want to stop the bleeding. You have no idea how much shit goes on when you own a restaurant. This thing with the sous-chef is just the latest horror story. Last year, when I was on my book tour, I put my chef in charge of buying the food. Disaster. Complete disaster.''

"Why? What happened? Didn't he buy the best quality?"

"No, but he *said* he did."

"I don't understand."

"He spent the restaurant's money—*my* money—on prime meats and free-range chicken and fresh fish, but what he had delivered to the restaurant was your basic, garden variety, supermarket crap."

"Why would he do that?"

Valerio laughed. "Judy, my darling. It's a good thing you're beautiful because you sure are naive. The man had a kickback scam going with the food boys. They billed us for top quality, sold us shit, and pocketed the difference—a percentage for the boys, a much bigger percentage for my chef."

"That's awful. How did you find out about it?"

"My accountant figured it out. I used to complain that he charged too much, but he saved me a lot of grief."

"Did you really need *him* to figure out that you were being ripped off? I mean, couldn't you taste the food and tell that the ingredients weren't up to your standards?"

"If I'd *been* there," said Valerio. "But thanks to Charlton House, I was getting up at five o'clock in the morning to show the viewers of 'Good Morning, Cleveland' how to prepare my Swordfish with Pistachio Nuts." He paused, waiting for my reaction. There was none, because I was deep in my own thoughts, busily pondering the implications of his little anecdote, wondering if Brendan Hardy might be pulling the same stunt on The Oaks as Valerio's chef had pulled on him. "Judy? Are you there?"

"Oh, sorry. Yes, I'm here." My mind raced. If Brendan was ripping off The Oaks and Claire found out about it, wouldn't that have given her an added reason for wanting him out of the club—and in jail? And wouldn't *that* have given him a real motive for killing her?

"Well, enough about me," said Valerio. "Tell me how you are, my gorgeous creature."

"Valerio, listen," I said. "Remember when you came up to Connecticut the Friday before July Fourth?"

"Of course I remember. You picked me up at the train. You were wearing a short little white skirt."

"Right. And Hunt and I took you to our country club for dinner, remember?"

"How could I forget? The fooda was sheet."

"Exactly. But you didn't say anything about the possibility that we were being ripped off, that our chef was doing the same thing to the members as your chef was doing to you."

"No, why should I? I just assumed that your club was like a lot of WASP clubs: great golf course, all the booze you can drink, lousy food. I figured the chef was a dud—period—and that, since members at a place like that don't care what they eat, nobody noticed. Anyway, why should *I* suspect something about some country club I don't belong to? Hunt said he was on the Finance Committee there, right? He'd know if something funny was going on. At least, that's what he said."

Yeah, but would he know? He was a commodities broker, not an accountant. Besides, he didn't know a thing about restaurants. You could tell him that the broiled flounder on his plate was fillet of horse mackerel and he wouldn't blink. What's more, he didn't even manage our family finances—I did. The last time he handled our tax returns, we were audited, for God's sake. He couldn't spot a restaurant scam if it hit him in the face.

And neither could the other members of the Finance Committee, I was sure. Evan Sutcliffe, the head of the committee and the club's treasurer, was in the Christmas tree business, and Logan Marshall was a former ambassador to Uruguay. Addison Bidwell didn't do much of anything except fritter away the family trust fund. And then, of course, there was Ducky, who worked with Hunt at F&F and knew about things like cattle and gas and crude oil. What did any of them know about running a country club and its three restaurants? Nothing, absolutely nothing. And the truth was, nobody cared whether anybody knew anything. These CEOs and former ambassadors and perennial trust-fund user-uppers came to the club every weekend to play golf, to see their friends, to score points with people who could help them in some way, to relax, be seen, hang out. The last thing they wanted to do on a sunny Saturday afternoon was sit in a hot, stuffy room and pore over the club's dining room receipts. Why not just sign the checks, pay the bills, and leave all the tough stuff to the accountants, who did the books once a year?

No, there was plenty of room for a scam at The Oaks, plenty of rope for someone to hang himself with.

"Judy? Are you there?" said Valerio into the phone, as I had completely forgotten about him. "You're really not holding up your end of the conversation today, darling."

"I know," I said. "But I've got to go now, Valerio. We'll talk soon, okay?"

I hung up and went to find Hunt. He was on the phone with Kimberley.

"I love you too, pumpkin," I heard him say. "I understand that. Of course I do. That sounds great, but I want to talk to Judy about it before I say yes. No, Kim, it *is* important what Judy thinks. Why? Because she's my wife and your stepmother. I'm sorry you feel that way. No. I don't care what your mother says. When you're with us, you'll abide by our rules. No. No. Kim, we've been all over that. Yes, I'll talk to Judy and call you back. Give my love to Grandma and Grandpa. Bye, sweetheart."

I walked over to him and threw my arms around his neck. "Whoever thought up the expression, 'You can't teach an old dog new tricks,' was an asshole," I said.

"You're referring to me, I presume?" Hunt grinned.

"Yes," I said, mussing his hair so it fell across his brow. "I was wrong to think you couldn't change where Kimberley and her mother were concerned. I heard you with my own ears. You said no to her—not once but three times! In one conversation! Do you realize what a milestone that is?"

"Yup."

"What's more, you gave her the message that you and I are a united front. I'm sure it was hard for you, but you did it, kid. I'm proud of you!"

I kissed him.

"What did she want you to say yes to, by the way?" I asked.

"She wants us to take her with us when we go to visit your folks in Florida," said Hunt.

"Now that's a surprise," I said. "I thought Kimberley hated taking trips with us. Or maybe it was just *me* she hated taking trips with."

"Well, apparently she's had a change of heart. How do you feel about her coming along, Jude?"

"The truth?"

Hunt nodded.

I took a deep breath. I didn't want to upset Hunt, not when we'd just reconciled. On the other hand, I'd envisioned our trip down to Boca Raton for my father's seventy-fifth birthday as a sort of second honeymoon for us, a respite from weekends at The Oaks, a break from the craziness of Hunt's job and my lack of one, a change of

scene at the very least. Bringing Kimberley along would put a different spin on the trip.

"I don't know if we can get another plane ticket," I said. "The
airlines get pretty booked up the weekend before Labor Day, don't
they?"

"Could be. But what if we could get a ticket for Kimberley? Your
parents have four bedrooms, and I don't think they'd mind having an
extra guest. What about you, Jude? How would *you* feel about her
joining us?"

The moment of truth. "I would rather she didn't, I admit it," I
said. "When Kimberley's around, things get very tense between us."

"What if I made sure they didn't get tense?" said Hunt. "What if I
swore to you that I wouldn't let her come between us, that the trip
would be just as much fun as if she weren't with us?"

I looked at Hunt and felt his conflict. Of course he wanted to spend
time with his daughter. I'd be a fool not to understand and support
that. She was his baby. He adored her. It killed him not to be able to
see her more often. Who was I to come between them?

"Under those conditions, I say yes, she can come with us," I said.
"Maybe the trip will be a fresh start for all of us."

"I love you," said Hunt. "I really love you."

"I love you too," I said. "But there's just one thing."

"I know. I'll call Delta about getting another ticket."

"No, it's something else. We can't go anywhere until Claire's murderer is arrested. I'm on the Belford Police Department's payroll
now, and Tom never said anything about vacation time."

"Oh, shit. I didn't think of that."

"Besides, I wouldn't feel right about leaving town before the case is
solved."

"Then we'd better solve it in a hurry, don't you think?"

I nodded and kissed Hunt. I couldn't wait for us to go to Florida,
even if it was unbearably hot and humid there in August and even if
Kimberley was coming along. The thought of getting out of Belford
thrilled me. But first, we had to find out who killed Claire.

I told Hunt about my conversation with Valerio.

"It struck me that Brendan might be ripping off the club," I said,
"that he might be in cahoots with his vendors. What if they've been
selling him inferior goods and he's been overcharging the club and
pocketing the money?"

"Why would he do that?" said Hunt.

"Because they all 'do that,' according to Valerio," I said. "He says the restaurant business is nothing but kickbacks and scams and dirty dealing."

"Okay, but let's not forget about Duncan Tewksbury. Why would Brendan go to work for his father and then steal from him?"

I thought for a minute. "Maybe Brendan isn't stealing *from* his father. Maybe he's stealing *for* his father. Maybe Duncan's in on the scam."

"Duncan? A crook?"

"Why not?"

"Because he doesn't have to steal from the club. He's already got plenty of money."

"Oh, yeah? What does he do for a living, anyway?"

"He does what a lot of the older members do: nothing. He's a retired something or other."

"I think we should find out what kind of a something or other he was before he retired," I suggested. "Maybe he spread himself a little too thin and now he's using the club to fatten himself up again. Maybe that's why he hired Brendan, Mr. Ex-Con, so they could cook up a rip-off scheme together."

"Jesus. This is all so crazy. I joined The Oaks so I could expose myself to people who were . . . who were 'nifty,' for want of a better word."

"Hunt, *any* word but 'nifty' would be a better word. I can't believe I'm married to a man who uses the word 'nifty.' "

"I can't believe I'm married to a woman who has involved me in a murder case."

"I think you're glad. I think you're enjoying all this."

"I hate to admit it but I am, just a little. It's very different from trading pork bellies."

"Yes, well, getting back to Brendan and Duncan, see if you can find out how Duncan made his money and whether he has any left."

"Right."

"But more important, see if you can get us into the bookkeeping office at the club."

"No trick to that. All we have to do is walk in. I've got a key."

"Fabulous! What do you say we go to that Tennis Tussle at the club tonight? Then after we get knocked out of the tournament in the first round, we'll sneak off to the bookkeeping office and have a look-see at the invoices?"

"What makes you think we'll get knocked out in the first round? I haven't played much tennis this summer, but I still have a wicked top-spin forehand."

"Really? Well, I have no forehand at all. Besides, I say we should lose in the first round on purpose. It'll give us more time to dig around before they start serving the Bloody Marys and barbecued chicken."

"Why rush back for the Bloody Marys and barbecued chicken? You hate barbecued chicken."

"Yeah, but it's included in the Tennis Tussle. We've already paid for it. Surely, you remember my mother's motto: 'If you've paid for it, you should eat it.' "

"That's one of the things I love about you, Booch. You've got such a good head on your shoulders."

"Oh, Hunt, I think we're close."

"You're darn right we're close, especially after that marathon in bed last night."

"I meant, I think we're close to solving this case. If we can prove that Brendan has been ripping off the club—and that Duncan knew about it—we've got our murderers."

"What do you say we celebrate?"

"How?"

Hunt checked his watch. "I'm all done with my calls to the office, and we don't have to be at the club for a few hours. How about a matinee?"

A matinee. The word transported me back to the first year Hunt and I were married. He used to call me at work in the middle of the day and ask me to meet him at our apartment. "For a quickie," he'd say. Sometimes I could get away from the office and sometimes I couldn't. Either way, I was enormously flattered by his interest. And then, seemingly overnight, his interest waned. Pretty soon, there were no phone calls suggesting a midday tryst. There were no phone calls suggesting much of anything—not even lunch. There were calls about who was picking Kimberley up at school and did I remember to call the plumber and was the termite guy coming this week or next. But no "Do you want to run home and make love?" Not until now. Now, seven years into our marriage, it appeared that Hunt had redis-covered sex. Had being involved in a murder investigation revved him up? Had the idea of working for the police turned him on? Or had our near separation and tearful reconciliation recharged his bat-tery?

Who cared *why* he was back, I decided. He was back—period. The man I married was back!

"A matinee sounds divine," I said. "Where would you like to have it?"

"In the Jacuzzi," he said.

"A hot bath? It's ninety degrees out."

"I'll make the water nice and cool."

"No, I'm not in the mood for the Jacuzzi. I hate it when my skin shrivels up. How about the living room floor? On the dhurrie rug in front of the fireplace?"

"No, that rug is wool. Too scratchy."

"Okay. What about the rug in the library? It's synthetic."

"I don't think I want to do it on the floor. My back's sore. I overswung on a drive last weekend and it hasn't been the same since. Let's do it on the couch in the library."

"I just had it recovered."

"How about the rattan chaise in the sun room?"

"Perfect," I said. "The fabric's Scotchguarded."

So off we went, arm in arm, our bodies poised for a thrilling half-hour or so, our minds secure in the knowledge that sex, like marriage, is a mysterious and wonderful thing.

CHAPTER SIXTEEN

♦

Hunt and I were a few minutes late for the Tennis Tussle. When we arrived at the club, Johnny, the head pro, had already posted the tournament ladder showing which couples we'd be playing in which order. Most of the teams had gone out to the courts and were warming up for their matches.

"Oh, shit. Look," I whispered to Hunt as I surveyed the ladder. "We're playing Susan and Conrad Dingle in the first round."

"What's wrong with that?" said Hunt. "Conrad's a neat guy, an orthopedic surgeon specializing in sports injuries. The last time I saw him he said he wanted my advice about commodities. He—"

"Hunt, would you stop with the networking?" I cut him off. Conrad Dingle was far from a "neat guy," but that was beside the point. The point was to get the tennis over with as quickly as possible so we could start snooping. "What I'm trying to say is that Susan and Conrad Dingle are as hopeless a mixed doubles team as we are."

"I'm hurt."

"Sorry, but it's true. She's a klutz and he's a hog."

"Which am I, in your opinion? A klutz or a hog?"

"A hog, of course. You're always poaching in mixed doubles. When I play with you, it's a miracle I get to hit the ball at all. But the reason

I'm bringing this up is that since we're evenly matched with the Dingles, we'll never get off the court unless we tank the match."

"You really want us to lose on purpose?"

"Yes. This is not the time to be macho. This is the time to solve Claire's murder so we can close the case, go to Florida, and have a wonderful time."

"I'm having a wonderful time right now," said Hunt, his eyes filled with love. He reminded me of a puppy dog. A golden retriever in a tennis outfit. I reached out to pet him.

"I love you," he said, looking at me adoringly.

Boy, it was nice to see that look again, that look that made me feel positively cherished.

"I love you too," I said softly. "But we've got a job to do, you know?"

"I know, but I can't help it if I'm happy," he said. "Happy to be back where we started."

I nodded and put my arms around him. We held each other for a few seconds. Then I spotted the Dingles on Court 13 and suggested that we walk over to join them.

Susan Dingle was thin and dark and humorless. She was so humorless that she never said "Good shot" to her opponent. Never. Not even if you hit the zippiest forehand or the snappiest backhand or the most hard-to-return serve. What's more, she always had this pinched, sour expression on her face, as if she spent every waking moment sucking on lemons. You'd never know she had gobs of money and loads of friends and every reason in the world to be happy. And as for her husband, "Con," as his intimates called him, he was an incredible asshole. No class whatsoever. For starters, he had the sense of humor of a fourth grader. Totally immature. He was also one of those tennis players who never shut up—not even while a point was in progress. You'd be playing your heart out, running to this side of the court, running to that side of the court, and he'd yell (and I do mean yell) things like: *"Oh, brother, that sun is hot!"* And: *"Wow! I thought that ball was out but it caught the line!"* And: *"I can't believe how much spin there was on that dropshot!"* All in the middle of a point! With him around, there was no way to maintain your concentration. But worst of all was the way he spit on the court. I swear to God, the man actually cleared his throat and spit—like those gross pigs you see in the street or in the subway—as if it were the most natural thing in the world to hurl little blobs of phlegm onto the ground, just inches from your feet. I tell you, it's amazing what members of a country club will put up with.

But then, that's what they get for being members of a country club: they get stuck with people like Susan and Conrad Dingle.

"Well, hello, you two," Conrad bellowed as Hunt and I approached him and his lovely wife. "Susan and I were wondering if you'd chickened out when you saw that *we* were your opponents!" Conrad flapped his arms and made clucking noises. Get it? *Chicken*ed out? God, what a jerk.

"Sorry we're late," said Hunt as he unzipped his racquet case and removed his mammoth Wilson Sledgehammer.

"If you'd been five minutes later, we would have won the match by default," said Susan. "It says so in the rule book: If your opponent's a no-show, you win automatically."

I smiled. "Yes, well we're *not* a no-show. We showed up."

"Just in time for us to whup your asses, right, Susie?" Conrad elbowed his wife, who winced and gave him a dirty look.

"Darn," said Hunt. "We forgot to bring balls."

"I have balls," said Conrad as he held up a can of Wilsons. Then, thinking he had just said something terribly double entendre-ish, he snickered like a goofy adolescent.

While Conrad Dingle struggled to open the screw-top can, he and Hunt chatted about the commodities market, interest rates, and the pros and cons of air bags, and I was forced to make conversation with Susan.

"How've you been, Susan?" I asked old pursed lips.

"Oh, you know how it is. We're redoing the house." She sighed in that plaintive, exhausted way people who are redoing their houses have. "The place is a mess. Completely uninhabitable. Especially the kitchen."

I'm sure I was supposed to fall to my knees and sob over Susan's trouble, but I really couldn't work up much sympathy. I mean, what is it with people who get their houses redone? Nobody is putting a gun to their head and saying, "Tear down the walls, refinish the floors, renovate the kitchen, or I'll blow your brains out!" And yet, they act so put-upon, so victimized, so . . . abused. Show me a person who whines about her contractor, her decorator, and her wallpaper hanger, and I'll show you a real pain in the ass.

"What do you say we get started?" I suggested. I was dying to get the match over with.

"Capital idea," said Conrad as he placed the head of his racquet on the Har-Tru surface before spinning it to determine which team would serve first. "Up or down?"

"Up," I said, just as Hunt was saying, "down."

Conrad laughed. "Hey, you two, with that kind of team work, you won't have a prayer of beating us. Yuk yuk."

He spun his racquet again. "Up or down?"

"Down," said Hunt. I remained silent this time.

"It's down," said Conrad. "You guys want to serve?"

I looked at Hunt, who had absolutely no control of his serve. Sometimes it would land in the court. Sometimes it would sail over the fence. Sometimes it would hit me in the back of the head.

"Sure, we'll serve," he said and picked up all three balls and put two of them in his shorts pocket.

We took our respective positions on the court. Then Hunt yelled, "These are good," as is customary when you're about to serve to begin a match.

"Whoa," said Conrad. "Don't you two want to warm up first? Susan and I hit for a while before you got here."

"No," I said, trying to hurry things along. "We warmed up at home." Yuk yuk.

"Suit yourselves," said Conrad.

Hunt served a double fault, and the match got under way. The good news is that I played miserably and so did Hunt. The bad news is that Susan and Conrad Dingle played even more miserably. Consequently, just when I thought we were about to lose the match and be ousted from the tournament, as per our plan, the Dingles tied the score. On and on it went. Hunt blew a forehand. Conrad blew a backhand. I hit a ball into the net. Susan hit a ball into the next court. We were god-awful, all of us, and our awfulness made us testy with each other. Like when Hunt was winding up to serve and Conrad put his hand up and yelled, "Foot fault!" Or when Susan hit a lob that resembled the launch of the Space Shuttle, and I called the ball out after it finally landed.

"Are you *sure* it was out?" she whined from across the net.

"Of course I'm sure," I said. How much do you hate when people who are supposed to be your friends (or at the very least, your fellow club members) question your integrity? If I didn't think the ball was out, I wouldn't have called it out. "Do you want to come over here and check the mark, Susan?"

"Yes," she said, then walked all the way over to the spot where her ball had landed and inspected the mark, all of which caused our already long match to last even longer. "It doesn't look out to me," she sniffed.

"Are you calling my wife a liar?" said Hunt as he and Conrad converged around the notorious spot.

"Hey, hey, simmer down," Conrad told Hunt. "Let's just do it over."

Oh great, I thought. If we keep playing points over, we'll be here till midnight.

Eventually and mercifully, the Dingles beat us.

"Wow. That was quite a match," Conrad chuckled as we all shook hands at the net.

"Congratulations," I said begrudgingly to the Dingles. "Who do you play next?"

"Probably the Winstons," said Susan. "But we'll never beat them. They're much better than you two."

"Gee, thanks," I said.

"Well, you know what I mean," said Susan. "Besides, even if we do beat them, we'll lose in the next round to Larkin and Perry Vail."

"Perry's not much of a tennis player," said Hunt. "Golf's his sport."

"Maybe, but he's got quite a partner in Larkin," Susan said. "She doesn't lose. Ever."

Hardly ever, I wanted to say but didn't. There was no point in bringing up Larkin's match with Claire—the one match she'd lost all summer.

Hunt and I wished the Dingles luck against the Winstons, said we'd see them later, and rushed over to the clubhouse.

"Did you bring the key?" I whispered to Hunt as we tiptoed toward the bookkeeping office, which was down the hall from the kitchen.

"Of course I brought the key," he said, looking annoyed.

"I was just asking," I said. "I remember the time we drove all the way out to Shea Stadium for a Mets game and you forgot to bring the tickets. And then there was the time you drove up to the cash machine and realized you'd left your ATM card in your other wallet."

"Thanks for the poignant retrospective," said Hunt as we stopped at the door to the office. He reached inside his tennis racquet case and pulled out his key chain, which was sterling silver and shaped like a golf club. "Jeez," he muttered as he fumbled with the half-dozen keys on the chain. "This could take a while. I forget which key opens the door."

I sighed. "Oh great. Why don't we just stand here with little signs saying, 'Look at us! We're planning to snoop around in the club's confidential files!' "

Hunt ignored me and kept inserting different keys into the lock on the door. When we both heard footsteps coming from down the hall, we froze.

"Now what are we going to do?" I moaned. "We'll be caught."

"We're not going to do anything," said Hunt. "We have every right to be here. I'm on the Finance Committee, remember?"

The footsteps grew louder and were accompanied by male voices.

"Just act normal," Hunt instructed. "Pretend we left something in the office and stopped by to pick it up."

"Left something? Like what?" I asked.

Just as Hunt was about to answer, Brendan Hardy and Duncan Tewksbury came around the corner and saw us.

"Hello," I said, smiling, and gave them a little wave.

Duncan would have kept going, I was sure, but Brendan stopped in his tracks and looked first at me, then at Hunt, then at me again. He seemed nervous, fidgety.

"We just came from the Tennis Tussle," I said, feeling the need to explain to them why we were standing in front of the bookkeeping office, even though it was none of their business and even though there was nothing in the bylaws of The Oaks that said we couldn't hang out in the bookkeeping office if we felt like it. "We lost in the first round," I went on, "so I suggested we take a little walk before dinner. That barbecued chicken of yours is so tempting, Brendan, that I wanted to be sure I made room for it."

"Glad you like it," he replied without emotion.

"Yes, well we really can't stay and chat," Duncan chuckled as he practically grabbed Brendan's arm and dragged him off. "Brendan and I have some business to discuss."

"Please, don't let us detain you," said Hunt.

"Right-o," said Duncan. "Have a pleasant evening, Hunt. You too, Mrs. Price."

Hunt. Mrs. Price. The man lived on Mars.

When they were out of earshot, I turned to Hunt and whispered, "What do you think all that was about? Duncan looked upset."

Hunt shrugged. "Maybe one of Brendan's soufflés fell."

"Cute. Or maybe Duncan knows we're on to their little kickback scam."

"You really think Duncan's in on it? He's the brother of the club's founder, Jude."

"And the father of a convicted felon. Can't you just picture the two of them plotting to silence Claire? I'll bet Duncan was the brains behind her murder and Brendan was the one who whacked her on the head. He's so big and strong he probably killed her with one awesome blow."

"Oh, neat. I found the right key."

"Yeah, neat." I rolled my eyes as Hunt jiggled the lock and opened the door. We were in!

"Now let's see if we can find something to incriminate the two of them," he said, then closed the door behind us and flipped on the light.

"Don't do that," I whispered. "People will know we're in here if they see there's a light on."

"Jude, we can't read the files in the dark."

"Right. Sorry."

"Now, I think the food bills are in here." He walked over to a filing cabinet and opened one of the drawers.

"What exactly are we looking for?" I asked as I scurried over to him.

"I don't know. Some kind of discrepancy in the invoices, I guess. Something that would show that the club has been paying for items it hasn't received."

He pulled out a manilla folder marked RHEINHARDT'S.

"What's Rheinhardt's?" I asked, looking over his shoulder.

"The food service company The Oaks uses. They specialize in country clubs. They function like a middle man, selling us all our meats, fruits, vegetables, everything."

"So if Brendan's got some kind of scam going, someone at Rheinhardt's is in on it, right?"

"I would think so. Apparently, we started using Rheinhardt's when Brendan came to the club a few years ago. It wouldn't be too much of a stretch to imagine him saying to somebody there, 'Overcharge me for x, y, and z and I'll give you some of the money back.' "

"Sure, and with Duncan protecting him, he'd never get caught," I said. "So what we've got to do is find a recent bill from Rheinhardt's and see what they've been charging us for."

Hunt leafed through the papers in the file and pulled out one of them.

"Here's one," he said. "Dated June first and marked 'Paid.' It's got Brendan's signature on it."

The bill listed various types of foods in varying quantities, along with prices.

"Wow! I never realized how expensive it is to feed three hundred members of a club," I said.

"Look, here's another one," said Hunt as he pulled a bill from the folder and examined it.

"Does it seem to be on the up-and-up?" I asked.

"Yeah, but I'm not an expert in this stuff. Ask me about cattle futures and I'll be able to help you."

"Well then, we'll have to take it."

"Take what?"

"The Rheinhardt's file."

"Jude, we can't take the whole file. Somebody's bound to notice that it's missing."

"We'll only keep it for a day or two," I said. "If somebody comes looking for it, they'll think it's been misplaced, that's all. The same goes for the budget file. It's here somewhere, isn't it?"

"The budget file? Yeah, it should be right in here."

Hunt opened another drawer and pulled out a file marked THE OAKS: 1995 BUDGET.

"Great," I said. "We'll take it, too."

"But what are we going to do with them?" said Hunt. "I've already told you that the invoices look okay to me."

"We're going to take both files to our accountant," I said. "When Valerio was getting ripped off at his restaurant, it was his accountant who saved the day."

"We can't take the files to our accountant," said Hunt.

"Why not?" I said.

"Because our accountant's a member of this club, remember? I switched us over to Peter Kendall six months ago when he opened an account with me at F&F. I thought it would be a nice quid pro quo, you know?"

"Oh, Hunt," I said, and sighed. "What am I going to do with you?"

I considered our predicament. Then an idea came to me.

"I know another accountant," I said, thinking of the woman who had been one of Claire's guests at the July Fourth Wild West party. "Her name's Sharon Klein."

"Klein. Klein," said Hunt as he tried to place the name. "Isn't she one of the women who applied for membership here?"

"Yes. Claire sponsored her. I bet she wants to see her friend's killer brought to justice just as badly as we do, and I bet she'll go through the files and be very discreet about it."

"It's worth a try," said Hunt.

I nodded and unzipped his tennis case, pulled out the Wilson Sledgehammer, and placed the files inside.

"Thank God for oversized racquet cases. These files would never have fit in mine," I said. "Now, let's go eat some barbecued chicken."

The Tennis Tussle dinners were casual affairs, held on the deck of the tennis house. When we arrived, the kitchen staff was setting the tables in anticipation of the end of the tournament, which was now in its final round with Larkin and Perry Vail pitted against Penelope and Reggie Etheridge. Everybody sipped Bloody Marys, watched the action, and offered their assessments of the match.

"Wow! Great shot," shouted Bailey Vanderhoff after Larkin blasted a blistering forehand past Penelope Etheridge's outstretched racquet. Then, while we all clapped for Larkin, Bailey turned to me and whispered, "The bitch can hit the ball, I'll give her that, but I'll never forgive her for showing up Penelope in front of all these people."

I laughed, marveling at how two-faced people at the club could be. And competitive. Couldn't they get it through their heads that the Friday night Tennis Tussles were supposed to be fun?

"He foot-faulted!" Conrad Dingle yelled onto the court after Perry stepped over the line while delivering his first serve.

"You need glasses," I told Conrad. "Not to mention a muzzle."

"*You* need glasses," Conrad shot back.

"I've already got a pair," I said, reaching into my purse for my new gold-wired Ralph Lauren specs, the ones that were supposed to help me read the newspaper without holding it three feet in front of me.

"Gee, that's funny," I said to Hunt, ignoring Conrad Dingle for the moment and concentrating on the fact that my eyeglass case was not in my purse. "I could have sworn I brought my glasses with me."

"You did," Hunt whispered. "You had them on when we were in the bookkeeping office."

"Right, but they're not in my purse."

Hunt turned pale. "You didn't leave them in there, did you, Jude?"

"God, I guess they could have dropped out of my purse and fallen on the floor. Or maybe onto the conference table."

"Oh, great," he muttered. "Now everyone will know that we took those files."

"They will not," I said. "The glasses could belong to anyone on the Finance Committee."

"No, they couldn't," he said. "They're women's glasses and we don't have any women on the committee."

"You would have if Claire had lived," I sighed.

"We'll just have to go back and get them," said Hunt.

I nodded.

We got up from our chairs, tossed our empty plastic cups into the garbage, and were about to walk back to the clubhouse when one of the boys from the kitchen staff rushed over to us.

"Mrs. Price?" he said, sounding out of breath, his accent thick with an Irish brogue.

"Yes?"

"Are these yours?" He handed me my eyeglass case.

"Why yes, they are," I said. "But where did you find them?"

"Mr. Hardy said to bring them to you," he said. "He said you'd left them."

Brendan? My heart jumped. "How did he know they were mine?" I asked the boy.

He shrugged. "He just said that I should tell you to be more careful in the future."

The boy turned and ran back to the kitchen.

"Did you hear that?" I asked Hunt, my mouth dry with fear. "Brendan just gave me another warning."

"Jesus. The guy must have been prowling around in the bookkeeping office after we left," he said. "I guess he wanted to know what we were up to—badly."

"That means he could be the killer, Hunt, *and* the person who broke into the house and disabled the elevator," I said. "All we have to do now is get the evidence."

Suddenly, there was thunderous applause coming from the tennis house. I suspected that Larkin and Perry had won the tournament and were being congratulated by the rest of the participants, many of whom had trashed them only minutes before.

"They're going to start serving dinner now," said Hunt. "We'd better head over there."

"Not a chance," I said. "The only place I'm heading is over to Sharon Klein's."

"But we don't even know where she lives," said Hunt.

"She lives in Belford," I said. "We'll look her up in the phone book."

"Are you sure about this, Jude?" he said.

"Sure, I'm sure," I said. "Sharon will help us. I know she will."

"No, I meant are you sure you want to leave before they serve dinner? You haven't missed a meal in all the years I've known you."

CHAPTER SEVENTEEN

♦

We hurried out to the parking lot.

"Do you see the car, Hunt?" I asked. It was twilight and hard to see much of anything.

"I think we parked over there," he said, pointing to the area near the driveway.

"Oh, right. I see it now," I said after spotting the BMW, all black and shiny and new. Well, almost new. We had bought the car the year before, when I still had my job at Charlton House and Hunt still thought he'd be made a partner at F&F any day. As we drew closer, Hunt grabbed my arm so hard he nearly broke it.

"What the hell's wrong with you?" I said, looking at him.

"That!" He pointed to the car and gasped.

All four tires had been slashed. "Who would have done such a thing?"

"Who do you think?" Hunt muttered.

"Brendan." It had to be. Or maybe he had one of his little kitchen boys do it. To send us yet another message. "Oh, Hunt. What are we going to do now?"

He didn't answer. I think he was calculating how much a complete set of new Michelins would cost him.

"Look, this has really gotten out of hand," I said. "We need Tom's help now, don't you think?"

He nodded. His complexion had turned a sickly shade of green, the way it always did when his car or his house or his daughter required a large and unexpected outlay of cash.

"You hang on to the racquet case and the files. I'll go inside the clubhouse and beep Tom. He'll be here in no time," I said.

"Make sure you tell him we want a flat-bed truck for the car, not one of those cheesy tow jobs," he called out, then sat on the hood of the BMW and put his head in his hands.

I ran to the pay phone in the ladies' locker room and beeped Tom, who called me back within five minutes. When I told him what had happened, he said Hunt and I should wait by the car, that he'd be there to pick us up in ten minutes and that he would send a tow truck—a flat-bed tow truck—right away.

"Are you okay?" he asked me.

"A little shaky, but that's probably because I haven't eaten since lunch," I said.

"I'll stop at Burger King and bring you a couple of Whoppers," he said. "Or are you a McDonald's person?"

"I'm a Lutèce person, but a couple of Whoppers would be just fine," I said.

Tom picked us up in his unmarked Chevy Caprice and took us over to police headquarters, where we sat in his office and wolfed down our burgers and fries. I know that some people simply can't eat a morsel of food when they're upset, but I was ravenous. My mother's daughter, apparently.

"You've got to help us find Sharon Klein," I told Tom between bites. "I think it's important that she look over these files and tell us if there's anything suspicious in them. If there is, you can arrest Brendan."

"Not so fast," Tom cautioned.

"Come on, we all know he's a crook," said Hunt. "Why can't you just lock him up?"

"Let's take one step at a time, huh?" said Tom. "Even if Brendan is ripping off the members of The Oaks, that doesn't mean he killed Claire Cox. I think our next step should be to find out where this Sharon Klein lives and then pay her a visit."

He grabbed the White Pages of the telephone book and started looking for Sharon's number.

"You shouldn't have much trouble finding it," I said. "This is Belford we're talking about, not Great Neck. There can't be more than one Klein in the book."

Tom ran his finger down the page of the phone book, then stopped. "Here's an 'S. Klein' on Rosebud Trail."

"Shame on her," I said. "Years ago, single women listed their first initial in the phone book instead of their whole first name, because they wanted rapists and robbers and phone fetishists to think they were a man and leave them alone. But hide the fact that you're a single woman in this day and age? Not very PC of Sharon. *Tsk tsk.*"

"I'll give her a call," said Tom, ignoring my sermon.

S. Klein did indeed turn out to be Sharon Klein, *the* Sharon Klein who was about to join The Oaks Country Club. When Tom explained the situation to her as well as the urgency, she agreed to see us right away.

"It's a good thing this isn't tax season," she said when we arrived at her house, a modest colonial on a couple of acres. "I would have been up to my ears in spreadsheets."

Sharon had short, no-nonsense brown hair, wore large, tortoise-shell-framed eyeglasses, and had a serious, almost pained expression. She fit my image of an accountant in every way except for the fact that each of her earlobes was pierced in six places and the T-shirt she was wearing read I'M A BIKER. YOU GOT A PROBLEM WITH THAT?

When we told her what we wanted her to do, she said to give her twenty-four hours.

"Normally, it would take me a few days to do this sort of audit, but I'll take a cursory look and try to get a sense of what's been going on," she said. "It's the least I can do for Claire."

The following afternoon, after Hunt and I returned home from Tire World with our newly outfitted vehicle, we received a call from Tom, saying that Sharon had indeed detected a problem with the club's accounting.

"I'm not exactly a whiz at numbers, but according to Sharon, who said something about analyzing The Oaks's food and liquor costs to sales, the food costs are way out of line with what they should be," he

said. "Sharon also mentioned something about 'phantom bills,'
money that was paid to the food supplier even though the goods were
never received. She said somebody at your club has definitely been
up to something—and has been for quite a while—and that she'll be
glad to testify to that effect in court."

"Great! What happens next?" I said.

"You're going to replace the files you took from the bookkeeping
office," he said.

"Replace them? But they're evidence," I said.

"Sharon's made copies of everything. I want you and Hunt to take
them back to the club and make sure Brendan sees you do it."

"Why? So he can slash our tires again? I don't think I could put
Hunt through that."

"No, so we can catch Brendan—and whoever else is in on the kickback scheme with him—trying to cover their tracks. We don't have
any hard evidence against Mr. Hardy, Judy. We need some. I'm betting he's going to go back into that office and either take the files or
falsify them somehow."

"Fine, but how will you know if it's Brendan who takes them?"

"I'll know if it's Brendan, because you're going to bug the place."

"I am?"

"Yup. When you go back into that bookkeeping office today,
you're going to put a little surveillance wire in there for us. Then we'll
know exactly who's doing what."

"But Tom, I don't know a thing about bugs, wires, whatever you
call them. And forget about Hunt. He's a disaster at anything electrical. He almost blew up the kitchen when he tried to fix the toaster
oven and—"

"Judy, relax," said Tom. "What I'm asking you to do isn't brain
surgery. Is there a tissue box in the bookkeeping office?"

"I have no idea. Why?"

"Because we've got a special surveillance antenna for tissue boxes.
It's easy to hide and it works great. So if there isn't a box of tissues
hanging around, bring one, okay?"

"I guess so. Any special brand? Kleenex makes this new kind where
there's moisturizing cream on each tissue. They're gentler on the
nose."

"Swell. I'll be sure to buy them the next time I have a cold. Now, I
assume there's a desk or a conference table in that office, right?"

"A conference table."

"Good. You'll mount the transmitter underneath that table and then hook the antenna up to the tissue box."

"But Tom, I'm not sure we'll know how to—"

"I'll be over in twenty minutes to show you everything you need to know. Is that convenient?"

"Yes, but there's just one thing."

"What?"

"Do I get extra for this or is bugging an office considered part of my work as an informant?"

"You get extra for this. I'll buy you another Whopper at Burger King."

As it was a gorgeous Saturday morning in August, The Oaks was packed. Hunt was supposed to play golf with Ducky and Perry and Addison Bidwell, but he dropped out in order to accompany me on my surveillance mission. Ever since the elevator incident, he'd been by my side. Protecting me. Supporting me. Loving me. Being the kind of husband I needed him to be. My mother was right when she'd said, "Hang on to him. You could do worse."

"I hate to take you away from your golf," I said as we walked past dozens of golfers on our way to the clubhouse. "You must be dying to play."

"I don't miss the game all that much," he said. "What I miss is the comraderie, the people-thing. I really like Perry and Ducky. Especially Ducky. He's a nifty guy, Jude."

"Yeah, nifty."

"Oh, come on, Booch. I know you suspected him at one time, but he's a real mild-mannered, low-key guy. He wouldn't hurt anyone, believe me. When I called him this morning to cancel, do you know what he was doing?"

"I know what he wasn't doing: making love to his wife. Nedra says they never do it."

"Nedra says they do it. Nedra says they never do it. Nedra says a lot of things. She loves to shock people."

"True."

"No, when I called, he was operating on Bartholomew."

"Nedra's little Yorkie?"

"Yeah. Old Bart had stepped on a tiny piece of glass, and Ducky was taking it out."

"Aw, isn't that sweet. Actually, I like Ducky well enough. Of all the

clowns at this club, he's probably the least clownish. It was just that
when I overheard him telling Claire how he wished they were still
together and all that mush . . . it made me a little queasy."

"Look, Claire Cox was a very attractive, passionate woman. It's not
hard to see how she would have made a huge impact on Ducky when
they were in college."

"I suppose you're right."

We arrived at the clubhouse with our "gear," which consisted of
the files, the transmitter, the antenna, and the box of Kleenex, all of
which we had stuffed into my Barnes & Noble canvas tote bag and
covered with a beach towel. As Tom had instructed, we went into the
main dining room and asked one of the waiters if Brendan was
around.

"He's in the kitchen," said the waiter.

"I know," I said, "but I'd like to speak with him. Just for a second."

The waiter said he'd be right back and disappeared into the
kitchen. A few minutes later, Brendan emerged.

"Oh, hi, Brendan," I said. "I just wanted to thank you personally
for finding my eyeglasses and then having one of your staff bring
them to me. That was so thoughtful."

"No problem," he said.

"I left them in that bookkeeping office when Hunt—he's on the
Finance Committee, as you know—was looking for some files. Now
we're going back there to return them, and I'll be *sure* not to leave my
glasses this time!"

I extended my hand to Brendan in a gesture of thanks, but he de-
clined to shake it.

"I'm greasy," he said. "I've been stuffing chicken breasts."

"I understand completely," I said. "Take care."

And off we went to the bookkeeping office.

Tom was right: setting up the surveillance equipment wasn't brain
surgery. Hunt and I returned the files, set up the transmitter and antenna, and were out of there in twenty minutes.

"Now, all we have to do is wait," Hunt said.

We didn't hear from Tom until four o'clock that afternoon.

"Did you get anything?" I asked.

"Yeah. Some guy blew his nose into one of your moisturized tissues."

"That's all?"

"That's all."

The next day, Tom called to say there were three people in the bookkeeping office.

"Was one of them Brendan?" I asked.

"No, all three of them were women. They were discussing the flower arrangements for the Labor Day Dance."

"Great. Well, tomorrow's Monday and most of the members will be at work. If Brendan's going to do anything funny, tomorrow just might be the day."

It was.

"I've got great news," said Tom when he called. "Brendan was in the bookkeeping office this morning, and he had someone else in there with him."

"Duncan Tewksbury?" I asked.

"I couldn't tell. The other guy only grunted a couple of times."

"You sure he didn't chuckle? Duncan chuckles a lot."

"No, these weren't chuckles. These were grunts."

"Okay, so did Brendan talk to this guy about the Rheinhardt's file?"

"No, it never came up."

"Then what *did* he talk about?"

"The new kitchen. Your club is planning to renovate the kitchen, right?"

"Yes, to the tune of three million dollars. Talk about a rip-off. Hunt showed me the architectural plans one night and I couldn't believe how little we were getting for our money. I had a better-laid-out kitchen in my studio apartment in Manhattan."

"Well, it turns out that Brendan and whoever was in the room with him have a little kickback thing going with the general contractor on that three-million-dollar kitchen. Those architectural plans you saw were for a two-million-dollar kitchen; Brendan and his accomplice are splitting the million-dollar difference with the contractor."

"God, what pigs. Between the food service rip-off and this thing with the kitchen, Brendan must be squirreling away a small fortune."

I sighed, thinking of how rotten people could be, how devious. "Well, at least we've got some evidence against Brendan now," I said. "When are you going to arrest him, Detective?"

"I'm not."

"What do you mean you're not?"

"The evidence isn't admissible in court, Judy. The only time I can use evidence gathered from technical surveillance equipment is when it falls under the heading of 'consensual monitoring.' "

"You mean you have to get Brendan's *consent* before recording him? How lame is that?"

"Look, here's the deal. We don't need his consent to obtain evidence of criminal activity *if* he has the conversation with a police officer or someone acting in an undercover capacity. According to Title 18 of the United States Code, Section 2511 (2), 'It shall not be unlawful for a person acting under the color of the law to intercept wire or oral communications, where such person is *party* to the communication.' "

"So you're saying that Brendan has to be talking about his evil deeds with a cop before you can arrest him?"

"Right. He's got to be talking either to a cop or to someone working for the cops."

"How likely is that?" I said, discouraged and not a little bit frustrated. Police procedures were beginning to sound as rigid and out-of-touch with reality as The Oaks's bylaws. "Brendan will never talk about his scams to a cop. He may be a lousy cook, but he's not a complete idiot."

"No, but he might talk to a member of your club who's helping the police," said Tom. "Especially if he felt he had no choice."

"I don't understand."

"Let's say a member of your club set up a meeting with Brendan in the bookkeeping office, where we've got our surveillance gear planted. Let's say this member confronted Brendan about all the kickbacks and then said something like, 'If you cut me in, Brendan, I won't go to the president of the club—or to the cops.' Then we can get Brendan agreeing to the deal and admitting everything on tape. *That* we'd be able to use as evidence in court."

"Brilliant, but you're not suggesting *I* be the member to confront him, are you? I know I'm working for you and all. But confront the guy who murdered Claire?" The man was a criminal, after all. Talking to him in public was one thing; having a secret meeting with him was another.

"No, Judy. I'm not suggesting that you confront Brendan," said Tom. "I'm suggesting that Hunt do it."

"Hunt?"

"Did you call me, Jude?" Hunt yelled from the living room, where he was poring over his commodities charts. He was supposed to be taking the week off, but so far, he'd been spending every minute agonizing over this trade and that trade. The truth was, Hunt didn't have the personality for commodities trading, which is high-risk and requires a strong stomach. He wasn't much of a risk taker, period, which was why I was surprised that Tom had thought of him for such a risky operation.

"You want Hunt to confront Brendan in the bookkeeping office?" I asked Tom.

"It's an idea," he said. "Brendan already suspects that you two are on to him. What if Hunt sat down with him and said, 'Listen, guy, I've been looking over the books and I know you've been pulling something. I'm having real problems at work and I'm desperate for money. If you give me a piece of the action, I'll keep my mouth shut.' Chances are, Brendan will feel squeezed and consider Hunt's offer. The minute he says something to incriminate himself, we'll go in and arrest him."

"But Tom," I said. "Look what happened to Claire. She probably found out about Brendan, confronted him, and threatened to blow the whistle on him. Now she's dead, something I don't want my husband to be."

"Nothing's going to happen to Hunt," Tom said. "We'll be sitting in the parking lot of the club, listening to every word they say. If it sounds like Brendan's getting riled up, we'll go in."

I considered the scenario. Obviously, I didn't want to put Hunt in jeopardy. On television, cop strategies backfired all the time, and the good guys didn't always win. But it was Hunt's decision whether or not to go along with Tom's plan, not mine.

I hung up the phone and went into the living room to talk to Hunt.

"Booch?" I said, cuddling up next to him on the sofa. "Can I talk to you for a minute?"

"Sure," he said, putting aside his papers. "Was that Tom you were on the phone with?"

I filled him in on my conversation with Tom, then posed the possibility of Hunt's playing undercover cop.

"He really wants me to do it?" Hunt said, his eyes wide.

I nodded. "But listen, Hunt. You don't have to do it," I said.

"Don't fall into that macho trap where you think you have to prove your manhood by putting yourself in danger. I love you just the way you are, whether you play undercover cop or not. Just remember that when you're weighing the pros and cons of Tom's idea and trying to decide what to—"

"I'm doing it," he interrupted me. "If it will bring this whole mess to a head, I'm doing it."

"Are you sure?" I said.

"I'm sure," he said. "Nothing's going to happen to me."

CHAPTER EIGHTEEN

♦

Tom arrived at the house and rehearsed Hunt for his undercover mission. Then Hunt called the club and asked to speak to Brendan, who wasn't available. Hunt left a message. About an hour later, Brendan returned the call.

"I'd like to talk to you," Hunt told him. "Tonight. At the club. It's in both our best interests to have this meeting right away."

"Why? Is something wrong?" Brendan asked.

"Yes, and I think you know what it is," said Hunt. "I'll see you at eight o'clock. In the bookkeeping office."

"I can't. I've got plans," Brendan said.

"Cancel them," said Hunt, in a voice I hardly recognized. Hunt had never been the bossy type, the sort of man who orders people around with nonchalance. Which was probably why he hadn't made partner at F&F, where they equated being a blow-hard with being smart. It struck me suddenly and with great clarity that Hunt would never ascend at F&F. He wasn't obnoxious enough.

Hunt drove over to the club in our BMW, while Tom and I followed in the Caprice. We parked in the lot, the only cars there.

"Good luck, Booch," I said as I kissed Hunt goodbye. "We'll be right here if you need us, listening to every word."

"I know," he said. "Everything's going to be fine. I'm going to get this guy to incriminate himself on tape, and we're going to put this whole murder thing behind us."

While Hunt walked toward the clubhouse, Tom set up his surveillance receiver on the front seat of the car. He adjusted the controls, put on a pair of headphones, and handed me a pair. Then we waited. I nearly jumped when I heard Hunt's voice. My own sweet Hunt, transmitted over that Kleenex antenna. So near and yet so far.

"Glad you decided to show up," I heard him tell Brendan. "We've got a few things to discuss."

I tried to picture them in that office, interacting. Who was where? Were they standing or sitting? Close together or on opposite sides of the room? Were they smiling at each other or glowering? The sensation of being able to hear Hunt but not see him was discomfiting, to say the least.

"What's this all about, Price?" asked Brendan.

I nudged Tom. Brendan's dropping the "Mr." when he spoke to Hunt was not a good sign. But then men often called each other by their last name, I reminded myself. It was a macho thing. You never hear women do that. You never hear women say: "I hear Goldberg is pregnant." Or: "Rudinsky just had her third face-lift." Maybe Brendan's "What's this all about, Price?" wasn't hostile, just male.

"I know you've got a little kickback scheme going here at the club," Hunt continued. "More than one. You've got the Rheinhardt's people in your pocket. The contractor on the new kitchen too."

"Have you been drinking, Price?" Brendan asked derisively. "You're not making any sense."

"Look, Brendan. There's no point in denying it. I've got proof. I've had an accountant check the figures and I've got a guy from Rheinhardt's who admitted you've been running a scam."

The latter remark was a bluff, part of Tom's plan to trap Brendan.

"Yeah? Who?" Brendan challenged.

"Joe Carabella," said Hunt, using the name of one of Rheinhardt's' employees. "He says you've been ripping the club off since you got here."

Silence. Then a sneeze. It wasn't Hunt who sneezed. I'd know his sneeze anywhere. Besides, he'd hardly ever sneezed since the doctor had switched his allergy medication.

No, it was Brendan who sneezed. Once. Twice. "Damn hay fever," he cursed. "Now look, what is it you want, Price?" he said. "You want to get me canned? Is that it? Because if you do, you're going to have to deal with Duncan—"

"You mean your father?" said Hunt. "Is Duncan in on this little scam of yours?"

"Just tell me what you want, huh?"

"I want a piece of the action," said Hunt, talking tough, like an actor in a gangster movie. "You cut me in and I'll keep my mouth shut."

Silence.

"Why are you looking at me like that?" Hunt asked.

"I'm surprised, that's all," said Brendan. "You didn't seem the type."

"The type to steal from the club, the way you have?" said Hunt, who was doing just what he'd been told to do: goad Brendan into a confession.

"I thought you were one of those holier-than-thou types," said Brendan. I could practically feel his smirk.

"I'm not a holier-than-thou type. I'm a commodities trader, and my trades haven't gone well lately. Not well at all," Hunt explained. "The truth is, I'm in a deep hole. My firm's about to dump me. I'm behind on my mortgage and I haven't paid my bills here at The Oaks. Plus, my wife's out of a job."

"Your wife's a piece of ass, you know that, Price?" said Brendan.

Tom and I looked at each other. Then he mouthed the words, "He's right," and smiled. I tried to smile back, but I couldn't. Not until Brendan Hardy was behind bars.

"Listen, Brendan. I've made you an offer," said Hunt, doing a remarkable job of maintaining his cool. "You give me a piece of the action, I won't tell the police what you've been up to. I imagine that, with your criminal record, the cops won't look kindly on you."

"How did you know I had a record?" asked Brendan.

"Your friend at Rheinhardt's told me," said Hunt. "He told me a lot of things."

"Bullshit," said Brendan. "Bullshit, he did."

"Okay, if that's the way you feel about it," said Hunt, "I guess I'll have to tell everybody what I know, starting with Evan Sutcliffe, the treasurer of The Oaks. I suppose he'll discuss the situation with your father and they'll go to the police together."

"My father," Brendan snorted, then sneezed again.

"Look, are you going to take my deal or aren't you?" said Hunt.

Silence. We were close. Very close. Any minute Brendan would admit—on tape and for the record—that he had been stealing from the club. And then Tom would throw him in jail and make him confess to killing Claire.

"Well? What'll it be?" Hunt asked.

More silence. I shifted in my seat. The wait was excruciating.

"Okay. I'll cut you in," said Brendan.

I looked at Tom and gave him the thumbs-up sign. It was over! Hunt had pulled it off! We had caught Brendan! My mind raced as I imagined how much better the food at The Oaks would be once we got a new chef.

"I thought you'd see it my way," Hunt said. "Now, I think you'd better tell me how the scam works. Who's in on it, how the money comes back, that kind of thing."

"You don't need to know any of that," Brendan snapped.

"Sure, I do. I want to know who at this club is in on the scam besides me. So why don't you just tell me about you and Duncan and all the—"

"You'll get your money. That's all you need to know," Brendan said again, then sneezed.

I heard movement, then a very loud noise.

"Shit," said Tom as he removed his headphones and motioned for me to remove mine. "I think he went for a tissue and dislodged the antenna."

"Then we have to go in there," I said. "We can't let Hunt stay in there without monitoring their conversation."

"*Shhh.* Wait." Tom put his headphones back on. "It's okay."

I put mine back on and listened.

"You sure you're not going to tell me who else is involved?" Hunt was asking Brendan.

"Why so curious?" Brendan asked before sneezing yet again.

He must have reached for another tissue and come to the end of the box because there was static in my headphones, then silence, then a voice.

"Hey, what the fuck is this?"

It was Brendan. Had he spotted the antenna? Was our cover blown? Was Hunt in danger?

"How should I know what it is?" said Hunt. "Looks like somebody was playing a little trick on us."

I grabbed Tom's arm.

"Let's go," I said. "Now!"

He took off his headphones, radioed for a patrol car, and bolted out of the car.

"Stay here," he ordered.

"Not a chance," I said and ran out of the car after him—or tried to. He was a much faster runner than I was and in much better shape. I vowed to sign up for an aerobics class as soon as this mess was over.

I had lost sight of Tom as I huffed and puffed and chugged breathlessly toward the bookkeeping office, and when I heard the shot, I froze.

"My God! Not Hunt!" I yelled and pushed myself forward. By the time I reached the office, things had quieted down considerably. Hunt was helping Tom handcuff Brendan. Tom was reading Brendan his Miranda rights. And the bullet that had been fired from Tom's gun was lodged in the office ceiling. Apparently Brendan had tried to flee, and Tom had fired the shot to get his attention.

"Oh, thank goodness. You're safe," I cried, flinging myself into Hunt's arms.

"Sure, I'm safe," said Hunt, as if his brush with death were merely another night in the life of a commodities broker. "We'll all be safe now that this pond scum is out of circulation." He glared at Brendan, who glared back.

Then, suddenly, there were sirens.

"Sounds like my backup has arrived," Tom said.

Seconds later, three uniformed police officers charged into the bookkeeping office. Tom gave them a few facts about the case and told them to take Brendan away. After they had gone, he turned to Hunt and me and said, "I'll take it from here, you two. Time for you to go home."

"With pleasure," I said, exhausted from worrying about Hunt—and from all that running.

"What happens next?" asked Hunt.

"We'll question Brendan—as much as his lawyer will allow us to," Tom replied. "I'm sure his father will get him some hotshot from New York. But that's not my problem. My problem is to gather as much evidence as I can and turn the case over to the prosecutor. We've got a lot more on Mr. Hardy than we did before. We've got him confessing to the scam at the club. And if we can find evidence that Claire Cox knew about the scam, we've got a motive for his killing her."

"You mean we still don't have enough evidence against him?" I asked.

"Not yet," he said. "We've got to prove that Ms. Cox knew what Brendan Hardy was up to."

"How?" I said. "The woman's dead."

Tom shrugged.

"Let's go home," said Hunt, who looked tired but triumphant. I had the feeling he was experiencing the type of high that people who survive a difficult ordeal experience. Sort of like the way I always felt after getting through a weekend with Kimberley.

"I'm very proud of you," I said as we walked to the parking lot. "Were you scared?"

Hunt shook his head. "Not at all," he said.

"Not even when Brendan found the antenna?" I said.

"Not even then," he said.

I didn't believe him, of course, but that's one of the things you do for the man you love: you let him believe that you believe him. You let him believe that you think he's big and strong and fearless, and that when push comes to shove, you'd take him over Arnold Schwarzenegger any old day.

Brendan's arrest sent shock waves throughout the membership of The Oaks, and even though none of the members was present when the arrest was made, word about how and when it happened got around—including the fact that Hunt and I had been working with the police on the Claire Cox murder investigation. As a result, we were instant celebrities at the club, but not in the way you might think. No, despite the fact that *we'd* been the ones who'd risked our lives to stop Brendan from stealing money from the club, the members of The Oaks not only didn't applaud when we walked by, they booed and hissed! One of the old dowagers even gave us the Bronx cheer! It was bizarre. People actually seemed angry at us. As if we were traitors. As if we had deliberately tried to bring disgrace and ignominy down on The Oaks's hallowed reputation.

Truthfully, the shunning didn't bother me all that much, but I felt bad for Hunt, who genuinely liked some of the members and enjoyed their company. Oh, Perry and Ducky were still his friends and told him they thought it had been very courageous, even noble, of him to put himself in jeopardy for the good of the club. But the rest of those slugs he played golf with acted as if *he* were the criminal, not Brendan.

"It's unbelievable," I said when I told Arlene the whole story. "Just when I think the people at The Oaks can't get any more loathsome, they do."

"At least you got this Brendan guy arrested," she said. "*I* think you and Hunt deserve a medal."

"Thanks for your support," I laughed. "How can I ever repay you?"

"Are you serious?" asked Arlene.

"About what?" I said.

"About repaying me?"

"What are you talking about?"

"Well, I was wondering, are you still planning to go down to Florida for your dad's birthday?"

"Don't tell me you want to come too?"

"Come too?"

"Yeah, Kimberley's coming with us. I couldn't *not* let her come."

We had gotten an extra plane ticket for Kimberley the morning after Brendan's arrest, figuring that Tom wouldn't need our services any longer. Unfortunately, it turned out that Tom had been right: Brendan's lawyer was a big shot New York attorney named Patrick Delaney, who was known in legal circles as "Teeth," not because his were remarkable, but because he apparently sank them into each case with a vengeance. Mr. Delaney went to the judge and claimed that his client had been the victim of entrapment on the part of the Belford Police. The judge refused to dismiss the case, but he did allow Brendan to put up bail money, despite the fact that his run-in with the law was not his first. So now the guy was running around loose again, while he awaited trial. And we were going to Florida—regardless.

"No, I wasn't angling for an invitation to Florida," said Arlene. "It's too hot there in the summer. I was hoping I could stay at your house while you're gone. You know, sort of house-sit the place?"

"Of course you can," I said. "I should have thought of it before. A few days in the country will be a nice break for you. Were you thinking of coming alone?"

"Yeah, that's kind of the point. Ever since I broke up with Randy, I haven't felt like going out much. I thought maybe a weekend in Connecticut would revive me a little."

"Absolutely. Use the house, the car, whatever."

"You're a good friend, Judy," said Arlene. "I really wish I could help you get a job."

"I know," I said. "Maybe things will open up for me in the fall."

"I hope so."

I hung up with Arlene and called Tom to tell him we were going to Florida and to give him the number at my parents' house in case anything exciting happened while we were gone.

"I was just going to call you," he said.

"What's up?" I said.

"Two things. Good news and bad news. Which do you want first?"

"The bad news. Then I'll have something to look forward to."

"Okay. The bad news is that my boss is making me pull our guard off your house. He says it costs the department a fortune to have the place watched twenty-four hours a day, and that, since we've arrested our chief suspect, you're no longer in any danger. Besides, we really can't spare the manpower. We're shorthanded as it is."

"That's okay," I said. "Brendan may be out on bail, but I can't believe he'd be stupid enough to try anything now. Besides, we'll be gone soon. We're going down to Boca Raton for a week for my father's seventy-fifth birthday. I know you and I have a deal, but now that Brendan's been arrested, I didn't think you'd mind if I left town for a few days."

"Of course, I mind," said Tom. "I'll miss you."

"Thanks, same here." Poor Tom, I thought. He must be so lonely since his wife died. "Tell you what," I went on. "When we get back from Florida, the three of us will have dinner. I'll cook one of my extravagant gourmet feasts, okay?"

"It's a date. My stomach and I can hardly wait."

"Great. Now, tell me the good-news part of this phone call."

"Right. Guess who I'm meeting with this afternoon?"

"Your father," I said. "You two are going to mend your fences and then you're going to tell him how wonderful I am and what a smart move it would be for him to hire me back at Charlton House."

"No, sorry. Dad and I are still on the outs."

"Figures. Then who are you seeing this afternoon?"

"Delia Tewksbury."

"You're kidding."

"Honest. She called and asked if I could come to her house."

"Interesting, considering how uncooperative her husband's been in your investigation. It was Duncan who got that slick lawyer for Brendan, wasn't it?"

"Not according to Delaney. He says Brendan hired him."

"Oh, come on. Brendan's not exactly plugged into big-time celebrity lawyers. Somebody must have called Patrick Delaney for him. And I'm betting that somebody was Duncan Tewksbury.''

"I don't know," said Tom. "Hopefully, Mrs. Tewksbury can shed some light on all this.''

"Call me after your meeting with her and tell me everything," I said.

"Absolutely.''

About three hours later, Tom showed up, bringing us a complete play-by-play of his meeting with Mrs. Tewksbury.

"I still can't figure out what made her want to see you," I said as the three of us sat in the living room.

"Panic, that's what made her want to see me," Tom replied. "She wanted to make sure she gave me *her* version of things before Brendan gave me his. This is a lady who's *very* big on controlling what people think of her. She's terrified of losing her stature in the community and, of course, in that club.''

"Well, what did she say?" I said, barely able to contain myself. The thought of Delia Tewksbury losing her stature in the community pleased me deeply. "Did she admit that Duncan is Brendan's father?''

"Yes," said Tom.

"Finally. Did she tell you who the mother is?''

"Yes again," said Tom.

"Well, don't keep us in suspense," I said. "Who is Lorraine Pennock? Wasn't that the name on the birth certificate?''

Tom nodded. "Pennock is Delia Tewksbury's maiden name," he said.

"Delia? Are you saying that *she's* Brendan's mother?''

"You got it.''

My mouth flew open. So did Hunt's.

"Her full name is Delia Lorraine Pennock Tewksbury," Tom explained.

"Wait, let me get this straight," I said. "Delia and Duncan Tewksbury are Brendan's parents, but they never told anybody?''

"Apparently," said Tom.

"Then what was all that business about her being barren?" I asked.

"A cover, I guess," said Tom. "She didn't want anyone to know that she and her husband gave Brendan up for adoption right after he was born.''

"Why did they do that?" Hunt asked.

"They weren't married when Delia got pregnant," said Tom. "They'd had a brief romance, then Duncan, an Army man, went off to the War. Meanwhile, Delia, who came from a prominent New England family that was humiliated by her unfortunate pregnancy, was shuttled off to some hospital in the Midwest, where she had the baby and then gave it up. When Duncan came back from Europe, he and Delia were married, and they never mentioned their son again. Brendan was simply their Little Mistake."

I shook my head. "Brother, you never know what goes on in families," I said. "The Tewksburys always seemed so proper, so . . . so . . . 'holier than thou,' to quote Brendan."

"And I'm only just getting started," said Tom. "It turns out that Brendan grew up in Ohio and bounced from one place to another, getting himself in and out of trouble. About ten years ago, he showed up on the Tewksburys' doorstep and announced that he was their long-lost son. They were mortified. What if all their fancy friends found out that they'd had an illegitimate son—and given the boy away? They told Brendan it would be best if he went back to wherever he came from, which, at the time, was prison, but he was not about to go quietly. First, he told the Tewksburys he needed money, which they gave him. Then, he told them he needed a job, which they helped him get at the Belford Athletic Club. Then, he told them he wanted to work at their club, so they got him the job at The Oaks. They kept going along with his demands because he threatened to tell everybody he was their son if they didn't."

"No wonder Duncan wouldn't let anybody fire Brendan," said Hunt.

"I still don't understand why Delia would volunteer all this information to the police if she's so paranoid about people finding out about her relationship to Brendan," I said, "especially now that he's been arrested for stealing from the club."

"Because she's even more paranoid that the members of The Oaks will think Mr. Tewksbury was in on the kickbacks," Tom explained. "Like son, like father? She wanted me to know that her husband is innocent, that he had absolutely no knowledge of any schemes, and that she'll testify in court to that effect."

"Do you believe her?" Hunt asked Tom. "We know Brendan must have had at least one accomplice at the club. He was talking to somebody about the kitchen renovation in the bookkeeping office that day."

Tom shrugged. "I don't know," he said. "And frankly, I'm not all that interested in whether Duncan Tewksbury was padding his wallet."

"Tom's right. We've gotten off the track here," I said. "Who cares about some dopey kickbacks when it's Claire's murder we've got to solve? Isn't that why we wanted to nab Brendan as a rip-off artist? So we could prove he had a motive for killing Claire, assuming she knew about the kickbacks and was about to blow the whistle on him?"

"Yes, and I'm getting to that," Tom said. "Mrs. Tewksbury dropped another bombshell this afternoon: she admitted that, a few days before Ms. Cox's death, she had gone to her grandniece's house and asked her advice about Brendan, about the fact that he was blackmailing them, harassing them. She figured that since Ms. Cox was a lawyer—and a member of the family—she'd keep their confidence and tell them how to handle the situation."

"What advice did Claire give Delia?" I asked.

"She told Mrs. Tewksbury that *she* would handle the situation with Brendan, that *she* would confront him and threaten him with legal action if he didn't leave the club and Belford."

"But why would Claire stick her neck out for the Tewksburys? She didn't get along with them," I pointed out. "Duncan didn't even want her to join the club. Why would she do them any favors?"

"Didn't you say Claire wanted the club to fire Brendan and hire a better chef?" Hunt asked. "She probably had her own reasons for wanting him gone."

"Good point," I said, then turned to Tom. "Well, Detective, it sounds like you can wrap this case up now. Brendan *has* to be our man. He had the opportunity to murder Claire, seeing as he was at The Oaks the night she was killed but admitted that he left the party, supposedly to go back to his cottage. He had access to the murder weapon, seeing as he often played golf on Mondays and used the golf pro's clubs. And he had the motive for killing Claire, seeing as he wanted to stop her from going to the police about him."

Tom nodded. "We'll see what the prosecutor says, but I'm pretty sure he'll go for it—especially since Delia Tewksbury has agreed to testify against her son."

"You mean you can't arrest Brendan for murder right away? This afternoon?" I asked.

"No," Tom said, grinning at my naiveté. "It may take a little while longer to get Mr. Hardy back in jail for good. But the hard part's over.

We've got enough evidence to make a case against your favorite chef—thanks to you two.''

I stood up and cheered. "Hooray for us!" I cried, then danced around the room.

Tom and Hunt stood and watched me celebrate. Then they smiled and shook hands and spoke of truth, justice, and whether or not the situation called for an ice-cold beer.

"Forget the beer," I said jubilantly. "Let's break out the Dom Perignon. It's not every day that we solve a murder.''

PART
T·H·R·E·E

CHAPTER NINETEEN

◆

Point O' Palms, where my parents have lived since the mid-eighties, is like every other gated, upscale "country club community" in south Florida—only more so.

Occupying several hundred acres in Boca Raton and developed by Westinghouse or General Electric or some other American corporate giant, it boasts two golf courses, a tennis stadium, three pools (in addition to the private screened-in pools that are de rigueur in the backyards of every house), a marina, several man-made lakes, an opulently appointed clubhouse, dozens of fountains, and a profusion of tropical shrubs and flowers. And then there are the homes themselves—ostentatious megastructures that the Point O' Palms sales agent who sold my parents their homesite referred to as "product."

"How can you live in a place where they call houses 'product'?" I had asked my parents when they'd announced their intention to build in Point O' Palms.

"That's the way they talk in Florida," my father had explained. "The communities are 'subdivisions,' the houses are 'product' and the people who live in the houses are 'units.' "

"Sounds dehumanizing," I'd said.

"It's not dehumanizing at all," my father had maintained. "The developers think of everything a human being could possibly need when they build the houses. Jacuzzis. Bidets. Subzero refrigerators. Three-car garages, plus a separate garage for your golf cart."

Presently, Point O' Palms consists of six "neighborhoods," although construction is under way for at least six more. The neighborhoods have names like "Crystal Isles," "Leeward Estates," and "Mangrove Way," and every house in its neighborhood looks exactly like the one on either side of it, right down to the landscaping. For example, the "Windemere Key" neighborhood is adjacent to the North golf course and features pastel-colored houses that are Bahamian in architecture. The "Coral Cove" neighborhood, where my parents live, is set close to the marina and offers Mediterranean-style homes complete with red tile roofs.

It was nearly noon when we drove through the Point O' Palms gatehouse in our rental car. Our plane had landed right on time at the Fort Lauderdale airport, thank goodness. Never a fan of flying (did they have to call the airline building a "terminal"?), I had been particularly on edge during the two-and-a-half-hour flight from LaGuardia, to the point where I'd needed three drinks to calm me down. It wasn't the occasional turbulence that had made me anxious, I knew, or Kimberley's presence, or even the fact that the man who sat in front of us insisted on leaving his window shade open during the movie. No, whatever had caused my anxiety was far less obvious. But there it was and continued to be—a very real sense of foreboding that I just couldn't shake, no matter how many Bloody Marys I threw back.

"It's probably from all those weeks of wondering who murdered Claire," Hunt suggested when I told him I had a bad case of the willies. "After what happened to you in our elevator, who would blame you for feeling shaky? You could be having a delayed reaction. 'Post-traumatic stress,' isn't that what they call it?"

I nodded and tried to concentrate on happy thoughts, on the fact that I had made it out of Belford alive; that I had escaped the lunacy of The Oaks; that I no longer had a murder case weighing on me; that the police knew who killed Claire and would put him away; and that I didn't have to worry about anyone breaking into my house, especially since Arlene was staying there and looking after it.

Kimberley had been remarkably pleasant during the flight. She even thanked me for letting her come along on the trip. She said she liked being included instead of left out. Maybe she was growing up. Maybe we all were.

"Here we are, everybody," I said as Hunt pulled into my parents' driveway.

Arthur and Lucille Mills were standing on the lawn waiting for us. My father waved, while my mother chatted with someone on her portable cellular phone.

"Lucille, hang up. They're here," my father nudged her.

"I can see that, Arthur. I have eyes," said my mother, who ended her call, rested the phone on the front steps of the house, and rushed over to our car. She was wearing a mauve jogging outfit, Reeboks, and a Florida Marlins baseball cap, which must have infuriated my father, the Mets fan. He had on *his* Florida uniform: madras shirt, white slacks, white shoes.

"Hello, hello," said my mother as she hugged and kissed me, then Hunt. "And look at Kimberley! What a big girl she is! And so bee-yew-tiful!"

Kimberley pretended to wince as my mother clasped her to her ample bosom and covered her cheeks with wet, sloppy kisses. But I could tell my stepdaughter was flattered by the attention. She never received that kind of overt affection from her mother—or, for that matter, from me.

We carried our bags inside as we talked about the flight down, the food on the flight down, the weather, how well we all looked, etc. After we had unpacked, we were summoned to the pool for the huge lunch my mother had prepared for us.

"You didn't have to do all this, Mom," I said as I surveyed the platters of food. There were salads, cold cuts, pastas, breads, cookies, pastries. My mother's idea of a light repast.

As we ate, I asked my parents what plans they had made for my father's birthday party the following evening.

"We're going to Stefano's," said my father. "I made a reservation for seven-thirty." Stefano's, an Italian eatery, was one of three restaurants in Point O' Palms. The other two were Chinese, and they delivered.

"I wanted to throw a party for your father here at the house, invite some friends, people from the club, go all the way," said my mother. "But Arthur wouldn't hear of it. The man didn't want me to exert myself. He's convinced I'm going to drop dead any second."

"Drop dead? What are you talking about?" I asked.

"Oh, you know Arthur. The way he worries."

I looked at my father, then back at her. "No, I don't know the way he worries. He's never struck me as much of a worrier."

"Well, he's a worrier now," she said. "Ever since I had that incident."

"What incident, Lucille?" said Hunt.

"Just some heart thing," said my mother.

"What heart thing?" I said, putting my fork down on the plate and looking at my mother expectantly. I was more than a little alarmed. She had always been so strong, so healthy. She'd certainly never said a word about a "heart thing."

"A few months ago. I had chest pains." She shrugged. "No big deal."

"Mom! You had chest pains and you didn't tell me?"

"What's to tell? The doctor sent me home from the hospital after a couple—"

"You were in the hospital?"

I had always thought my relationship with my parents was a close one, considering that they lived in Florida and I lived in Connecticut. We spoke on the phone every Sunday. We visited each other at least once a year. We didn't have periods of estrangement. We didn't go on "Oprah" and accuse each other of heinous crimes. Besides, my mother had always been somewhat of a kvetch, who told you more about her aches and pains that you ever wanted to know. So why had I been kept in the dark about her chest pains and hospitalization? Why hadn't my parents said a word about something so potentially serious? Instead, they'd acted as if my mother had been in perfect health when they'd been up North the previous month.

"We didn't want to worry you," was my father's explanation. "What was the point?"

"The point?" I said, my voice rising. "The point is that I'm your daughter. Your only daughter. You're supposed to be honest with me. When I call you every Sunday and say, 'How are you?,' you're supposed to tell me. You're supposed to tell me what's *really* going on with you, even if it's bad. Especially if it's bad."

"Excuse me," Kimberley interjected, her mouth full of egg salad. "But I'm *your* only daughter and you and Daddy don't tell *me* what's really going on with you. I always feel like you tell me one thing but really mean another."

I was too stunned to speak. I had just arrived in Florida for a few days of vacation, and suddenly I was in the middle of a psychodrama.

"What do you mean, pumpkin?" Hunt asked Kimberley. "I've never heard you say those things before."

"I never heard Judy say those things to her parents before," she replied. "It made me realize that you two treat me exactly like they treat her."

"Oh, now Kim," I said. "Let's not get carried away here. You—"

"I'm telling you," she went on, ignoring my interruption and directing her comments to Hunt, "that whenever there's a problem—like when Judy lost her job or when you two are mad at each other—you always try to pretend everything's fine. You treat me like a total retard. Like I'm too stupid to understand anything."

Hunt patted Kimberley's knee and said, "I had no idea you felt that way, Kim. Neither did Judy, I'm sure. I guess our only excuse is that we know that you have a lot to deal with in your life—your schoolwork, your friends, your mom—and we don't want to add to it by laying our problems on you."

"Well put, Hunt," my mother applauded. "Now you all understand why your father and I didn't mention my heart thing."

"Look, Mom, Dad. I can appreciate the desire to protect me," I said. "But if there's a serious medical problem, I really should have been told."

"All right. So we're telling you," said my father. "The doctor says your mother has early signs of clogged arteries. But you know Lucille. She knows everything. She thinks she can carry on as if she's seventeen."

"Now, Arthur. Don't exaggerate. So I had some chest pains," my mother said. "I'm supposed to exercise and watch the cholesterol now, Judy. But does anybody really expect me to change my lifestyle—at my age?" She rolled her eyes and shoved a large forkful of chopped liver into her mouth.

I felt sick. My mother had heart trouble, yet she didn't seem to care. Was this what my sense of foreboding had been about? Had I somehow known that my mother was going to reveal that she had health problems? "Mom, no wonder Daddy's worried about you," I sighed. "Do you still have the pains?"

"Not really," she said. "The doctor gave me some pills. Now. Let's forget all about this business and talk about your father's birthday. A man doesn't turn seventy-five every day, you know."

My mother began to describe the new set of golf clubs she'd bought my father for his birthday, but Kimberley cut her off. She wanted to keep talking about the way Hunt and I never treated her like a real person.

"Take the time we were at the country club and I found Judy's beeper in her purse," she told my parents. "Dad was real mad because he didn't even know that Judy *had* a beeper. And then when he saw the message that this guy sent her, he went nuts. He got real jealous and accused her of sleeping with the guy. The next thing I know, Dad is taking me to my grandparents' house and not telling me a thing!"

My parents eyed me.

"Sleeping with *what* guy?" they said simultaneously.

I shook my head. "It's not what you think," I told them.

"Judy. Not you. Not our daughter," said my father. "We didn't bring you up to—"

"You see that, Arthur?" my mother interrupted. "I knew something was funny when we visited them in July. I even asked her about it. Remember, Judy?"

"Hunt, tell them," I said. "Tell them I wasn't fooling around. Tell them I was doing a job, for God's sake."

"I thought you couldn't get a job," said my mother. "You told me your friend Arlene found another job but you couldn't."

"Right," I said. "But I meant that I couldn't get a publishing job. The job I got was a police job."

"A police job?" my parents said, once again in unison.

I took a deep breath and told everybody all about my job as a police informant.

"You were involved in that Claire Cox murder case and didn't tell your parents about it?" said my father.

"Or your stepdaughter?" said Kimberley.

"I didn't want any of you to worry," I said. "You would have worried if you'd known."

"Aha! Now you see why we didn't tell you about your mother's chest pains," said my father. "Nobody wants to worry anybody."

"So nobody tells anybody the truth," said Kimberley with a pout.

"Look, everybody. Let's just agree that, from now on, we'll stop protecting each other and be honest," I said.

Hunt lifted his water glass. "A toast," he said. "To honesty."

We all clinked glasses and drank.

"On second thought," said my mother, setting her glass down. "I want to hear more about the murder case, Judy. How do we know you're not in any danger?"

"I told you," I said. "The police caught the guy who killed Claire. He was the chef at the club."

"But you said he hasn't been arrested for the murder yet," said my father. "Only for the kickbacks. And that he's still out on bail."

"Detective Cunningham said that, by the time we come home from Florida, Brendan Hardy will be back in jail," I said. "For good."

"I certainly hope so," said my mother.

"Hey, let's drink to that," Hunt said, lifting his glass once more. "To putting Claire Cox's murderer away—for good."

"Here, here," I said.

We all clinked glasses again. Then Hunt and my father volunteered to clear the table and do the dishes.

"What do you say you and I go swimming?" I asked Kimberley, bracing myself for her usual reluctance to do anything with me.

She considered the question, then did something truly startling: she smiled at me and said, "Sure." Then she jumped off her seat and went into her room to put on her bathing suit.

"See that?" said my mother, who had observed the scene. "All it took was a little food. You feed the girl and she's happy."

That night the five of us enjoyed a relaxing evening. Well, it would have been if I had been able to relax. But I couldn't. The anxiety hovered, made worse by the revelation of my mother's heart trouble.

We cooked swordfish on the grill, took a swim, and watched *Goodbye Columbus,* my parents' favorite movie. Everything's fine, I told myself. Just fine.

My father's birthday began on a cheerful note. Hunt and I were just waking up when Kimberley knocked on our door about eight-thirty and said she was taking a walk with my parents, who had recently started walking one or two miles each morning. After I heard the front door slam, I rolled over and tapped Hunt on the shoulder.

"Booch?" I said. "It's just the two of us in the house. What do you say we take advantage of our good fortune?"

"I say, 'I'd love to. Come closer.' "

And so I did.

We made sweet, languorous love in my parents' sunny guest room overlooking the pool. Afterward, I clung to Hunt and said, "Am I being paranoid or are things going a little too well on this trip so far, aside from the stuff about my mother's chest pains, I mean?"

"Why shouldn't they go well?" he said. "We're on vacation. Besides, they only kept your mother in the hospital for observation. If she was seriously ill, they would have recommended open heart surgery or some other procedure. She's going to be fine, if she watches her diet."

"That's a big 'if,' " I said. "My mother's never met a piece of cheesecake she didn't like."

The weather on Saturday was as hot and humid as the day before. Hunt and my father intended to play golf. My mother had a bridge game. And Kimberley and I decided to check out the mall.

"I like malls," Kimberley said as we strolled past the shops. "I wish they had them in New York. We don't have anything good in New York. Everybody's always rushing around and forgetting you exist."

"Forgetting you exist?" It was a strange thing to say, and I turned to look at her. She had always tried to seem so tough, so sophisticated, so urbane. It was easy to forget that she was young and vulnerable—a little girl who'd been left by her daddy at a young age and would probably never get over it, no matter how often he visited her.

"Who forgets you exist, Kim?" I asked. "Are things okay between you and your mom?" I wondered if Bree had found herself a boyfriend. Or maybe Bree had found herself a job. Fat chance.

"My mother is busy with her acting classes," she said. "And my dad is busy with his job. And *you're* busy with . . . I don't know what you're busy with, but you never have time for me."

I felt a wave of tenderness toward her—and of confusion. Kimberley had never given me the impression that she wanted to spend even five minutes with me. I'd always thought she wished I'd drop off the face of the earth.

"I'm sorry you feel that way," I said. We were standing in front of an electronics store, and a half a dozen boom boxes were booming with rap music. "Why don't we sit down somewhere," I suggested. "I'll buy you a soda and we can talk quietly, huh?"

She agreed and we found an ice cream parlor on the second level of the mall and ordered a couple of Cokes.

We talked for an hour and a half. About the divorce. About her mother and father. About me. About how I act as if I don't have time for her and, worse, as if I don't like her.

"Is that why you're so angry whenever you come to Belford?" I asked, grateful that Kimberley was unburdening herself to me this way. It was the first time.

"I don't know," she said. "I guess so. I get mad when you act like

Daddy is all you care about and that you have to be with me because he says so."

I shook my head and put my hand on hers. "I'm so sorry if I've made you feel that way," I said, and began to describe to Kimberley how much I cared for her, how much I wanted us to be close. She listened intently as she sipped her soda, her lower lip quivering occasionally.

"I'm so sorry," I said again. "I'll try to be a better stepmother. But you have to try too, Kim. You have to try to understand that it takes both of us to make our relationship work. We have to treat each other with love and respect."

At the mention of the word "respect," she sat up very straight in her chair, looked me right in the eye, and said in her most grown-up voice, "No problem."

I smiled. "Good. Want to get back out there and do some serious shopping?"

She did, and so we did.

We pulled into my parents' driveway just after one o'clock and found Hunt pacing on the front lawn, a worried look on his face.

"Jude! Where have you been?" was the way he greeted us.

"At the mall," I said. "I thought you were playing golf with Dad."

"I was, but something's happened."

My hand flew to my mouth. My mother! "Okay," I said. "You can tell me, Hunt. We promised we'd tell each other everything, no matter how serious."

"That's right, Dad," said Kimberley as she got out of the car and joined us on the lawn. "You've got to tell us."

I reached for her hand and squeezed it. She inched closer to me.

"Go on, Hunt. Tell us," I said. "How bad is she?"

"She's in the hospital," he frowned.

"Oh, God," I said. "Is she . . . ?"

He shook his head. "But it's serious," he admitted.

I gasped. "We've got to go to her," I managed. "Right away!"

"Okay," said Hunt. "I didn't know what you'd want to do about your father's birthday party tonight, but there's a flight out of here at five o'clock this afternoon, and we could—"

"Flight out of here?" I said. "What are you talking about?"

"I know it's Arthur's birthday," said Hunt, "but I thought you'd want to get right to the—"

"Hunt! If my mother is in serious condition, why on earth would I want to leave Boca?"

"It's not your mother who's in serious condition," he said.

"Not my mother?" I looked at Hunt, who was obviously in such a state that he wasn't thinking clearly. "Then who is it?"

"Arlene," he said.

I stared at him. "Arlene Handlebaum?"

He nodded. "Somebody broke into our house last night and tried to kill her. The police have arrested Brendan Hardy. He denies it, of course, but then he denied killing Claire too."

I grabbed Kimberley and clutched her to me.

"I still don't understand," I said as my heart raced and my mouth went dry. "Why would Brendan—"

"Come inside," Hunt said, "and I'll tell you what I know."

What Hunt knew was what Tom Cunningham told him when he had called my parents' house, just as Hunt and my father were about to leave for the golf course. Apparently, at ten o'clock on Friday night, Tom had been summoned to the scene of the crime—our house— after Arlene had been viciously beaten about the head and face and, after she had been left for dead, had managed to drag herself to the phone and call 911. From what the police had been able to piece together, it seemed that Arlene had been upstairs in our guest room, reading a manuscript, when she heard someone enter through the front door. She must have called out and surprised the person, who then panicked and attacked her. When the police found her, she was lying on the floor near the telephone, dazed, in shock, her head a mass of contusions, her memory a combination of incomprehensible images and terrifying nothingness. She was rushed to the hospital and diagnosed as suffering from a subdural hematoma as well as cerebral edema, which had required several hours of delicate brain surgery to remove. But instead of recovering, she had lapsed into a coma, which the doctors had pronounced rare but not unheard of. They were hopeful that she would emerge very quickly from her sleeplike state. So were the police, who were eager for her to wake up and identify Brendan as her attacker.

"The doctors really think she's going to come out of the coma and be all right?" I asked, barely able to process the information I was being given. My friend, Arlene, was in a coma! After spending the night at *my* house!

"According to Tom, there's a good possibility she'll be fine. In time," said Hunt. "He's been right on top of things at the hospital. Hardly left Arlene's side. And I don't think it's just because he's waiting for her to regain consciousness and identify Brendan. I think he genuinely feels bad about what happened to her."

"I'm sure he does," I said. "He's a very sensitive man. But what about Brendan? How did they figure out that he was the one who did it?" I suddenly flashed back to my ordeal in the elevator and recalled the way Brendan had disguised his voice, calling me on the elevator phone and threatening me in that bizarre, singsong pitch. "Mrs. Price," he had teased. "Mrs. Price, I have a message for you." I shuddered, despite the Florida heat.

"There was a cigarette butt in the kitchen sink," said Hunt. "It was too wet for them to get prints on it, but there was one thing they *could* determine: it was Brendan's brand—Merit."

"But why?" I asked. "Why would Brendan go back to our house? He was out on bail for the kickback scheme at the club. He was about to be arrested for Claire's murder. Why would he make matters worse for himself?"

"Tom says it has to do with the criminal mentality," said Hunt. "That if Brendan knew he could break into our house once, he also knew he could break into our house twice, the theory being that hardcore criminals always need that one last hit, that one last thrill, that one last high before they're caught." Hunt paused to consider his words. "And then there was the more practical reason."

"Which was?"

"That there was something in our house he wanted."

"Such as?"

"Evidence against him. His lawyer, the illustrious Patrick Delaney, must have advised him that he was about to be arrested for Claire's murder. Tom thinks Brendan found out we were in Florida and decided to come looking for evidence, afraid we might have something in the house, something that would put him away for life, something he could steal. Unfortunately for Arlene, he had no idea there was anybody home."

"I can't believe this happened," I said angrily. "Brendan should have been in jail weeks ago. If only the Tewksburys had gone to the police about him, instead of to their grand-niece. If only we hadn't taken so long to discover his kickback scheme. If we'd been able to put all the pieces together faster, Arlene would be all right and this whole mess would be well behind us."

"Does all this mean we have to leave Florida tonight?" asked Kimberley with obvious disappointment.

"I don't know what to do," I said. "I hate to miss my father's birthday. But I can't enjoy it either, knowing that Arlene is lying in a hospital bed, half-dead, because she decided to spend a relaxing weekend at our house."

"Would you like to stay here, pumpkin?" Hunt asked his daughter. "Even if Judy and I go home, you could probably stay here with Grandma and Grandpa Mills."

She shook her head. "I want to be with you and Judy," she said firmly.

When my parents came home twenty minutes later, we discussed whether we should return to Connecticut or stay in Florida.

"You can't do anything for your friend tonight," my mother said. "Why not stay for Arthur's birthday and go back in the morning?"

Which was what we did.

I tried my best to enjoy the evening, but thoughts of Arlene, Brendan, and our house of horrors continued to haunt me. The only consolation was that Brendan had finally been arrested and jailed and, according to Tom, would not be roaming the streets anytime soon.

We left Boca Raton early the next morning and arrived in Belford around noon. I dropped Hunt and Kimberley at the house, then drove to the hospital to see Arlene.

There was a policeman posted at her door and her parents were sitting at her bedside. I told them how sorry I was about what had happened to their daughter at my house. They told me not to blame myself and left me alone with Arlene.

It was difficult to be in the same room with her, painful to see how ill she was. She looked so pale, so fragile, as she lay in bed, her right cheek bruised and swollen, her newly shorn head wrapped in bandages that were held in place by something called a "neurocap," a sort of beanie that, in happier times, would have made her laugh. "How did this all happen?" I whispered to her, tears rolling slowly down my cheeks. It seemed only days ago that we were sitting in my office at Charlton House, gabbing about Loathsome Leeza and wondering when she would reveal herself as the Know-Nothing she was and be tossed out on her butt the way we eventually were. How had we come to this: I becoming a police informant, she slipping into a coma? And when would our lives get back to normal?

Normal, I thought, as I watched Arlene sleep. My life hadn't been normal for a very long time, not since Hunt joined that dopey country club and put us all in jeopardy.

"Judy?"

I looked up from the bed. It was Tom. I stood up and went to him. He hugged me for several seconds, patting my back and telling me everything was going to be all right. Then, he pulled away.

"I'm glad you're here," he said. "Glad you're safe."

I nodded.

He looked over at Arlene. "How is she?"

"The same, I guess. Oh, Tom. She's *got* to be all right. She's such a wonderful person. Such a good friend. And such a romantic."

"Tell me," he said. "I want to know all about her."

There was something in the way he said it that made me do a double take. He reminded me of Dana Andrews in the movie *Laura*—the cop who found himself mooning over a woman he'd never met but should have saved. But then Tom had once told me he was a sucker for damsels in distress. And Arlene Handlebaum was definitely in distress.

"Well," I began, "Arlene's the best romance editor in publishing . . ." and I proceeded to give Detective Tom Cunningham a thumbnail sketch of the woman who had been my closest friend in the book business. He seemed very moved when I explained that, despite her talent, attractiveness, and good nature, Arlene had never been married or even had a long-term relationship with a man. "She always aimed high when it came to men," I said. "She was looking for Prince Charming and never found him."

He smiled. "Then there's no way she won't come out of this coma," he said. "Not when her Prince Charming is still out there waiting for her."

CHAPTER TWENTY

♦

While Arlene languished in the hospital and Brendan languished in jail, The Oaks geared up for Labor Day Weekend, the final hurrah of the season. Despite the torrent of negative publicity about the club in the tabloid media, which covered Claire's murder and Brendan's evil deeds with lip-smacking excess, the longtime members carried on as if nothing much had occurred. Larkin Vail was still favored to win the women's singles tournament, Curtis Lamb was everybody's pick to be the year's golf champion, and the Tewksburys, those rascals, were as popular as ever. Instead of being shunned for having given birth to a monster like Brendan and neglecting to tell any of their friends about it, they were sympathized with, fussed over, treated as heroic victims. It was sickening.

Given that my job as a police informant was over, there didn't seem to be any reason for me to go to the club again—ever. Addison Bidwell, Perry Vail, and the other traditionalists viewed Hunt and me as traitors; there was nobody there who would help me get a job in publishing; my tennis game was never going to be any better than mediocre; and after Labor Day weekend the place essentially shut down anyway. But Hunt missed the club and yearned to play golf with Ducky, who was one of the few members who supported our efforts in crime-busting and was grateful that we'd helped the police nail Claire's killer.

"The hell with those people. Why don't you go ahead and play golf with Ducky this weekend?" I asked Hunt. "He's invited you several times. And you know you're dying to play. Don't stay away from The Oaks because those plaid-panted jerks have turned on you."

"You're right, I do miss the golf," said Hunt. "And why should I care what people are saying about us? We did the right thing by working with the police. I know we did."

"Of course we did," I said. "So get Ducky on the phone and tell him you'll play this weekend."

"I have a better idea: I'll tell him *we'll* play this weekend."

"Not me. Golf is your thing, not mine."

"Fine. Don't play. Just come with us. We can make a foursome of it: you and I and Ducky and Nedra."

"Nedra? Come on," I said. "She'd never tear herself away from the tennis courts and Rob."

"I think that's over with," Hunt said. "Ducky mentioned something about Nedra wanting to work harder on the marriage."

"Really?" I said. "The last time I saw her, she gave me the distinct impression that their marriage was a sham. She had nothing but disdain for Ducky and said they hadn't had sex in years."

"Oh, Nedra's got a screw loose," Hunt scoffed. "Ducky Laughton is a good guy. Much too good for Nedra. He doesn't deserve to be humiliated the way she's humiliated him at the club."

"No, he doesn't," I conceded. "Although he sounded like he would have put the moves on Claire if she'd let him. You make Ducky out to be a saint, but I heard him tell Claire she was his grand passion. He wanted to have an affair with her, Hunt. There was no doubt about it."

He shrugged. "Maybe. But Claire's gone and Ducky's still the best friend I've got at The Oaks."

"Exactly. So play golf with him."

"Only if you join us."

"Nope."

"Aw come on, Jude. Ride along in the cart while Ducky and I play eighteen holes."

I sighed. "I'd love to spend time with you, Booch, but eighteen holes will take hours. I couldn't bear to be out on a golf course that long. It would be torture. Total boredom."

"All right. Then how about a compromise: come along for nine holes? It'll only take *half* as long. The scenery will be nice and the company even better."

I kissed him. "All right, I'll come—as long as we can take a golf cart. I realize that walking the course is great exercise, but you know how I feel about exercise."

"About the same way you feel about The Oaks."

"Exactly."

"No problem. We'll take a cart. Actually, we'll probably take two carts. Ducky doesn't like to walk the course any more than you do. So he'll drive his; you can drive ours."

The golf date with Ducky was for Sunday afternoon at five o'clock. "It doesn't get dark until seven-thirty or so," Ducky had said to Hunt when they were making plans. "And if we play late in the day, you won't have to face all the Neanderthals. By five, they're all in the bar, getting smashed. We'll probably have the entire course to ourselves." Hunt and I liked the idea of avoiding the members' disapproving stares, so five o'clock it was.

On the way to the club, we stopped at the hospital to check on Arlene. When we arrived, her parents and sister had just stepped out for a dinner break, and Tom had taken their place at her bedside. He had been there every time I'd visited.

"Is your interest professional or personal?" I'd asked him earlier in the week. I knew he was eager for Arlene to wake up from the coma and identify Brendan Hardy as her attacker. I also knew Tom Cunningham was a lonely man who had a penchant for reaching out to women in need.

"Both, I guess," he'd admitted. "There's something about her that just gets to me. Something about her face. Something about the way she . . . oh, I don't know. It's pretty ridiculous, but I have this feeling that if she ever . . . oh, never mind."

He stopped.

"Ever what?" I prodded. "Comes out of the coma?"

He nodded. "I just have this feeling that we'd hit it off," he said shyly. "Stupid, huh?"

"Of course not," I said.

"I'm just a romantic, I guess," he said.

"Then you and Arlene *will* hit it off," I said. "There's no doubt in my mind."

"We'll see," he said. "We'll just see what happens."

Wouldn't it be wonderful? I thought to myself. Wouldn't it be wonderful if Arlene recovered and fell in love with Tom? And didn't we all deserve some good news after what we'd been through?

As Hunt and I entered Arlene's hospital room the following Sunday afternoon, Tom greeted us, looking grim and exhausted.

"No change," he told us. "She's still in the coma. But that's not necessarily bad," he added. "The doctor says she's stable, whatever that means. He says she could come out of the coma at any time and be perfectly fine."

"I hope that's what happens. In the meantime, how are *you* doing?" I asked Tom.

"Okay. I just stopped in to check on her." He glanced at Arlene, his eyes full of compassion.

"You look pretty beat to me, buddy," said Hunt. "Don't they give cops a day off?"

"Yeah, actually this *is* my day off," said Tom.

"Then how about relaxing a little?" said Hunt. "Judy and I are on our way to The Oaks. I'm playing golf with Ducky Laughton, and she's going to cheer me on—if she can stay awake. Want to come along? Maybe play nine holes with us?"

"Thanks but no thanks," said Tom.

"Aw, come on," Hunt said. "You met Ducky during your investigation. He's a neat guy, really. Nothing like the rest of the folks there."

"I'm sure he is, but no cigar."

"Now Tom, we've got a new chef at the club," I teased. "He's only temporary, until they find a real replacement for Brendan, but I hear he can make a mean cheeseburger."

Tom shook his head. "I think I'm going home and get some sleep. I could use it."

I nodded. "Maybe we'll call you later, to see if you changed your mind and feel like company. We could have dinner."

"I'll see," said Tom. "You've got my home number, right?"

"Yup. Now go on," I urged. "We'll check on you later. Meanwhile, we'll sit with Arlene until her family comes back."

Tom gave Arlene a last look, waved goodbye to us, and left.

"He's torturing himself," I said to Hunt. "He thinks he could have prevented Arlene from getting hurt. Just the way he probably thinks he could have prevented his wife from getting killed."

"Poor guy," said Hunt. "I wish there was something we could do."

"There was something we could do and we did it," I said. "We got Brendan to incriminate himself in the kickback scheme at the club, which provided the police with the motive for Claire's murder. It wasn't our fault that the justice system moves at a snail's pace."

Hunt and I drove over to the club and walked to the golf course, where Ducky was waiting for us. He looked jaunty and full of pep in his kelly green slacks and bright yellow polo shirt, his chubby cheeks rosy with the outdoors. I tried to picture him as a college student at Berkeley, protesting the war and romancing Claire. But the only image that came to mind was the one Nedra had planted in my mind: the asexual husband who "got his rocks off in other ways," whatever that meant.

"Judy," he said, then kissed me on the cheek. "So good to see you."

"Thanks, Ducky. You too," I said and patted his arm. "It's a relief to find someone at this club who doesn't throw things at us."

"Don't pay any attention to the Neanderthals," he advised. "They just don't get it."

"Ducky's right," said Hunt. "Who needs 'em."

I looked at my husband and blinked. Was this the same man who had spent the past two years courting the members of The Oaks, the same man who had *campaigned* for their friendship? Was this the same man who'd been so desperate for a partnership at F&F that he was willing to suck up to people like Duncan Tewksbury and Addison Bidwell? Was this the same man who'd been willing to make a complete ass of himself in exchange for a chance to invest their money in crude oil, natural gas, and pork bellies? I blinked again.

"Yeah, fuck 'em," Hunt went on. "It's a beautiful evening. The course looks great. Brendan Hardy's in jail and we're healthy. So let's forget all the bullshit and play nine holes before it gets dark."

"Atta boy," said Ducky, who slapped Hunt on the back and winked at me.

We were on the fourth hole when it happened. I know it was the fourth hole, not because I was ever able to tell one hole from another, but because it was on the fourth hole that Claire Cox had met her untimely death, and one doesn't forget things like that.

In an attempt to fortify myself against the inevitable boredom that came over me every time I tried to watch Hunt play golf, I'd brought along the September issue of *Gourmet,* and as Hunt and Ducky drove and putted and chipped their way onto the green, I sat in the golf cart in the late afternoon sun and immersed myself in articles extolling the virtues of Chicken Breasts with Horseradish-Scallion Crust, Peppered Pork Tenderloin with Cherry Salsa, and Raspberry Chocolate Meringue Pie.

I was deeply involved in a recipe for Grilled Tortilla and Onion Cake when I heard Hunt calling me. I looked up and saw that he and Ducky were standing on the green, their balls a few feet away from the cup. The other golfers had long since departed for the bar, so the course was deserted; the three of us were the only ones around.

"Jude!" Hunt waved excitedly. "You've got to watch me sink this putt. God willing, I'm about to birdie the hole."

I saluted him. "I'm sure you'll birdie the hole," I said, "but you know how I feel about watching you putt. It's about as riveting as watching the man who comes to the house to read the gas meter."

Hunt pretended to pout, while Ducky laughed, shook a finger at me, and said in a high, falsetto voice, meant, I supposed, to mimic a nagging wife, "Mrs. Price, you're not being very supportive of your husband's golf addiction."

Ducky was joking, just as I had been, and so his words didn't register at first. In fact, I went back to my magazine and promptly forgot all about them. Then, as I was rereading the recipe for Grilled Tortilla and Onion Cake and wondering whether I'd screw it up if I substituted vidalia onions for the Spanish ones, Ducky's remark came back to me—with a vengeance—and I gasped.

"Mrs. Price, you're not being very supportive of your husband's golf addiction," he'd scolded.

I felt a chill, then a wave of dizziness, then a mixture of feelings—confusion, revulsion, and fear.

"Mrs. Price, you're not being very supportive of your husband's golf addiction."

The words reverberated in my mind, and as they did, my throat closed.

"Mrs. Price." . . . "Mrs. Price." . . . "Mrs. Price."

It wasn't *what* Ducky had said that made me drop the magazine onto the floor of the golf cart and sit straight up, my body taut with terror. It was the way he'd said my *name,* the tone he'd used, the high-pitched, singsong *voice* he'd used. The same eery, sickeningly sweet voice that had belonged to the person who'd trapped me in my elevator and warned me to stop snooping around at the club.

"Someone who just wants to send you a little message, Mrs. Price."

That's what the voice had said that awful afternoon. At the time, I'd been unable to determine whether it belonged to a man or a woman. All I knew was that, despite the playful quality of the voice, it had been intended to disguise the speaker's identity and frighten me away from the club, warning me to stop asking questions about Claire's murder . . . or else.

"Mrs. Price, you're not being very supportive of your husband's golf addiction."

I shook my head and tried to shake off the thoughts that threatened to strangle me, tried to tell myself they weren't true, tried to tell myself *it* wasn't true. But I couldn't.

"Mrs. Price." . . . "Mrs. Price."

I hadn't been the only one to blame Brendan for breaking into the house and holding me hostage in the elevator. The police had blamed him too. We'd all thought it was Brendan who had disguised his voice; Brendan who had killed Claire and nearly killed Arlene. He'd been ripping off the members of The Oaks with his kickbacks schemes; it had seemed perfectly logical that he had killed Claire to prevent her from turning him in. Even his own parents had blamed him for killing her. But we'd been wrong—all of us. Ducky was the guilty one. The question was why? Why would respectable, mild-mannered, politically correct Ducky kill Claire, a woman he admired? Because she'd jilted him when they were in college?

"Jude! I made the putt! I birdied the hole!" Hunt said as he patted Ducky on the butt.

"See that, Mrs. Price? You're married to a pro!" said Ducky in That Voice. That same falsetto, singsong voice.

So it was Ducky, I realized with devastating clarity. Ducky who had killed Claire the night of the July Fourth party. Ducky who had warned me off the case. Ducky who had struck Arlene and sent her into a coma. Ducky who was Hunt's friend, colleague, and business associate. But why? Was he crazy? He had to be. But what had set him off? Claire's admission to The Oaks? Her unwillingness to resume their relationship? Nedra's affair with Rob, the tennis pro? What?

There wasn't time to figure out why Ducky was a monster. There was only time to get the hell away from him.

"Hunt," I said, trying desperately not to look Ducky in the eye. "We have to leave. Now."

He nudged Ducky and laughed. "There she goes again," he sighed. "My wife, the golf nut."

"Hunt, I'm serious," I said. "I don't feel well. I want to get out of here."

He and Ducky looked at each other, then began to walk toward me.

"Do you think it was something you ate?" asked Ducky.

I tried not to look at him, tried to avoid his gaze, but I couldn't help myself. And in that precise moment of eye contact, Ducky Laughton knew the truth: that he had inadvertently revealed himself to me—and that I was a golf cart ride away from telling the police.

"Hunt, please. Just take me home," I said.

"But Ducky and I have another five holes to play, Jude," said Hunt. "Are you sure you don't want to wait in the ladies' locker room? Or maybe get something cold to drink while we finish—"

"No!" I cried. I turned the ignition key and started up the golf cart. "Please, Hunt. Get in the cart."

Hunt looked at Ducky, shrugged, and hopped into the cart next to me. "Sorry, pal," he told his golfing buddy. "Can we reschedule?"

"Sure, but not until we're sure that Judy's all right," said Ducky, feigning concern.

"I'll be all right as soon as they put you away," I said, unable to control the rage that surged through me. Ducky Laughton had proposed Hunt and me for membership in The Oaks, pretended to be our friend, pretended to be our lone supporter at the club, when all the while he was responsible for Claire's murder and God knows what else.

"What did you say, Judy?" he asked.

"You heard me," I said, my voice quivering. "I said I'm going to make sure you're put away for life, make sure you don't hurt anyone ever again."

Ducky's eyes were locked on mine as his expression darkened. He turned to Hunt and said, "I'm awfully sorry this happened, old boy. Awfully sorry."

"Awfully sorry *what* happened?" said Hunt, who looked at Ducky, then at me, then back at Ducky. "Am I missing something here?"

Before I could respond, Ducky reached for the key to our golf cart and turned it to shut the cart off. I batted his hand away and restarted the cart.

"Hey, what's going on, you two?" Hunt asked.

Without responding, I shifted the cart into the forward gear, put my foot on the accelerator, and attempted to drive us down the path, past the fourth hole, around the course, and back to the first tee. All

I could think about was getting away from Ducky, getting to a phone, and calling Tom.

But Ducky had other ideas. He jumped into his cart and began to chase us.

Dear God, I thought, as we chugged across the course in our battery-operated cart. Where in the world is everybody? The one time I want to attract the attention of the members of this dopey club, they're nowhere to be found!

Golf carts aren't exactly Maseratis, but I had managed to give us a nice head start. Unfortunately, because there were two of us in our cart, it carried a heavier load and moved slower than Ducky's. Not only that, Ducky was a more experienced golf cart driver than I was. He was able to zigzag his way along the path and gain on us very quickly.

"Judy! Will you tell me what the hell is going on here?" Hunt yelled as he turned around and saw Ducky following in hot pursuit.

"He did it!" I cried. "He killed Claire!"

"Are you crazy? You know Brendan did it. So do the police."

"We were wrong. It was Ducky."

I was breathing so hard I thought I might faint, but I kept driving, kept steering the golf cart up and down the pathways that meandered across the course.

"Jude, listen to me," said Hunt. "I know how bored you get watching me play golf, but this is ridiculous. There are more subtle ways of telling me you've had enough."

"Hunt," I said, "you're going to have to trust me on this. Ducky Laughton is a cold-blooded killer. He killed Claire, he tried to kill Arlene, and if we don't get off this golf course, he's going to kill us."

"But how do you—"

Before Hunt could finish his question, we felt a jolt from behind. Then another. And another. Ducky was crashing the front of his golf cart into the rear of ours!

"Ducky!" Hunt yelled back to him. "Take it easy, would you?"

Ducky rammed into our cart once more, harder and more insistently. We were on an elevated path that overlooked the course's second hole, the hole that sloped steeply down to one of The Oaks's two man-made lakes.

"Oh, my God!" I cried out. "He's trying to tip us over!"

"But why?" said Hunt, who had finally realized there was cause for alarm.

"Hunt, listen to me," I said, trying to stay calm. "Ducky killed

Claire and he knows I know. We've got to figure a way out of this. We've got to get away from him and call Tom."

Hunt shook his head, as if he still couldn't believe what I was telling him about his friend and colleague. Then Ducky drove into the back of our cart again, this time harder and with more speed. Our tiny wheels began to wobble and the cart pitched back and forth, and before Hunt and I knew it, we were going over.

I grabbed Hunt's hand as the cart rolled over, spilling us out onto the green below.

We landed on the ground with a thud, the cart having rolled away from us and into the lake, sinking like a stone. Several seconds passed. I was so dazed, so shocked by what had happened, that I couldn't move, couldn't speak. My left arm throbbed, but I was otherwise unhurt. It was just that I was terrified. Terrified of what Ducky would do to us, now that we had no way to escape.

"Jude, are you okay?" Hunt whispered as he lay next to me, not far from the hole he had bogeyed only minutes before.

"She's just fine."

It was Ducky, and he was standing over us as we remained on the ground, captive. In his right hand was a gun—one of those compact, oh-so-handy silvery models that fits in the palm of one's hand. I tried not to gag.

"Stand up, both of you," he commanded us.

I nodded and started to pull myself up, while Hunt remained on the ground, stunned by his friend's bizarre actions.

"Come on, old boy," Ducky exhorted Hunt. "Up, up, up."

Hunt rose slowly, taking his place beside me on the second green, midway between the cup and the lake.

"Now then," said Ducky. "Here we are, just the three of us." He sighed, glancing up at the sky, which was beginning to redden in anticipation of a spectacular sunset. He returned his gaze to us. "I suppose you both want to know why," he said matter of factly, as if he were about to explain to us why he'd played a hole with a nine-iron instead of a three-iron.

"Ducky," Hunt said, wide-eyed with fear and confusion. "Tell me this is all some kind of a joke."

Ducky laughed his genial, avuncular laugh and tightened his grip on the gun.

"No, it's no joke," he said. "It's a sad story, actually. And since neither of you is in a big hurry to leave, I suppose I'll give you the unabridged version."

CHAPTER TWENTY-ONE

◆

"First, let me apologize to you, Hunt, for all the anxiety I've caused you," Ducky began as he continued to point the gun at us. "I don't want you to think I haven't valued our friendship. I've enjoyed working with you at F&F and playing golf with you here at The Oaks. You've even made serving on the Finance Committee tolerable."

Hunt shook his head. "Then why?" he asked plaintively. "Why all this? Why the gun?"

"The gun?" he shrugged. "Just for extra protection. When you play the games I play, you tend to need extra protection."

"The games?" I said disgustedly. "Is that what you call murdering the woman you considered your grand passion?"

Ducky cocked his head and looked at me. "So you did overhear that little conversation," he said. "I thought you might have. No, killing Claire was not a game. Not a game at all."

"I can't believe this. You really did it," Hunt said, finally accepting the fact that his friend was a murderer. "Back in July, when Judy told me she suspected you, I actually defended you. I kept telling her and the detective she was working with that you were an honest, stand-up guy. And now I find out that you're not. You're a fucking murderer."

"Guilty," said Ducky, nodding his head.

"You God damn son of a bitch! Why, I ought to—" Suddenly,

Hunt was charging toward Ducky, as if he wanted to tear him apart, but Ducky shoved the gun into Hunt's chest and pushed him back.

"Let's not get emotional," said Ducky, straightening the collar of his polo shirt. "Not if you want to hear the whole story."

"Hunt!" I cried. "He could have shot you!"

Hunt composed himself and stood next to me. We joined hands and waited for Ducky to speak.

"Now, you two. I wonder if you'd mind stepping back just a few feet," he said, using the gun as his pointer. "That's right. Closer to the lake. A little closer. Yes, that's perfect. I love being near the water, always have. And besides, I'd rather we stay out of sight, in case one of our fellow club members comes moseying along on this balmy evening."

We were on the edge of the lake then. The mosquitoes that had emerged in the humid dusk air began to nip at my bare legs, but I had bigger problems. Much bigger problems.

"So," Ducky said. "I'd like to start by telling you that I hadn't planned things to turn out this way today. I had fully expected to play nine holes of golf and go home. But then I had to use that silly voice of mine, and Judy had to notice. *Tant pis,* eh?"

I squeezed Hunt's hand and tried to silence my heart, which was thumping so loud in my chest I thought I'd die within seconds.

"I was always a risk taker," Ducky said wistfully, like a favorite uncle about to tell the story of his glory days on the high school basketball team. "But I was a closet risk taker. I didn't *seem* the type to take the more dangerous, less cautious route, but that was precisely what I always did. Sweet, mild-mannered Ducky, the boy who played with fire." He chuckled. I shuddered. "Yes, I was the kid who didn't study until the night before the exam, knowing he might fail. The kid who stole money from his father, knowing he'd get six lashes with the belt if he got caught. The kid who 'pushed the envelope,' as they say, always staying one step ahead of disaster. It was sport, you see. Strictly sport." He paused to swat mosquitoes with his gun. "I decided to go to Berkeley, instead of U.Va., Dad's alma mater, just to piss the old boy off. But soon after I arrived there, I found that I was bored stiff. The academics didn't interest me, nor did they challenge me particularly. And the social life—well, it was dreary, to say the least, all that rah-rah fraternity stuff. I kept myself from going stir-crazy by running card games in the dorms. Poker. Gin rummy. That sort of thing. Betting—gambling, as it were—was against the school rules, of course, but I had to feed my need for danger, didn't I? Breaking the rules was my addiction, you see?"

Hunt and I were supposed to nod, I guessed, but we clung to each other, offering Ducky nothing in the way of understanding.

"Then came the antiwar movement and the protest marches and rallies. Talk about breaking the rules! The movement was made for me. I could break rules and be thought of as a selfless activist! And then I met Clissy. Beautiful Clissy."

Ducky looked like a lovesick teenager suddenly, and I felt a wave of revulsion toward him. How could this man who had seemed so normal, so harmless, turn out to be such a monster? I'd suspected him, and Tom had talked me out of it. If only I hadn't been so quick to dismiss my feelings and examined his behavior more closely. It wouldn't have saved Claire, but it would surely have saved Arlene.

"It wasn't hard to fall in love with Claire Cox," Ducky continued. "Every guy with half a brain fell in love with her. Every guy who wasn't threatened by her, that is. She was lovely and passionate and alive. She had principles, which, of course, I did not, and when I was in her presence, I felt as if I were the most moral, principled guy in the world. Her goodness made me good. Her righteousness made me righteous. I volunteered for the committees she was on. I raised money for all the causes she supported. I made her care for me, through planning and hard work and, yes, cunning. Obviously, I wasn't going to win her with my dashing good looks. I'm a chipmunk, my charming wife never ceases to remind me. Look at me."

He patted his paunch and laughed.

"But it worked, you see," he went on. "Gradually, she realized how grateful she was for all the money I'd raised, how comfortable she felt with me, how much we had in common. We both came from old New England stock and we both angered our families with our antiestablishment stances. We were Claire and Ducky against the world, and when we finally became lovers, I felt as if I'd accomplished something important. Something that would last forever. Something that went beyond the games and plots and schemes that had been my sickness and salvation since I was a kid."

"What went wrong between you?" I asked hesitantly, aware that I might upset Ducky with my question and provoke him to use the gun. But I needed to know how his romance with Claire had led to murder, how two lives full of promise had ended in tragedy.

"Oh, there was someone else," said Ducky offhandedly. "For Claire, of course, not for me. Never for me." He swallowed hard. "He was a Russian exchange student, and he lasted a few months at the most.''

"And after they broke up? You and Claire couldn't pick up where you left off?" I asked.

"Regretfully, no. I had left Berkeley and transferred to my father's alma mater by then. I'd been banished, you see. Bounced out on my bloody ass.''

So Arlene's boyfriend Randy had recounted the story accurately. Ducky *had* left Berkeley under a cloud of suspicion.

"You see, I had been found out," he explained, his eyes becoming glassy and unfocused. "For the first time in my life, I'd gotten caught.''

"Caught at what?" asked Hunt.

"Remember when I said I'd helped Claire raise money for her causes?" said Ducky. "Well, how do you think I came up with the money? From my father, Mr. John Birch Society? Hardly.''

"You stole it?" I ventured.

"Oh, Judy. You underestimate me," Ducky chuckled. "I was never a thief. Not really. I was a game player, a sportsman.''

"Just tell us what you did," Hunt said impatiently.

"Easy, easy. I'm getting to it," Ducky replied. "Actually, my first idea *was* to ask my father for the money. I thought it would impress Claire if I came up with some cash myself, rather than to take the time to stage rallies and lectures and all that. I was always one for shortcuts, you know?" He didn't wait for a response. "But old Dad turned me down flat. He said that my 'Communist' activities were an embarrassment to the family. That's Dad for you. Conservative to a fault.'' He sighed. "So I came up with another idea: I stole tests. English lit. Poly sci. Economics. The whole lot.''

"I don't understand," I said.

"And *I* thought you said you weren't a thief," said Hunt.

"Now, now, you two. Let me finish," said Ducky. "I stole the tests, complete with the *answers* to the tests, and sold them to students. Lots of students. Students who were warned that if they breathed a word to anyone, they'd be risking expulsion. And since nobody wanted to get expelled, the scheme was a grand success. I made good money and gave it to Claire. For her antiwar causes. She thought I was wonderful, which was the point, of course.''

I shook my head. The man was sick, and his sickness was terrifying.

"Sad to say that the school eventually conducted an investigation," Ducky went on. "And it led to me.''

"They found out that you stole the tests?" I asked.

"Exactly. One of the kids fessed up, to my grave disappointment. Claire found out about it and wanted nothing to do with me. No surprise there. My father exerted his considerable influence and talked the dean at U.Va. into letting me come to Charlottesville after Berkeley threw me out."

"That explains why Claire avoided you when she joined the club," I said. "It doesn't explain why you killed her."

"No, it doesn't," Ducky conceded. "When I heard she was joining The Oaks, I was thrilled. I thought perhaps she had forgotten what had happened in college. It *was* so long ago, after all. I wanted the chance to show her I'd changed, that I'd made a life for myself as a respected and respectable member of society, that I could be trusted, that I was worthy of her at last. But it was Claire who played games, Claire who tried to pull a scam on me."

"What on earth are you talking about?" Hunt snapped.

"Claire tried to ruin me, folks," said Ducky. "Yup. Our Lady of Truth and Justice tried to destroy my life."

"Why would she want to do that?" I said. "If you ask me, it seemed as if she didn't give two shits about you."

"Oh, you're right there, Judy," Ducky said. "She certainly didn't, and she made that very clear. You see, when she found out that I had been skimming a little money off the club's—"

"You!" I interrupted him, suddenly putting things together. "So it wasn't Duncan Tewksbury. It was *you* who helped Brendan rip off the club! We suspected that one of the members was in on the kickback schemes, but we didn't suspect you, Ducky."

"Don't be too hard on yourself. Neither did anybody else," he said. "And I was on the Finance Committee, for God's sake."

"On second thought," I added, "I'll bet you engineered the schemes and used Brendan to do *your* dirty work. Am I right?"

"Right as rain," said Ducky, almost proudly.

"Jesus," said Hunt as he drew me to him. "You need help, Ducky. Big-time help."

Ducky threw his head back and laughed out loud. "I need help all right," he said. "I need to finish this story and get out of here. Nedra's having the Vails and the Bidwells over for dinner and I'm running late."

"Jesus," Hunt said again.

"Now, may I go on?" Ducky said. "Claire called me at the office, just before the July Fourth weekend, and told me she wanted to talk to me. In my naiveté, I thought she wanted to rekindle the romance, reconsider what we had together, see if she felt anything for me after twenty-five years. So I suggested we meet in a romantic place, away from Nedra and everybody else. The golf course at The Oaks seemed like a good idea—at the time. When I arrived at the fourth hole, where we'd agreed to meet the night of the party, Claire hadn't shown up yet. I noticed that someone had left the pro's pitching wedge in the sand trap. While I waited, I dug it out, walked onto the green, and took a few swings. I was all keyed up about being alone with Claire, and the exercise sort of helped me work off the tension. Then Claire came. She walked toward me, and she didn't look happy. I dropped the pitching wedge and put my arm around her. She pulled away. When I asked her what was wrong, she told me she knew all about the kickbacks and threatened to have me arrested. She brought up what happened at Berkeley and said just what you said, Hunt: that I needed help. I told her the only thing I needed was her. We quarreled. I told her I loved her. I even promised to see someone, a shrink, anything. But she wouldn't budge. She said I was a menace to society and should be put away. Not very sporting of her, eh?"

Ducky was still pointing the gun at us, but he was gripping it tighter and waving it slightly as he gestured. I squeezed Hunt's hand and prayed our ordeal was coming to an end, that Ducky would finish his story and let us go. Fat chance.

"She said she'd heard enough and started to walk away from me," Ducky continued, becoming more agitated. "I couldn't let her go. I couldn't let her go back to that party and tell everybody what I'd done. There was my marriage to think of. My job at F&F. My membership at the club. Everything. I panicked. I spotted the golf club on the ground and grabbed it. The next thing I knew I was hitting Claire on the back of the head. Over and over. I never saw her face again. I just watched her sink to the ground, then I dragged her body a few feet and laid it in the sand trap, facedown. I waited a few minutes to compose myself and then went back to the party."

Hunt and I were silent. What could we say? Or do? We were in the presence of a madman with no means of escape. Our golf cart was at the bottom of the lake. Our captor had a gun which he seemed quite capable of using. We were stuck there, alone with Ducky, at his very mercy.

"And then, of course, you two started snooping around," said Ducky wearily. "I tried to scare you off in the elevator that day, Judy. Then when you wouldn't leave it alone and got Brendan to incriminate himself in the bookkeeping office at the club, I figured I'd be the next one on your hit list. And I couldn't let that happen. I needed to find out if you had evidence against me. I knew you were going down to Florida, so I broke into your house. I had no idea you had a houseguest, obviously. Poor woman. Attractive too. I left one of Brendan's cigarettes in your kitchen sink, just in case the police wondered who hurt your friend. I try to think of everything, you know?''

I did know, and suddenly the tears came. Big, fat tears that rolled down my cheeks onto my blouse. I had dreaded the moment when Ducky would come to the end of his gruesome tale, for I knew it probably meant the end of me. And now he had.

"Ducky, listen," I said. "I can understand why you did what you did. Honestly. You're the type of person who loves a good prank, and you did those things—stealing the tests in college, overcharging the club for food, etc.—for sport, just like you said. They were pranks, that's all. Now as far as Claire's . . . accident, well I'm sure that a good lawyer will—''

"That's going to have to be all," Ducky cut me off after checking his watch. "As I told you, we've got company coming for a little Sunday night supper. Now, Hunt, I'd like you to stand here." Ducky pointed to a spot near the lake. "And Judy, you stand here." He pointed to the ground just to the left of where he was standing.

We followed his instructions, having no choice in the matter.

"What are you planning to do with us?" Hunt asked through clenched teeth.

"I'm planning to arrange a murder-suicide," he said matter of factly. "You read about them all the time in the newspaper. Dreadful stuff, don't you think?''

I gasped. "Please, Ducky," I said, the tears continuing to fall. "Please don't do this. If you let us go we'll—''

"There's been so much talk about the two of you at this club," he went on. "People have wondered about your marriage, about what the stress of working for the police has done to you, about the fact that Judy can't get a job in publishing and Hunt isn't going anywhere at F&F. And then there's Hunt's daughter who's always coming between you. I'll just explain that we went to play golf this afternoon, but that you two had a disagreement. I'll say that I left you alone, to work things out, and went home. I'll say what a tragedy it was that Hunt couldn't control his temper, how sad that he had to shoot his wife and then himself. Sad, sad, sad.''

"You don't really think anybody will believe you, do you, Ducky?" Hunt said. "People who know us know I would never—"

"Please!" Ducky snapped. "I'd like you both to be quiet, while I explain the sequence of events. Now, I'm going to shoot you first, Judy. I'm not a bad shot, considering my lack of practice. Do you have any final words for Hunt? A goodbye? Something?"

I was about to speak when I watched in horror as Hunt charged toward Ducky a second time, tackling him around the knees and wrestling him to the ground. Miraculously, the gun dropped out of Ducky's hand without going off. I raced over and grabbed it, then pointed it at Ducky's head.

"Okay, okay," I said breathlessly. "Now you're going to do what I say, Ducky."

Ducky stood up, his hands in the air, and laughed. Laughed!

"You're not going to shoot me, Judy," he said. "We both know that. Now give me the gun." He walked toward me. I backed up, then realized that if I backed up anymore, I'd be in the lake, along with my golf cart. I stopped and tried to hold the gun steady. "Give me the gun, Judy," Ducky repeated as he drew closer to me.

Hunt went at him again, this time with his fist. He overswung wildly, missing Ducky's head. Then Ducky swung at Hunt and caught him in the eye. They fought, while I stood there, holding the gun, knowing that I didn't know the first thing about guns, knowing that if I fired I'd very likely shoot Hunt, not Ducky, or maybe even myself.

I was nearly frozen with panic, overwhelmed by my own impotence, when I heard footsteps, then voices.

"Judy! Hunt!"

It sounded like Tom, I thought. But no. How could it be? He was home sleeping. And even if he weren't, why would he come to the—

"Judy! Hunt! Can you hear me?"

It *was* Tom!

In the distance I could see him running toward us, along with four or five other police officers. Within seconds, they had surrounded Ducky, their guns pointed right at his head.

"That's enough, Mr. Laughton," Tom said as Ducky and Hunt were pulled apart.

I dropped the gun and ran toward Hunt, who cradled me in his arms and rocked me. He had a bloody lip and his left eye was beginning to swell. "I love you," I whispered and rested my head on his chest.

Ducky stood by the lake, his hands above his head. His mouth formed an O and he seemed genuinely stunned by the dramatic turn of events.

"Don't move, Mr. Laughton," Tom commanded him. "We're gonna do this nice and easy. Nice and slow."

Tom moved slowly toward Ducky, handcuffs ready, his fellow officers poised to fire their guns if necessary.

Tom was inches away from Ducky and about to handcuff his wrists, when Ducky suddenly bolted and dove headfirst into the lake!

I screamed as the officers began firing into the water, the gunshots echoing over the vast, deserted golf course. It was deafening and I buried my head farther into Hunt's chest. I didn't want to look, couldn't bear to. Let them shoot Ducky and take his body away, I thought. I've seen enough violence for one day.

After several seconds of gunfire, Tom instructed the officers to put their weapons down.

"We got him," he said. "I saw him take a bullet on the side of the face. I would rather have brought him in alive, but he didn't give us much choice. It was either watch him drown or shoot him."

I lifted my head and looked out over the lake. It was nearly dark, and there was a fine mist over the water. It was a peaceful, tranquil sight that belied the horror of what had just transpired.

"So he's dead?" I asked.

"Looks that way," said Hunt. "The nightmare's over. Finally."

Tom told one of the officers to radio for the police divers. "Tell them to get here in a hurry. I want the body out of there before it's too dark to see anything."

He turned to Hunt and me. "You both okay?"

"I'm fine, but Hunt's got a few scratches," I said.

"Aw, it's nothing," said Hunt in his most macho voice. He could barely see out of his left eye, but he wasn't about to complain. At least, not in front of Tom and the boys.

"Thank God this whole mess is over," I said. "And thank you, Tom Cunningham, for saving our lives. But how did you know? What made you come to the club to look for us?"

Tom wiped his brow and replied, "About an hour after you left the hospital this afternoon, Arlene came out of the coma."

"She did! That's wonderful!" I said, hugging Hunt.

"Her doctor examined her and said something about how lucky we all were that she didn't have any 'retrograde amnesia'—just some residual neurological problems," Tom continued.

"What kind of neurological problems?" I asked.

"Jude, let Tom finish," Hunt advised. "The important thing is that she's out of the coma." He turned to Tom. "Were you able to talk to her?" he asked.

"Absolutely," he replied. "Once I got the okay from the doctor, I drove over to the hospital with a photograph of Brendan, hoping Arlene would be up to identifying him. When I got there, she was groggy, but she was very eager to talk to me. I showed her the photograph, and she said positively that Brendan Hardy was not the man who attacked her. I asked her if she could describe her attacker, and she said, 'I can do better than that. I can tell you his name. It's Ducky something or other. I met him at Judy's club.' I remembered that you said you were going over to The Oaks to play golf with Mr. Laughton. I thought I'd better come along—with reinforcements."

"We're very glad you did," said Hunt.

"So Arlene remembered meeting Ducky at the club that day," I said. "We were having lunch and he stopped by to say hello."

"She remembered that—and his name," Tom reported. "As the doctor said: no retrograde amnesia, something that's not uncommon in patients who've made it through a trauma. She's a trooper, your friend. She said to tell you that, aside from the fact that Mr. Laughton tried to kill her, she enjoyed staying at your house while you were in Florida and hopes she can come again."

I laughed. "How did she react when she woke up from the coma and met you, Tom?" I asked with a grin. "You're her type, you know."

"What type is that?" he said shyly, lowering his eyes.

"Dark. Handsome. Rugged. Sexy. Just like all her favorite romance heroes."

Tom smiled. "I'm just glad she's all right," he said. "I'm glad everybody's all right."

CHAPTER TWENTY-TWO

♦

Everybody wasn't all right. Not exactly. Arlene did come out of her coma to identify Ducky as her attacker, but she was far from cured.

After Hunt and I left the club at about seven o'clock—we did not stick around to watch the police divers fish Ducky's body out of the lake—we went straight to the hospital to talk to Arlene. We arrived, naively expecting her to be in tiptop shape all of a sudden—despite Tom's remark about neurological problems—and discovered that, not only was she pale and thin and terribly weak, she was lopsided. It seems that the blows that Ducky had dealt to her cheek had created what the doctors termed "residual neurologic deficit." The result was that the right side of her face drooped.

"They call it traumatic Bell's palsy," Arlene explained when she realized that Hunt and I were trying to act as if we didn't notice. The truth was, she was quite a sight, particularly when she attempted to smile—one half of her mouth did, the other half didn't—and the effect, combined with her nearly bald head, was rather ghoulish. "The doctor's optimistic that the paralysis will go away in time," she added. "But you know, if it doesn't, it doesn't. I'm alive, and I have to be grateful for that."

I took Arlene's hand in mine and squeezed it. What a gal, I thought with admiration and envy. If half of my face sagged like that, I doubted I would be so philosophical about it.

"Can you ever forgive us for involving you in this mess?" I asked her.

"I invited myself to your house, remember?" she pointed out.

I nodded and felt my throat close at the very thought of what poor Arlene had been through. Still, if she hadn't spent the night at our house and been able to identify Ducky, Hunt and I would be lying on the bottom of the lake on The Oaks's famed golf course with bullet-holes in our heads.

"Do you have any idea how long you'll have to stay in the hospital?" Hunt asked Arlene.

She shook her head. "They just told me that I'll be here awhile," she replied. "And that after I go home, I won't be able to go right back to work, which really bums me out."

At least you have work to go back to, I thought but did not say. It didn't escape me that now that Claire's case had been solved and the summer was over, I really did have to start job hunting.

"Well, if you have to be stuck in the hospital, the good news is that you'll be stuck in a place that's five minutes from my house," I said. "I'll be able to visit you a lot. And I know Tom Cunningham will too."

Arlene's face brightened at the sound of Tom's name. Or should I say, *half* of it did. "Tell me about Tom," she urged as she lay back on her pillows. "He says he came to see me every day since I've been here, but of course, I don't remember."

"Oh, he came to see you, all right," said Hunt with a twinkle in his eye. "You've been his Sleeping Beauty, and now that you've awakened, I bet you'll see a lot more of him."

"He's a terrific guy, Arlene," I told her. "He's a widower—his wife was killed early in the marriage—and the murder inspired him to become a cop instead of a lawyer, much to his father's chagrin."

"His father is William Cunningham, the head of Pubtel," Hunt added.

"Oh?" said Arlene. Her eyes opened and closed, then opened again, and I could tell that her energy level was beginning to ebb.

"Yup," I said. "It's true."

"Does that mean Tom can talk to his father about you and Charlton House?" Arlene asked. "Or maybe help you get a job in one of the sister companies?"

"I doubt it," I said. "Tom and his father don't talk to each other. But look, the last thing I want you to worry about now is *my* employ-

ment status. You need to concentrate on getting well. In fact, I can
see you're getting tired. We're going to go home now and let you
rest."

Hunt nodded in agreement and we stood together next to Arlene's
bed and said goodbye.

"See you soon," I whispered, bending down to kiss the droopy side
of her face. "Sleep tight."

She smiled and I watched as her eyelids grew heavy. I guessed that
by the time we were in the elevator heading to the lobby of the hospital, she was fast asleep. I prayed that her dreams would be free of
murders and hospitals; that, instead, she would dream of Tom.

If I thought our lives would get back to normal once Claire's murderer was laid to rest, I thought wrong. First came the media on-
slaught, as Hunt and I became the reluctant recipients of Fifteen
Minutes of Fame. Once we gave our statements to the police, we were
fair game, according to the reporters and television crews who pur-
sued us as if *we* were the criminals. We agreed to talk to *Time* and
Newsweek, as well as the "Today" show and "Good Morning America," but refused to appear on "A Current Affair," despite the ob-
scene amount of money they were willing to pay us.

Second, there was Brendan's trial. Obviously, he was no longer
being held on suspicion of murdering Claire and attacking Arlene,
but he *had* committed several other, albeit less violent, crimes: he had
been stealing money from the members of The Oaks, thanks to all of
his and Ducky's kickback schemes, and he had been extorting money
from his biological and very rich parents. A trial date was set for mid-
October, and Hunt and I were being asked to testify for the prosecu-
tion, which we were glad to do.

Then, there were the visits from our family members, none of
whom wanted to miss any of the excitement of our brush with celebrity. My parents flew up from Florida to spend a few days with us.
Kimberley skipped her first week of school and camped out at our
house, bringing along her new gerbil, whom she had named Madonna, after you know who. Even Hunt's parents, Mr. and Mrs. Im-
passive, stopped by several times, asking us how we were holding up,
saying that they were proud of how we had brought a murderer to
justice, wanting to know whether the big shots at F&F had made Hunt
a partner yet, seeing as he had done something so heroic (they
hadn't).

And if all *that* wasn't enough, on the tenth of September, I received some news that really took the cake.

In fact, it was *cake* that I was eating when the problem first came to light. A Sara Lee pound cake, to be specific.

Normally, I'm a snob when it comes to store-bought cakes, but my mother, who had not cut down on her cholesterol despite her cardiologist's advice, had bought six Sara Lee pound cakes, insisting that they made terrific breakfast treats as well as delicious desserts. She had defrosted one of them and was heating up a slice in the toaster oven when I came downstairs for breakfast.

" 'Morning, Mom," I said, padding over to the coffee maker which, thanks to my mother, was already filled with fully-brewed java. I poured myself a cup and sat down at the counter.

"Good morning," she replied, then looked at me, cocking her head to the right, then to the left, then sticking out her tongue.

"What on earth is the matter?" I asked.

"That's what I was wondering," she said, still giving me the once-over. "Stick out your tongue."

"Why?"

"Just listen to your mother."

I stuck out my tongue, which she inspected. Then she shrugged.

"It looks okay," she said. "But your color's terrible. Green. Like when you were little and you had worms."

I laughed. "Thanks for the memory."

"I'm serious, Judy. Do you feel all right?" she asked, laying her hand on my forehead to see if I had any fever.

"I'm exhausted, but otherwise okay," I said. "There's been so much going on around here lately, I guess I haven't had much sleep."

"Or much food. Now, have some pound cake," she said, cutting another slice off the newly defrosted loaf.

"Pound cake? In the morning?" I said, making a face.

"Just taste it," she insisted, removing her piece from the toaster oven, putting it on a plate, slathering it with butter, and pushing it in front of me. "Go on. Take my piece." She placed a second slice in the toaster oven. "It's good for you. Eat."

I took one bite of the pound cake and felt a wave of nausea that nearly knocked me off the chair.

"Maybe I do have worms," I said as I pushed the plate away and held my stomach.

"Either that or you're pregnant," said my mother.

"Pregnant? What did you put in your coffee, Mom, a hallucinagen? I'm forty years old and have never been pregnant in my life. I'd say that's a stretch."

"Maybe, but I've never known you to push food away."

"It's probably one of those twenty-four-hour viruses," I said before I felt another wave, this one more intense than the first. "I think I'll go back upstairs," I told my mother, barely able to speak without gagging.

"Good idea. And while you're up there, call your doctor. *Your gynecologist.* You may think you have a bug in your stomach, but if you ask me, you have a bun in the oven. A mother knows these things," said Lucille Mills as she devoured the pound cake I had left behind.

In between trips to the restroom, which, over the next two months, came to be known around the house as "the retchroom," I tried to remember the date of my last period. And when I really thought about it, I realized that I *had* skipped a period but had chalked it up to all the stress I'd been under. The same thing had happened when I was a senior in college and was crazed over final exams and the boy who had just jilted me for a perky little freshman he'd met on line in the cafeteria. But pregnant? Me? I had long given up on the idea that Hunt and I would ever have children of our own. For one thing, there had been my career as a cookbook editor, and becoming pregnant would have put a crimp in my ability to focus on my work, I was sure. For another thing, Hunt already had a child, and while he'd never actually gone on record as saying he was against our having children of our own, he'd seemed content to lavish his paternal affection on Kimberley. And for a third, I'd always assumed I was infertile—"barren," as Delia Tewksbury would have put it. I'd stopped using contraceptives years ago and decided to let nature take its course.

Had it taken its course? Was I pregnant at forty? It was possible, I knew. After our frustrating, seemingly endless drought, Hunt and I had been having sex again—lots of sex. It wasn't completely absurd to think that during one of those torrid, overheated summer nights of lovemaking I had . . . *we* had . . . conceived a child.

The very thought made me feel both joyous and panic-stricken.

I considered going out and buying one of those home pregnancy tests, but what was the point? I didn't trust them, the same way I didn't trust telephone answering machines. Whenever I'd leave someone a message on their answering machine, I never believed they'd ever get it. Similarly, if I gave myself a home pregnancy test, I'd never know for sure if I was really pregnant. On the other hand, if Dr. Higginbottom, my gynecologist for the past five years, looked me in the eye and said, "Judy, dear"—he calls all his patients "dear," which infuriates some of them but doesn't bother me at all because of the kindly, unpatronizing way he says it—"you're going to have a baby," I would believe him. I would not only believe him, I would run right out and buy the kid a nursery full of mobiles.

So off to Dr. Higginbottom I went, without telling anyone but my mother.

"I'll be a grandmother—finally," she said as I was walking out the door.

"Don't count your chickens yet, Ma," I called out. "They could be worms."

"Not on your life," she muttered as I closed the door behind me.

Dr. Higginbottom was a very nice man. He wasn't one of those misogynist gynecologists who kneads your breasts just a little too hard while he's searching for lumps or goes silent on you while he's got his hands up your privates. No, Dr. Higginbottom was a friendly, chatty sort, his only obvious hang-up being that he was a kindly Connecticut country doctor who felt a great deal of rage toward his wealthier, flashier colleagues in Manhattan. For example, he was forever saying things like, "The big boys in New York would probably charge you an arm and a leg for a Pap smear and then send it to a lab that would screw up the results." Or: "The big boys in New York keep you waiting for hours in their fancy waiting rooms but have no compunction about canceling *your* appointment if you're five minutes late." Dr. Higginbottom may have been a little too caught up in the My-stethoscope-is-bigger-than-your-stethoscope thing, but he was right about the big boys in New York more than he was wrong about them.

"Hello, Dr. Higginbottom," I said when he entered the examining room, where I sat on the table wearing one of those impossibly uncomfortable disposable "gowns."

"Judy, dear," he smiled. "Didn't we see each other a few weeks ago?"

"Yes, but I just couldn't stay away," I deadpanned.

He laughed, then his expression became one of concern. "Is there a problem?"

I shrugged. "My mother seems to think I'm pregnant, do you believe that? Me. After all these years."

"Pregnant, huh?" he mused. "Let's have a look."

Dr. Higginbottom looked, and while he looked he delivered a lecture on how the big boys in New York were making a mockery of the medical profession the way they were advertising their services on television.

"See anything?" I asked as I lay there, more than a little curious.

He stood up, pulled off his white rubber gloves, and grinned.

"Tell your mother she's a better diagnostician than most of the big boys in New York," he said, chuckling.

My heart thundered in my chest and my jaw dropped. "You mean it's true? I *am* pregnant?"

He nodded. "About two months along," he said.

I continued to stare at him. "But how could this have . . ." I stammered. "How could I be. . . . How could . . ."

"It didn't happen while you were sitting on a park bench, dear," he chuckled again.

"Yes, I know that, but . . . why now? Why at this time of my life? Why would I suddenly be able to have a child when I'd never been able to have one before?" My jaw had returned to its normal position, but my eyes had filled with tears. Tears of joy and wonder and complete and utter incredulity.

"God works in mysterious ways, dear," said Dr. Higginbottom as he pulled up a chair and sat beside me. "Look at all you've been through lately, with your friend, Ms. Cox, taken from you so abruptly." Obviously, Dr. Higginbottom had been following the case along with everyone else in town. "Perhaps, the good Lord is replacing the life that was lost."

I regarded him, all sweet and fatherly and sixtysomething, and then I leaned toward him and began to cry on his shoulder. For what must have been several minutes, I cried for it all—for Claire, for Arlene, for the job I had lost, for the marriage I had nearly lost, and especially, for the sheer miracle that now grew inside me. I was overwhelmed by my emotions, flooded with the enormity of the situation in which I now found myself, astonished that, without my expecting it or worrying about it or even wishing for it, Hunt and I had created a life. A life that would change ours in ways I couldn't begin to anticipate. The very idea of my having a baby was thrilling and terrifying, and despite the fact that women had babies every day, totally awe-inspiring.

"There, there," Dr. Higginbottom comforted me. "Surely, you're happy about this?"

I picked my head up off his shoulder and wiped my tears.

"Oh, yes," I said. "Very happy and very shocked."

Dr. Higginbottom chuckled once again and began a speech about pregnancy—how the first trimester was critical in terms of miscarriage, what I should and shouldn't eat, etc., etc.

"Dr. Higginbottom," I said, interrupting him just as he was getting to down-the-road stuff like amniocentesis, "I appreciate the talk, but I'd really like to go home and tell my family about the baby. I'll call you later and you can finish your speech then, okay?"

He laughed. "Okay," he said and helped me off the examining table. "Tell your husband I said congratulations, will you?"

"I sure will," I said. "Don't you worry."

When I got home, nobody was there. I had driven like a madwoman, barely able to contain my excitement, rehearsing how I would tell them, figuring out exactly what I would say, and they had all gone out! Hunt, who was doing more and more work from home these days, had taken Kimberley over to his parents' house, according to the note on the kitchen table, and my parents had gone grocery shopping.

Momentarily deflated, I went upstairs and tried to keep busy until everybody came home. My parents arrived first, and not wanting them to hear the news before Hunt did, I pretended I was asleep. It was only when I heard Hunt and Kimberley enter the house that I made my entrance in the kitchen.

"There's something I'd like to tell everyone," I announced.

Only my mother registered a reaction. Her eyes opened as wide as I'd ever seen them, and she was about to blurt something out when I shushed her.

"Hunt, Kimberley, Dad, I said I have something to tell you all," I repeated, hoping to get their attention away from Kimberley's gerbil, which was racing around in its cage on the kitchen counter and, apparently, behaving in a very entertaining way. Its namesake would have been proud.

Hunt turned around to face me. "What is it, Jude?" he asked.

"I'll tell you as soon as I have everybody's attention," I said, eyeing my father and Kimberley.

"Arthur! Kimberley! Listen to Judy," my mother scolded.

They turned to look at me.

Now, I thought. Now I have their attention. Now I can tell them my wonderful, amazing news.

I cleared my throat and began to speak, but nothing came out! I was mute!

"Jude? You okay?" asked Hunt, walking over to me. "I thought that bug was a stomach virus. Has it gone to your throat now?"

My mother guffawed, and I shushed her again.

I tried once more. "It turns out that I'm not sick after all," I said, gathering strength for the big punch line.

"But the vomiting," Hunt said.

"Yeah, you sure look sick to me," said Kimberley, as tactful as ever.

"Well," I said slowly, dragging the whole thing out just a tad.

"Oh, tell them already," my mother said, bursting with the realization that she would be a grandmother at last.

"I will, I will," I said, then paused for dramatic effect and fixed my eyes on Hunt. "It turns out that I'm not sick. I'm . . . I'm pregnant."

He looked confused, as if I had just spoken in Bangladesh.

"It's true," I said, throwing my arms around his neck and pulling him toward me. "We're going to have a baby, Booch. Isn't that something?"

Before he could respond, Kimberley rushed over to us and threw her arms around us, wanting to be part of our little huddle, not wanting to be left out. "A baby!" she cried, jumping up and down. "I've always wanted a little brother or sister!"

"Oh, I'm so glad," I told her, bending down to hug her back. "You'll be a terrific big sister, Kim. I know you will." I stood back up and looked at Hunt. "And you'll be a wonderful father. Are you happy, Booch? Tell me you are."

He answered with his eyes, which were brimming with tears, just as mine had when I'd first heard the news.

"A baby," he murmured, a little dazed and not quite sure he believed what I had told him.

"Yes, Dr. Higginbottom confirmed what my mother already guessed," I said, winking at my mother. "He said to send you his congratulations."

"A baby," Hunt said again, shaking his head and beginning to grin. "When?"

"April," I told him and then watched as his grin grew wider and his expression changed from one of confusion, disbelief, and uncertainty, to one of joy, pride, and most apparent of all, abiding love. For the family he already cherished. And for the family that was yet to be.

EPILOGUE

♦

"How do I look?" I asked Hunt as I smoothed the skirt of my dress, which was frilly and lacy and not at all *me*. My look was a little more tailored, but when you're a bridesmaid, you're stuck with the bride's taste in dresses.

"You look . . . let's see." Hunt eyed me—all of me. "You look like a woman I'd like to throw down on the bed and ravish," he said.

"So I look ravishing?"

"Yes."

"So do you." Hunt was wearing a white dinner jacket over a pale blue and white striped shirt and navy blue slacks. I walked over to him, combed back an errant lock of his hair with my fingers, and kissed him on the mouth.

He moaned with gratitude, then said, "Do you think we have time?" His voice was low and husky.

I checked the clock on the night table, then shook my head. "Arlene and Tom want us at the club at two-thirty. It's one-thirty now and we still have to make sure the girls are ready."

"Megan's dressing them. They'll be fine."

"Yes, but it's not every day that an eleven-year-old girl and her five-month-old sister are flower girls in a wedding," I pointed out, thinking of how adorable Kimberley and Heather (that's what we named the baby) would look in their frilly little dresses. Actually, the question of what to name the baby had become quite a topic of discussion in the house in the months leading up to the birth. Three generations of male children in Hunt's family had been named Hunter. But what was I supposed to name Hunt's daughter: Huntress? My mother wanted me to name the baby Adelaide, after her dead sister with whom she feuded most of their lives. And Kimberley wanted us to name the child Madonna, after her gerbil. Hunt and I vetoed all their suggestions and settled on Heather, the closest we could get to Hunter without resorting to Helen or Hester. Her full name was Heather Mills Price. We hoped she'd be happy with it when she was old enough to care.

"It only takes ten minutes to get to the club from here," Hunt said.

"True, but we're already dressed in our party clothes. We'd have to get undressed, then redressed," I said.

"Okay. Figure another five minutes to get undressed and five more to get redressed."

"That's a total of twenty minutes."

"You're quite the math whiz."

"It's one-thirty now, and if we add twenty minutes, that would put us at one-fifty."

"Right. If we had a quickie, we'd definitely make it to the club by two-thirty."

"A quickie. A *quiet* quickie." I was warming to the idea, but didn't want to offend the other members of the household. "Where should we do it?"

Hunt began to loosen his tie. "How about the bed?"

"No, we always do it on the bed. I'm up for something different. What about the floor?"

"I'm not supposed to. My back, remember?"

"Oh, right."

"I'll think of someplace else," said Hunt. I could tell he was ready because he had his "hooded eyes" look. I was ready too. I quickly pulled my dress over my head and removed my undergarments. Then I unbuttoned Hunt's shirt, while he unzipped his pants and stepped out of his boxer shorts.

"How about doing it standing up?" he said, keeping up his end of our little game. "In the bathroom? Against the sink?"

"Nooo!" I shivered. "The porcelain's too cold. I'll freeze."

"Come here," said Hunt.

As I came into his arms, he threw me down on the bed and ravished me, keeping one eye on me, the other on the clock.

Arlene and Tom wanted a simple, early September, Saturday afternoon wedding—a small affair attended by members of their immediate families and a few close friends. Hunt was Tom's best man, I was Arlene's matron of honor and her sister was her maid of honor. And as she didn't have children or even young cousins, Kimberley and Heather were the so-called flower girls (Kimberley tossed rose petals along the aisle and Heather sat in my arms, gurgling and cooing and pulling on my hair). Tom's father, Wild Bill Cunningham, head of Pubtel, was there too, since he and his son had mended their fences the year before, a few weeks after Tom apprehended Ducky on the golf course and saved our lives. Apparently, Wild Bill had watched his son receive a great deal of favorable publicity surrounding the Claire Cox murder case, and had decided that having a cop for a son wasn't such a terrible thing after all.

Tom and Arlene had begun dating after she left the hospital. He visited her in the city, took her on walks through Central Park, brought her cookies and candies to fatten her up, read her passages from her favorite romance novels, and ignored her Bell's palsy, which eventually disappeared, just as the doctor had predicted it might. Tom was every bit the romantic hero, and she fell madly, passionately in love with him. Three months before the wedding, they had decided to get married at The Oaks, where Arlene was a new and very enthusiastic member.

She had joined the club at the suggestion of her physical therapist, who thought it would be good for her to drive up to Connecticut on weekends and play a little golf or tennis. I had heartily seconded the idea, of course, seeing as I was spending more and more time at the club myself. I had concluded that since Hunt loved The Oaks's golf course with such ferocity, I should learn to love it too. And the only way I was going to learn to love it was if I had women I liked and respected to play golf with. So I became friends with the women whom Claire had recruited for membership, including Sharon Klein, the accountant. And then Arlene joined. And then I persuaded her to convince some of her authors to join. Before I knew it, I had a real circle of friends at the club—*my* circle. And since I had hired a wonderful young Irish woman named Megan to help me take care of Heather, I actually looked forward to spending weekends there.

As for my week*days,* they were spent at home, either in the nursery with Heather or at the computer, working on my second book. Yes, my second book. I had planned to start looking for a publishing job after the whole mess with Ducky was over, but then came the pregnancy and the morning sickness and the trips to Dr. Higginbottom, and before I knew it, time was marching on. I did get one job offer though: from my old company, good old Charlton House. Tom had introduced me to his father, who tried to talk me into coming back to the company, coming back to work for Loathsome Leeza Grummond. While I was weighing the offer, I got a phone call from Dorothy Ohlmeyer, Claire's agent, who invited me to lunch. It seemed that Dorothy had found a sort of culinary diary that Claire had kept—a journal in which she had described the meals she prepared for her retreats, complete with actual recipes. Dorothy had the idea that I should draw from the diary and write the cookbook that Claire and I were going to write together. I agreed instantly, we sold the proposal to a publisher, and I told Wild Bill that Charlton House would just have to do without me and that, if he were smart, he'd get rid of Loathsome Leeza. I spent the rest of the year writing the book, which was due to be released the following year. In the meantime, Dorothy had gotten me a contract to write another cookbook. It was titled *Country Club Cuisine,* and my co-author was Armand Rossier, the new chef at The Oaks. A native of Paris, and the former sous-chef at La Bouche, one of Connecticut's premier restaurants, Armand was brought into the club after I became chairperson of the Dining Committee. Yes, things at The Oaks had definitely changed in the past year. Larkin Vail was still the women's singles tennis champion and Duncan and Delia Tewksbury still behaved as if they were from a previous century and there was still no valet parking. But Ducky's death—and the revelation that a man everyone had trusted and respected was a murderer—had a sobering affect on the people at the club. Some of the old guard actually resigned their memberships in an effort to distance themselves from the sordidness of Claire's death and its aftermath. Others simply came to the conclusion that times were changing and The Oaks would have to change too. As a result, those of us who felt the club needed updating and upgrading were able to persuade the rest of the members to cough up the money for a top-notch chef, a redecorated clubhouse, refurbished locker rooms and tennis pros who actually taught tennis.

As for Hunt, he decided he'd waited long enough for F&F to make him a partner and quit his job. He also decided that he didn't have the stomach for the commodities market and turned, instead, to mutual funds. He set up a consulting business out of our house and continued to represent many of his old clients. He found being self-employed very satisfying, and it gave him more time to spend with Kimberley, who was still giving me grief but not as often, and with little Heather, who wasn't giving me any grief—yet.

The weather was glorious for the wedding—crisp, clear, fragrant. The ceremony was held in the living room of the clubhouse, the cocktail reception outside on the terrace. Arlene, whose hair had grown to chin-length, looked radiant in her nineteenth-century bridal gown, the exact replica of the gown worn by the heroine of one of Kathleen Woodiwiss's novels. Tom wore a dark suit and looked like the happiest man on the planet. He beamed and hugged people and said corny things like, "Pinch me. I can't believe this is happening."

Speaking of corny, I cried my eyes out as the minister asked Tom and Arlene if they promised to love each other till death do them part. I was so moved by the fact that they had found each other, that they had been able to turn adversity into happiness. At the word "death," I was reminded of the terrible ordeal Arlene had been through, of the terrible ordeal we all had been through, of Claire and Brendan and Ducky, of the summer we were still trying to forget.

Obviously, last summer hadn't been a total disaster. I'd met Tom, and Tom had met Arlene, and Hunt and I had rekindled our love for each other and conceived Heather. Yes, there were positives about last summer, I thought, as I watched Hunt raise his champagne glass and toast the bride and groom at the start of the reception.

About an hour into the party, I was standing with Hunt, sipping champagne, nibbling on one of Armand's perfectly divine hors d'oeuvres, and keeping my eye on Kimberley, who was holding Heather and trying not to drop her, when Arlene came scurrying over.

"In all the excitement, I completely forgot to tell you," she said breathlessly.

"Tell me what?" I said.

"About Leeza," she said.

"What about Leeza?" asked Hunt, who was no longer Leeza Grummond's financial advisor. Several months before, she had abruptly fired him, just as she had abruptly fired me.

"She's leaving Charlton House," said Arlene.

"Well, what do you know," I said, a self-satisfied grin on my face. "The geniuses over there finally figured out what a zero she is."

"Wrong," said Arlene. "She wasn't canned. She quit. To go to Remington House. As president of the company!"

My mouth dropped open. Leeza Grummond had ascended yet again! She was actually being rewarded for her incompetence! Instead of getting the heave-ho, she was given the go-ahead to run one of the most prestigious companies in the industry! I was nonplussed, not to mention resentful.

"The woman's an idiot," I said charitably. "And she doesn't know a thing about books. She once let it slip that the only novel she'd ever read all the way through was *Jaws.*"

"I guess she enjoys reading about her ancestors," Hunt smirked.

"Exactly," I said. "But Arlene, are you sure about Leeza becoming president of Remington House? I mean, the rumor mill isn't always a hundred percent accurate."

"Oh, I'm sure all right," Arlene said. "I heard it straight from the shark's mouth."

"From Leeza? She told you?" I said.

"Yup. She called me at work a few days ago," said Arlene.

"But why?" I asked. "You and she aren't exactly bosom buddies. She fired you at Charlton House, let's not forget."

"Oh, I haven't forgotten," Arlene laughed.

"So why did she call *you?* Don't tell me she wants to hire you back—to work for her at Remington House?" I said.

Arlene shook her head. "Leeza's phone call had nothing to do with business. She only mentioned her move to Remington House in passing. No, she called because she found out that I was a member of The Oaks. She said she heard it's *the* country club to join these days, that it has the best food of all the clubs and the most challenging golf course, that she's taken up golf in order to 'maintain parity' with the male executives in the book business, that she simply must become a member right away, and that she wondered if I would sponsor her for membership and convince you to be her co-sponsor."

I burst out laughing, and I laughed so hard the other guests turned around to look at me.

"She's got some set of balls, huh?" said Hunt.

"Does she ever," said Arlene.

"What did you tell her?" I asked, after catching my breath.

"I told her that she was absolutely correct, that in order to become a member of The Oaks, she would need a sponsor and a co-sponsor," said Arlene.

"Sponsor, my ass," I said. "You should have told her that if she ever tried to get into this club, we'd blackball her so fast her head would spin.''

''Those were my exact words,'' said Arlene.

''Bravo!'' I cheered, holding up my glass, then taking another sip of champagne. ''Now that we've dispensed with Loathsome Leeza, how about turning to more pleasant subjects. Where's the groom?''

''Over there,'' said Arlene as she looked lovingly across the terrace at her new husband, who was chatting with her parents and sister. ''This is all so wonderful, isn't it?'' she asked, her eyes sparkling the way a bride's should.

I glanced down at my children, who were content for the time being. Then I gazed at Hunt, gazed at the man whose weaknesses I had come to accept, whose love I had come to treasure. I knew in that single moment how lucky I was. How lucky we all were. There was no telling what would come later, what indignities, tragedies, losses we would suffer. But right then, right when Arlene asked the question, I knew with absolute certainty what my answer would be.

''Yes, it's wonderful,'' I agreed. ''Yes, it really is.''